A CRIMSON GRACE

A CRIMSON GRACE

JOHN RIHERD

DUSTIVUS

MEDIA

ISBN: 978-0-9907019-0-3 (Trade Paperback)

DUSTIVUS

MEDIA

C03

Published by:
Dustivus Media
P.O. Box 1432
Genoa, NV 89411
www.dustivusmedia.com

For my wife Jan.
Your patience is astounding.

And for my children:
Morgan and Mike
Nicole and Joey
Debi and Dustin

Each of you is my joy
and my reason.

Dustin, you should have stayed longer.
I told you I would finish.

This book is done and, starting on the very next page, the fiction begins.

A special thanks to my wife Jan for always giving me a time and place to pursue my creative efforts. She says the kids will laugh that I laud her patience because the kids know she has no patience. She says it is her hardheadedness that is actually behind her willingness to let me spend so much time in the effort it takes to write. I thank her for whichever it is.

A special thanks to the thousands of people out there keeping the internet running and full of almost everything a person needs to write a book. As distracting as the internet is to the wandering mind, it is a blessing to have maps and dictionaries and the rules of grammar right at hand.

I have mentioned a few real places in this book. I did so with the utmost respect and affection. I have taken some liberties with geography and the topography of the bays of the Gulf Coast. If you notice, I thank you for reading around those variations from reality. If mistakes remain, they are mine.

John Riherd

Your blood has not
  been spilled for naught,
Your redemption's found
  in battle fought,
Your sins absolved by
  sword and mace,
Your blessing won
  by crimson grace.

-An caoineadh na peacaigh
-Na scríbhneoirí

CHAPTER ONE

S HE SAID, "I intend to save at least two teenage girls from a life of prostitution and sexual slavery." It was a startling, unexpected thing to hear on such a beautiful spring day.

The day started as expected. Joshua Bell and I finished a custom barbecue smoker and grill commissioned by the Scamp Boat Company. Intended for use on the professional barbecue cook-off circuit, the cooking machine was a thing of beauty. Luckily, the customer agreed it did not have to look like a bass boat.

It stretched over twelve feet long and six feet wide. I'd finished it with an attention-getting brass steam whistle. Polished brass letters spelled "Scamp" in an arch bookended by etched brass replicas of the company's logo, a playful puppy, forepaws on the ground, tail curved over a raised rump. I'd gone for a circus calliope look.

I did not want to hear about somebody's problem with prostitution and sexual slavery. With what Scamp Boats paid me, I could pay Joshua's salary for the rest of the year, buy myself a couple of new and expensive fishing rods, fill my boat's fuel tanks and still have a respectful sum left in the bank. When my responsibilities slowed in the fall, I intended to leave the shop in Joshua's care, pay him extra to watch over the rentals I managed, let Harry Faulks take over any legal matters I couldn't finish in time, and, then, I would take a meandering journey down the Intracoastal Waterway to the Florida Keys. I planned to spend Christmas in Key West craziness, drinking mojitos and enjoying spicy Cuban cuisine.

So far I only had one trial scheduled, an argument over travel restrictions the other side sought to impose on my client, the father of three children. I did not want any other involved case. I intended to be careful and not take any case that might interfere with my plans to disappear for a while at the end of the year.

That day, a Saturday, started gloriously free of responsibilities. Joshua and I finished early before the workshop heated up. I thought it might be a good day to go fishing.

Joshua, whistling softly, applied a steel brush to the last of the weld slag while I stood back to admire our handiwork. A car crunched to a stop on the driveway just outside the open doors to the shop. Doors slammed. Preacher came around the edge of the door and into the shop in the company of three others, strangers to me.

They made an interesting group. Preacher is large, well over my six feet and an inch, beefy, but coordinated enough to be a skilled surfer and an amiable competitor at volleyball games on the beach. I never saw Preacher in anything other than loud Hawaiian style shirts, well-worn jeans or shorts, and leather sandals.

With sun-bleached hair pulled into a long ponytail and his always available sunglasses, Preacher looked like an aging surfer. He was a genuine minister of sorts. He arrived on the coast a few years earlier and set up a church in an abandoned convenience store on the bay side of the Blue Water Highway on Follets Island. He ministered to an ever-changing congregation of the fringe who gravitate to the coast. He sought me out early on to handle legal issues arising with members of his congregation.

I liked Preacher. He was well off-center and that made him interesting. Besides, any minister who rescheduled

Sunday morning services if there was good surfing available was my kind of minister.

Two of his companions, a man and a woman, looked as though they belonged together. The man, wiry with close-cropped dark hair, wore a black t-shirt fitted tight over what could have been a middleweight boxer's body. The dark edges of a tattoo appeared beneath the sleeve of his shirt.

The woman, who stayed close to his side, also dressed in no-nonsense black. Her dark hair was only a little longer than his. Their lace-up boots added to their combat-ready appearance. The man glanced around the shop, looked at his similarly clad partner, and gave a subtle shake of his head. Tight-lipped, neither appeared pleased with what they saw.

The third stranger looked out of place by sheer normality. She'd pulled her dark hair into a ponytail. She wore starched khaki Capri pants, a white short-sleeved blouse, and crisp white tennis shoes. She carried a large, flat handbag. Her intelligent, wary, blue-gray eyes looked at me as I walked toward the group. She had a pleasant, if somewhat nervous, smile.

Preacher's companions did not look like they'd come to buy a grill or hire a fishing guide. That left only one thing. I picked the nicely dressed dark-haired beauty as the one with a legal problem. In that group, she was the misfit, and the misfits usually had the legal problem. She didn't look like one of Preacher's usual projects. He often brought by some member of his congregation for legal attention, drug possession or unpaid child support or this or that. I usually took on Preacher's people projects for free as my contribution to his good works and out of some sense of obligation as an attorney.

"Brother Sam, we need your counsel."

Preacher talks like that.

"Let's go up to the house."

I led them out of the acrid, hot metal atmosphere of the shop into the fresh air outside. Leaning against their car was a girl. I guessed thirteen or fourteen years old. Her short, bleached blonde, shaggy hair had dark roots of her natural hair color. She leaned against their car with her arms crossed in front of her chest. Diminutive and shrinking into herself, she moved only her eyes. She watched us, unblinking with a fearful intensity. After one brief glance at all of us, she focused on the nicely dressed woman and did not look away from her. The woman directed a smile and nod at the girl.

I revised my speculation about who needed legal counsel. It would be the girl. She would be caught in some sad custody battle or she would need to escape some terrible home life or she would have done something that brought her to the attention of legal authorities. There are rarely good answers for the children. In the legal arena, children need crusaders. I am not a crusader. I would refer the problem to someone who practiced in whatever area she needed and do my best to talk that lawyer into doing what needed doing for free or for as low a price as possible.

The five of us crossed the yard and went up the steps to my screened in porch. The girl did not move from where she leaned against the car. With a gesture, I invited them to choose from the chairs on the porch, and said, "I'm having coffee. Anybody else? Iced tea? Dr Pepper?" I directed the last offer to Preacher. He consumes a lot of Dr Pepper. He nodded yes.

The normal looking dark-haired woman said, "Coffee would be good."

"No, I'm fine." That was the man in black. The

woman in black said nothing.

I returned with the drinks, sipped my coffee, and looked expectantly at Preacher.

"Sam, this is Sister Mary Elizabeth Kincaid."

The normal looking lady set her coffee cup down and put her hand out. I leaned forward to shake it. She took a deep breath and started to say something, but the man spoke first, "What are you exactly?"

"Excuse me?"

He was rude. In my lawyer role, I expected rude people coming for help. A client's rudeness arose from insecurity, fear, or anger because of their circumstances. I'd learned to deflect the rudeness, hear their story, and dispassionately do what I could to help. Having just deposited a sizable check from Scamp Boats, I could indulge in a lower tolerance for rudeness.

"Like the sign says, I build grills and smokers." I pointed at the steel sign hung from a post by the driveway. They couldn't have missed it as they drove in. Joshua made it for me as a Christmas gift the year before. My name and anachronistic appellation, "Samuel Locke, Esquire," was arched in brass plated six-inch tall letters at the top. Joshua often called me squire. It amused him.

The profile of a speckled trout curved beneath my name on the sign. Two rows of four-inch tall letters spelled out "Custom Barbecue Smokers and Grills" beneath my name. Below that it said "Fishing Guide." Hanging at the bottom, in two-inch letters, it said "Lawyering."

The unfriendly lady made a sound of disapproval. Mary Elizabeth Kincaid gave both of her companions a sharper look than expected from such a gentle-looking lady. Preacher spoke, ignoring them completely. "Sam, we need your expertise."

"What's going on?"

Mary Elizabeth spoke up. "Mr. Locke, I intend to save two girls from a life of prostitution and sexual slavery. Preacher thinks you can help."

If Preacher started a conversation about sexual slavery and prostitution, I would not have been terribly surprised. Not much Preacher said surprised me, but the declaration came from his companion, the coolly attractive Mary Elizabeth Kincaid. She looked like she should be sipping her coffee at a country club, talking about her child's latest swim meet or soccer game, not sitting on my porch in the company of an eccentric like Preacher telling a beach bum like me she intended to save girls from the clutches of sexual slavery.

I leaned back in my chair absorbing what she'd said. I looked at Preacher. He sat serenely with hands clasped across his belly saying nothing. The other two looked at me, scowling. I turned back to Mary Elizabeth.

"Ms. Kincaid ... "

"Mary Elizabeth, please."

I nodded. "Mary Elizabeth, what are you talking about?"

"Just what I said. Out of the thousands of girls coerced into prostitution every year, I intend to save at least two. I need to pick the brain of somebody who knows the coast. We could use a boat. Preacher speaks highly of you. He told me you are a good man with a good boat."

She smiled. Although enormously self-contained, half-formed tears glistened in her eyes suggesting a crack in her calm demeanor.

The lady in black tentatively reached toward her and spoke for the first time, "Mary Elizabeth ... "

Mary Elizabeth jerked away from the hand reaching

toward her. "No. I know you think it was a mistake to come down here. I know you think this whole thing is a mistake. I know you think there's nothing I can do. I know. I know. I know. Okay?"

"We all want to do something. We always do. It's just that it really would be best to take this one to the authorities."

"No. I tried that. You know what would happen. I cannot walk away from this one. I have to try to do this one right. You don't have to stay. Go back. I have to try."

The man in black remained quiet. Arms crossed, he looked toward the bay glistening beyond the grass flats. A muscle tensed at the base of his jaw. The emotional atmosphere crackled. On the outside looking in, I didn't like the shape of things, but she had captured my curiosity.

"Could I at least get your names?"

The man turned from the window. "Jason Edwards." We nodded at each other.

"Patricia Carr." She actually leaned toward me and held out her hand for a short, firm handshake.

The atmosphere remained leaden with emotion. I asked Mary Elizabeth, "Would you be more comfortable speaking in private?"

She glanced at her companions. "No. It will be okay."

Jason Edwards looked at her for a moment and nodded. Patricia Carr reached toward her touching her arm and smiling. "It will. You just know ... "

"Yes, I know. But we won't know for sure, will we? Not until we try."

I really needed to catch up. "Okay, it doesn't hurt to talk. Somebody tell me what's going on."

Mary Elizabeth looked at her companions with a do not interrupt me look and turned back to me.

"Mr. Locke ... "

"Sam."

"Sam." She smiled. She waved a hand toward her friends and continued. "We work in Chicago with The Beacon, an organization assisting children who are with homeless families or who are alone on the streets for one reason or another. In December, one of our street kids brought a girl to The Beacon. The girl's name is Mina. Mina Verenka."

I looked out at the girl still leaning against the car in the drive. "Her?"

"Yes. Mina is sixteen. She showed up in the freezing cold with hardly any clothes and badly beaten. She wouldn't talk. She wouldn't cry. She let me bathe her and treat her abrasions. We checked her out at a clinic. We made sure she did not need a hospital for her injuries. We checked to make sure she was not pregnant and that she had not picked up some disease. She was compliant, but she would not talk much. She gave minimal answers to only basic questions.

"Eventually, she opened up to me." She turned to look at the girl and took a deep breath. "They brought Mina to this country illegally from Ukraine. She thought she was going to work as a housekeeper or a nanny. Instead, her captors forced her to work as a prostitute. It took me a month of gaining her trust and working with her to learn that about her. No one else could connect with her."

I looked at the girl outside again. She was too young, too tiny. Damn the animals of this world.

"Yes, I know. Hard to believe isn't it?" Mary Elizabeth said, leaning toward me.

No way did I want a part of this ugliness. Somebody else should handle it. Someone else should hear Mary Elizabeth's story, but there was no gracious way to stop her from telling me.

"Once she learned I draw, she opened up to me. Here, let me show you."

She unzipped the bag she carried and pulled out a drawing pad, placing it on the table between us.

"One of the things I do at The Beacon is help the children communicate and express their feelings. I have degrees in psychology, and I draw. I use drawing to get the kids to communicate. Some children will draw something they cannot say."

I nodded my understanding.

"I tried it with Mina, and she finally got excited. She draws and does so with considerable talent. Drawing is how I gained her trust and friendship. It's how I learned her story. It created an affinity between us."

She opened the drawing pad and turned it toward me. "This is how I started. I showed her where I grew up."

The sketch was a two-story house, suburban America, unremarkable in any way. Mary Elizabeth turned the page to the next drawing. "She drew this."

Though not as refined as Mary Elizabeth's, Mina's skill showed in the drawing of a bleak and ugly building. The building's facade framed a collection of anonymous, dark windows.

Mary Elizabeth turned several pages, saying, "These are people we know. I drew my family and she drew hers. These are her parents, her brothers, and her twin sister Zoio. Her parents died in a bus crash. Mina and her brothers and sister lived with an uncle and aunt." She pointed out another pair of portraits, the uncle and aunt.

Mina certainly could draw haunted eyes. The faces of the adults were gaunt, lined with weariness. Her twin had a small, sad smile, but she wasn't happy. She looked as lost and haunted as the adults. The brothers looked sullen and angry.

I looked at the stark picture of the sister and back out at Mina. I had a feeling. "You said you intended to save two girls."

"Yes." She tapped the drawing with a finger. "They have her twin."

I looked at the group on the porch with me. Mary Elizabeth watched me quietly, calmly reposed, but with a tightness around her mouth and eyes. Preacher sat still, his fingers interlaced, nothing moving except his eyes. He looked back and forth between Mary Elizabeth and me. Edwards stared out the window, his face etched in hard lines. Patricia Carr stared at me, pale with spots of pink high on each cheek. Outside, the girl had not moved from where she leaned against the car.

"Okay. Tell me the story."

Mary Elizabeth turned to a drawing in the sketchpad and pushed it toward me. It was a picture of a man. He loomed tall and thin, standing in a doorway, wearing a full-length coat ending just below his knees. A hat shadowed his face. Mina had drawn his eyes deep in black hollows, rimmed in white, gleaming in the recessed darkness of his face. His were not sad eyes. His eyes were soulless. His were the feral eyes of a predator.

I looked at Mary Elizabeth. "That's the man," she said. "He's the one who came to her home and paid her uncle. He explained how they would train Mina as a housemaid or a nanny. Mina's family has a difficult struggle and her aunt and uncle didn't ask many questions. The family wanted to believe what they heard."

I glanced at Preacher. A tear rolled down his cheek. "Sam, that man and all those like him will spend eternity in hell. And the sooner they get started the better. You've not heard the worst of it."

Mary Elizabeth nodded at Preacher with a small smile. She continued in a quiet voice. "They treated her okay for a while. They cleaned her up and gave her new clothes. A woman taught her to use make-up. Mina was fifteen. She thought that was wonderful. They told her she could earn the most money in the United States and started teaching her English. They told her that in America she would earn enough money to bring her entire family over to live. They told her she could visit Disneyland. After a couple of months of anticipation, it excited her to be coming to the States."

Mary Elizabeth flipped the pages in the drawing pad to drawings of what looked like the interior of a small, cheap apartment. "These are drawings of where she lived for a while with several other girls after she left home."

I held up a hand to stop her. "You keep talking about 'they' and how they bought her and how they did this and that. You are talking about an extensive criminal organization. You need the FBI. You need Interpol. Have you talked to the authorities at all?"

"Yes, but it does no good. Everybody knows there's a problem, but it overwhelms. They don't like to discuss it. I do not have enough information to get the police interested."

"But you have a girl who was involved. Somebody who can give the police specific information."

"First, I don't think she could give them useful concrete information, at least not enough to help. She couldn't even find the apartment from which she'd escaped in Chicago. We looked for it. I told them everything Mina could tell them. Second, I don't think she should talk to the authorities."

"Why?"

"The police would have no choice but to turn her over to child services. She might be deported."

"Surely they wouldn't deport anybody in her situation."

"Oh yes, they would. It happens. International politics often make governments blind to harsh realities. She would become a playing piece. Do you remember the hoopla surrounding the boy from Cuba they sent back? Eventually, they'd send her back to the custody of the Ukraine government. I don't think that's the best solution. The social service agencies in Ukraine are overloaded. At best, once there, they'd send her home and that man in the hat and coat would find her again. Her entire family would be at risk.

"Sam, authorities know about the problem. Governments pass laws all the time. There are meetings at the United Nations. Scholars make speeches and write papers on the subject. People study the problem to death. Meanwhile, girls are bought and sold every day." Her voice rose in pitch as she fought to control her emotions.

Mina had a lot of concrete information. She had drawings. I thought her story compelling enough to get the necessary attention. But maybe the girl would be swallowed in the process. I had no idea.

Mary Elizabeth closed the drawing pad. Her lips grew tight. The skin around her eyes went slack. She suddenly looked ten years older and very tired. Her voice cracked with emotion. Patricia put a hand on her shoulder. Edwards turned from the window.

"I know I cannot stop them. Perhaps no one can. It's been going on for centuries. This one little part of it is personal to me. The big picture will swallow the girls I want to save if authorities get involved. These girls are nothing to the people who buy and sell them. In the end, they are nothing to the governments that might stop this travesty.

"I don't expect to stop everything that's going on. I will tell the authorities what I know and what I learn, but first, Mina will be safe. If possible, her sister will be safe. That's something I can try to do."

Obviously, Mary Elizabeth's quest was personal. Her reluctance to involve authorities did not bother me. I appreciated her sense of futility about fixing the big picture and her desire to fix the personal part. I had no problem with her desire to work outside the strict boundaries of the law. I argued only because I believed whatever she planned was a lost cause. Fighting lost causes is noble but ends in tragedy and heartache. I stopped fighting lost causes some time ago. I preferred beer and barbecue to heartache. Selfishness or survival? I didn't know and I didn't care. I had no reason to analyze the whys of my preference.

Preacher continued to sit there like Buddha in a Hawaiian shirt, hands folded, saying nothing. I turned to him. "Preacher, you're not saying much. That's unusual for you."

"She has a quiet power, Sam. I'm confident that once you've heard enough you will help. Probably more than you think you will."

Out of respect for Mary Elizabeth, I didn't articulate what I thought, but I made a sound. He smiled. I poured more coffee and turned back toward her.

"Look, why don't you tell me exactly what you intend to do and what you think you need me to do."

"Okay." She leaned toward me. "After Mina opened up to me, I realized she had tremendous visual memory about her experience in getting to Chicago. She, along with five other girls, traveled on a cargo ship to the States. They actually cooked and did laundry on the ship. Free labor. They had little English, and nobody on the ship spoke their native language.

"After a long trip at sea, they put the girls on a small boat. They must have been some distance from shore. The girls had no idea where they were, but I'm sure the boat brought them somewhere along the Texas coast close to Galveston. They stayed some place next to the ocean that first night. The next night, they left in a van driven by a woman. They stopped one time in a big city where they took two of the girls out of the van. From the way Mina describes the timing and the city, I'm guessing that was Dallas."

"How did you decide on Galveston?"

"Let me show you." She turned the pages of the sketchpad. "As I said, Mina has an excellent visual memory. She was excited and very observant about what was happening. I got her to draw what she could remember about her trip. She drew this. She saw it that first night she traveled in the van."

She turned the book toward me. I recognized it immediately. Mina had drawn a picture of General Sam Houston a hero of the Texas revolution and a two-term President of the Republic of Texas. The statue she'd drawn stood nearly ninety feet tall beside Interstate 45 north of Houston. Mile marker zero for the Interstate was in Galveston a couple of miles from the Gulf of Mexico.

The statue was solid white. At night, it rose out of the darkness of the surrounding forest, brightly lit by spotlights, gleaming like alabaster. It could startle an unwary motorist. To Mina, in a strange country traveling in the dark into the unknown, it would be a memorable sight.

Mina had not drawn many details of the statue, but she had the looming bulk of the piece, and she had the cane. The statue of Sam Houston leaned on a cane. That's what I recognized first.

Mary Elizabeth said, "It didn't take me long to find a picture of that statue on the internet. Mina recognized the photograph."

I nodded. "Have you been up to see it yet?"

"Yes. Mina confirmed it is the statue. That's the highway they took on their way to Chicago."

Preacher tapped a finger against the drawing. "Do you have doubts Brother Sam? I've never seen the statue."

"No. I agree. It's the statue. Okay. It looks like they took her up I-45 from Houston. I still can't imagine what you plan to do about it without official help."

"Sam, I don't expect to stop the smuggling. I know I can't do that. I do intend to get as much information as I can and put it in the hands of somebody official, but not until I try to save Zoio."

"Tell me about her. How do you know she's involved?"

"You cannot imagine the horror of Mina's life in Chicago. She didn't learn what they planned for her until she got there. They locked her in a room all alone. They told her there was no way she could get the work she'd been promised until she or her family paid what it cost to get her to the United States. She was powerless, beaten for the slightest reason. She had no refuge. The man in charge of her told her the debt for feeding and housing her increased daily. He told her at some point it would be cheaper to just kill her. Finally, at her most hopeless moment, he told her how she could make the money necessary to repay her debt."

A breeze rustled across the flats, the air gentle and scented of salt and the sea. I started to hear the sounds that are usually unnoticed, the flip of a fish in the flats, the squawk of a gull. I knew there were unfortunate and terrible circumstances in the world. It angered me that Preacher brought this sincere, naive social worker and her sullen friends to my house. I didn't see a thing she could do. I couldn't imagine what she expected me to do.

"I can imagine what they did ... "

Preacher interrupted me in a quiet, sincere voice. "No, Sam. You cannot imagine the evil of these people. They auctioned off this child's virginity."

"You don't know that."

Mary Elizabeth said, "I do. I've heard her tell it. They stood her in a room in front of three men and made her strip for inspection. She lost her virginity to one of those men. That is one picture I cannot ask her to draw."

"Okay, I can't imagine the evil." I was getting angrier at the intrusion in my life. "I also can't imagine how you can do anything. What's up with her sister?"

"Mina knew the man in charge of her as John. Just before she ran away from him, John told her he had good news. Her twin was coming to work with her. By that time, Mina had pretty much given up. She'd become very compliant. He must have thought he had total power. He told Mina she could help teach her sister what to do. He told her the two of them would have to pay off her sister's debt, but they'd be able to earn even more money working as a team.

"Mina decided she could not let Zoio do what she'd had to do. She objected. He beat her. She continued to resist. He beat her unconscious. She waited for her chance. She'd never had the courage to try to escape. She knew the punishment for trying would be unimaginably bad. This country terrifies her. To her, it is a place of shame and horror. She'd lost all hope and had no will to try to escape before he told her about her sister. Mina could not live with the possibility of her sister suffering the same fate. Knowing the risk to her sister gave her strength and she ran. She didn't know where she would go or what she would do, but she knew she had to try. One of our kids found her on the street and brought her to the Beacon."

"How do you expect to save her sister?"

"Through connections of the Church, we were able to get a priest to go see Mina's family in Ukraine. Someone had already approached the family and told them a glowing tale about Mina. They'd made a better financial arrangement for the sister than they did for Mina. By the time the priest got to the family, they'd bought and paid for Zoio. They took her from the home at the end of February. Based on what I know from Mina's story, and if Zoio makes a similar trip, I think she'll get to Galveston on a boat sometime this month or the first of next month."

"But you have no idea exactly where do you?"

"No."

"She could already be here. Or once Mina ran, maybe her sister got sent to another country."

"Maybe. I pray not. They are looking for Mina in Chicago. Somebody came by the Beacon. Luckily, the staff is trained to be careful, and nobody mentioned Mina."

"You have contacts in Ukraine. Is there some way you can find out what ship her sister is on?"

"I'm trying, but it is incredibly dangerous to make inquiries about these things in Ukraine."

I shook my head. "You don't have many threads to hang on to, do you?"

"That's why we're here. Preacher said if anybody can help, you can."

I looked at Preacher. Preacher said, "Show him what you have. Let's see if he can help. Brother Sam, you might not even have to move from that chair to help us get one step closer to figuring out what to do."

Mary Elizabeth clutched the sketchpad to her chest. "Mina drew a couple of pictures of the boat they put her in to come to shore. It was very loud and very fast. It had an open area where the driver sat and a place up front where he put the girls. She could see out a small round window."

Preacher said, "Sounds to me like one of those offshore racing boats."

"Yeah," I said. "Could be. They're certainly popular with smugglers. Can she describe the boat?"

"It was black. Or her impression of it was that it was solid black."

"I wonder why they don't just sneak them off the freighter when it's in port. That seems like the safest thing."

"I don't know. I just know what happened with Mina. That's all I have to go on."

"It sounds like you have a network of people working on this. How many are down here to help you try to save Mina's sister?"

"Just us."

"Just the three of you?"

"Patricia and Jason have to leave soon. There's just Preacher and me."

I looked at Preacher.

"And you, Sam," he said. "We need your help."

I stared at them. "Let me get this straight. International traffickers may be bringing in Mina's sister. If so, you don't know the name of the ship. You don't know where or when the unknown ship will arrive. You need the Coast Guard and Immigration and the FBI and something like Interpol and you won't call any of them."

Mary Elizabeth's tears broke free. Patricia Carr moved to put an arm around her and angrily stared at me.

Edwards actually nodded at me with approval and a slim smile. Gently, he said, "See Mary Elizabeth, he agrees. You really have to turn this over to somebody. You have Mina. Let the authorities work on saving Zoio and all the others."

"No." Mary Elizabeth's reply was sharp and angry. "Maybe it's impossible. If it is, then I have to question everything I've ever done in my life. If God sees fit to make me aware of what's going on but gives me no power to intervene in this evil, then my dedication has been a joke."

She began crying. I'd thought her tears were born of sadness, but they weren't. They were tears of frustration and anger. The evil that would do this thing angered her. She was angry at God for letting it happen and frustrated at her inability to do something. There were complex motives involved in Mary Elizabeth's passionate desire to correct some small result of the evil forced upon her.

Mary Elizabeth invoked God. I did not want to be involved in her desire to be an instrument of heavenly intervention. I did my best to not complicate my life with issues of such weight. But I did want to hear the next part of the story.

"What is it you have? What do you need me for?"

Mary Elizabeth turned to a page in her sketchpad but kept it clutched to her chest. "Remember, at first all Mina could do was look out one small window in the speedboat. She was anxious. She was scared and excited about a country she'd only heard about. She still thought everything was a new and grand opportunity. With that incredible mind of hers, she saw and remembered visual details of her journey."

I nodded. I almost told her to call the small window a porthole, but that was only out of irritation at the futility of whatever she wanted to do.

"She remembers the trip in the small boat as being fast and noisy and rough. The girls had a hard time sitting on the cushions in the cabin. Mina wedged herself where she could see out. For the longest time, she saw nothing but darkness and spray bouncing off the window." Mary Elizabeth smiled. "I think it was exhilarating for her the way a roller coaster ride is for a normal teenager. This is something that might get us close to where she came to shore."

She pushed the sketchpad toward me. "She told me she thought they were going to crash. They were going fast and headed right toward a rock wall. It was dark, and she didn't see it until they were right on top of it. Just when she thought they would all die, the boat made a sharp turn and passed through an opening in the wall."

The drawing was almost abstract in its depiction of the darkness and waves rising into spray on what Mina and Mary Elizabeth called a rock wall.

Preacher said, "I told her if anyone could find such a place it would be you. The coast is your backyard."

She looked at me expectantly. "I thought if there's a place like this where he comes to shore I could watch for him. I'll sit there every night if necessary."

"And do what?"

"I don't know." Her frustration spilled over. "I need to see this place first. Will you help me find it?"

I shook my head at her simplistic plan.

"So, all you want right now is to see this place?" I tapped the drawing with a finger.

"Yes. Do you think you can you find it?"

"I know where it is."

"I knew it, Sam. I knew it." Preacher sat back in his chair triumphantly. "Where is it? How do we get there?"

"I can't imagine that seeing it will help you. Not without a lot of help from the Coast Guard."

"Exactly," said Jason Edwards.

"Please." Mary Elizabeth ignored everyone in the room but me.

"I need coffee." I needed a moment alone. "Anybody else?" Everybody declined. I got up and went to the kitchen. There was a quiet, intense murmur of conversation from the porch.

I debated the possibilities. I could show them. It couldn't hurt. I didn't think showing her would increase Mary Elizabeth's resolution to do something foolhardy. She was determined to do that no matter what. It didn't mean I had to get involved any further.

I went back to the porch without having refilled my coffee cup.

"What do you have planned for the day?"

"Not a thing, Sam," Preacher said. "Not a thing."

"I'll show you this place. We'll take my boat. It will save us a long walk. It'll take us a while to get there. I'll buy you lunch at Stingaree after we see it."

Mary Elizabeth beamed. Jason Edwards looked at me like I'd betrayed him.

I would show them the place Mina had drawn. I'd show Mary Elizabeth how ridiculous it was to think you could stake it out and catch a smuggler. I had no illusion she could save the child Zoio by sitting on what she called a rock wall.

I KEPT MY BOAT ten minutes away from my house in the marina at Sol de Mer, the community on the bay developed by my Uncle Harlan's company. I owned a couple of rental properties there and managed several more for Harlan. I called the guys at the marina and asked them to get my boat ready.

Outside, Mary Elizabeth introduced me to Mina and told her I was going to take everybody to see the rock wall. Mina shook my hand weakly and said hello, the timbre of her voice rich with the consonants and vowels of her homeland. Her hand trembled. Her eyes stayed steady, looking intensely at my shoes.

I told Joshua to clean up the shop and take the rest of the day off. I took my Range Rover to the marina. Preacher's group followed in their car. *The Lonely Star* was my thirty-eight-foot indulgence. Tied dockside, she glistened with water where they had sprayed off her overnight collection of cobwebs. She was plugged into shore power, and they'd turned on the air conditioner to cool the cabin.

"Nice," Mary Elizabeth said as I helped her aboard. She helped the girl. Patricia Carr said nothing as she took my hand and stepped aboard. I went to the topside controls, switched to battery power, and flipped on the blowers. I disconnected and stored the power cable. Preacher and Edwards held her to the dock while I started the engines. They pushed us off, and I turned tightly in the basin.

I left the marina's channel and turned east. The length of West Bay stretched out in front of us. Between the Gulf of Mexico and us lay Galveston Island. East of Galveston Island was the Bolivar Peninsula. On Bolivar, Mina had entered hell.

CHAPTER TWO

I STOOD TOPSIDE TO STEER. Mary Elizabeth and Jason Edwards started out on a bench in the well of the boat, talking fast and quiet. She had her arm around Mina. Patricia Carr sat across the well, maintaining her anti-social demeanor. Preacher took up his favorite place on the boat, right on the bow, straddling the anchor chain, his legs dangling, one over each side. He made a colorful figurehead in his Hawaiian shirt.

I usually enjoyed an early morning cruise across the bay, watching the wildlife, feeling the hum of the bay. The day I set out with Mary Elizabeth and friends would have been perfect for a leisurely boat ride, the sun warm, the air cool and sweet with the scent of the sea. The bays were smooth, the water clear.

I thought about Mina's experiences and those of her twin sister. Zoio might be journeying across the Atlantic at that very moment. I thought about soulless predators who traded in the bodies of children, stealing their innocence and the essence of their lives. The scenery of the bay could not hold my interest. Everything seemed shabby.

"You don't think I have a chance of saving Zoio like this, do you?" I hadn't heard Mary Elizabeth come topside. She was speaking just loud enough for me to hear over the rumble of the engines and the rush of the wind. Mina had gone forward to sit by Preacher.

I shook my head. "I don't see how. I know it's not what you want to hear, but the Coast Guard is your best bet."

"I can't run the risk. The corruption surrounding the girls is pervasive. The ship may have papers sufficient to document the girls as legitimate crew. What will happen if the Coast Guard can't do anything? For weeks, they train the girls not to trust the authorities. The girls think they're heading for a paradise. They will participate in the deception. Plus, the girls are less than nothing to these people. If the crew on the ship finds out they're to be searched, what do you think will happen to them?"

"Mina can tell the authorities what's going on. I'm sure they'd be careful."

"Then, I might lose both of them. I can't take that risk. I want to save both, but I will at least save Mina."

"What if they get to shore? What do you plan to do?"

"Mina says the lady that drove the van was real nice. I don't think they're worried about anybody being on their trail. I'm hoping that Preacher and I can just follow the van and take the girls off when they make a rest stop. What are they going to do? Call the police on us for kidnapping? I don't think so." She paused. "You could help."

I ignored that. "What if they get to shore and you never see them?"

"I will find a way to have Mina tell somebody in authority what's happening. Her sister and the others will at least have a chance that way." Without seeing anything, she looked out over the water. "And I will not stop looking for them. Ever."

"You said you intend to go to the authorities anyway. Are you sure it wouldn't be best to just do that now?"

"No. I cannot tell them what they insist on knowing. I believe they'll send Mina back to Ukraine and I don't think she'll survive." She turned and faced forward. Her voice broke when she said, "I've got to save somebody. I've got to save at least one of them."

I looked at her. Tears welled in her eyes. Her hands

clutched the handrail on the console. Her knuckles turned white with strain. She was complex, with undercurrents and motives I did not fully appreciate. As with all good zealots, Mary Elizabeth's hopeless quest was as much about herself as it was about her cause.

"Okay, look, I'm going to show you the only place I know that fits her drawing. It has to be the place she saw. We'll cruise around a bit and see what you think."

"Thank you, Sam." She smiled. "I'm sorry for being emotional. Please don't think I'm trying to use tears on you."

"I don't think that. You've lived with this longer than I have. I know there's evil out there but very little of it is ever personal to me. I appreciate that it's personal to you. I'll show you around. I just think the odds are against what you want to do." I checked the gauges, adjusted the throttles, and swerved a little to keep Preacher awake. "I wish I had a good idea."

"Thanks for helping. You're right. It is personal. God help me. It is personal."

"We're going to take our time to get there. It'll take a while. Enjoy the ride."

She smiled. "I will. This really is a great boat. You must enjoy it."

"I do. I toy with the idea of living on it, but it's not quite set up for that."

I pushed the throttles up a couple of notches. Up front, Preacher raised his face to the breeze. He took Mina's hand and stretched their arms high as if to fly. For the first time, I saw Mina smile as she looked at Preacher. I smiled and shook my head.

Mary Elizabeth said, "He thinks highly of you. He says you are integrated."

"Integrated? I wonder what that means. He's a friend. I like Preacher." I looked at her. "I do wonder, though, how in the world did you meet Preacher? You're not like most of his flock."

"I'm borrowing a house on the beach. He spoke to me the first day we were here. I confess it took me a little while to realize that he is not anywhere close to being an ordinary minister. I felt so overwhelmed and alone. I eventually talked to him more than I intended. He has a way about him, and he listens well. It didn't take long to realize that he was not likely to go to the police if I told him the whole story. And I do need some help."

"Preacher does have a way about him. I think, perhaps, you both have a way about you. I'm worried about what you might be getting into."

She smiled again.

"Sam, I do appreciate what you're doing. I won't let Preacher do anything dangerous."

"You know you're involved in something evil. You're concerned about the girls on that ship. You are just as expendable as they are if you get in somebody's way. Somebody has a lot invested in Mina and her sister and the other girls. Whoever that is will not be happy that you are screwing up their investment."

"One thing about being as insignificant as I am is that we'll be awfully hard to find if I can get Zoio out of there. I've got places to hide."

"What about the other girls?"

"Arrangements can be made for them as well. I'll see to it."

I shrugged. The fervor behind hopeless causes saddens me.

I pointed out sights to Mary Elizabeth along the way.

We saw Rosette Spoonbills and Brown Pelicans. I told her about their comeback from an endangered existence. From time to time, flocks of noisy, hungry gulls hovered in our wake grabbing morsels churned up by our passing.

I shouted to Preacher and Mina to hang on.

I pushed the throttles forward. The sound of both engines increased with a satisfying surge. The smooth surface of the bay slipped beneath us. I could hear the constant splash of the bow wave. *The Lonely Star* went on plane. The wind whipped Mary Elizabeth's hair. I smiled and looked at her. She laughed with pleasure.

I leaned toward her so she could hear. "We're going about thirty-five miles an hour. It's probably half as fast as he brings them in from offshore. Plus, he does it over waves in the surf in the dark. He is nuts."

Preacher looked back at her and waved. He, too, had a grin on his face. He put his arm around Mina. I ran half the length of Galveston Island at that gas-guzzling rate. I swerved once or twice to chase seagulls scattering before us.

She pointed toward the island and shouted, "Galveston looks different from out here. I've driven it, but I've never seen it like this."

I slowed to navigate safely through the channel across Carancahua Reef. I told Mary Elizabeth how the Carancahua Indians crossed the reef to get to Galveston Island and how some historians think mosquitoes ran them back to the mainland.

Just as we crossed the reef, the scent of ripe watermelon freshened the air. "Smell that?" I asked. "The smell of watermelon?"

"Yes."

"That's a school of speckled trout feeding on shrimp washed over the reef. They eat more than they need and disgorge to eat some more. That's what we smell."

To me, that scent usually meant all is right with the world. That morning it created a selfish longing, a wish that I'd skipped work and left the dock early that day. The bays were my refuge. It angered me to waste my day on somebody's quixotic quest. It angered me that a stain of such magnitude tainted my world. It didn't help my self-esteem that Mary Elizabeth was a much better person than I.

"May we come up?" Edwards and Patricia stood at the bottom of the steps. I waved them up.

I slowed as we passed under the interstate and through the gate of the railroad bridge. I took the channel to the middle of the pass between Galveston Island and Bolivar Peninsula. I turned seaward and headed toward the Gulf of Mexico. A freighter made way toward Houston. I slowed, so I could talk to them without interference from the wind.

"This is the Houston Ship Channel." I pointed at freighters anchored just offshore. "Those ships are waiting to make their way up the channel to Houston or Texas City. There are two jetties that protect the entry to the channel." I pointed right to the jetty extending from the tip of Galveston Island. It was dotted with people enjoying the day. "That's the South Jetty." I pointed at the jetty that ran out to sea from the peninsula. "That's the North Jetty. Those are the longest jetties in the world. They stretch over five miles out to sea."

"That's the rock wall, isn't it?" I could see the excitement in Mary Elizabeth's eyes. On the bow, Mina pointed at the jetty and talked rapidly to Preacher. She turned and nodded with excitement at Mary Elizabeth, her hands gripping Preacher's arm. Preacher aimed a finger at me with a satisfied smile.

"Yes. The North Jetty has a boat cut about a mile out.

We're headed there. They built the boat cut to let small boats get back to the bays without running five miles out to sea. It can be a lifesaver if you're up the coast and a storm pops up. Your guy must have brought the girls through the boat cut."

She put her hand on my arm and squeezed.

I said, "He'd be a fool to take it at night at high speed. For one thing, he might crash into a boat fishing at the cut. Maybe he times it so there's a slack high tide. That's what I'd do. Fewer people fishing then. Maybe he has a lookout with a cell phone or radio."

There were boats anchored at the cut, their occupants fishing the current flowing through the cut.

"I caught the biggest redfish I've ever caught right there."

I slowed as we approached, staying a respectful distance from those fishing. The boat cut made me nervous anytime. *The Lonely Star* was way too big to take through the cut. It was narrow and the current strong. Unyielding slabs of granite jumbled crazily on each side. The sea swirled on the rocks as it picked up speed through the cut. It got crowded in the console as Preacher and Mina joined us.

"This is it, Sam." He gripped Mary Elizabeth's shoulders. "I told you Sam would know."

"What do you think?" Mary Elizabeth asked Mina.

"Yes." Mina nodded and moved to closer to Mary Elizabeth, who put her arm tightly around the girl.

I slowed just off the cut, keeping the throttles up just enough to maintain control and make headway against the incoming current. The fishermen in other boats were starting to give me wary looks. I pointed out a sunken shrimp boat sitting on the bottom just on the other side of the cut, its masts and the top of its pilothouse above water.

"That's what a storm can do to you. I won't take my boat through the cut. Let's go look at it from the other side." I moved away slowly turning away from the jetty. I pushed the throttles forward heading out to sea.

The boat rocked through the surf. I braced my legs against the motion. Everybody else held on with both hands. Waves broke to our left on the granite of the jetty. I tried to imagine aiming for the cut while running at high speed in the dark. It might have been possible with good radar or someone at the cut with a light, or both. The noise of my engines and the wind limited the obligation to talk.

In fifteen minutes I circled the end of the jetty and another fifteen brought us to the boat cut again. I watched the depth finder carefully as we approached. I held the *Star* fifty yards away from the cut. It got quiet as I cut back the engines to hold us steady, rocking in the surf.

"Yes," Mary Elizabeth said. "That's it. It has to be."

"That means he met Mina's ship back that way." I pointed out to the sea over our stern. "The first land you run into that way is Florida or Cuba, then the Bahamas, then Africa. He met the ship out at sea, safe from observation and brought them back through here. I don't know why he wouldn't just go through the mouth of the channel. I think he'd be a lot less noticeable coming in between the jetties. Maybe he's a cowboy, scaring the girls, showing off. Maybe it's how he dodges the Coast Guard."

Mary Elizabeth asked, "Can you walk out to the boat cut?"

"Yes. People do it all the time to fish."

"So, someone could sit there, and they'd definitely see him if he came through."

"Yes. You'd see him if you were sitting there at the right time on the right night, unless that night he took a different route. What if you did see him? Then what? You wouldn't know where he was going, and you'd be a mile from your car. And the more I think about it, the more I think his lookout would be sitting there, too."

She continued to stare at the boat cut. "But we're closer. Thank you so much, Sam." I could see a strengthening of her will. She was starting to appreciate the difficulties of what she wanted to do, but it was the unknown that made her problem most difficult. We'd cleared up some of the unknown.

"Let's go to lunch." I turned back toward the gulf and ran fast enough to bounce everybody. I hoped the immensity and surging power of the sea would discourage Mary Elizabeth from her foolhardy quest to do something on her own.

Everybody but Preacher went down to the boat well and started talking. I couldn't hear what they said. Jason Edwards leaned toward Mary Elizabeth, undoubtedly arguing the futility of what she was trying to do. Occasionally Patricia would say something. Mary Elizabeth sat with her arm around the girl, never looking as though she was losing an argument.

"Thank you, Sam."

I shook my head at Preacher. "You know this is impossible, don't you?"

"I have faith."

"In what? God? Please. You are a more pragmatic preacher than that. At best, this is a waste of time. At worst, it is extremely dangerous. Deadly dangerous."

He smiled. "Well, thanks for doing this much. Maybe you'll have some more ideas that will help make it not so much a waste of time. Or to limit the danger."

I turned around the end of the jetty and headed back

up the ship channel, passing the looming bulk of anchored freighters. Each flagged by some small foreign country. Here, close to shore, the ships were immense. At sea, traversing the world, they would be smaller, capable of disappearing without a trace.

Every year there were ships that left some port and simply disappeared. Some were lost, but many became incognito by choice. Pirates stole entire ships and not just off the coast of Somalia. Often a ship carried something somewhere it should not have been going and disappeared by choice. They carried missile parts or guns to despots and freedom fighters. They carried food and medicine to countries subject to political embargo. They carried frightened people to countries where they were not supposed to be.

The freedom of the sea made our oceans a large, lawless frontier, attracting unbound free spirits and self-serving anarchists. It attracted me. I liked living where I lived and knowing that with a little work and some drums for fuel, I could have left my pier and traveled the world. With a sailboat, I wouldn't even need the fuel drums.

I looked back at my guests and opened the compartment where I keep sunscreen. "Hey," I shouted to get attention. I tossed the tube to Edwards. "Y'all better put some of this on, you're getting sun."

A few minutes later, Mary Elizabeth climbed back up, handed me the sunscreen and said, "Thanks. Thanks for everything."

"We're going to eat lunch at one of the best places on this part of the coast. I hope you enjoy seafood."

"Yes."

After several minutes, I swung wide to avoid a ferry traveling between Galveston Island and Bolivar Peninsula. I pointed out a couple of porpoises arching through the water at the side of the ferry. Mary Elizabeth pointed them out to Mina.

We passed the ferry landing and the old, rust covered and unused lighthouse. Turning into East Bay I punched up the speed. The mainland was an indistinct smudge to the north. The low profile of Bolivar Peninsula lay between the Gulf and us. In less than twenty minutes, we could see boats clustered over Hannah's Reef.

It was almost noon and almost peak high tide. Shrimp were riding the slow tidal flow over the reef and there were fifteen or twenty boats drifting with them. There have been good days when I would anchor the *Star* off the reef and launch a kayak to join the drift over the reef. On really good days there would be a friend or three with me. We would sit at anchor for the afternoon. There would be some soft music going while freshly caught speckled trout met the charcoal grill hung over the transom. Margaritas under the moon had a special flavor.

This day, I made the turn through the channel to Stingaree Marina and slowly approached the docking area. Preacher and Jason tossed the fenders over and jumped ashore to hold the lines, waiting for me to tie them fore and aft. We all went upstairs to the restaurant.

Stingaree Restaurant perched on the Intracoastal Waterway. We sat overlooking the Waterway, enjoying the weather and watching barges move down the canal. We shared barbecued, fried, and blackened shrimp and crispy fresh bread.

The conversation was strange. We were together in that place because of a global sex trade smuggling enterprise and we talked about the scenery and the excellent food. The girl who started it all ate slowly and talked only in quiet whispers to Mary Elizabeth.

Eventually, Mary Elizabeth became distracted, staring out over the marina. She said, "I had hoped that what Mina saw that night led to one particular place, a marina or something. Somewhere we could get behind the van when it left."

"Well, you can see that it doesn't. It's just the entrance to the bays. There's West Bay behind Galveston, East Bay right over there." I gestured at the bay on the other side of the Waterway. "Between them are the Galveston Bay and the largest of them all, Trinity Bay. He could go anywhere in there."

"There has to be something."

Preacher reached across the table and took her hand. "There will be. God is on your side."

Jason and Patricia murmured consolation, but they, like me, hoped Mary Elizabeth would accept the futility of her cause and do something other than try to be personally involved.

I should have kept my mouth shut.

"Mina," I said, "what do you remember about where you spent that first night?"

She looked at Mary Elizabeth, who nodded encouragingly. Mina turned toward me, her head tilted down in shyness, or fear. I couldn't imagine what she must think of men at that point.

In the rich timbre of her voice and her elementary English, she said, "We got off the boat and all of us slept inside. It was one big room."

"Were there windows?"

She shook her head.

"Do you know how long you stayed there?"

She shrugged. "It was night when we left."

"So, you think you stayed there all the next day and left the next night?"

She shrugged and nodded in the affirmative.

"What do you remember about the van?"

"It was brown. It had crosses on the side."

"Crosses?"

"Like church."

A church van full of kids would look normal. And distinctive. To Mary Elizabeth, I said, "A church bus might be easy to spot if every cop between here and Chicago was watching."

"Exactly," said Edwards.

Mary Elizabeth shook her head. "No. I've tried. Nothing is going to happen unless they get to talk to Mina and that is not going to happen. She is not going back."

Mary Elizabeth put both hands on the edge of the table and looked square at me. "Look, thanks for what you did. If you have any ideas other than let's go to the police, I'd like to hear them, but I've made up my mind. I will not put Mina in harm's way by putting her in the hands of the government."

I raised my hands. It wasn't my place to argue. Before I could frame a noncommittal response, Mina jumped and swiveled to look down the stretch of the pier toward the marina's entrance. I wondered for a moment what had grabbed her attention and then I noticed the reverberating rumble of two massive engines.

An offshore powerboat entered the marina through the channel. It was glossy white and turquoise with its name, *Lawless*, painted on the side in large yellow letters. Multicolored splash designs decorated its bow and stern. Its cockpit was an expanse of white leather. Unmuffled chrome tailpipes made noise like never-ending, distant thunder. The man at the wheel turned carefully to the dock and moved in just behind *The Lonely Star*. His passenger, a young lady very nicely clad in a turquoise bikini that matched the boat, stood ready with a fender. Every person on the deck of the restaurant turned to watch its arrival.

"That," I said, "is the kind of boat you took the night time ride in, isn't it?"

Mina's eyes were wide and the corner of her lip trembled. She nodded.

"It's okay, sweetie. That's not the one." Mary Elizabeth patted her on the shoulder. To me, she said, "It's bigger than I'd imagined. You're right. It would be scary taking that through the jetty at night."

"Mina," I asked, "do you remember what the boat you rode in looked like? How was it painted?"

"Not like that. It was black. It had no color."

Preacher asked, "Have you seen a black one, Sam?"

"No, but I don't pay that much attention to them. I know most of them are garishly painted. Like that one. A solid black boat would be exceptionable and noticeable for its lack of color. Those guys pay attention to the boats of others. I know somebody to ask."

Preacher nodded and smiled. He winked at Mary Elizabeth. She smiled. I ignored them.

We watched the girl in the bikini tie the boat with practiced ease while the captain raised the engine cover. Raising the cover made sure no fumes collected and gave those of us watching a chance to see his two impeccably clean muscular engines, bright with chrome and almost pulsing with testosterone.

I paid for lunch. We walked along the pier to admire the *Lawless* before we boarded *The Lonely Star*. I gave the blowers a couple of minutes to work. Preacher and Jason pushed us away from the pier and jumped on as I started the engines.

Stingaree Restaurant sits on a wharf that crosses a T. The leg of the T is a channel dead-ending opposite the entrance to the restaurant and bar. Houses line the channel and range from neatly painted homes with lawns and little plaster figurines fishing from their docks to shabby, weathered buildings that look like they're just waiting for a push to collapse into a pile of scrap. Some of them have enclosed boathouses. Instead of heading straight out to the bay, I turned and paused at the entrance to the dead-end channel

I gestured at the houses lining the channel. "There are a lot of these kinds of places all over the bay system."

"Do you think he lives somewhere like this?"

"I have no idea. He has to keep that boat somewhere. I doubt if he's trailering it. As noticeable as they are on the water, they're more so when out of their element on a trailer. He probably doesn't park his boat this close to anybody, but you never know. He could hole up in any one of many isolated places. There are entire communities down here that mind their own business and protect their own."

Preacher grinned.

"What are you smiling at?"

"You. You are getting on his trail."

"No. I'm just pointing out how hard it will be for anybody to get on his trail."

He grinned and nodded and made his way to his perch on the bow. I followed the channel out of the marina and across the Intracoastal Waterway to enter East Bay, where I turned to the northwest. Mary Elizabeth stood beside me. Mina went to sit by Preacher. Edwards and Patricia took refuge in the cabin out of the sun and wind.

"Mary Elizabeth, look at his options once he gets into the bay system." I motioned at the expanse of water around us. "This is the smallest of the bays. We're about halfway down its length."

She nodded.

"As fast as we're going, it's going to take us twenty minutes to get out of East Bay. At that point, we'll be at the lower edge of Trinity Bay. Trinity Bay goes over forty miles inland. Jean Lafitte hid his pirate fleet in there. You know how far we had to come from my place. On the other side of where I live is Christmas Bay and then Matagorda Bay and then bay after bay all the way to Mexico."

She nodded, starting to look defeated. I felt bad about extinguishing the spark she'd had since I'd shown her the boat cut.

"Listen, you're further along than you were. The worst that can happen is you have to get the authorities involved. Maybe you'll find out what ship Zoio is on and they'll check it out."

She nodded. She looked so hopeless, I was close to trying to convince her she could still win, that there would be a way for her to save the girl, but I just didn't see it.

I told myself to keep quiet, don't encourage her. To her, I said, "Look, you got Mina to talking. She must have been in bad shape when she came to you. You extracted her from some nastiness. You literally saved her life. That's something. You found where she came into the country. You've already done well. Maybe something else will come up."

She nodded again.

The long ride back to my slip in the marina was quiet. I pushed the boat to get there as quickly as possible. I backed into my slip. Preacher jumped ashore to tie the boat.

Mary Elizabeth said, "Thank you, Sam. I really do appreciate you showing us the jetty. And for lunch. I understand the difficulties. I just need to think. Maybe you're right. Maybe it is hopeless."

Preacher stood waiting to help her ashore. "There is hope. Sam, thanks. I knew you would help."

"No problem Preacher."

Edwards shook my hand and said, "Thank you." He squeezed my hand and nodded at me once, with a tight, satisfied smile. He thought I'd almost convinced Mary Elizabeth of the foolishness of her quest.

Patricia Carr nodded in my direction. She still didn't like me. I wondered if she liked anything.

They climbed into their car and left.

I sprayed down the boat trying to not think that the day had been a waste. I spent the rest of the afternoon tending to a few of the endless chores generated by a boat for its caretaker. I used the routine to limit my thinking about the sale and rape of girls. How convenient for me. Finally, I locked up the boat and headed to my house.

THAT EVENING, back at my place, I started charcoal burning in the grill. I took a snapper fillet out of the refrigerator and seasoned it. I got in the shower and stood there for a while, letting hot water hit me in the back of the neck, trying to wash away knots of tension.

I usually looked forward to grilling on the deck, watching the sunset, enjoying the slowly appearing night sky over the bay. I was and happy to have carved out a peaceful place. That night, as I showered, I was unsettled. I thought about the horrors inflicted on Mina. Sixteen-year-old girls should enjoy the joyful mysteries of life with boys their own age.

Mina's captors had forced horrible truths on her about the insatiable desires of flawed men. The animal devoured her before she'd had the chance to enjoy the first physical expressions of love. She might be so messed up she would never know what it meant to make love in a good way.

Mina's country, like so many others, struggled in its freedom from the smothering care of the Soviet Union. Gone was the oppression of the communist state and gone was the shelter it provided. Those countries struggled to catch up in a world moving at an ever-increasing rate. Economic and spiritual poverty threatened to overwhelm those trying to create a modern state from scratch.

The less fortunate citizens of every country on earth hungered for things dangling just out of their reach. I wondered if Mina's family heard the horror stories of what happened to young girls taken to foreign lands. Maybe the dark man in Mina's drawing had been convincing. Maybe I just couldn't fathom the desperation and despair that caused people to send children away. Maybe it was a tragic choice Mina's relatives had to make in order to save the rest of the family.

The crime was not that of the family. The crime was the merciless grip of the monster whose tentacles stretched around the world. The crime belonged to those who fed the monster by purchasing the innocence of children and to those who consumed that innocence. Now, that monster had reached my refuge on the edge of the sea. I could smell its stink like the rotting carcass of a large fish.

I slammed the shower faucets off. I was a fool and it made me angry.

The odds were several hundred to one, but if all else failed, I knew how Mary Elizabeth and Preacher would have the best chance at grabbing the tail of the monster. I hoped there was a better way. If not, it would take more than the two of them.

I grilled and ate my snapper. I didn't enjoy it.

CHAPTER THREE

THE NEXT MORNING I got out of bed before sunrise. I took a mug of coffee and sat at the end of the boardwalk. I sat there, listening to mullet flipping at the surface and the lonesome calls of birds of the night. The dawn turned from gray to the pastels of a blue and yellow morning. The breeze blew gentle and sweet from the southeast.

In the tranquility of the morning, I imagined a freighter at sea. In my mind, it was not a gentle sea. It rolled in slick, foamed flecked swells, sending the rusty ship crashing down in geysers of spray that covered the decks. Terrified passengers were somewhere in the fetid bowels of that ship praying in whatever language their God understood. They prayed to survive the sickness inducing pitch and roll of the ship. They prayed for the families they'd left behind. They prayed the myths of America were true and worth the price they paid.

All week long I'd planned to fish that day, but fishing would feel trivial. I needed to know more about bringing dispossessed souls to shore in the dark. With enough information, I'd be able to find somebody with the resources to intervene and save the girls.

Sunday is a play day for the power boaters. To get one on the phone, I had to call early. I went to the house and dialed Leeland Cook's cell phone. I met Leeland three miles offshore one day. The day before we'd met, he'd made a run down the coast to Corpus Christi and failed to take into account an approaching storm. It slowed him up halfway back. He ran out of gas and I heard his radio call. He and the two gorgeously suntanned and scantily clad ladies in his boat were happy to see me.

My boat doesn't run on the high octane his engines require so I towed him in. In appreciation, he bought me one beer and then another. I bought him the third one. We discovered mutual interests and agreed that The Big Easy Social Club in Houston was the best bar outside of Louisiana for live blues. We drove to Houston that night and listened to Thumper Lee play some blues. We consumed more than an appropriate quantity of Jack Daniels. We've been friends ever since. Leeland took me on my first eighty miles an hour boat ride.

I caught him on his cell phone before he left the marina.

"Samuel, come join us for a boat ride. There are five of us. We have an extra lady."

"I can't. I'm too far away, but if you have a few minutes I want to ask you something."

"Sure. We're still waiting on the extra lady. What's up?"

"Do you know anybody who owns an all-black or mostly black power boat?"

"You mean one like mine?"

"Yes."

"No. All black would be unusual. Why?"

"It has to do with a legal matter I'm handling. I'm not free to discuss details, but it may be involved in a smuggling operation. Could you very discretely ask around?"

"Sure. I'd have seen it if it's owned by one of the regulars. Do you think it's on our water?"

"It's been seen here. Be very discrete. Don't make a big deal out of it. There's a chance it could be dangerous. I wouldn't want to spook the owner or anything."

"Okay, I'll ask, and someday you will tell me what it is

all about."

"If at all possible."

I asked Leeland about the range of a boat like his. Like all the boat guys, he loved to talk about his boat. Its two engines each directed almost four hundred horsepower to the water. It had a hundred and twenty-gallon gas tank, and Leeland was thinking about having another tank installed. If conservative, he got about four miles a gallon. When having fun, he'd get a couple of miles per gallon. He knew some people who didn't get that good of mileage out of their boats. He knew some people who carried over three hundred gallons of gas.

I thanked him for the information and agreed we needed to get together soon.

I logged into the internet, did a search for "human trafficking," and got over seven and a half million hits. I didn't even search for "forced prostitution" or any of the other possibilities. I learned enough. The Baltic States, and primarily Ukraine, had supplanted the Philippines and Thailand as the leading source for women fed into the prostitution trade. Most ended up in countries where prostitution was legal or tolerated. Relatively few ended up in the United States, but it was a growing number.

There were plenty of scholarly articles on the problem, complete with footnotes and bibliographies. There were references to studies conducted by the United Nations. There were news articles and summaries of the laws of countries around the world. Documentaries existed. There were thousands of sad stories. It was a centuries old problem and a multimillion-dollar industry. I turned the computer off. Mary Elizabeth was right. The big picture would chew up and swallow two lonely teenage girls.

I couldn't think of anybody I knew who did

immigration law. I checked the time to make sure it wasn't too early and called Harlan. He answered the phone as he always does, "Yes?"

"Harlan, it's Sam. Good morning."

"Good morning Sam. Is there a problem?"

"No. No problem that concerns you, anyway. I need to ask a favor."

"What?"

"Would you ask your lawyers if they have anybody who does immigration law? If they don't, will you ask them to find me the name of somebody I could talk to?"

"I can do that. Anything else?"

"No. That's it. The weather is nice, though. You need to let me know when you want to take a fishing trip."

"I'll do that. I have a couple of gentlemen from Florida who might enjoy a fishing trip. I'm trying to do a little deal with them."

"Just let me know. That was it. I'll let you go."

"Okay, Sam. I'll have somebody call you. Good-bye."

Harlan respected my privacy, as I respected his. It's a product of our satisfying and unusual relationship. Unusual because I was the only person in the family with whom he socialized. Our friendship drove certain members of my family nuts. Harlan's wealth was a family legend. My mother took great delight in mentioning my relationship with Harlan in casual conservation with her sisters. The sisters thought I was selfish and mean because I did not get jobs with Harlan for a variety of my cousins. I hoped Harlan realized that I really did not care about his money.

It was like Harlan to not act the least bit curious about why I needed to talk to an immigration lawyer. He respected my privacy and my ability to take care of my own problems, asking for assistance if needed. I valued and returned that respect.

Harlan's lawyers had an office in the building he owned and where he maintained his office in downtown Houston. The firm of Sherwood, Thomas, and Cain had been with Harlan for decades and made a lot of money off him. I hoped, as a matter of courtesy, acting on his request, they would have somebody I could talk to without having to pay for the privilege.

Thirty minutes after I called Harlan, I received a phone call from Rosalyn Myers, secretary to Clancy Sherwood.

"Mr. Locke, Rosalyn Myers. I understand you need to talk to an immigration attorney."

"Yes. Do you have somebody?"

"No. Not at the firm, but there are a few with whom we maintain relationships. We could refer you. May I inquire as to the nature of your problem? If you need a green card for a maid, I will send you to one person. If it's something more complicated there would be a choice of others."

"It is more complicated than a green card. I need someone familiar with illegal immigration from Eastern Europe. Best of all would be somebody with an understanding of persons forced into prostitution and brought to this country illegally."

"Mr. Locke, what have you got yourself into? Okay. I know someone. Let me give her a call. Is it an emergency? Do you need to see her today?"

"No. Sometime next week will be fine. At her convenience."

"Can you meet downtown?"

"Sure. Just let me know when. And Rosalyn, I don't have a paying client."

She sighed. "Mr. Locke, all clients should pay, but I

understand. I think she'll give you some time at no charge. We send her work from time to time. I'll call you after I talk to her."

"Call me on my cell. I may be out. And thanks. You are a sweetheart."

"I'm just doing my job, Mr. Locke."

It did not surprise me that Rosalyn knew someone she could call about my problem. An assistant like Rosalyn was worth several attorneys to a law firm.

When Preacher and friends left the day before, we'd made no plans or promises about getting back in touch. Preacher has no phone, and I had no idea how to get in touch with the others. I left a message for Preacher with Clara's Bar and Grill asking him to call my cell. He checks in with Clara most every day for beer and messages.

I dressed scruffy but put some decent clothes in a bag. I put three casting rods and four surf rods in the back of my fishing truck, a seasoned four-wheel drive Ford with rod holders welded to it front and rear. It sat high on wide tires. With a bench seat and no carpet. I could sleep in it and wash sand from the floorboard with a water hose. The truck had spent its life trudging up and down beaches and looked like it. I loved that truck.

I filled a cooler with ice from the ice machine in the shop and loaded it with salami, goat cheese, Dr Pepper, Shiner Bock beer, bottles of green tea, one pack of frozen squid, and two of shrimp. I looked like a typical Gulf Coast fisherman. I was ready for a little undercover work.

Possibly, the smuggling operation that brought Mina into the country was a one-shot deal. I doubted it though. A boat painted solid black and a van painted like a church bus had the earmarks of an ongoing operation. A boat ripping through the boat cut in the middle of the night must have attracted attention at some point. Of course, Mina's ride might have coincidentally been a one-time evasive action, but it wouldn't hurt to check it out. I headed toward Bolivar to nose around.

I passed the entrance to Sol de Mer on my left and thought about my canceled plan to spend the day on my boat. My cell phone chirped. It was Rosalyn.

"Mr. Locke, I've scheduled an appointment for you tomorrow in our offices at ten in the morning with Cathy Winwood. She specializes in immigration matters and should be able to answer questions for you or direct you to someone who can."

"Thank you."

"No problem. Is there anything you need for your meeting or anything else I can do for you?"

"No. I didn't mean to bother you on a Sunday. Shouldn't you be in church?"

"Probably not as much as you, Mr. Locke. I'm just doing my job. It's no bother."

"You are a peach."

"Why, yes. Yes, I am. You be sure and mention that to Mr. Sherwood shortly before bonus time. Have a nice day."

I drove the length of Galveston Island. Joggers, skaters, and walkers were starting to populate the Seawall. Early arrivers staked out places on the beach with umbrellas and towels. Frisbees and boogie boards were in use. A few people were fishing the rock groins jutting into the Gulf at regular intervals. Filtered through my awareness of the trafficking in girls that touched these shores, the carefree pulse of life seemed strained, with no intelligent direction.

Later in the spring, there would be a long wait for the ferry connecting Galveston Island to the Bolivar Peninsula. I only waited through one departure before my truck bounced onto the ferry and, directed by a yellow vested attendant, tucked in close to the car in front of me. Children tumbled out of that car with a bag of breadcrumbs and headed to the rear of the ferry, laughing and excited, ready to feed the whirling mass of seagulls following the ferry on its twenty-minute cruise across the channel.

Usually, I went up to the observation deck for the ride, but that morning I just leaned my head back, closed my eyes, and contemplated Mary Elizabeth's quest. No brilliant inspiration came to light.

The ferry bumped to its pier on Bolivar. The cars left the ferry, spreading out along the highway. I left the pack after a mile, turning right toward the sea. The road led to the base of the jetty. There was a store there selling bait, fishing supplies, and sundries. I parked in the gravel lot and went in, letting the screen door slam behind me.

I browsed the aisles and picked up a couple of lures I could use.

The man behind the counter was dusty brown. His hair, his eyes, his skin, and his clothes were a washed-out earth color. I believed the message on his t-shirt. It said: I work so I can fish.

"That all?" he asked. "Need some bait?"

"No. This is it. I'm having to slowly replace a lot of tackle."

"Oh?" He was ringing up the sale.

"Yeah. I was fishing out at the cut a while back and about two in the morning some damn fool in one of those jacked-up offshore racing boats came through like a bat out of hell. Boat was solid black, throwing water everywhere. Snagged my lines. Dragged a couple of expensive rods into the water. I'd tied my bait bucket to my tackle box, and he got them both. I couldn't salvage a thing."

The clerk shook his head and handed me my purchase.

"You ever hear of anybody doing that? I'd like to have a discussion with the jackass who drove that boat through there. He could kill somebody."

"Nah. Not me. I ain't heard nothing like that."

"I have." The voice came from behind me. It was a boy, in his prime, seventeen or eighteen years old with good shoulders and tapered waist. He was probably a running back on his high school football team. He was dumping boxes of frozen squid into the iceboxes at the back of the shop.

"A while back old man Jackson saw the same thing."

"Oh?" I turned toward him.

"Yeah. Jackson fishes the jetty a lot from a skiff. He came in one Sunday a while ago, cussing and fuming. He saw one of those boats come through there. I think it scared him off the water."

"Do you know where Mr. Jackson lives? I'd like to compare notes. See if he noticed anything."

"Nah. I don't know where he lives. How about you Houge?"

"No."

The boy never stopped cutting open boxes and dumping bait into the ice. "He must live on the peninsula somewhere. Drives an old beat up Chevy. He'll be around somewhere fishing."

"Well, maybe I'll catch up with him sometime."

I debated leaving a message for the man Jackson, but I was leery of attracting too much attention. Besides, I doubted I'd learn more than I'd already learned. Somebody, probably more than once, had come through the cut at high speed in the boat that had my interest. It wasn't a one-time thing. I took my lures, grabbed a rod out of the truck and walked out onto the jetty.

The first part of the jetty was easy to walk with a sidewalk-like concrete finish. When the concrete ended, I walked on spray and algae slick blocks of granite, taking care to avoid banged up shins or worse. It took a while to walk the mile to the boat cut.

Early on there were a couple of children slinging crab nets into the water. They had a bucket of chicken parts for bait and another bucket starting to fill with crabs. They pranced in bare feet as sure-footed as a couple of mountain goats.

I nodded to the occasional fisherman. Halfway to the cut the sounds of the surf drowned out all noise of the highway. There, a young lady, her long dark hair blowing in the wind, sat facing the sea, absorbed in thoughts of her own. She did not even glance at me as I walked past. I hoped she sought and enjoyed a pleasurable loneliness.

There wasn't much to see at the cut. Being there reinforced my awareness of the risk the smuggler faced when he went through the cut. I decided he must have help. Somebody had to stand where I stood with a radio or phone to warn of obstructions, holding a lantern to mark the escape route.

I saw nothing to back up my conjecture. Plenty of cigarette butts populated crevices in the rocks, litter of more than one person who chose to fish from this spot. But, I envisioned another man, faceless for the moment, sitting with a two-way radio or cell phone, smoking in the offshore breeze, waiting for the driver of the boat to let him know when to turn on the light.

The ocean usually enveloped me in a comforting aloneness I enjoyed, but that day it did not comfort. Standing there, I appreciated the frustration of Mary

Elizabeth at being alone in a search for acceptable options for Mina and Zoio. I started walking back toward the peninsula. The girl who had been sitting in solitude was gone, but the kids were still at their crabbing.

As I approached the place where the concrete walkway begins, I noticed someone walking purposefully toward me. Again, she was out of place. Mary Elizabeth was furthering her quest by coming to the cut. I had a choice, either jump in the water and take a dangerous swim or wait for her.

Swimming away would be embarrassing. Mary Elizabeth saw me before I noticed her. She walked toward me purposefully, with a knowing smile on her face. I hurried to meet her before the sidewalk ended.

"Mr. Locke," she said, her hand reaching out to touch my arm, "I'm somewhat surprised to see you here. Fishing?"

I felt like a school kid caught doing something I shouldn't be doing. "Ms. Kincaid ... "

"Mary Elizabeth, please."

I nodded. "There's not much to see out there."

She shrugged. "Maybe not. But I want to see it. I have nothing else to do."

"Where's Mina?"

"With Patricia. They're going to do a little shopping in Houston. I worry about her being in public. Perhaps that's silly, but I know the ones who took her are trying to recover their investment. I know she must be safe down here. Plus, she's bored. And a teenager. In any event, The Galleria is safer than the streets of Galveston."

She spoke like a parent, the role she had assumed. I looked back over the length of the jetty. It stretched into the distance, fading into the sprays and mists of waves breaking along its length.

"Come on," I said. "I'll show you. Watch your step. It

can be slick out here."

The children who had been crabbing passed by us on our way toward the cut. They were laughing and almost running toward shore, carrying their buckets and nets with the mysteriously unbound energy of their age.

Mary Elizabeth turned to look after them and said, "They took that from Mina."

I doubted if Mina's life would have ever been that carefree. I recognized the subtle pressure being brought to bear on me, but I kept my mouth shut and continued to lead Mary Elizabeth toward the horizon.

At the cut, she stood with her hands tucked into the back pockets of her jeans. I sat on the edge of a granite block and watched her. The wind whipped her hair and it struck me, in other circumstances, I would be very interested in getting to know her on a personal level. As it was, the only passion she had room for was her battle for Mina and her sister.

She spoke loudly over the sound of the restless surge of sea and wind. "Thank you."

I nodded. She walked over and put a hand on my shoulder.

"No. I'm serious. I know you think this is all a bad idea and you took all this time for me." She smiled. "I know you weren't out here fishing. I thank you. Your willingness to spend time when you think it is wasted makes it all the more special."

I nodded again. I might as well stop ignoring the truth of things. I knew I'd signed up for her crusade. I just hadn't said it out loud yet. I looked out to sea, scanning the horizon slowly until I was looking at her.

"I have an appointment with an immigration lawyer tomorrow. I have some questions for her."

I noticed her look of concern and doubt.

"Don't worry," I said. "I'll take care to protect Mina's privacy." That's a lawyer's rationalization, doing stupid things in the interest of protecting a client.

"I trust you. Do you want me there?"

I hadn't considered that possibility and gave it several seconds of thought. I decided my best chance of getting brutal truth from the lawyer would be without the weight of Mary Elizabeth's subtle charisma and her quiet belief and fervor.

"No. Let me see her alone. She'll be available in the future if necessary. I just want more information on your legal options, that's all."

"Okay." She took a deep breath. "Thank you, Sam. Thank you." She sat down next to me. "What else do we need to do?"

"The most important thing is to find out when Zoio leaves Ukraine."

"I'm trying. There is a priest working with his counterparts in the Greek Orthodox Church trying to get the information for me. It is just so dangerous."

"Meanwhile, I guess we need to take a drive with Mina and get her best guess at the exact route they took. That could take a while." She nodded, her hand on my arm, her eyes alive with energy. "It wouldn't hurt to try to run down the smuggler's boat. I've already made some inquiries. He's used this cut more than once." She squeezed my arm on that one. "I still want to try to figure out a safe way to enlist law enforcement. We need them." She removed her hand from my arm.

"Sam ... " I raised a hand to stop her.

"Let me talk to the immigration lawyer tomorrow. I accept that the most important thing is to keep Mina safe.

Face it, we don't know what we're doing and we don't know what's possible. We need to explore all our options."

"Okay. I don't mean to cause trouble ... "

I interrupted. "Yes you do. You mean to cause trouble in a big way."

She smiled. "Yes," she said. She paused and her smile grew larger. "Yes I do." She drew her knees up, wrapped her arms around them and looked out over the ocean. We sat silently side by side for several minutes.

She took in a deep breath, held it for a couple of seconds, and visibly exhaled.

"Well," she said, "there's nothing else we can do today?"

"No. I can't think of anything."

She looked out over the ocean.

"I like it out here. It is primal." Now that we'd done everything we could about the Mina problem, she saw the sea for the first time.

"Yes."

We sat in comfortable silence. It is difficult to talk over the sounds of the wind and the sea on the rocks. I was intensely aware of her. Good looks, courage, and passion is a very attractive mix.

"So," I asked, "do you spend all your time saving children of other people, or do you have children of your own?"

She turned to me, almost laughing. "You don't know, do you?"

"I guess not. Know what?"

"I'm a nun, Sam. A real nun."

"Ah. So, when Preacher calls you Sister Mary Elizabeth, he really means it."

"Yes." She smiled. "I thought you knew."

"I guess I was a little dense about that. Not that I've known many nuns, but you must be undercover. I'd never have guessed."

"Undercover nun. I like that."

"It's just that you dress like a soccer mom, but are acting a little militant."

"Well, where I come from, nuns, at least the good ones, have a history of causing trouble."

"Guess I better not ask you out on a date."

She laughed. "No. The Church frowns on us dating. Thanks for the thought though."

We were quiet for a moment, letting my embarrassment dissipate in the breeze.

"You know," she said, "Patricia is no longer a nun."

"No longer?"

"She used to be. We are similar in that we both grew frustrated with the passivity of the Church in some areas. Perhaps she grew more frustrated than me. We both feel compelled to try to do more than the Church is comfortable with." She paused, continuing to look out over the sea. A freighter moved slowly in the distance. She looked at me. "You know, since Patricia left the order, she's dated. She's had boyfriends. She's single now. She's going to stay here and try to convince me to do the smart thing. I'm sure she could use a fun diversion when there's time."

She was being a matchmaker. "It would be nice if she lightened up. I don't think she likes me much."

"She is just over protective of me, that's all. Give her a chance."

"Okay, but I don't think we'll be dating."

"I'm surprised you aren't married or at least have a girlfriend. You are obviously a nice guy, you have that great boat, a wonderful place to live. There's nobody special?"

"Nah. I'm not as good as I appear."

"I don't believe that."

"There are ladies, but nobody serious. I even married once, but it didn't take."

"Children?"

"No. Thank God. I mean thank goodness."

"You can thank God if you want. Sam, don't go weird on me now that you know I'm a nun."

"Sorry, but it is just a little weird."

She punched me on the arm. "No, it's not. Nothing has changed. You just can't date me."

"Okay. But I can buy you lunch. Let's go, I'm hungry."

I helped her up and we made the long walk back to shore. She followed me in her car back to the ferry and over to the island. We ate outside in the courtyard of a sandwich place on The Strand, the heart of Galveston's tourist baiting entertainment district. She was pleasant company and easy to talk to. Later, I realized I'd shared a lot more about myself than I would on a real first date.

That lunch gave me additional motivation for helping her. I was, of course, outraged at the slimy business entrapping Mina and her sister, but the more I got to know Mary Elizabeth the more I realized she was genuinely nice and straightforward in rare ways. Mary Elizabeth Kincaid deserved to get what she sought. She deserved to win this battle for the souls of two children.

I'd dealt with lawyers for so long, her dedication to doing what was right was enlightening. The quiet people who get things done without accolades are humbling examples of what people should be.

The immigration lawyer I met the next day turned out to be no exception. She, too, was a quiet warrior.

CHAPTER FOUR

I MET CATHY WINWOOD on Monday at ten in the conference room of Sherwood, Thomas, and Cain. Rosalyn provided fruit and sandwiches for refreshment.

Cathy Winwood was younger than I expected, late twenties or early thirties. The attorneys at Sherwood, Thomas, and Cain tend to wear expensive business suits and sport razor cut hair, even the ladies. Cathy was in jeans and a t-shirt, her hair long and pulled into a ponytail.

After introductions by Rosalyn, I said, "Thank you for seeing me." We shook hands, and she sat down across the table from me.

"No problem. Rosalyn tells me you want to consult about an immigration matter. What's up?"

"What do you know about smuggling women into the States and forcing them to work as prostitutes?"

Her eyes narrowed and her smile lessened as she studied me for the briefest of moments. "It's an age-old problem of tragic proportions that, like a lot of criminal activity, is becoming worse as it spreads. The number of people adversely affected is rising. The number of enterprises in the industry, large and small, is growing. There is competition and, like the drug business, there are struggles to carve out territory and to consolidate. The winners in the battle win because they are the most vicious. The product often suffers, but so far, there is an adequate supply." She paused for a moment. "Mr. Locke, what have you gotten into?"

"I have a client who is sheltering a sixteen-year-old Ukrainian girl who escaped from those that brought her over here." I told her Mina's story and asked what I should expect to be the best possible solution for her.

"The best possible legal solution would be that the girl gets turned over to the Children's Protection Service which then finds a suitable foster home where she'd be safe while proceedings went forward. The police agencies of all the states involved would competently investigate and gather enough information so that the pimps and purveyors and smugglers would all be rounded up and prosecuted. They would all serve maximum sentences or be put to death. Internationally, the FBI, the Ukrainian police forces and Interpol would cooperate, and those involved overseas would suffer the same fate. The girl would be reunited with her family, go to school, learn a profession, get married, and enjoy a happy family with children who would never face the same problem.

"The reality will be different, but there's only so much you can do. You represent her the best you can within the bounds of the law and, as I'm sure you do with other clients, hope for the best."

She spoke with all the appearance of professional detachment, but her eyes, unwavering in their focus on me, narrowed, the small lines at the corners of her eyes deepened. With her, the issue had depth beyond its complexity as a frustrating legal problem. I could tell she monitored my reaction to things she said, trying to decide about me, trying to determine whether I had an interest beyond representing a client "zealously within the bounds of the law" as required by the written rules of the profession.

Cathy Winwood was willing to fight in this sordid war as much as Mary Elizabeth. Suddenly, I wanted to be as good at my core as the two of them.

"Well, then," I said, "thanks for the fantasy and lecture on legal ethics. How about some reality?"

She took a sip of coffee. For a couple of seconds, she focused her eyes somewhere over my head.

"Your client is in for some heartbreak. And as for the girl … " She didn't finish. She looked sad, reminding me of Mary Elizabeth in one of her reflective moments, succumbing to the strain of futility.

Taking a deep breath, she continued, "There are actually immigration measures put in place to assist and protect victims of trafficking. It is possible for your client to get what is known as a "T" visa. You said she's sixteen?"

"Yes."

She shook her head. "The T visa is designed to let a person have non-immigrant status in exchange for assisting in the prosecution of those who traffic. But, being under the age of eighteen she doesn't even have to cooperate. The visa would probably allow her to stay in the states for four years. She would need a tremendous support system. Does she have parents who could come over or that she could go back to?"

"Her parents are deceased. She lives with relatives, but those are the people who, knowingly or not, put her in this predicament."

She nodded sadly.

I watched for tears, but she took another deep breath and with intense, angry eyes that did not waver from looking at me, said, "Currently, if the girl ends up with CPS, it is likely she will eventually be deported to Ukraine. Once there, chances are she will have no refuge. At best, she'll end up back with her family, which is ill equipped to deal with her return. The people over there who sold her into the states once are flagrant. She is an investment and will likely be made an example. They will find her, take her, punish her in ways you don't want to imagine and sell her again, perhaps to a different buyer in a different country, probably into a situation more horrible than she must have experienced over here. They won't kill her because she is worth more to them as a warm receptacle for a penis than as a cold corpse. There is a very slim chance that the law over there will work, and she'll be okay, but I would not bet a dime on it. There's too much burden, too much corruption, too much darkness.

"Maybe, just maybe, you can make enough noise that somebody will get arrested over here and either disappear while on bond or plea-bargain their way to eventual probation where, depending on the size of the criminal organization you're dealing with, he will bide his time or disappear with a new identity."

"Okay, thanks. There is no good legal solution. How about a creative solution?"

"Creative?"

"Ms. Winwood, I do not want to dance with you. I intend to help save this girl by whatever means are necessary. I intend to try to take at least one other girl from the hands of these people. I will break the law to do that. If that offends your principles or violates your professional ethics in an untenable way, then let's enjoy lunch. But, I could sure use some help if you have any."

She centered herself, clasping her hands together on the table in front of her. She sat quietly for a long time. Her eyes expressive as she thought. I waited and decided that if she and I ever met in court as adversaries, I would always try to sit so I could watch her eyes. Eventually, she decided the issues in her mind in my favor.

"Who is the other girl?"

"Her twin sister."

"Let's start at the end. There are certain things you could do with the girl you have, or both if you can get her sister safely away. Either actually, or on paper, you get them to another country, one that allows the flexibility necessary to achieve a just result without political concern. Maybe Canada. You or another zealot adopt the girls and do those things necessary to slip them past the legal barriers. There are organizations that can help. I don't know what to tell you about how to get them away from their kidnappers. I don't get involved with that side of things. Perhaps I can put you in touch with someone."

I sat forward, leaning over the table toward her. "Really? You are plugged in with someone who does that kind of thing?"

She shrugged. "There are people willing to do what the authorities cannot when the demands of justice are clear but too cumbersome for the law or politics. I do what I can in my field. Others have different expertise."

I leaned back. It was my turn to evaluate her. My world continued to shift. In a three-day period, beginning the Saturday morning I met Mary Elizabeth Kinkaid and Mina, I found myself on the edges of a new reality.

"That sounds like something you've said before. I'm not sure what it means."

She smiled. "Perhaps it is merely a well-practiced rationalization I continuously repeat to myself to help me sleep at night. That it is right to do things I personally feel are important even if there is not exactly an accepted legal solution.

"And, yes, there are people willing to take proactive steps about the possession of a person when the facts warrant such action. I can have someone call you. If I do, you be sure and tell them the absolute truth about what's going on. They deserve no less, and they will keep it confidential. Their efforts and their freedom, often their existence, depend on confidentiality."

"You have my card. I don't know where this is all going, but I might as well learn about as many resources as possible." She'd introduced me to an intriguing possibility, professionals who do this kind of thing and actually know what they're doing.

I asked, "Can I call on you in the future, either for more advice or if I need to slip some things past some legal barriers?"

"Yes." We'd traded cards earlier. She pulled her card back across the table, turned it over and wrote on the back. "There. I added my cell phone. Call me if you need any help."

She'd made me a provisional member of her frightening club.

"What do I owe you for today?"

"Lunch. And you've already paid. From time to time Sherwood, Thomas, and Cain is good to me."

I walked her to the elevator. She turned, put her hand flat against my chest and no longer in her professional tone of voice, said, "Mr. Locke, be very careful. You know that the best thing to do is call law enforcement, but I understand there may be a multitude of reasons why you don't. Trafficking is entrenched and very organized. It is a violent and remorseless business. It operates in dark places, and the people involved have no souls, no moral compass and tons of money. If you do this thing be very, very careful. Try not to let anybody know who you are. Stay in the dark as much as possible. Get it done, get away, get lost."

"I'll be very careful. And I'm sure I'll call you."

I wondered which persona she used most in a courtroom, the intelligent and skillful lawyer or the passionate true believer. The passionate Cathy Winwood would resonate with a jury. I cleaned up the conference room, thanked Rosalyn for a perfect referral, and drove back to Galveston.

I TURNED INTO THE DRIVE to my house at about half past two. As I parked on the slab under the house Mary Elizabeth came down the stairs, her sketch pad under her arm.

"Hi," I said.

"Hi. How did it go? Did you meet with a lawyer? What did he have to say? How much did you tell him?"

"Let me change clothes, and we'll talk about it. Something to drink?"

"Sure. A Dr Pepper. Preacher has converted me."

I changed, got the drinks and a can of bug spray. We sprayed on a layer of protection from mosquitoes and walked out the boardwalk over the grassy flats toward the bay.

As we walked, I started talking and couldn't stop. I explained to her I was lucky to have the boardwalk and the pier at its end. Huge sections of the bay system's environmentally vital grass flats are diminished, some to the natural erosion of time and weather, but way too much to the ignorance of those who live on or develop the coast. People like my great-grandfather and my grandfather who didn't think twice about dredging channels through the flats or building bulkheads to create more land by filling in what had been marshy salt flats at the edge of their property. In the past, property owners used and developed acres out of grass flats all around the bays. In the minds of those early residents, the flats were too shallow and too dense with grass to navigate easily by boat. That made them useless.

Later, we learned the importance of those immense areas of sea and grass as filters keeping the bay healthy and as giant nurseries protecting and feeding young shrimp, mullet, and mud minnows, the significant lower tier of the ocean's food chain. The state passed laws to protect the remaining grass flats and mandating the redemption of areas previously lost.

Harlan financially supported ecological research projects at Texas A&M University and allowed the University to use his land for research. The University maintained the boardwalk as a minor blemish on the grasslands to provide scientists and students minimally invasive access to the expanse of grasslands on the edge of his property. Not only did they study the ecology of the grassy flats, they eagerly replenished long lost grasses, diligently pushing back the waste of history and extending the pier closer to the deeper channels of the bay.

The University got its research platform, and I got a good place to sit and watch the sunset and a great place to fish. Large, smart, hungry fish patroled the edges of grass flats just waiting to consume a share of the bountiful goodness nurtured in the flats and washed out to deeper water with the surge of an outgoing tide. Some percentage of the shrimp and fishes born in the flats fed those stalking fish. Some percentage of those hungry predatory fish fed me. There was another bonus, one I didn't share with Mary Elizabeth. During the spring and summer, I often got to watch healthy, bikini-clad co-eds doing college fieldwork off the boardwalk. That was a win-win-win situation.

Mary Elizabeth and I sat on the sun-warmed boards of the pier, our feet dangling over the edge and I finally quit talking. It embarrassed me that I'd talked non-stop about the irrelevant history of grass-flats restoration. Silently, I watched her move her head from right to left, looking out over the mostly featureless expanse of the bay.

I analyzed what it was about her that made me babble. It started with her eyes, intelligent and encompassing. She listened with her eyes, scanning my face, looking at my eyes and my mouth as I talked, even while we were walking out to the pier. By watching so closely, she quietly demanded more than a social veneer. With a knowing smile, she encouraged more depth, more me. I may have been talking pedantically about the importance of the grass-flats, but the way she listened made me want to make her understand my personal and visceral connection to the environment in which I lived.

Her face completed its arc of observation and once again her eyes and her attention focused on me. I recognized in myself that I distanced myself from others. It amused me that she so easily cracked that barrier.

"I'll shut up now," I said.

I saw in her eyes that she recognized my moment of wry self-awareness and her smile deepened. "You are a part of this place, aren't you? You find that it suits you."

I nodded. "Yes. Yes, I am, and yes it does."

She looked out over the bay. "You enjoy sharing it. I think you want others to feel how special it is. I'm still a little surprised that you aren't married, that you don't have someone special living here to be a part of it all."

I shook my head. "I told you I was married once, and it didn't take. She lives with her next husband in Houston. The big city is more her speed than this."

Mary Elizabeth nodded. I liked that she did not extend an empty sympathy.

"Being a nun and all, perhaps I can't completely relate. But you strike me as someone with tremendous compassion for others, someone marriage would suit."

"And I think you're still just being nice, trying to recruit me for your crusade." I didn't feel like telling her about Anna, the lady I loved and who was happily married to another. I didn't think she would understand or approve of my relationship with Cecelia, also married, who occasionally made the drive to my place where we would draw the shades for an afternoon of making love, careful to ignore the reality of life beyond the bed we shared. "Perhaps I really prefer a life alone, away from the world's complexities."

Her smile changed a bit and clearly communicated her disbelief, but she said, "Okay."

"Why are we talking about me anyway, don't you want to hear what the lawyer had to say?"

"Of course. Tell me about it."

I told her what Cathy Winwood said, how she agreed with Mary Elizabeth about the slim chance of a happy result if Mina ended up in the hands of officials. I told her Cathy was more interested in results than strict compliance with what the law might expect. I told her Cathy could provide needed expertise and assistance with Mina's status and that of Zoio, if somehow the two were miraculously reunited.

I did not mention that Cathy might put me in touch with an organization more experienced with self-help. I needed to know more about that before sharing it with Mary Elizabeth.

Mary Elizabeth listened, nodding. She was learning nothing new. She didn't even look at me except when I mentioned that Cathy would be willing to help with the legal status of the sisters without raising too many questions. She nodded at that and said, "Good." Then she looked back out over the horizon. When a fish slapped the surface within twenty yards of where we sat, she did not turn her head to look. She didn't seem to have noticed at all. Something was on her mind. Something more than what I'd told her about my morning meeting with the lawyer.

"So," I said, "what's up? You have something on your mind."

She looked at me. This time her eyes did not project an expression of probing curiosity or optimistic competence. Something had cracked. She looked vulnerable. Frightened.

She turned toward me, took my hand, and squeezed it as she said, "Something's happened. It's Zoio. She's on her way. I'm sure of it. And I don't know what to do."

"What makes you think she's on her way? What happened?"

"Remember how I told you that priests in Ukraine were trying to get any kind of information?"

"Yes."

"Well, they may have learned something."

"May have?"

"There is a lady in Odessa who has been cooking meals for an apartment full of girls. Her sister knows the Ukrainian priest who has been quietly asking questions."

Mary Elizabeth paused and, breathing deeply, looked out over the bay for several seconds before she continued.

"Five days ago she stopped cooking because the girls are gone from the apartment. At some point, she'd overheard them talking about coming to the United States. The timing is perfect. I know Zoio is in that group."

She turned from looking at the bay and looked at me, her eyes rimmed in tears, her lip trembling, pausing between breaths as if she had to make herself inhale.

"What do I do?" she asked.

"We take it a step at a time. Step one is to see if we can

figure out the name of the ship they're on and when it's expected to arrive. I don't guess your folks in Ukraine have any idea?"

"No. How do we find out?"

"Let's go up to the house and get on the internet."

I helped her up, and we walked back toward the house without so much talking this time. Step at a time, I'd said. I didn't say it out loud, but, in my mind, the next step was to get in touch with Cathy Winwood's mysterious friends, the ones in the business of snatching children. After that, turn the problem over to them.

I'd already done some research on container ships traveling from Ukraine to the states. I'd bookmarked a website dedicated to worldwide shipping. There weren't that many ships departing Odessa in Ukraine and going to Houston, especially when we ignored the large, well-known shipping companies like Maersk and Hapag-Lloyd. There might be some freelance smugglers on the crews of their ships, but I didn't think there would be the ship-wide corruption described by Mina.

I ignored any ships going to any U.S. port other than Houston. If Zoio was headed for another port, there just wasn't a thing we could do, except try to alert authorities. But there was a ship headed for Houston, the *Soliez*, flagged in Panama, owned by a Singapore company, and crewed by Taiwanese. The ship left four days previously with an estimated travel time of thirty-one days to Houston. That would be within the first couple of weeks in May, a little less than four weeks away.

Suddenly, the theoretical became reality. All the intellectual research I'd done felt inadequate. Something needed to be done involving muscle and blood and guts instead of the talk I'd been applying. We needed Cathy

Winwood's shadowy acquaintances.

"Go," I said. "Go to Mina. See if she heard or saw or recognizes in any way the name of the ship. I have some ideas, but I need to give the whole thing a lot of thought."

After a couple of visible breaths and then one big breath, where she raised and lowered her shoulders, she said, "Okay." The corners of her mouth tightened into a smile.

I could see her resolve once again taking control. And, an almost annoying understanding on her part that I was finally fully committed and committed to her battle.

She grasped both of my arms. "Thank you."

"Go. I have work to do."

She left. I called both numbers Cathy Winwood gave me and had to leave a message on her voicemail.

I spread out a roadmap showing Houston and Galveston. I studied the map, measuring distances, thinking about the gigantic, serpentine system of highways in and around Houston. It took Cathy about thirty minutes to call me back.

CHAPTER FIVE

CATHY AND I MADE OUR POLITE, professional greetings over the phone, and she said, "How can I help you?"

"We've received some information. I need the number for your friends, the ones who might be able to help get the girl."

"Give me a number, preferably not a cell phone, where you can be reached for the next couple of hours. I'll have somebody call you."

The only landline I had that was not answered by my answering service was the one listed for my shop. I gave it to her. "Warn them," I said, "it is not my law office line. It is the number for my welding business."

She laughed. "Welding? You are an interesting man. Are you sure you know what you're getting into?"

"Yes. I know. The welding is how I maintain my sanity. I am a lawyer. I know enough about what I'm doing to want to consult with your experts."

"No problem. They won't care." She paused, emphasizing the seriousness of what she said next. "I'm vetting you, Mr. Locke. Do not make me sorry I did that. Follow whatever instructions you get over the phone and do not hold back from what you tell them."

"I understand. Thanks."

"You're welcome. Be careful. Call me if you need help with your immigration matters."

"And you call me if you need any welding done."

She laughed and hung up.

The line to the shop had an extension in the house. I knew the ringer was turned on, but I double-checked to make sure. I didn't have anything else to do.

It took an hour and fifteen minutes for a callback and for me to get the chance to say, "Locke Welding."

"Hello." It was a ladies voice, cool and noninflected. "May I ask to whom I am speaking?"

"Samuel Locke."

"Mr. Locke, you called earlier and left a message. I was asked to call and let you know that your package will be available for pick up at the front desk of the Marriott at Houston Intercontinental any time between ten and eleven in the morning the day after tomorrow."

"Thank you."

"You're welcome. Goodbye."

"Goodbye."

That was it. Very civilized. Very professional. Very calm. And I felt like a man must feel after slipping and beginning to fall over the edge of a cliff too steep and too high to survive, the way he feels just as he realizes the big blunder. He is not going to recover, he is going to make the fall.

My cell phone rang and interrupted my mental vertigo. Mary Elizabeth did not even say hello. "Sam. Mina did recognize the name of the ship. She saw the name *Soliez*. Zoio is on that ship and on her way. I know she is. What are we going to do?"

"First, we're going to calm down. Let's get everybody together tonight. I'd like to talk some more to Mina and I'll tell you what I think we ought to do."

"Where?"

"Here. I'll grill burgers. Bring Patricia and Jason. I'll try to get word to Preacher. If he checks in with you, let him know."

"When?"

"Seven o'clock." I called Clara's Bar and Grill to leave a

message for Preacher and thought, not for the first time, I might buy him a cell phone and add him to my plan.

Preacher called while I was driving to the market to buy some hamburger meat and buns. I made a u-turn and drove over to Follets Island to pick him up at Clara's. I filled him in on the drive to buy groceries in Surfside and on the way back to my house. That took up most of an hour. We'd been back at my place about fifteen minutes when Mary Elizabeth drove up with Mina, Patricia, and Jason. At least Patricia was in jeans, and Jason was wearing khakis. They looked much less militant.

I'd fired up the grill, iced down some drinks, and had Preacher slicing potatoes when they arrived. Mina went straight to Preacher's side. He handed her a Dr Pepper and a knife. She began slicing potatoes, watching him closely to learn the technique.

Mary Elizabeth had a glass of wine. Patricia and Jason each took a beer. The atmosphere relaxed. Unlike our last get together, it started as a party with an agreeable lightness to the conversation. At one point Patricia joined me by the grill. Mary Elizabeth had drifted over to talk to Mina and Preacher. Patricia did not look as hard as when first we met.

While watching Mary Elizabeth and Mina, she said, "So, Zoio is on her way."

"Looks like it."

She turned to me. "Do you really think you can do something?"

Now that she wasn't glaring at me as the enemy, her eyes had lost their stony glint and were as expressive and vulnerable as Mary Elizabeth's. Even though Patricia and Mary Elizabeth had taken different paths, she, too, had a passionate desire for something good to come from Mary Elizabeth's quest.

"I'm not sure. I have an idea. I'll explain it to everybody after we eat."

She nodded. "Please make sure Mary Elizabeth is kept safe."

"Absolutely. She will not be directly involved in whatever happens. If anything actually does happen."

"Good." She turned toward me and took a sip of beer. "I'm sorry if Jason and I were kind of unfriendly when we met. It's just that this whole thing scares the hell out of me. Mary Elizabeth is not going to quit on this one, even if it really is impossible to get anything accomplished."

She looked at Mary Elizabeth laughing at something and Mina smiling shyly. Preacher winked at me. Patricia turned back to me and put her hand on my arm. "She will not back off this one even if it kills her."

"Well, trust me, I don't want her or Preacher hurt, or me for that matter. I want to tell everybody the details at the same time, but I think there is somebody who has done this before who will help us."

She looked at me for a long time, studying my face. "Good. Thank you."

I looked over the group. Preacher loaded a tray with sliced potatoes while Mina watched carefully. A connection existed between the two. After Mina's experiences with men, it encouraged me that she willingly befriended a male. At that moment I realized some part of my desire to actively participate in this venture was to prove something to Mina and Mary Elizabeth and Patricia and my mother and sister and every woman I'd ever known. I wanted to prove those men taking the innocence of girls like Mina were the aberrations. There were more good guys than bad guys and the good guys would win.

Mina brought the tray of potatoes. "Thank you," I said.

"You're welcome." She didn't hang out with me but headed straight back to Preacher's side, helping him set the table. He waved off Patricia's help.

Mary Elizabeth sat talking to Patricia and Jason. She was animated. Patricia remained more relaxed, but I could not be sure about Jason. Self-contained, he did not show emotion. He participated in conversation but was hard to read. Perhaps it was the battle-weary countenance of someone fighting daily in the gritty trenches of social work. Maybe he was the only realist present and most appreciated the folly the rest of us seemed determined to see through.

We ate hamburgers and fries and Blue Bell ice cream with chocolate sauce and the conversation slowly focused in on my plan.

We moved inside. Mina and Preacher carried all the dishes into the kitchen. Returning to the living room, Preacher said, "We'll clean them later." He looked at me meaningfully. I thought for a fleeting moment that Mina should be protected from the details for some reason, but she was no longer a child. She deserved to be in on what was going on.

"I've been in touch with an organization that does the kind of thing we want to do."

Jason leaned forward, "What's that mean?"

"There is a group willing to take matters into their own hands regarding matters of child custody when it is clearly warranted. I am going to meet with someone day after tomorrow."

Everyone started talking at once, except for Mina, whose eyes darted from one to another.

I raised my hand to quiet them all. "I don't know much else about the group other than what I've told you. Someone much more experienced in these matters put me in touch with them. There are still things we need to do.

"I'll know more after my meeting, but we can plan. Mina, you need to draw us a few portraits of your sister from different viewpoints, something we can give them to help recognize her. Did you dye your hair before you left or after you got to Chicago?"

"In Chicago."

"You look like her, right?"

She nodded.

"Mary Elizabeth, why don't you take Mina to a hairdresser, get her hair back as close as you can to its original color? We'll take her picture before and after to use as ID, as well."

Mary Elizabeth and Mina were nodding at that. Mina actually smiled. I went a little further with that idea. "In fact, why don't you and Patricia and Mina all have a spa day on me. It's time to be less gloomy."

Mina turned to Mary Elizabeth talking quietly, but obviously excitedly, asking what I meant by spa day.

"That's not necessary," Mary Elizabeth said. "Getting her picture is a good idea, and we should do that."

"You certainly don't have to do anything like that for me. I don't do spa days." This from Patricia.

"Okay," I said, "maybe it's not necessary to go all out and maybe nuns and ex-nuns aren't allowed to pamper themselves, but there are a couple of reasons it should be done. One is that a picture of Mina looking as close to her sister as possible will be very helpful. Second, we have a while before we can expect the ship to arrive, the distraction and the relaxation will refresh you. Relaxing will help your thinking. Thinking the best we can is vitally important.

"In fact, now that I think about it, we can all use a relaxing day. The day you go have your spa day, us guys will do something to relax. We'll go to a ball game, or we'll go fishing or golf, whatever." I looked quizzically at Jason.

"I'm going to have to get back to Chicago at some point, especially if you have help coming in."

"Well, we can do it before you go. Do you enjoy fishing?"

He shrugged and nodded.

"Preacher?"

"I'm in."

"What if I would rather go fishing?" This from Patricia.

"Fine. Then you can go fishing with us. Better yet, we'll all go fishing and then, whoever wants can have their spa day. We have the time."

"Good," Preacher said, "I need to get my hair done. And perhaps a pedicure."

The laughter was good, but it faded.

Everybody looked at me expectantly. Preacher leaned back, hands folded on his stomach, Mary Elizabeth sat forward, waiting for more hope. Jason was resigned and stoic. Mina was a heartbreaking combination of curiosity, fear, and bewilderment, an ingénue aged in some bad ways but with a youthful resilience I hoped would win the battle for her soul.

Patricia had changed most during the little time I'd known this crowd, softening somehow. She stayed close by Mary Elizabeth's side, but no longer appeared steely-eyed protective, as if Mary Elizabeth's faithful expectations had rubbed off. She looked as if she wanted us to win.

At the center of their focused attention, I was glad I had a meeting scheduled with someone who knew what to do. I saw our role as support by providing facts and by answering any questions we could. Although relieved to have somebody to turn to for the retrieval problem, I had an urge to go along, to be a part of whatever happened to grab Zoio. Ego trumped common sense.

"First, as I said, there are people who specialize in taking physical custody of at-risk children without regard to the law when circumstances clearly indicate it is necessary. I have a meeting in Houston with someone about that day after tomorrow. We will rely on their expertise. They have experience and the people necessary to get this done." Lawyers are practiced at saying things about which they have no knowledge and making it sound like gospel.

"Okay," I said, "let's run down what we know. We're pretty sure we know the name of the ship Zoio is on. We can, to some degree, track it's schedule and expected time of arrival in Houston. We have no choice but to assume that the smuggling will occur as it did when Mina came in.

"He meets them at some distance offshore and comes in through the ship channel. I don't see how we can narrow a window of arrival shorter than ten days or so." There were nods from some of my audience.

Mary Elizabeth sat forward and said, "I will sit at the boat cut every night for ten days. Or however long it takes."

"There are a couple of problems with that," I said. "I think somebody watches the cut from the jetty or from a boat anchored there to help him navigate the cut. The one thing we do not want to do is attract any kind of attention. Secondly, the more I think about it, the more I think he only uses the cut when he has a reason. It is the one thing he's done that attracts a lot of attention. It's how we got on his trail. It's where location makes him most vulnerable while coming in. Unless he has reason to use it the night he brings in the girls, I just don't think he'll be there."

"You don't think it's worth the risk? How else do you

get close to him?" When that came from Patricia, it earned a sideways glance from Jason.

Everyone turned to look at me. I wished I'd waited until one of Cathy Winwood's experts could be in attendance to take charge.

"Remember, I'm going to talk to experts, but I agree we need to get on their trail as early as possible. If we can catch him coming through the ship channel, great. We'll know when to try to find them on the road. I'm thinking the people I'm going to talk to will be able to help watch the channel. We'll also have to watch for them on the highway."

Jason finally had something to say, "Do you really think this is possible?"

Mary Elizabeth drew a breath to respond, but I raised a hand. "I think our chances are slim but not as bad as you're imagining if they do not change up their timing and their route. We'll sit somewhere, maybe on my boat and watch and listen for him. Here, let me show you."

I stood up and got a roadmap. Everybody leaned in as I spread it out on the table.

Jason said, "You don't think that's going to be a little like a needle in a haystack. I've seen Houston traffic."

I shrugged. "Maybe the people I'm meeting with will have a better idea, but I don't know what else to do. If we do catch up with them coming in on the boat, the only way we could follow them is with a boat as fast as his. A boat like that would be highly noticeable. Plus, if we spook them and lose them, we wouldn't have a chance."

Jason turned back to the map shaking his head.

"Feels impossible, I know."

"Yes," he said, looking up at me.

"But here's why it might work. This is the East Bay." I

put my finger on the bay. Everybody leaned in and focused on the map. Mina looked from me to Mary Elizabeth who, without looking up from the map, put her arm around the girl's shoulders.

"We have to go with what we know and what we can assume." I drew a circle on Trinity Bay and East Bay on the map. "Because these two bays are less built up than the other bays, I assume his boathouse is on one of these two bays. Thanks to Mina, we know they were on the interstate before Huntsville." Mina looked up and smiled shyly at that. "I am going to go with the assumption that he doesn't take any out of the way roads. He prefers to hide in plain sight by getting on the interstate. From where I assume he is coming from, there are three main highways that will get him there the fastest."

I traced the routes on the map.

"He can get on ten, head west and get on forty-five just north of downtown Houston. Or, he can take either Loop Six-Ten or the Beltway. The Beltway is a toll road for a lot of the way, and I think he would avoid the toll booths. In any event, if I'm right, he hits the Interstate a few miles north of Houston. There will be a lot of places to sit and watch for the church van on the Interstate on the other side of those routes."

Mary Elizabeth hugged Mina and said, "I know this is going to work."

Jason made a noise.

"Yeah," I said, "I know, but it's the best I can come up with. Like I said, maybe the experts we're going to talk to will have a better idea. In any event, we'll take Mina for a ride around Houston on the loop and see if it looks like what she recalls seeing."

Mary Elizabeth said, "It will work, I know it."

Patricia took Mary Elizabeth's hand and gave me a look. At least it wasn't a look of complete disgust.

Everybody stared at the map. Jason shook his head. There were high points of color on Mary Elizabeth's cheeks.

Jason said, "Mary Elizabeth, it is impossible. Maybe it will work with dozens of people. Go to law enforcement."

"No," she said. Tears were suddenly shining in her eyes. "Not yet." She turned to me. "Maybe the people you're going to see can help?"

I shrugged. "I know little to nothing about them. Maybe all they'll do is advise that we call in the FBI. I don't know. We cannot worry much about things over which we have no control. All we can do is take this thing a step at a time. And take that step the best we can. All you religious folks should do some powerful praying because that may be the only way this thing will work."

Preacher said, "That we will Samuel. That we will. Personally, I will pray for the strength not to strangle the sons of bitches when we catch up with them. Or, for the strength to strangle them if it should prove necessary."

Mary Elizabeth patted him on the arm. Jason made one of his noises. Mina sank against the side of Mary Elizabeth, her eyes moving back and forth as she watched us all. Patricia looked at me in a disconcerting way.

The party wound down, each person's appreciation of reality putting a damper on the earlier lightheartedness. I assured them I could clean up the mess, and they all left except Preacher.

As we loaded the dishwasher, he said, "It is a good thing you are doing."

"It is a foolhardy thing we are all doing. I sure hope the people I'm meeting will take on this whole thing."

"Doesn't matter. You at least had the resources to find

folks that will help."

We were quiet for a while, getting things done.

He dried his hands on a towel and leaned against my counter. "You know, Patricia is no longer a nun."

"What are you talking about?"

"Patricia and Jason just have a professional relationship. They are not a couple. She is no longer a nun."

"Preacher ..."

"She has said some nice things about you and what you're doing. You have impressed her."

First Mary Elizabeth made a suggestion about Patricia and now Preacher. I shook my head. "If she is impressed then she misjudges me. I've not done anything impressive. Believe me. And romance has no place in all of this."

He shrugged. He smiled. "I'll just sleep on your couch tonight."

IN THE MORNING PREACHER had coffee and breakfast going by the time I got out of bed. We spoke only of mundane things.

I did not want to spend that night at my house and have to drive in morning commuter traffic to the other side of Houston to meet with the experts. I called my uncle to invite him to dinner and to ask if I could spend the night at his place. He answered his cell in Florida where he was doing some business, but told me to get a key from Rosalind at the law firm.

After breakfast, I put a bag with a change of clothes in the Range Rover along with a briefcase full of files to work on and drove Preacher to his storefront church. Sitting on the steps were a couple of scruffy young people, a boy and a girl, typical of Preacher's flock. He greeted them loudly and, with an arm around each of them, escorted them into his church.

Driving up 288 toward Houston, I caught myself looking for church vans loaded with scared young girls.

The closer I got to Houston, the more traffic increased. The outbound lanes were bumper to bumper and moving at a snail's pace. My side of the highway moved a bit faster, but the density of cars on the highway kept increasing. The number of driving lanes grew, and the number of cars swelled to fill the space.

I moved to the lane I would need to be in to turn north toward downtown Houston and I, too, came to a dead stop in traffic. The hundreds of thousands of cars and trucks began to overcome my optimism that we had any kind of chance of finding the one van we sought.

I finally made my creeping way into downtown and parked in the underground parking of my uncle's building. My eroded optimism must have been apparent because Rosalind asked me what was wrong as she handed me the key to Harlan's office and apartment.

"Nothing," I said, "I just hate Houston traffic."

I busied myself for the afternoon by reviewing client files and making a few phone calls. There was a child support matter, a minor drug and paraphernalia possession charge, and a group of kids charged with public indecency for having the audacity to enjoy swimming naked in the sea in the moonlight.

Later, I picked up a basket of fish and chips from the restaurant on the ground floor. I ate back in the apartment while I surfed through the television channels. After dinner, I went out on the balcony and sipped a bit of Harlan's single malt scotch while looking out over the lights and movements of the city. The pulses and vibrations of the city, the flow of traffic, the hum of energy—it was easy to see the city as something alive, especially when viewed from fifteen floors above the streets after an ounce or two of Scotland's finest.

I went to bed early and spent a restless night high above the sounds of the streets.

CHAPTER SIX

I GOT UP AND WAS SHOWERED, shaved, bageled, and caffeinated by eight o'clock. The morning news included a story about an unidentified teenage girl found dead in a vacant lot. I thought about that story more than I would have a week before.

Again, I enjoyed the advantage of driving against the flow of morning traffic, reaching the Marriott next to the airport by nine-thirty. Cathy Winwood said to follow their instructions to the letter. The lady on the phone said after ten o'clock. I stopped at a Denny's for a cup of coffee to burn a little time. Two minutes after ten I gave the desk clerk my name and asked if she had any messages for me. She handed me an envelope.

I walked away while opening the envelope. Written on a sheet of hotel letterhead was: "Room 608." On the way up the elevator, I decided whatever price the people in room 608 asked, I would find a way to pay. I should have felt relief while walking down that long carpeted hallway from the elevator to the room, but I didn't. More nerve-wracked than waiting for a jury to return, my sense of dread increased with every step. Instead of feeling like I was walking out of the problem, it felt like I was walking deeper into the whole mess.

I knocked on the door expecting, perhaps, a squad of Navy Seals, but when the door opened I could not have been more surprised. She was older, with short, permed gray hair, and looked something like my grandmother, right down to her spotless white tennis shoes.

"Yes?" she said, peering up at me through her glasses

with a smile on her plump, round face. Her eyes were brown and looked large behind the lenses of her glasses.

I looked down at the paper in my hand and at the number on the door to make sure I had not made a mistake. "Um, I was told to meet somebody here."

"Who would that be?"

"I'm not sure." There was an awkward pause when nothing was said. She just kept looking at me benignly with a soft smile. "My name is Samuel Locke. I got a note asking me to come to this room."

"Well, then, come on in Mr. Locke."

She opened the door wider, and I entered her room. She looked up and down the hall before she closed the door and turned to me.

"Now, Mr. Locke. How can I help you?"

"I got a message at the desk to come to this room. I was sent by Cathy Winwood."

"How delightful. But, Mr. Locke, I must say, you don't look like a police officer."

It was turning into an even more confusing conversation, but I finally realized what was going on. We were playing some kind of game meant to assure my bona fides.

"I'm not a police officer. I'm a lawyer. I came to consult on a child custody matter."

"Of course. How can I help?" She looked at me carefully, with much more than casual attention. It was getting weirder and weirder until I realized she was looking for any surreptitious pin-hole camera or recording devices. She picked up a card on the desk and held it up to me. That's when I noticed she was wearing gloves.

Typed on the card was "please remove your shirt and pants."

Now that I realized what she was doing, it no longer felt strange. It felt very competent. I sat on the edge of the bed and removed my shoes. She pointed at my socks, and I took those off. She pointed at the end of the bed and I laid my shoes and socks out in a line for easy inspection. She smiled and nodded. From the drawer of the bedside table, she removed a scanning wand which she ran over the shoes and socks while I removed my shirt and pants and laid them out for her inspection.

I stood there in my briefs. She ran her wand over my clothes and turned to me. With her hands, she indicated I should raise my arms and turn in front of her. She ran the wand over the covered part of me and startled me with a professional, thorough pat down to make sure I had no microphones tucked away anywhere she couldn't see.

With that grandmotherly smile, she waved at my clothes and indicated I should get dressed. She punched a number on her cell phone and said, "I'm through with my shopping. All is good here." She listened for a moment. "Okay dear. Good-bye."

While I tied my shoes, she put her scanning wand into her purse. There was the sound of someone opening the door, and she turned to me. "It was a pleasure to meet you, Mr. Locke. Good luck."

I nodded to her and turned to see the man who walked into the room. He looked more like what I'd thought I'd find when the door to the room first opened. He was shorter than me with dark curly hair cut close to his scalp. Dressed in gray slacks and a blue blazer over a crisp white shirt with a red tie, he looked like a young professional something or other.

The older lady paused on the way out the door and turned to him. "Have a nice flight, dear. You be careful."

She hugged him.

"I will mom, thanks."

Mom left, closing the door behind her and the man turned to me. He had intense, dark brown eyes that gave me as good a visual pat-down as his mom's more physical effort.

"Hi. Call me Tom."

Call me cynical, but for some reason, I didn't think that was his real name. We shook hands. "Tom. I'm Samuel Locke."

He nodded and removed his jacket revealing a brown leather shoulder holster holding a pistol under his left arm. The weapon's black block of a barrel looked like a Glock. Two spare magazines were hanging on the straps of the holster running over his right arm.

"Now, how can I help you?"

"You were referred to me as somebody who could help me regarding possession of a child."

"Is there a custody order?"

"No. It involves a sixteen-year-old girl I believe is about to arrive in this country illegally."

"Tell me about it."

I told him the story of the two sisters, what we knew, what we'd learned, and what we'd guessed. I told him about our incomplete, rudimentary, and amateurishly designed surveillance and snatch plan. He asked a few pertinent questions about geography and about who we were and who we might have available to call for extra help.

I didn't like that last part, where he inquired about our resources and us. I was hoping his organization would take over the whole operation. "I don't know that there is anybody else. I'm hoping your people can take on the job."

"Law enforcement?"

"There are issues. Getting the girls into the hands of

the government is not as good a solution as getting them into hands of people who care about them personally."

He nodded with an understanding of the occasional shortcomings of relying strictly on the legal procedures. And then, he shook his head and said, "What do you know about me?"

"Not much. Cathy Winwood sent me to you as somebody who had experience in what we're trying to do, somebody with an organization with the resources to get it done."

"You have four other people helping you out, right?"

"Yes."

"That makes your organization the same size as my organization. Well, the same size, not counting my mom."

That set me back. I'd thought Tom was a part of something much bigger. "At least you have the experience to do this much better than us."

"Mr. Locke, I can assure you none of us have any experience dealing with any Ukrainian crime organization."

"But you know what you're doing."

"Look, all we really have is will. We are willing to circumvent the law. We are willing to ignore court imposed custodial orders. We are willing to spend time and effort to do what we think is right. We run the risk of being charged with kidnapping, and we have the will to accept that risk.

"Each person involved with me has a reason to do what we do, to do what is right instead of what's legal, but we are not impulsive. We are not hired guns available to anybody who doesn't like a custody arrangement. We research, first to get the truth about the people involved. To know that what we're being asked to do is right. We have to know that if we do help, somebody is prepared to follow up. They have to be willing to disappear, sometimes to another country.

Then we take the time to carefully research the situation to make sure we can proceed safely, with no chance of harm to the child or to us."

I glanced at his gun. He smiled.

"Yes. I am armed. I don't know you and there are a lot of angry people out there unhappy with what we've done. Some number of those people are criminals earnestly seeking to exact revenge. A greater number of people unhappy with me may not be criminals, but they have enormous resources and long memories and are capable of hiring people to right the wrongs they think I have facilitated. I have no illusions. Somebody, somewhere who doesn't like what I've done is spending a lot of money and doing everything possible to get a line on me and those with whom I work. Frankly, there is usually a cut-out or two standing between us and the people for whom we do what we do. If you had not come so highly vetted you would not have met me."

"Even if you've never had a situation involving trafficking, you've had more relevant experience than any of us. The criminals have no idea about me or the people I am involved with. If we can secure the girl, one of us has the resources and will to disappear. Besides, we're dealing with a criminal organization. In the end it is a business. We're talking two girls out of probably hundreds. The bad guys are not going to have the desire to spend too much time or resources trying to exact revenge or recover their assets. Sure, there will be some anger and if anybody gets caught, the results will not be pretty, but, in the end, the businessmen will cut their losses. They will not want to spend the money or draw too much attention to their business interests. I'm confident the girls can safely disappear."

Tom stood up and walked over to the window, looking

out over the cement landscape outside. "That may be. And I'd like to help you, but there's a problem."

"What's that?"

"What's your timeline again?"

"I can track the ship we're pretty sure is involved. I expect it to arrive sometime in the next twenty-five to thirty-five days."

"That's the problem. I leave here this afternoon for South America. The reason you got to see me so quickly is that I stayed here last night to catch a connecting flight out. I'll be joining my associates there. I expect to be gone for forty-five to sixty days on a job. A job we've planned for months."

My stomach took a tumble. I'd been so confident of being able to turn this over to the experts.

"Besides," he said, "we've been planning that operation for months and it's not nearly as complicated and risky as your situation." He shook his head. "I understand you have no control over your timing. I understand how you have to try to do something. Frankly, if I was not committed I'd be happy to be in on your job. At least there is no moral fuzziness about what you want to do."

"Can you direct me somewhere? There must be others who do what you do."

He shrugged. "I'm sure there are, but it's not like we attend trade shows. I honestly don't know who I could send you to. I would if I could."

I slumped back on the bed at a loss and stared at the floor.

"Look," he said, "your plan is not that bad. Logistically, the hardest part is going to be finding them timely. If you can actually do that and get behind their van, your plan is good. Wait until they stop somewhere fairly public, do what you have to do to get to your girl and run to somewhere very public. They're not going to be calling the police. If you surprise them quickly in as public a place as possible and you're careful, I wouldn't expect them to start shooting at you. I would expect them to scurry as quickly as possible back into the dark. Like cockroaches. Worse comes to worst, you yell for the police and deal with that lesser of two evils."

I nodded with some resignation, trying to think of other solutions.

He said, "I have your phone number. If this thing I'm on falls apart, I'll call you. If not, I'll call when I get back from South America. We'll meet for a beer somewhere. Hopefully, you'll tell me everything went perfectly. If not, well, you get together all the information you can. Talk to the girl you have. Talk to whoever it is you're doing this for. Get all the possible information. Maybe we can find a way to go after the other girl."

I nodded, but had no illusions. If we tried and failed, and lived to talk about it, it was not likely Zoio would ever be seen again. She'd be too big a liability to be easily traced. They'd hide her beyond discovery, perhaps take her to another country, one that doesn't cooperate well with the United States, or, thinking that somebody was too close, cut out the connection by disposing of her. My big plan was not going to work. I needed to think.

Tom and I talked for a while, but I learned nothing extremely helpful. We went over my amateurish plan in detail and he had a few suggestions. He agreed that those transporting the girls had no reason to be leery just because Mina had escaped. He agreed it was likely that the Houston smugglers had no idea she'd gone missing.

We talked about communication, and he suggested we

stake out our surveillance points and check for dead spots in cell coverage. He suggested everybody involved use untraceable cell phones dedicated just to our mission and have multiple phones with multiple service providers if possible.

We talked more about mobility and how important we needed to be able to consolidate our forces quickly. I was felt let-down. I thought we'd just dump our problem into the hands of experts. I'd been kind of smug with Mary Elizabeth and the others about coming up with a solution, but I felt less sure about the possibilities of our success than I'd felt the day Preacher brought everybody to my workshop.

I gave him my cell phone number. As I was leaving, Tom extended a hand to shake mine. He grasped my hand and pulled me a half-step closer. He looked me in the eye and, with his free hand, gripped my shoulder. It felt like a salute from a comrade in arms.

As I walked down the hall, I recited lines from "Charge of the Light Brigade": "Boldly they rode and well, into the jaws of death, into the mouth of Hell."

Having no desire to drive back to Galveston and spread the deflating news, I went to Harlan's apartment and pretended to work for the rest of the day. Preacher called as I napped on Harlan's sofa. I told him we'd talk when I got back to the island in the morning. I deflected his inquiries, telling him we all needed to have a conversation. He picked up on my mood, but I didn't feel like explaining anything. My mind worked overtime trying to come up with the best alternative. Going to bed that night, I'd firmly decided that the only solution was to enlist law enforcement. There was nothing else to do.

To my eternal regret I did not stick to that plan.

I WOKE BEFORE DAWN the next morning. I made a pot of coffee and stood on Harlan's terrace to watch the sunrise in hazy determination over the industrial area beyond the ballpark. The city was gray there, low, flat-roofed buildings built for utility, not show. There were railroad tracks running between old brick buildings, monuments to the economies and industries of the past.

A train moved slowly up the tracks. It was one of what were the lengthiest trains passing through Houston. They ran from the ports in the south, loaded with new cars from overseas, each wrapped in a thin, white plastic covering. Those trains did not stop in what used to be the downtown heart of commerce. They went north to a huge expanse of concrete. There, surrounded by a chain link fence, the cars were prepped for delivery to dealers, waiting to be fed into the endless streams of cars on the streets of Houston.

Behind me, the sun lit up the towers of the city, the metallic and glass representatives of Houston's life-blood. In those corporate towers, people who sought oil and gas and money struggled to acquire more of each than the occupants of the building across the street. Those buildings, built during the heady oil and gas boom days, made for a gorgeous, modern skyline.

I mused over the fact that Harlan's building, almost a hundred years old, stood right between the historical industrial area to the east, spread out over the landscape gray and dusty, and the modern business area to the west, glittering glass and steel, rising hundreds of stories toward the sky. The city started to hum, oblivious to my melancholy.

I straightened the apartment, gathered my files, put the apartment keys in an envelope with Rosalind's name on the outside, and pushed them through the delivery slot on the law firm's door. I drove back to the coast, thinking as hard as possible about our next course of action. I arrived home no smarter than when I'd left Houston.

Preacher stood up from my porch when I drove up to the house.

"So, brother Locke, what's the story?"

"Not good Preacher. I don't think we're going to get any outside help. We have to go to the FBI." I filled him in on the results of my meeting in Houston.

He listened to the story, sighed, and with infuriating optimism said, "We'll think of something. There are too many souls at stake to get this wrong."

I did not want to argue. I wasn't in the mood. I just leaned on my porch rail looking out over the grass flats. Out there, the well-ordered life of predators and prey was not as complicated as it is onshore.

"Sam, don't worry. You'll think of the best thing to do. Let's not tell the others just yet. No matter what happens, there is no reason for us to skip going fishing. Relaxing will do us all good. We should go ahead and get photos of Mina looking like her sister. That can't hurt and ought to help whoever takes this on. We probably have almost a month, let's take at least a week to think this through. If we have to call in the FBI, they'll be able to move quickly and won't miss the week."

I thought the FBI might appreciate all the time we could give them, but it was attractive to not have to immediately tell the others we were screwed.

Pushing off the porch rail, I said, "Well, there's certainly no reason the others have to know anything for the next two or three days. Let's make plans for our relaxation."

I called the others. Everybody agreed to meet at my

place that afternoon. Preacher and I talked of other things, drove to Clara's Bar and Grill for shrimp po'boys at lunch, and returned to my place by driving slowly on the beach, each of us quiet in our own thoughts, Preacher softly whistling a nameless tune.

The others arrived together at three.

I described my meeting by telling them the gentleman with whom I met impressed me. He certainly had the experience and skills to help us. I said I'd fully briefed him and that he'd made some helpful suggestions. I told them he'd had to leave on another job, but he would be calling me on his return. I told them we should have our day of relaxation, and Mina should have her spa day so we could get a photograph of her looking most like her sister.

Mary Elizabeth looked at me with a trust I did not deserve. "Thanks, Sam. Thank you so much for what you're doing."

I gave her a smile and nodded.

Of course, Jason remained skeptical, "I'd hoped he would return with you and we'd be done."

I shrugged.

"Patricia and I have to get back to Chicago soon. Keep in touch with us and keep us updated. Let us know if there's anything we can do from there." He'd read between the lines. I saw it on his face.

I looked him in the eyes and nodded my understanding. I expected to pull the plug soon. He smiled and gave me a nod. No one saw our silent understanding, they were all talking, obviously feeling some relief thinking we'd made a giant step forward. Preacher caught my eye and nodded my way, adding his silent approval of my misdirection.

I nodded his way, thinking maybe I could just nod my

way out of my growing predicament.

Oh, well, I thought, what was done was done. At least for the day. I clapped my hands to get their attention. "We should get the photograph of Mina as Zoio done tomorrow before we go fishing and before she gets any sun. You ladies will get your day at the hairdresser tomorrow. It doesn't make much sense to do it before a day fishing, but I'll spring for manicures, pedicures, and whatever you want done with your hair. You'll have to let the hairdresser know just how to best make Mina look like her sister. Mary Elizabeth, maybe you and Mina can sit down tonight and draw a picture of her that doesn't look quite as sad as the ones you have." She turned, took Mina's hands in hers and spoke to her softly.

I said, "I need to make a phone call to somebody who can get that done."

In my study, I pulled up my client files to get the number and called Marie, a hairdresser client of mine. I explained that I had a girl involved in a legal matter who needed her hair dyed and arranged to look as much as possible as it did some time ago. And I needed it tomorrow. As incentive, I used the fact that I'd be paying for three clients coming to her shop for full service.

Marie is a good client of my law business. That means every month she pays something on a legal bill that goes up and down depending on how long it's been since I'd written a letter, or dragged into court, one of her two ex-boyfriends to encourage him to pay child support.

After hearing what I needed done, she said, "Three cut and style jobs, one color treatment, pedicures and manicures for all will set you back at least three hundred fifty dollars, maybe more. Plus, I will expect you to pay a premium if I lose anybody I have to move the last minute to work on your friends. You're being a major pain in the ass, but if you send a hundred dollars along for supplies, forty dollars for tips to the other girls, and knock five-hundred dollars off what I owe you, I'll get it done."

Her economic theory was interesting, but I, too, charged more when a client promised to be a pain in the ass. She expected me to haggle, but I didn't. Her three children were all under the age of ten and child support would be owed for years. Besides, she was young enough to have another child or two and near as I could tell, did not want to get married. She is a good client. I agreed to her terms immediately, and she told me to have all three ladies at her shop at ten the next morning. It didn't sound like she was worried about any existing appointments.

I told the ladies about their appointment and gave Mary Elizabeth two hundred in cash, telling her to make sure Marie got all the cash because it included all expenses and tips.

Patricia said, "I'm fine. You don't have to pay for any of that stuff for me."

"It's a done deal," I told her. "You're part of a negotiated package deal. A hundred and forty dollars plus tip for all of you is a steal."

I wrote out directions to Marie's shop.

"While you get that done, I'll get my boat ready for a fishing trip day after tomorrow. It should be a nice day with a calm sea. We can talk about what we do next on the boat."

Preacher said, "I notice you didn't pay for me a haircut, but I'm going along with them tomorrow."

Surprising me, Jason said, "If you don't mind, I'll get them to drop me off here. I can help get your boat ready."

"Sure." I could tell he felt there were things for us to discuss.

Everybody left and, except for Jason, each seemed to have an excited energy. I didn't feel the energy. I spent a melancholy evening sitting on the pier, slowly sipping a glass of Jack Daniels. I watched the sun drop below the horizon, taking no comfort in the peaceful moment or the whiskey.

CHAPTER SEVEN

THE NEXT MORNING everybody showed up at nine o'clock. I took a few before photographs of Mina. With Preacher's help, she actually smiled in a few of them. But, sadly, no matter what we did, she looked like a victim in every shot.

There had to be some way to save her sister Zoio from the dark ordeal Mina had suffered.

I thought of all the children caught in the horror Mina had experienced. I tried to put the thousands of other victims out of my mind, but knowing they were out there intensified the desire to do something for Mina and Zoio. I understood Mary Elizabeth's fervor, her desire to make one small change, her desire to scrape one shiny spot in that disgusting veneer of ugliness.

The ladies, plus Preacher, left in Mary Elizabeth's car for Marie's hair salon. Jason helped me carry boxes of food and drinks to my truck. I'd already loaded the off-shore rods. We drove toward the marina.

For a minute he looked out his window, quietly watching the low dunes between the road and the sea. Then, he asked, "So, what's really going on with the man you met Wednesday?"

"Was it that obvious I wasn't as happy as possible?"

He shrugged. "You didn't seem as relieved as I expected at handing off the problem to somebody else. The others are blindly following your lead. I could tell there was a problem."

"Yes, there's a problem. He and his associates will be in South America for two or three months. They are not available on the date I expect the *Soliez* to arrive."

He nodded and looked back down the highway.

"I'm going to try to find somebody else, but I don't know where to look. I'll ask the person who put me in touch with those guys, but I'm not sure there is anybody else."

He nodded again, his mouth drawn tight. He looked back at me. "So, what do you plan to do?"

It was my turn to respond with a shrug and shake of my head.

"You know this is foolhardy. Right?"

To that, I nodded.

"And," he said, with resignation, "she will try. No matter what, she will try. You've given her too much information. You've given her the road map she will try to follow." He wasn't actually talking to me.

"Something happened, didn't it? Something in Chicago? Something besides just Mina that made Mary Elizabeth take up this crusade."

He nodded, lowered his head and scratched an eyebrow, obviously thinking.

"Yes." He looked out over the beach toward the ocean. "There was another girl. Alexis. Fourteen when she came to us, the victim of sexual abuse by her mother's boyfriend. Another lost child Mary Elizabeth took under her wing. I don't know what causes her to form a special attachment to some of the kids we help, but there's something.

"We care for them. All of us do. And we do everything humanly possible to help them. We do pretty well, but there will always be those we lose. Some come in and after a while just disappear. Some go back to a lifestyle that is inappropriate. It is just easier for some of them. It is a fact of life, and you have to move on, keep helping those that remain."

He lost himself in thought again, looking out over the beach and sea. I slowed down a bit. He was talking, and I didn't want to get to the marina before he'd finished Mary Elizabeth's history.

He looked back at me. "Like parents, we cannot afford to have favorites. We have to take care of all of them, but sometimes, you'll connect with one of them for some reason."

"Like she has with Mina?"

"You know, not really. Mina's situation for Mary Elizabeth is something much more complex. It's not exactly what I'm talking about.

"She did connect with Alexis. There was something special about the girl to Mary Elizabeth. I don't know what it was. I don't know if Mary Elizabeth could even articulate exactly what it was, but there was something. Sometimes I think it's because she is a nun. She would make a great mother. Maybe that's what she's seeking.

"It took no time at all to get the story out of Alexis. She ran away one night to get away from the boyfriend. She came to The Beacon the next afternoon after sleeping outside somewhere. She had no problem telling us about what had happened to her, and she had no problem repeating it to the police.

"By the time the police got to her mom's house, the boyfriend was gone. He'd left town. Everything about the mom suggested that what had been going on while she was at her night job was a surprise to her. She was devastated and gave the police a lot of information about where her boyfriend might have gone.

"Alexis was only with us the one night. Children's Protective Services took her the next day and put her with a foster home while they investigated and got some counseling done with Alexis and her mom. Mary Elizabeth followed up and stayed in touch with both of them. Mom got some help, and everything seemed to have been resolved. The police never were able to track down the boyfriend."

He was quiet again. I turned down the road to the marina, parked, and waited for him.

"Long story short, Alexis and her mom disappeared and we had no idea where they'd gone. Protective Services couldn't tell us. We found out months later that mom had moved to Phoenix to be with the boyfriend. I can't pretend to know what she was thinking. Maybe he was on good behavior for a while. Eventually, he came after Alexis again. This time she didn't run. She fought. He killed her."

"Wow."

"Yeah. Wow. Now the boyfriend is in jail for the murder, and mom is in jail for felony child abuse."

"And Mary Elizabeth took that particularly hard, I guess."

"To say the least. It broke her in some ways. Obviously, it's something that's been growing in Mary Elizabeth. She did not deal with the death of Alexis very well. She didn't get a lot of relief from counseling the church provided. After a life dedicated to serving God in her order, trusting what she believed true, it crushed her spirit. She is suffering some kind of crisis of faith. I can't pretend to understand. Without knowing exactly how, I do know that Mina and her situation has monumental meaning to Mary Elizabeth. The fervor you see is as much about saving herself as it about saving Mina."

Jason helped carry stuff to the boat. He watched as I did the necessary things, check the engine over, check the batteries, check the oil, check for forgotten food in the fridge, store the rods and do all the other things on my list of things to do before any trip off-shore.

We didn't talk much. As I went through the routine, I thought about the story he'd told me.

I've had clients go to prison, but only one I didn't think deserved to go. I kept many out of jail who should have been there. I didn't lose much sleep over any of them. I could only imagine the emotional turmoil and toll of doing the work done by Jason and Patricia and Mary Elizabeth. I didn't want the turmoil. Emotional turmoil was why I shied away from representing juveniles caught up in the justice system.

Juvenile cases had a high incidence of tragedy. Society no longer expected parents to take care of the problems that happen. Too often for the parents, it was pass or fail. Fail, and your child got fed into a system that doesn't work too well. We even commercialized aspects of the system. There was private money to be made in the system and campaign contributions to make. There were fiscal incentives to feed the system. Others were better equipped to pay the emotional price of dealing with those types of cases.

It didn't take me long to be happy with the condition of the boat. Jason and I went to the marina's office where I made arrangements to have the fuel and water tanks topped off.

"We're done," I said. "Would you like lunch?"

"Sure, but let me pay."

"Nope. The marina is owned by my uncle. We won't be charged." That wasn't exactly true. A discounted charge would go on my account. I'd pay that and full price for the beer, but not until the end of the month. We got shrimp po'boys and a beer each and went back to the cabin of my boat.

"Look," he said, "I want to apologize for the way I

acted that first day we met you. I think this whole thing is wrong. I don't understand Preacher. He acts like there's no problem. Mary Elizabeth wraps herself in his mindless assurance. I know she won't listen to anybody anyway, but it is frustrating that he seems to agree with her that a bunch of amateurs can do something. When he suggested we visit his lawyer friend, I thought maybe a lawyer could talk some sense into her. Then, when we came to your place, I jumped to the conclusion that you're just another flake."

I laughed. "I could tell I wasn't what you were expecting. I am another flake, certainly more beach bum than lawyer."

He smiled. "Then, I thought you were doing a decent job of pointing out the problems. I hoped maybe the added weight of your opinion would make her stop. But she is not going to stop."

"I guess you could just call the cops and tell them what she's planning. Maybe they would be willing to stop her even if they don't have enough to go after the bad guys. Client confidentiality means, right now, I have to keep things confidential."

He shook his head. "I've thought about doing that, going to the cops, but I think that would be worse than her trying and failing. At least as far as the part of this whole thing that is about her. Besides, she would see it as a betrayal and she'd be lost to us. They might end up taking Mina, and that would be untenable for her. I don't know that she'd be better off failing, but I think having Mina to care for would at least give her some direction."

There was a long pause with him just looking at nothing somewhere to the left of me.

"This is where I am," he said. "At least you can keep her safe, keep her away from any possibility of confronting anybody who might do her harm. You can keep Mina out of the spotlight. That way there's something for her to focus on afterward."

I laughed. "You mean after the bad guys kill me?"

He smiled. "No. In fact, I think the thing to do is act like you're doing something. Plan it. Practice it. Get prepared. Then, make sure she stays behind and report back how you tried, but you just couldn't get it done."

"That's likely to happen even if I seriously try to rescue the girl."

"I'm saying you shouldn't put yourself into harm's way. The best possible solution is for everybody to stay safe, even if that means you have to fail on purpose and let her move on with saving Mina."

"Perhaps. But you know what will happen. She'll be walking the streets of Chicago searching for Zoio and asking questions that might get her and the girl in trouble."

He nodded grimly. "All I can tell you is if you fail and she thinks you tried, I'll back you up and I'll do whatever I have to do to keep her safe in Chicago. Even if I have to get the Church to send her to Bolivia."

Driving back to the house, before I realized it was happening, he and I formulated the backup plan, the plan to follow when nothing else worked. He preferred it as the main plan, but I still hoped to find some way to reunite the sisters. His plan was to follow the safest course and fail on purpose.

At the house, as we waited for the return of everybody who went to get their hair done, I learned a little bit about Jason. He'd grown up in Los Angeles where he got into some trouble in his youth. A part of his community service was to work at a homeless shelter. There he met another nun, one that inspired him and taught him he was choosing the path he was on simply because it was the easiest path to follow.

He learned it was tougher to be a good man than a follower of his peers. The harder path attracted him. He went back to school and earned his high school diploma in order to be eligible to enlist in the army. The army is how he made the final escape from a world threatening to drag him down.

Out of the military, he went back to college and earned a degree in social services. That led him to The Beacon, an outreach program created in the late sixties. He'd been there a few years when Patricia and Mary Elizabeth walked in and asked what they could do to help. Both of them were seeking a way to better serve their faith. Surprisingly, it was Patricia who came seeking something new. Mary Elizabeth had just tagged along. They both became invaluable working with the children served by The Beacon. Reluctantly, their church officially sponsored their work at The Beacon. The work did not assuage Patricia's disenchantment, and she left her order. She and Mary Elizabeth remained the best of friends.

The others returned from the hairdresser and made a show of presenting Mina, making us close our eyes before she got out of the car. Then, there she was, standing in front of us. Not only had her hair been returned to a rich, dark brown, it had grown. She'd left with a shaggy haircut barely covering her ears and now her hair was down to her shoulders.

"Wow." Jason and I both exclaimed.

Mina glowed with pride. She looked like a normal teenager. It made thinking about her recent history much more sharply bittersweet, emphasizing what had been taken from her.

"You look amazing," I said. She beamed and took Mary

Elizabeth's hand. "How did you grow your hair?"

Preacher spoke up. "Marie loaned us a wig when Mina told her how long her hair used to be. She told me to tell you that if she didn't get it back in good shape you owe her another hundred and fifty dollars in cash."

Mary Elizabeth said, "She says this is exactly what she looked like before she left home." Mina, still smiling, nodded. "I thought we'd get a picture of her both with and without the wig. If her sister has not yet cut or dyed her hair she'll probably be wearing it like this."

"Okay," I said. I finally took a moment to look at the others. "You all look great. That was a good thing to do." Mary Elizabeth's hair had been trimmed. Her fingernails had been tended to but not polished.

They'd spiked Patricia's short hair with gel. Her fingers and toes sported a rose-colored nail polish. Her eyes really got my attention. Her lashes were dark, and whoever did her makeup used a smokey gray eyeliner. Somehow, it made me notice for the first time that her eyes were blue. I guess I looked at her a bit too long. I saw her eyes narrow.

"Look at you. Nice."

"Thanks." She actually smiled.

"Okay," I said. "Let's get her photo."

We took photos of Mina and a few snapshots of the group just for fun. Preacher insisted I use the timer to get in a photo. Mary Elizabeth and Patricia took off Mina's wig, and I made some photos of her with short hair.

Later, I compared the first photos I took, those of her with her bleached blonde hair with those made after the do-over. The difference was heartbreaking and hopeful. I saw with greater clarity the story of her ordeal. I saw there was a chance for her salvation. Perhaps she had what it would take.

I took a phone call from my lover Cecilia, asking if we could meet the next day. I declined, explaining I had a group going fishing. If anything, our affair is accommodating. She took the news gently with whispered promises for a next time.

Frankly, I thought about canceling the fishing trip. Everybody was relaxed and happy after the visit to the beauty shop. Fishing was my thing. I didn't want to push it on the others, but everybody said something about looking forward to a day on the boat. I decided having that day would make us closer as a group. Whether we followed through on seriously going after Zoio or if we had to do some variation of Jason's plan to pretend to try, it would not hurt to be as close a group as possible. I could always cut the day short if it became the obvious thing to do.

Eventually, Jason said, "I think that if we're going fishing we're going to need to get up early." He looked at me.

"Absolutely. If possible, I'd like to leave the marina no later than six in the morning."

If it had been just me, I would have left closer to four, but six would get us out to where we could do some fishing and not have a rough ride against the tide moving through San Luis Pass.

"I think I'll sleep on the boat tonight, so just meet me there."

Preacher asked, "Do you mind if I join you? That way I'll be sure to be on time."

"Sure. Do you have everything you need?"

"My backpack is in the car. It's all there."

The others left. I closed up the house, made sure the shop was secure, and Preacher and I headed out for the marina. He jumped out to tend to the gate, and we turned left heading east toward the marina.

Preacher inviting himself along irritated me a bit. A boat enforces closeness, and I wasn't sure I wanted to share the evening. I had too much to think about. But, Preacher doesn't demand attention. He would respect my moodiness.

The evening ended nicely. I tossed my small suitcase on the bed in the forward cabin. Preacher helped me put the netting over the back deck to stymie the mosquitoes. I turned on the air conditioning to keep the cabin fresh and puttered around inside for a bit, dumping ice into an ice chest, using the little hand vacuum to pick up some sand.

Preacher reads people well. He stayed to himself out on the deck, reading something he pulled out of his backpack. I enjoyed the solitude accented by the night sounds and moments of the marina, the muffled conversations and small sounds of others tending to their boats, the scent of somebody's barbecue grill, the darting of fish gathered where lights spread their glow over the water. It was a good place to be, even if a little way off, somebody had a television out on their deck, its blue light and canned laughter the only things out of place.

I piped some soft rhythm and blues to the speakers outside. I held up the bottle of Macallan single malt and waved it at Preacher. He put his hands together as if to pray and said, "Yes. Bless you, my son."

I joined him on the deck. The scotch tasted of smoke and caramel, creamy on the tongue. It was perfect with the soft, restrained passion of Etta James singing about the comfort, joy, and pain of love. We talked about things. It was a good evening, and I went to bed early. Preacher did as he usually does and made himself comfortable by piling cushions on the deck so he could sleep outside.

THE RUMBLE OF CHARLIE BOTSWORTH'S Bertram vibrated through the hull waking me at four. Charlie ran a fishing charter out of the marina. I sprayed off *The Lonely Star*, ridding it of the salt haze and spider webs. I washed and stowed the glasses Preacher and I used the night before. He shook out the cushions he'd slept on and return them to their rightful places. Shortly before six I started water circulating in the bait well and sent Preacher up to the restaurant for the breakfast burritos I'd ordered the night before.

At the bait shop, I paid for a couple of quarts of live shrimp, some frozen squid, and some cut bait. Randy from the bait shop brought it all to the boat and gently released the shrimp into my bait well. The others arrived a few minutes before six. I turned on the exhaust blowers when I saw them pull up and park.

Jason and Preacher cast off the lines and I took the *Star* slowly out of the slip and into the channel. Preacher took everybody below and gave them a lesson on how to use the head and showed them where to find the drinks, snacks, and sunscreen. About the time I turned to the southwest toward the pass, Preacher came to the bridge and asked what kind of fishing did I expect to do.

"Nothing big. Put a couple of the big rods up and ready, but we probably won't be using them."

"Aye, aye, sir." He scurried back to the deck to make the fishing rods ready.

The water was not rough and everybody enjoyed breakfast as we made our way into the Gulf through the San Luis Pass. I put the coordinates of an abandoned drilling platform into the GPS and sent its data to the autopilot. The electronics took over, and I kicked back to enjoy the trip, sipping coffee and appreciating the lively talk and laughter from everybody sitting below.

"May I come up?"

I turned to see Patricia's head just peeking over the edge of the deck. "Of course. Come on up and enjoy this glorious morning."

She was a surprise. She'd come aboard with a jacket zipped up almost to her neck. She'd unzipped it to disclose a bikini top over her shorts. There have been a few scantily clad women on *The Lonely Star*. Occasionally, some of them wear nothing up top and some enjoy the sun with even less. Perhaps it was the on edge emotion of our mission, or perhaps it was that she had once been a nun. I don't know, but of all the women who have graced the decks of my boat, not a one looked as sexy as Patricia did wearing that bikini and the coconut scent of sunblock.

I guess I looked at her a bit too long. I recovered quickly, but not quick enough. I noticed a smile touch the corners of her mouth and eyes. It amused her to see my momentary distraction.

"What a great morning," she said.

"Yes. Welcome to the big blue nothing." I glanced at the beige water that hugs the coast. "Well, it will be blue in a bit."

"This is great. How far are we going?"

"We're headed for an abandoned offshore drilling platform about thirty miles out. It works as a terrific artificial reef."

She looked back to where Mary Elizabeth and Mina were laughing at something Preacher said. Even Jason was smiling. Mary Elizabeth wore a short-sleeved yellow top, a windbreaker, and white Capri pants. Mina wore shorts and a tank top but held a jacket in her lap.

"Help me make sure everybody stays covered in

sunscreen. It can sneak up on you out here."

"We are well slathered."

We talked about nothing important. I zoomed out the map on the GPS to show here where we were and where we were going. I was in no hurry, this being more of a leisure trip than a fishing trip. I estimated our travel time at an hour and a half.

Everyone came up top at least once. It would have been a fun day on the water except for the ever-present knowledge about our ongoing mission. They'd walked into my shop one week previously and, for the rest of the week, I operated with a buzz of heightened energy and an anticipation of tremendous, undefined things.

Perhaps it was that heightened state of emotion or some visceral response of the primeval urge. I don't know. But I was very aware of Patricia, that she was very attractive, and that she had an energy of purpose. I kept looking at her. She noticed me looking and accepted it. A few times, when I glanced over at her, she was looking at me. Neither of us said a word about the looks. I kept telling myself it was just the heightened energy of shared purpose. I reminded myself of the possibly terrible consequences of losing focus. But I argued with myself. After all, nothing big would happen for three or four weeks.

At one point the conversation in my mind caused me to shake my head at the enormity of what we were doing.

"What?" she asked.

"Nothing, really. Just thinking about the situation and trying to decide what to do."

"You've been pretty perfect so far."

I snorted my disagreement.

"In one week you've done more than any of us thought possible. Trust yourself. I do. We'll take one step at a time, and something will work out or it won't. Even if we don't find Zoio, you have helped."

She stood next to me as we cruised in silence. I continued to process random thoughts. I shook my head again in frustration at too many unknowns and too many variables. Without looking over at me and without saying a word, Patricia put her hand on my shoulder, squeezed once, and left it there for a bit.

We tied up to the platform on a calm sea. I was not serious about the fishing, but it turned out to be pretty good. In the morning we caught several Spanish Mackerel and, later, after an early lunch, we started catching Kings. Those who wanted took turns pulling in the fish. Mina took a big interest after her first and she ended up landing most of the fish.

A lassitude settled over my crew in the afternoon. Preacher and Mina both fell asleep. I announced an end to the fishing and asked if they wanted to head straight back or take the long way home for a little cruise. The vote was unanimous for a cruise. I roused Preacher to get the fishing gear stowed, and I punched in coordinates on the GPS to take us to a point offshore Galveston where we could make our way home through the jetties into Galveston Bay.

At one point Jason and I were alone up top.

"When are you going to tell them?"

"Tonight, when we get back."

He nodded. "Thanks for this. I can't imagine what it has cost you in fuel and haircuts and wigs to join Mary Elizabeth's crusade."

"It's no big deal." I tried to think how to say what I felt without sounding silly. "She is a very good person and deserves the help."

"Yes. To a point. Just don't do anything foolish."

I nodded.

Patricia was a little overdone with a glow promising she would be a bit too red by the next day. Everybody else had been careful with the sunscreen and shelter. It was late afternoon by the time we made our way between Galveston Island and Bolivar Peninsula.

The sun lost its strength as we made way down Galveston Bay. By the time we were halfway down West Bay, the sun spread color in the coastal haze. Clouds gathered in layers where the moist air over the Gulf encountered the air mass of the coast. I slowed a bit to enjoy the spectacular sunset.

The day had been as lighthearted as possible. I knew I could no longer keep to myself that we had no mercenary force coming to assist us. The only viable plan was Jason's plan. After failure, we could do what we should do first, go to the authorities. I realized when we finally did that, we would have to do so carefully to avoid harmful repercussions. It would have to be done in a way that protected Mina and those protecting her. I'd been convinced that putting Mina in the hands of legal authorities would not be in her best interest.

Everybody was tired, but I needed to let them know what was happening. They began to gather their belongings and straighten up the boat as I guided the boat into its slip.

Holding up a hand as Preacher started to thank me for the great day, I said, "We all need to talk for a moment. Let's do it here, in the cabin."

Jason and Preacher helped get the boat securely in place. I connected the onshore electricity and water connections. Randy came down and collected our fish. He would have them cleaned and packaged by the time I left to go home.

We gathered in the cabin. Mary Elizabeth sat on the bench behind the table close by Mina's side, within hand-holding reach if necessary. Patricia sat next to Mary Elizabeth, close like a watchdog, but not as close to her as Mina. Preacher leaned over the navigation table, and Jason sat on the bench against the other side of the cabin, leaning back, relaxed with his legs crossed at the ankles. He knew I was going to break the news.

Their looks made me pause. I'd become the leader of this group. Now, I was about to tell them my best bet had fallen through. There was a good chance, if I did lead them further, I would be misleading them all, intentionally planning to fail. That would assure a very scared, sixteen-year-old Zoio ended up in a world of horror.

It was time to get it done.

CHAPTER EIGHT

I SAID, "FIRST. I HAVE TO TELL YOU ALL SOMETHING. This may change, but right now, the experts I talked to are not available to help us."

The cabin deflated. Mary Elizabeth slumped back against the bench. Mina looked from me to Mary Elizabeth, back to me, and back to Mary Elizabeth. She pressed closer to Mary Elizabeth's side.

Patricia said, "Oh, no." She and Preacher were shaking their heads.

Only Jason did not seem to react. He kept the same tight, almost satisfied smile.

I continued. "The folks I talked to have another operation out of the country. It's possible they'll be back before the *Soliez* gets here, but it's doubtful, and we cannot count on it."

"What are we going to do?" Mary Elizabeth said while patting Mina lightly on the knee.

"We do what we've already planned. Get as prepared as possible. I'll talk to the lawyer who helped me before. Maybe she'll know somebody else to call. If not, then we will have to decide what to do without help."

For the first time ever, Mina spoke directly to me without any kind of prompting. "Mr. Locke. You have to save my sister." Tears welled in her eyes. It was another first, seeing her cry, seeing tears track down each of her cheeks.

"I understand Mina. We are going to do everything we can possibly do." I carefully did not look at Jason.

Once again, I was at a loss. Mina was so young and so fragile. The unsettling emotion of her tears felt like one more link in the chain of things confusing the issues. I was determined to not put anybody at risk. But somebody, somewhere, had to be willing to enter the arena on behalf of these tragically lost children.

Mary Elizabeth took in a big breath and shook her head as if casting off my bad news. "So," she said, "what do we do next?"

I, too, took a big breath, gathering my thoughts. Jason and I were right of course. It was too risky to do anything on our own. For the moment, though, I had to continue the charade. Otherwise, Mary Elizabeth might try to do something on her own.

"We do what we need to do. Tomorrow night we take a drive to see if Mina can confirm the route they took. We start scouting for locations from which we can watch for their van. We decide whether there is a way we can watch for their boat. I continue to look for info on the boat they use. I get the before and after photographs of Mina printed. Mina teaches us how to say a few things in Ukrainian."

Mina's eyes opened wide at that.

"Mina, you need to teach us to say a few things. Things we can say to your sister. We need to be able to tell her that she is with bad men, that you sent us to save her, that she needs to come with us. Now that I think about it, you need to come up with something that only you would know so we can convince her that you did send us."

Mina said something in her own language and then said, "Yes. I can do that. I will help."

Mary Elizabeth said, "Are you sure there's no way to find where he lives? Trace his boat? Something?"

"I don't know what we can do. Even if we sit and wait for his boat, we couldn't follow him if we saw him. Our focus has to be on making sure the van does not get away before we find it."

"But you said every little thing we can come up with might help. We need to look for them."

"Yes, but the closer we get to the date we expect them to get here, the more we need to focus on the most possible things. I'm not even sure we need to sit and watch for his boat. We might miss seeing the van if we spend too much time on that."

It was quiet for a moment.

"Surely he smuggles more than just girls off the Soliez."

We all turned to look at Patricia when she said that.

"What do you mean?" asked Mary Elizabeth.

"We have some time before we expect the ship with the girls. We've talked about how the guy down here is probably just a smuggler and not a part of the whole big deal. You've said his boat is unusual and unknown. Surely, he's using it for other things. Drugs or something. Maybe we couldn't follow him, but you said every bit of knowledge might be important. If we don't have anything else to do, we will watch for him before we expect him to have the girls. You never know, we might get lucky."

I looked at her, feeling stupid. She misread my silence and looked embarrassed.

"You are exactly right," I said. "I should have thought about that. There's no reason we couldn't spend some of the time doing just that thing. Even if we can't follow him, we might get an idea about which bay he hides in."

She shrugged and smiled at me.

"Good idea," Mary Elizabeth said. "I am still willing to go sit all night on that jetty."

"No," I said. "You are absolutely not going to do that. I will resign from your little project if you decide to put yourself unnecessarily at risk. Sitting there is more dangerous than wise."

She didn't seem fazed by my potential mutiny. "Then how do you propose we watch for him?"

"From my boat. I will decide exactly how."

She nodded at that.

"Okay, then," I said. "Go home. Get some sleep. We start again tomorrow night."

Mary Elizabeth gave me a hug and said, "I know God sent you to me." That didn't help the way I felt.

Mina spoke directly to me again. "Thank you, Mr. Locke." That made me feel worse than what Mary Elizabeth had said.

Preacher added his two cents. "You are doing good."

Patricia looked at me intently as she reached out to shake my hand. Then, she hugged me. Quietly, with her mouth close to my ear she said, "You better not screw this up. You better not get them hurt." I nodded. She tightened her hug one time before she let me go.

Jason stayed behind as the rest of them filed out of the cabin and climbed to the decking of the pier. He said, "You haven't changed your mind, have you? You know you can't do this alone. Right?"

"I know. But there is a chance we'll have help. There's a chance I'll be able to find somebody who knows what he's doing. I might think of a way to safely get the law to take over. We have a little bit of time before we have to leave Zoio to those bastards."

It took a moment before he spoke. "Okay. Is there anything I can do to help you put your boat to bed?"

"No. There's not much to do, wash it down, lock it up. I'll take care of it. Thanks."

Jason followed the others, leaving me in the gently rocking sanctuary of my boat with a strong desire to top off the tanks, turn off my cell phone and start my trip to Key West. In a week, I had tripped and fallen to a place at the edge of hell, responsible for things for which I had no desire to be responsible.

I did those things the boat required, picked up our fish, and drove home to my bed. It took some time to fall asleep.

I WOKE THE NEXT MORNING with resolve. Something needed to be done about Zoio. If there were no available mercenaries with the required experience, then something needed to be done by law enforcement. Somebody had to know what to do.

I called Cathy Winwood. Whoever answered took my name and number and said Ms. Winwood would call as soon as possible. That turned out to be about forty-five minutes later.

"How may I help you, Mr. Locke?"

"I met with the gentleman to whom you referred me."

"How did that go?"

"He and his mom were impressive but unavailable in the time frame I need."

"I'm so sorry."

"Is there anybody else you can recommend?"

"No. That is really the only person I know with the expertise you need."

"Then I may need to hire you. For advice and as a go-between. Would you be willing to talk to whatever law enforcement agency we might need?"

There was a pause. "Let's get together. Are you in town?"

"No, but I can be."

"I am preparing for a hearing in the morning. Let's meet at six tomorrow evening. My office."

"Okay."

"Will anybody be with you?"

"No. Just me. I'm the one trying to figure out how to proceed."

"Okay. See you then."

I called Mary Elizabeth's and told her I'd made another appointment in Houston to find somebody else who could assist.

"I want to go with you."

I knew she would not like what I intended to do. "No. Not this time. The people with whom I consult are very skittish and reluctant to talk in front of anybody."

"Fine. I can sit outside and wait."

"Mary Elizabeth, I know you are anxious to be in on everything I'm doing. You and I share two concerns, saving Mina and saving Zoio, but I have another which you do not share."

"What's that?"

"Keeping you safe."

"Thank you, but you do not have to worry about me."

She irritated me. "I do not have to worry about any of you. I could tell you there's nothing I can do, that this whole thing is too big for us. I have other things I can do. If you want me concerned about the girls, then you will just have to accept the fact that my concern extends to you."

"Thank you again. But you have to promise me that your concern for me will not, in any way, stop you from doing what we have to do for the girls."

"I haven't made any promises about this whole deal. I've already done way more than I expected. And I'm not done. We'll see where this goes, but I am going to the meeting tomorrow alone."

She was unhappy. "I guess that's settled then."

"You can trust me, you know. I understand your concerns. I agree that in this whole foolish crusade we have to protect Mina not only from the bad guys but from the officials as well. That protection extends to you. There's nothing you can say about that."

"Sam, I do trust you. You have been honest and more helpful than I ever expected. Perhaps it is just that for the first time things are looking possible and I don't want to be in the dark."

"I will not leave you in the dark."

"Okay. But you have to promise to tell me, whatever the outcome of your meeting. Don't let another day go by like you did with the last bit of bad news."

"Promise." I don't know if the childhood rules applied at my age, but I crossed my fingers as I promised.

There were two ocean-going vessels I could check on. I called Leeland to ask if he'd learned anything about the all black boat. I left a message and trusted his electronics to get the message to him.

Though modern electronics sheltered Leeland from my inquiry, it made tracking the Soliez much easier.

On the freighter tracking website, much of the data was exact. The database gave the location of many of the freighters at a particular time by GPS location, obviously electronically provided and kept timely by the ship. For many, like the Soliez, the data was not so exact. The website reported its location as an approximate location. A notation stated that the position of the ship was an estimation based on the best available data. Its estimated arrival time at the Port of Houston was a vague eighteen to twenty-five days. I, too, would keep my whereabouts vague if I trafficked in humans.

My phone rang. It was Jason. "Sam, I've got to get back

to Chicago. I'm leaving in the morning. Please keep me posted on everything."

"I will. Don't worry, I know what the priorities are."

"Good. Look, despite my worries, it has been nice to meet you and get to know you."

"Likewise."

"I feel better knowing you are keeping Mary Elizabeth from doing something foolish."

"Keeping her and Mina safe is my number one priority."

"Okay then. I'll say good-bye for now. Again, let me know what's going on."

"Is Patricia going back with you?"

"No. She should, but she won't. She wants to be a part of whatever is going on and take care of Mary Elizabeth."

"Don't worry. I'll watch out for her, too."

It hadn't been long before the phone rang again. It was Leeland.

"Leeland, have you asked around about an all-black boat?

"I have."

"Discreetly I hope."

"Yes. I've told some folks I heard a rumor there was a solid black boat doing stupid things at high speed in the middle of the night. We all worry about one bad apple drawing too much attention to us all. When it happens, we all get stopped more often by the pleasure police."

"And?"

"Not much. I heard from one guy that a friend of his had mentioned a middle of the night sighting of a black boat going way too fast without running lights. But there was no real good description of the boat. He just figured it was somebody drunk or smuggling. Frankly, you know how it is, you hear a lot of boats at night without being able to see where they are. I'll keep looking for your solid black one."

"Okay. Thanks. Let me know if you hear anything more concrete, but do not attract attention."

"Will do. Talk to you later. Let me know when you're ready to make a run with me."

A car crunched to a stop on my driveway. I went out on the porch. It was the car that Mary Elizabeth drove, but Patricia was the only occupant.

"Hi," she said.

"Hi. Wow. You're alone."

She smiled. "Yes. I guess we usually all show up on your doorstep together, don't we? Does that make you feel outnumbered?"

"Nah. I guess we're all in it together." I held the screen door open for her. "How about some coffee?"

"Sure. I don't know what I'm doing here, actually."

"Well, it's good to know that you are no different from the rest of us. Come on in."

I made coffee while she stood in my living room looking at the photographs and prints on the walls.

She turned toward me as I brought in two cups of coffee. "I guess I've always been focused on other things when I was here. I never really paid attention to your place before."

"Not much to it."

"Did you take these?" She waved a hand at the photographs on the wall.

"No. They're done by a friend."

"They're nice." She sat down on my sofa. "I guess that's part of the reason I wanted to come over. I feel like we are taking advantage of you. I wanted to see you when we're not all here and focusing on our big problem."

"I'm glad you did."

She smiled. "I guess I still feel bad about my first impression and how I treated you."

"No reason. You had nothing to judge me by except for what you could see. Actually, you don't know. You might not have been that far off."

She shook her head. "No. You are much more than what I first thought. It's hard to believe it's only been a week, given all you've accomplished. For the first time, I think this whole thing might actually be possible and safe."

My turn to shake my head. "Do not start thinking anything we're doing is safe. Remember, whoever is behind this whole enterprise sent somebody to the Beacon. We're not the only ones out looking for information."

"Yes, I know. But, they certainly can't know about you or what you're planning."

Suddenly, Patricia sat up straight and slapped her hands on her knees, and said, "But I came over here today because a strategy session was not planned. One more thing and I will take you to lunch."

"Okay. What?"

"I'm curious, what's next on our agenda?"

"We're going to drive Mina around tonight and see if we get any better idea of the route she took. I don't think it's that important, but everything helps. After that, I don't think there is much we can do other than maybe learn some Ukrainian phrases and scope out where Preacher and I can watch the highway up north. I know it's not much, but it will either work or it won't. I'm still trying to find some pros to help. In fact, I'm meeting somebody in Houston about that tomorrow, but I don't think we'll find somebody in time. Other than that, I guess I'm going to go sit on my boat and listen for the smuggler. That's really silly and undoubtedly useless, but it's something to do."

She nodded. "Okay, then. Let's not talk about the problem again until absolutely necessary and I'll buy you lunch. Where are we going?"

"How about something other than seafood."

"Thank you. Yes."

I took her to Cranks, an unassuming place off a side street in downtown Galveston. Russell Franks, its owner, works hard fifty-one weeks out of the year and parties hard one week a year. It is his partying that made him a client of mine. At Cranks, we enjoyed barbecue, served up on paper plates accompanied by coleslaw, beans, white bread, and tea.

We talked a little about her. There were things about her life when she was young she talked around without revealing much, things that led her to become a nun. I got the impression being a nun gave her a place to grow up. Once she was grown, she realized she had not truly been called to be a nun, and she needed to do other things.

We talked about my boring life growing up, my unlikely friendship with my Uncle Harlan, and my growing disenchantment with the things a person needs to do to practice law. With our mugs of iced tea, we toasted the fact that each of us finally stepped out and changed our lifestyles in ways others did not appreciate.

My impression of her changed. I was resisting the urge to ask her out on a real date when she said, "Sam, when are you going to go sit on your boat and try to catch a glimpse of the bad guy."

"I'll probably start tomorrow night if I get back from Houston on time. Might as well. I can sit on my boat and accomplish nothing as easily as I can accomplish nothing in my living room."

"I want to go with you."

"Are you sure? It will probably be boring."

"I can be bored on your boat as easily as I can be bored in my room. At least we'd each have somebody to talk to if we wanted."

She misunderstood my hesitation. "Only if it is okay with you. You won't be obligated to talk to me. I can sit quietly. I'll bring a book."

"Sure. It won't hurt to have two sets of ears and eyes."

We drove back to my place and said goodbye.

That evening everybody but Jason got to my place about an hour before sunset. It took us a couple of hours to drive the length of Galveston Island, take the ferry across the channel, drive the length of Bolivar Peninsula, turn north to skirt the Anahuac Wildlife Refuge, and drive up to the town of Winnie where we got on Interstate 10 toward Houston.

The entire trip, from my place to the north of Houston and back to my place, took four and a half hours. We ate fast food on the trip. We didn't learn much. Mina confirmed that she remembered seeing Houston all lit up at night.

The brightly lit Budweiser bottling plant looms just before the interstate crosses the 610 Loop. Mina leaned over the seat back and excitedly pointed it out saying, "Yes. Yes. I saw that. I remember that." For sure, the van had taken the 610 Loop to get north of Houston.

Although she'd not seen anything else as memorable as the bottling plant, Mina's energy stayed elevated. She sat looking forward, searching for anything that might help us. She was trying and her interest was palatable. She, too, was putting trust in me to do more than I thought possible.

Back home, it took me a while to get to sleep. There

were too many people thinking I could do things. There were too many things to do and too many unknowns. Not to mention there were too many things we did know that were way too dangerous to mess with.

EARLY THE NEXT MORNING I called Ben Marsh, the harbormaster at Sol de Mer.

"Hey, Ben, do me a favor. I want to park my boat at the Channel Marina for a couple of weeks. Can you call and make the arrangements?"

"Yes, sir. Two weeks?"

"Actually, I'd like to keep it as flexible as possible. I don't know how long I'll be down there."

"Okay, we trade favors all the time. It shouldn't be a problem. Everybody has space these days. I'll have them pass any charges to your account here."

"One more big favor. Could you get a couple of your guys to take her down on their own time? I'll pay them. That way, when I get back to town tonight, I can go straight there."

"Sure thing."

The Channel Marina is on the other end of Galveston Island from my home marina, across the channel from Bolivar. If I was going to sit up all night doing surveillance in the channel, I wanted to stay close and not have to make the trip back and forth to my slip.

I considered using a smaller, faster boat for my night-time surveillance, something more capable of following a high-performance boat but concluded that a chase at night would not be wise. The most I could hope for was to catch a glimpse of the mysterious, all black offshore racing boat. Chasing the wary driver would not likely be successful and might be counterproductive if it caught his attention. I might as well watch for him from the comfort of the *Star*.

That done, I handled a few calls related to my legal business, sent out a bid to somebody wanting a custom grill for their backyard and a proposal to a brewery wanting a grill to advertise their beer. My idea was a massive reproduction of a six pack of long neck beer bottles. I wanted to try a ceramic finish that would look like glass beer bottles. The finish would take on the bright color and detailed design of their packaging. Smoke would escape through the neck of one or more of the bottles.

Two weeks earlier the complexities of building a beer bottle barbeque smoker would have consumed me. Now, it was nothing I could think about. That afternoon, as I drove toward Houston to meet with Cathy Winwood, there were other thoughts on my mind. Those thoughts were interrupted by my phone.

"Mr. Locke? Cathy Winwood. Change in plans. Do you like beer?"

"Sure."

"Do you know the Petrol?"

"No."

"It's a true beer lover's mecca. We're meeting someone there."

"Somebody who can take this mess off my hands?"

"No. Sorry. I don't have a suggestion in that regard. It's just somebody who might answer some questions or provide some insight. We need to meet quietly, and he really likes beer."

"Okay, then. Text me the address of the Petrol. I'll meet you there. I'm probably thirty minutes from downtown Houston."

"The address is on the way. We'll expect you in forty-five minutes or so. We'll be sitting outside in the back."

I converted her text to a GPS reference. It routed me to what looked like a residential neighborhood northwest of downtown Houston, but the GPS confirmed the Petrol Station was at that location. Houston's lack of zoning laws often created an interesting mix of retail and residential, especially in some of the older neighborhoods.

The Petrol Station was housed in what was a gas station many years ago. Judging from the number of cars parked on the street and in the lot across the street, it was a popular place. A lot of beer poured from a lot of taps. I made my way through the bar to the outdoor seating area out back.

Cathy Winwood sat at a small wooden picnic table in a corner with a gentleman. He wore the remnants of a suit, minus a suit coat and tie. Cathy waved at me and he turned to look at me. He had short brown hair parted in good business fashion. His foot fidgeted. I got the impression he operated at a rate of metabolism faster than most. He sat with the toes of his dress shoes on the ground, but both heels were vibrating like his engine was at a fast idle. He smiled but was obviously assessing me, as I was him.

Cathy indicated a place on the bench next to her, and I sat down. "Sam, this is Bill Dodge, a friend." We shook hands. Cathy stood up and said, "The service here is best if you do it yourself. Can I get you a beer? If you're hungry, they have some killer food here."

"A beer would be nice. I can get it."

"No, you sit. I'll get it." She was already moving away. "They have an eclectic collection of beer, trust me?"

"Sure."

She left. Dodge wasted no time. "Sam, I'm here at Cathy's request. I can answer some questions about immigration enforcement. There are some things I will not discuss and if you and I ever run across each other again, I will not know you and I trust you will not know me."

That was kind of strange, but quite fitting in the new, complicated world I'd joined. "Sure."

"I'm trusting you on Cathy's word."

"Not a problem. Where do you fit in?"

"I work for the feds. I'm a lawyer. Let's just leave it at that for now."

"Okay. Did she explain about my client and what I'm trying to do."

"Somewhat."

Cathy returned juggling three mugs of beer. I took a sip. It was an excellent beer.

"So, have y'all made each other's acquaintance?"

I realized she'd gone to get the beer to give Dodge time to tell me he worked for the government and this meeting was not taking place. It created a fiction in which to operate in the future.

"Yes, we have," he said.

She sat down next to me. "I told Bill a very broad outline of what we discussed. He can answer any questions you might have about your client's immigration status. And he might be very useful in the future if things need to be done officially."

Bill Dodge was another good-guy in the dark world into which I had fallen. Being such while working for the federal government must have been a significant career risk.

"Tell him what you can," Cathy said.

So, I did. I gave him the facts, but not the names. I described my snatching plan without mentioning that intentional failure might be the option of choice.

He turned to Cathy. "What about you know who?"

"He talked to them. They're out of the country."

Bill nodded and turned back to me. "Be very careful."

"Being very careful is my priority."

He spent some time talking about the T visa, designed to establish a legal, non-immigrant status for victims of trafficking. He was honest and not too hopeful about its application to Mina. He, too, confirmed the risk that if we did everything strictly legal, Mina and Zoio, if we got our hands on her, would likely be repatriated to Ukraine. He agreed with Mary Elizabeth that was not the ideal solution, even if it was the legal solution.

I learned nothing new from Bill Dodge and it irritated me a bit that Cathy had me drive all the way to Houston for this meeting.

He left, telling us he had to get home, and Cathy said, "I know what he had to say was nothing new to you, but I wanted the two of you to meet. I'm sure you've picked up on where he works. He shares our philosophy of getting things done when necessary. In his position, he can be a tremendous asset to you in the future when it comes to the fate of your girl. It was important for him to meet you before you get into the position of needing him."

That made sense. Breaking the law needs to be done carefully. There are a lot of politics and nonsense in the practice of law, things that play with people's lives in unsavory ways. The stuff I'd seen in the past paled in comparison to the complexities and absurdities of achieving something right in Mary Elizabeth's cause.

Tired on the drive back to the coast, I looked forward to parking the boat somewhere and spending the night. I called Channel Marina and talked to the evening manager. He confirmed the arrival of my boat and gave me her slip number. I told him I'd be taking her out that night. I told him a guest might be showing up before I could get there and, if so, he could give her the keys. He confirmed the power was hooked up so Patricia could run the air conditioning if necessary.

I called Patricia's cell phone.

"Patricia, Sam. I've had my boat moved to the other end of Galveston Island. I'm about an hour away. I plan to sleep on her tonight somewhere I can watch for our smuggler coming through the channel. If you want to join me, you should get to the marina. I've left your name with the manager. He'll give you the keys so you can get into the cabin. If you have any questions about running the air conditioning or anything you can ask him."

"Okay. I'll do that. How did your meeting go."

"It was not what I expected and not a lot of help when it comes to actually getting our hands on Zoio. I'll tell you about it later." I gave her the address of the marina and directions on how to get there.

Patricia's car was in the parking lot when I got to the marina. I was torn between looking forward to her company and wanting to be alone on the boat to think and try to organize my plans. But it was nice to walk up to the boat and see lights on in the cabin. It felt like somebody was home, waiting for me to get there.

Chapter Nine

It wasn't just the lights there to welcome me. Patricia had take-out Chinese food ready to heat in the microwave, a chocolate cream pie in the refrigerator, and, in the center of the table, a bowl of jelly beans.

"Wow," I said.

"I didn't know if you'd be hungry or not. If you don't want any, it will all keep."

"No. It's all good. A pie and jelly beans?"

She smiled. "Jelly beans are my secret sin."

"As sins go that one is fairly benign."

"Once, when a novice, a Sister ordered me to confession because she found a bag of jelly beans in my room. I'm still not sure exactly what the sin of that was, but I confessed that I had a bag of jelly beans. I heard the priest laugh. The next week he gave me a bag of them."

"Okay. Now I know something important about you. If I'd known before, I'd have made jelly beans a part of ship's stores."

"How about Chinese?"

"Yes, but if you can wait, let's go ahead and get anchored out past the channel where I intend to spend the night."

"Sure. What do I need to do?"

"Not a thing. Enjoy the very short ride."

I'd picked a spot just inside the bay off the point of Bolivar Peninsula, tucked next to the spoil island on that side of the Intracoastal Waterway. It was as close to the channel between Galveston Island and Bolivar as I could be while staying outside a Coast Guard controlled traffic area.

If my guesses were on point, our quarry would pass within a mile of where we anchored. I thought he'd stay closer to the more sparsely populated Bolivar than to Galveston. If so, he might pass within a quarter mile of us. We should be able to hear those engines of his.

In that area, I had to be careful where I anchored to avoid losing an anchor to an abandoned drilling platform on the bottom, or I'd hook a five-inch thick high voltage cable traversing the bottom. I'd spent the night there several times and had the location in the GPS.

I'd checked and expected calm weather and water all week. We would feel the wake of ships going up the Houston Ship Channel, but there should be few of those at night. I didn't know how long I would sit and watch for our quarry, but at some point, we'd have to do something else. I expected the *Soliez* to arrive in the next two to three weeks.

I secured the mosquito netting over the rear deck before we crossed the channel. I liked the bays at night. There was the non-ending industrial hum, but overall it was quieter and the world shrunk to a smaller diameter around my boat. Galveston and the refineries and chemical plants of Texas City lit up the sky, but sitting on the boat in the dark was like sitting in a dark theater, a voyeur to things on a stage.

I watched the GPS and the depth finder, found my spot and backed down against the anchor, making sure there was enough scope to allow the *Star* to swing fully as the tides changed.

We ate on the deck, protected by the mosquito netting. The conversation was easy. We talked about television, music, and trips we'd made. Patricia was animated, and I became very aware of her as a woman. If we'd been dining casually on my boat and enjoying a night on the water instead of being on a stakeout, I would be thinking the chances were good we would happily end up in the same berth. But we were there on a stakeout, playing a part in a dangerous mission with mortal stakes. There was the very real possibility of a tragic ending.

I told myself to not confuse the emotion, intimacy, and awareness of the moment as anything other than a reaction to the Adrenalin fueled exhilaration caused by our dangerous mission.

Finally, I said, "I hate to say this, but I have got to try to get some sleep if I'm going to get up at midnight and watch for our guy."

"I'll clean up. Do you think I should take the first shift and watch until midnight?"

"No. I think if he comes through here it will be after midnight. We won't see him, but we ought to be able to hear his boat. We won't know for sure if a powerboat we hear is his. We won't be able to follow him far. If we hear somebody, we'll follow as long as we can, but I won't be able to keep up with him and I do not want to spook him. We'll try to hear and maybe track him on my radar. I'd like to know whether he turns into East Bay or heads up into Trinity Bay."

"We're not going to be able to do much are we?"

"No. I just don't know what else to do right now. I'm going to turn on my radar and have it wake me up when it detects any boats passing in the channel. The alarm will be going off all night. You may hear it squeal. That's why I'm sleeping on deck. There's a speaker out here through which I'll pipe the radar alarm.

"The radar is going to pull some power, so you may hear the generator kick on at some point. I'm afraid it's going to be a noisy night."

She shrugged. "No problem. Maybe we'll get lucky. I remember what you said about gathering every shred of information we can. I'll sleep out here, too."

We hauled bedding and pillows up from the bunks and made our beds on the benches on deck. As we were doing that my cell phone sounded. It was Preacher.

"Hey, Sam. You all set?"

"Yes. We're anchored. We've eaten. We're about to bed down for a while."

"We were thinking and it seems like there is something we could do instead of just leaving you out there alone."

That set off alarms with me to the point where Patricia noticed the expression on my face. She stood, took a step closer to me and raised her eyebrows in silent inquiry. I shook my head. "What do you mean? What are you doing?"

"We're driving down to the jetty. We're going to sit and watch for the lookout while you sit and watch for the smuggler."

"No."

"We'll be careful, and we might get a license plate number or a description of the bad guy or something. Mina is safe. She's not with us."

"No."

"Sam, Mary Elizabeth is insistent that we don't just sit and do nothing. This is how we can help."

"Listen to me. And tell her. We are at a point where there's not much anybody can do. My one overriding objective is to not put anybody in harm's way. You tell her that if the both of you cannot promise me you are turning around and going home I will pull up anchor and I will not do this. I will be going straight to the cops."

"Sam ... "

"No. Call me when you decide." I hung up.

I breathed deep and leaned on the table, thinking.

Patricia asked, "What's going on?"

"Preacher and Mary Elizabeth decided to go park at the jetty."

Patricia stepped closer, wrapped her arms around my waist, pressed the side of her face against my chest, and said, "Thank you."

I put an arm around her and returned the hug. "But there's a problem."

She stepped back and looked at me for a moment but kept her arms around my waist. "What's the problem?"

The phone rang.

"Yes."

"Sam. She's not happy, but we're headed back home."

"Good."

"Do you want to talk to her?"

"No. We'll all talk later." I hung up.

"So," Patricia said, "what's the problem?" She took her arms from around me and stepped back.

"They may have had the better idea."

"What do you mean?"

"We're sitting out here on a long shot, hoping to maybe hear a high-powered boat come through the channel in the dark. We already know he comes through here, but I don't know what we're going to accomplish by hearing some boat that might or might not be him.

"They, on the other hand, were going to a specific spot where I'm pretty sure one of the bad guys will park. Maybe we're all fighting the odds. But if something happens, there's a much better chance of learning something useful if it happens at the jetty. The results of watching there would be something concrete, not just a sound in the dark."

"Maybe somebody should go there."

"Maybe. But not without some preparation. Those two are primed to do something stupid."

"What do we do? You and I go sit there? I could do it by myself. I promise I'd be careful."

"I'm thinking about something better. We'll talk about it later. There's nothing to do tonight." Suddenly tired, I felt the great weight of the futility of our efforts and our lack of information. Patricia must have noticed me sinking. She put her arms around me again.

"You've already done so much. Everybody knows we're working in the dark with no great chance of success. You'll decide the best course based on what we know."

I nodded and rolled my neck to shed some tension.

"And now," she said, "set your alarms and sleep. What happens, happens. We'll learn something or we won't."

Before I could get to sleep I lay there thinking, trying to determine what else I should do. There were too many unknowns.

Eventually, I got to sleep, waking periodically to check a few radar hits. Sounds carry well over the water, amplified by the quiet of the night. I heard no loud boat engines. I got up shortly before one o'clock and sat, listening to the night. I turned off the audible alarm and monitored the radar screen. I tried to be quiet, but after a short while Patricia was up and sipping coffee with me in the dark. We sat side by side, speaking little.

We heard nothing and, as the sky brightened to the east, I pulled up anchor and motored back to the marina. Patricia took our bedding below and made up the bunks. It was too early to call, but I didn't care and called Mary Elizabeth's cell phone. Preacher answered.

"Hey, Sam. We came back last night. She didn't like it,

but we did it. I sacked out on her sofa. She's probably still upset. What's up? Did anything happen?"

"No. Just as expected, nothing. First, let me apologize if I was harsh last night."

"No. I understand."

"Secondly, you had a good idea to stake out the jetty. It makes a lot more sense than sitting on my boat hoping to hear something that might or might not be our guy."

"It was her idea. Not mine. She really wants to do something."

"She's doing plenty. I will not agree to her putting herself in danger, but we need to consider having somebody parked at the jetty at night. We just need to figure out how to do it safely."

"I'll do it. I'll start tonight."

"Let's get together and talk about it later. I need to get some sleep. I'm going to nap for a while here on the boat. Let's all meet at my house this afternoon at three, and we'll make some plans."

"Okay, and I'll get some sleep, too. I'll be ready to stay up all night at the jetty."

I did sleep, eventually, but first, while Patricia napped in one of the guest bunks, I made a call to Wallace Rockwell. Occasionally I need a private investigator. Rockwell is the man I call.

He has no receptionist and no answering service. If he's not available, he simply doesn't answer the phone. He was not busy and opened the call as he does every call, "Investigations."

"Rocky. This is Samuel Locke. How are you?"

"Sam. Good. What's up?

"Are you busy?"

"I have a few small things I can do to be busy unless

you're offering a fishing trip, then I'm not busy at all."

"Soon. Unfortunately, I'm caught up in something for a client and need a couple of things, one of which is some overnight surveillance."

"Where and when?"

"Over the next couple of weeks, I need someone to watch the parking areas at the north jetty over on Bolivar between midnight and four in the morning. I don't really know who I'm looking for, but license plates and descriptions of anybody there at that time would be helpful. I'm not getting paid and probably cannot afford you every night. I've got someone else willing to do it, but he might need some relief." That last bit was me fishing for a discount. I was quickly going through my Scamp Boat money.

"Perfect. I have an idea. Your back, my back mutually scratched by economic need. I have taken on an apprentice who needs some experience, and sitting in the dark all night will be an excellent lesson. Half price to you plus expenses."

"Sounds very nice, but I'm not sure I'll use him every night. This is all out of my pocket."

"What exactly is going on?"

"I'm trying to get on the trail of a smuggler, somebody trafficking in children, and who I suspect is smuggling in other contraband. I think he posts a look-out on the jetty."

"Bastard. I hate trafficking. How dangerous is it going to be for my person?"

"Shouldn't be dangerous at all. He doesn't know I'm trying to find him. I would just as soon he never knows who I am. I'm not even trying to stop him. I'm just looking for one particular girl he may get his hands on. I'm thinking somebody in a pickup with a camper would not be seen. The truck would not look out of place, and he could just park and record the license plates of anybody going out on the jetty, getting a description of the vehicles and the people if possible."

"Do you have the truck or do I have to rent?"

"I know where I can get one that will be perfect. If its license plate is current."

"Okay. I'll charge you a hundred bucks a night. That'll cover what I'm paying my person. Plus, you'll owe me one overnight fishing trip for a couple of my clients and me. I'll buy the bait, the food, and split the gas. You provide the boat and the bikini-clad deckhand."

"Great. Can do. One more thing. Can I rent a pair of night vision goggles from you?"

"My person will have a pair. Do you need another?"

"Yes. I'm sitting on my boat watching for the bad guy's boat. Night vision might come in handy."

"I'll loan you something. When do you want to get together?"

"I'm meeting with my clients at three at my house. Can you come there about three-thirty."

"I'll be there, and I'll bring my operative."

I thought about how what we were doing was becoming more complicated. The odds were still against us, but at least I was trying to influence some direction to the flow of what felt like out of control events. I knew the more I found solutions to problems, the further I moved from Jason's plan to make moves only to satisfy Mary Elizabeth until we could fail gracefully. Hiring somebody to watch the jetty was unnecessary if I was just playing that game. I was investing not only time and money. I was investing some ego and moral outrage. I really wanted to beat the bad guys. That was scary foolish.

I lay on my bed in the boat and tried to not think

about all the things I should be doing. I didn't have the experience to do what we were trying to do. Sleep came, fitfully, and was little more than a theater of abstract dreams of frustration and failure.

Subtle shifts in the movement of the boat and the sounds of Patricia moving around woke me from my nap for the final time. I splashed water on my face and went into the salon to find Patricia making coffee.

"Sorry if I woke you up, but I could not sleep anymore."

"No problem. I wasn't sleeping much anyway."

She held up a cup. "I have coffee, though."

"Bless you." I took the cup.

"Did I hear you on the phone?"

"Yep. Scheduled a client meeting at three and added somebody else to our ill-fated army."

She held up her cup to tap with mine in a toast and said, "Here's to the red sword of virtue."

I must have looked confused. She smiled, and said, "A Stephen Crane poem. 'Supposing that I should have the courage to let a red sword of virtue plunge into my heart, letting to the weeds of the ground my sinful blood, what can you offer me? A gardened castle? A flowery kingdom? What? A hope? Then hence with your red sword of virtue.'"

I touched my cup to hers again. "Ah. Yes. To hope. I hope our blood will not be let into the weeds."

She laughed. I looked into her eyes as we sipped our coffee. Her eyes suggested the possibility of other complications.

WE GATHERED AT THREE. Mary Elizabeth pouted.

I spoke directly to her. "I know you want to help. I know you want to do everything we can do. I've already told Preacher it is probably a better idea to watch who parks at the jetty than to sit on my boat."

"Then ... "

"No. I will not do this job if I'm worried about any of you getting in harm's way."

"You said it was a good idea."

"It is a good idea. That's why I'm hiring my private investigator to sit there. He has trained people and he has night vision equipment. We'll get it covered without danger."

She took a deep breath, wanting to say more. Finally, she said, "Okay. But there has to be something I can do."

"Yes. Keep Mina safe. You've gathered your army. Let us do what we can."

She sat down by Mina and took her hand.

"What else do we have planned?" she asked.

"Nothing. Unless somebody can think of anything."

"I can drive around and look for the van."

"You've already done that, right? After you first got here?"

"Yes."

"Then let's not waste any more time and gas doing so. If we learn something from all this surveillance we're doing, maybe we'll have an idea where we can do that effectively."

She sat on the edge of the sofa not as relaxed as she always seemed to be in the past. Things were getting closer to a climax of some sort. She needed to do something.

"I have an idea," I said. "I just checked again for its position and there is no way the *Soliez* will get within range of our guy for another week. I know it's driving you crazy to just sit and wait. Why don't you and Preacher drive to Dallas and take Mina to Six Flags. On the way, she can watch and see if she recognizes where they stopped on the road when she made the trip. That would be helpful information."

Preacher said, "Six Flags would be fun, but shouldn't I stay here in case you need help."

"I cannot think of another thing we can do. When it is time to go sit on a highway somewhere, you'll be with me. But that's a week away. You can take care of them and practice speaking Ukrainian with Mina on the way."

Mary Elizabeth looked at Mina and said, "I don't know."

Mina asked, "What is Six Flags."

"I hear it's a great amusement park," Preacher said. "Have you ever ridden a roller coaster?"

"Okay, I guess," said Mary Elizabeth. "But, I will not be gone when it is time for the ship to arrive."

"No. Drive up there tomorrow, go to the park the next day, and drive home on Friday. I can't imagine anything new coming up, but if it does, I promise I will call you guys."

Preacher quietly explained Six Flags to Mina. Mary Elizabeth looked at me and nodded. Having made the decision, she visibly relaxed. She turned to Patricia and, with a look, said, "So, Patricia, you want to go?"

There were undercurrents in her question. Patricia gave Mary Elizabeth a look and actually blushed. "No," she said, "I'll stay with Sam and make coffee."

Ignoring the exchange and its undercurrents, I went to the computer. It took only a few minutes to find a Six Flags and hotel package deal at which I could focus my credit card. I pulled up the Six Flags website and turned the computer over to Preacher and Mina.

To Mary Elizabeth, I said, "I'll have to get to an ATM machine to get you gas and spending money."

"I've got some money, and I've got a credit card. We'll let The Beacon pay our way."

Preacher piped in, "I've got some cash, too."

Patricia smiled and nodded my way. That's when the crunch of tires on the drive signaled the arrival of Wallace Rockford and his protégé.

I went out to greet them. The person with him was a surprise. I thought at first it was a teenage boy getting out of the passenger side of his car. Rocky's apprentice was a girl. Thin, dressed in scruffy jeans, a t-shirt, and a ball cap, she looked fourteen years old. He noticed my double take and grinned.

"Hey Sam, I'd like you to meet Genevieve Mills. She's coming on to help me."

She held out her hand to shake my hand with a firm grip and said, "Hello. Mr. Locke, it is a pleasure to meet you. I look forward to helping you out. Call me Jenny."

Her hazel eyes were steady and unwavering. "It's a pleasure," I said, "and I'm Sam." Up close her female shape was more apparent, but she still looked about fourteen.

Rocky laughed. "Don't worry. She's twenty-three and perfectly capable of watching out for your bad guy."

"Just surprised. I'm sure she's most capable."

"I am," she said.

"Okay, then, y'all come on in. You can meet the client."

In my living room, I introduced everybody. I gave Rocky and Jenny a summary of the situation. I noticed that Mina kept her eyes on Jenny. Jenny smiled and nodded at her getting a smile in return. Rocky and I signed one of our typical contracts for investigative service. That put his work under the attorney-client privilege.

I ended my summary by saying, "I'm going to watch for them on the highway when the *Soliez* is scheduled to arrive, but in the meantime, I'm thinking if he's in the business of smuggling, we might see him on another run before then. I'm sitting close to the channel in my boat all night. All I want Jenny to do is get information about anybody on the jetty from midnight until daybreak. If she can get a description of individuals and a copy of license plates it might come in handy."

"I can do that," she said. "In fact, I'll take the night vision binoculars and a camera. I'll get the best photos I can of anybody going on the jetty. They won't be great, but who knows, we might get something."

"So, we good?" asked Rocky.

"We're good. Let me see if I can borrow the truck with the camper."

"If necessary I can sit in a car."

"Thanks for the enthusiasm, but you'll be more comfortable in a camper. And it will be easier for you remain hidden. Let me call my neighbors."

The ladies next door have a pickup with a camper they only use occasionally. They've had it since it was new, but that was twenty years ago. It looks like something some coastal fisherman might use, but it is in good running condition. I called and got Maude on the phone. She took a moment to ask Joanne if there was a problem and said I could use their truck as long as necessary.

"I'll walk over and pick it up."

Rocky said, "I'll go with you. Jenny, you can stay here."

He and I walked across the pasture bordering my property, gaining the attention of Joanne's and Maude's goat herd. As expected, Rocky wanted to have a private discussion.

"Sam, this doesn't sound like an easy deal you've got yourselves into. Where is the FBI?"

"Yeah, I know. I'll explain as much as I can." I gave him our reasons about protecting Mina and her sister from the possible legal compulsions of the government. He nodded his understanding.

"Okay. I hope this works out for you. I'm not sure I'm comfortable confronting the traffickers, but I'll help you all I can. Jenny is my niece. Her parents died in a wreck a couple of years ago and she bounced around a bit. I'm trying to give her something to do and help her find something she enjoys to do for a living. I offered her an office job. That lasted about a week. She's taken to fieldwork nicely, but I'm unwilling to put her at significant risk. She's a little overconfident right now."

"I understand. You make it very clear to her that I do not want her in any way to get into a confrontation with anybody at the jetty. The chances of us actually seeing these guys are pretty slim, but, if we do, it could be bad on everybody if they know we're on to them."

"Understand. Looks to me like you've done a remarkable job in running down some details. Like I said, I'll help all I can. I have some contacts at the port. I'll see if I can get better info on when to expect the ship. Let me know what else I can do."

"That would be a good thing. Based on what Mina told me I think he probably meets the ship well out to sea, maybe a hundred miles or more. Pinning down when the smuggling of the girls will happen is important and cannot be done with a great deal of accuracy. Any help would be nice."

"I hate to say this but you better write all this down. Just in case. Leave me a copy. If something bad happens, I'll get somebody official to follow up."

"Good idea. You'll have it tomorrow. That will give me something to do on the boat tonight. I'll leave a copy with instructions with the lawyers at Sherwood, Thomas, and

Cain as well."

The goats assured the ladies heard us coming and Joanne met us on the porch with the keys to the truck.

"It's gassed up," she said, "and the battery is good. You know how to use the generator if you need to charge the service batteries."

"Thanks, Joanne. It's going to be a big help."

We drove the truck the short distance to my house. I invited Rocky and Jenny to stick around for an early dinner and he accepted.

Mary Elizabeth, Preacher, and Mina all made a trip to the nearest place to get take-out pizza while I showed Jenny the camper and explained how to use the generator if needed. The camper has a propane fired stove top and a chemical toilet. It has a crawl-through window from the cab to the camper. She checked it all over and nodded her head in satisfaction saying it would make a great vehicle to stake out a parking lot.

"It won't be very cool and you'll have to run the generator to run the air conditioner," I said.

"I won't use the air conditioner. The generator might attract attention."

"Going to get warm."

"I'll take a chest full of ice and sit in my underwear. I can open some windows for air. There shouldn't be a problem. I'll be fine."

"I have ice. We'll stock you up, buy some coffee and whatever you want to snack on. What else do you need? A notepad?"

"I have my stuff. I won't need a notepad. Rocky would chew me out if I was unprepared with the basics."

Rocky nodded his agreement and his pride.

"What do you think Rocky?" she said. "Think I could

use that infrared alarm thing to let me know when a car is coming down the road."

"We'll pick it up. That's a good idea if there's a place we can put it. Speaking of gadgets, Sam. Let me get you some night vision equipment."

He retrieved a case from his car and showed me how to use the night vision goggles.

"It has an infrared boost if you push this switch, but I'm not sure it will help at the range you're looking at. You should have enough light to at least make out the profile of the boat you're looking for. Keep in mind, he might have a bunch of shore lights behind him that could mess you up. Try getting up high and looking down to keep as much water behind him as you can."

"Good idea. The tower on the boat might work."

"Okay, then. There are plenty of spare batteries in the case."

I started to feel competently organized for the first time since we started this foolhardy mission.

The pizza arrived, and we ate hurriedly. We took three vehicles toward Bolivar. Patricia and I were in mine. Jenny drove the camper, and Rocky was in his car. Rocky left the caravan in Galveston to go to his office to get the infrared alarm thing Jenny asked about. We stopped and stocked the camper with granola bars, energy drinks, and toilet paper. Patricia and I picked out groceries for us to use on the boat.

I followed the camper onto the ferry and down the road to the base of the jetty. There were a few vehicles parked in the unorganized dirt parking lot at the bait shop. Jenny slowed to consider her options and pulled into space at the edge of the lot close to a jumbled pile of broken concrete and lumber leftover from a rebuild after the last hurricane. Anybody else parking would have to park between her and the beach. She got out and joined Patricia and me as we walked toward the jetty.

"Good parking spot. The bait shop will close soon. Nobody will pay attention to you," I said.

Jenny nodded. "I can hide the infrared alert Rocky is getting in that jumble of trash. It will send an alarm to a receiver I'll have. I shouldn't miss anything where I'm parked, but backup never hurts."

I looked over toward the beach where a few vehicles were parked. "I guess he could already be parked on the beach. Take a stroll down to the beach in a bit and get their license plates. Any that leave will have to pass by you. Any that stay you'll have their info."

She nodded and smiled, giving me a look that made me realize she'd already thought to do all of that.

Patricia asked, "Are we about to leave?"

"No. We're in no real rush."

"I'm going to walk a little way out on the jetty."'

Jenny and I went to the camper and I watched her unpack a Nikon with a large zoom lens from the bag she'd brought along.

"There's enough light I might get decent photos of anybody walking on the jetty."

She had a bottle of spray glass cleaner and walked around the outside of the camper washing all the windows.

"Why all of them?" I asked.

"One clean one might attract attention. This way they all look the same."

She also cleaned the inside of every window facing the jetty and those facing the road at the back of the camper. She attached a monopod to the base of the camera, checked its battery level and nodded with satisfaction. She had a stack of books in her bag. She shuffled through them and pulled out a birdwatcher's field guide to birds of the Gulf coast. I laughed. She shrugged and said, "Just in case anybody gets curious about what I'm doing."

A pocket digital recorder, a notebook, three pens, and three sharpened pencils completed her supplies. The backside of her equipment bag had a small clip where she clipped her notepad.

She also had a duffle bag. From it she removed a can of pepper spray, a large tactical flashlight, and a pistol grip shotgun. Those she laid in a line on the front bunk of the camper and covered them with a blanket. She smiled, arched her eyebrows and said, "Just in case some beach bum falls in love with me."

"I'll be sure to knock politely when I return."

"After Rocky and I get the alarm on the road, I'll stroll down the beach with my recorder and camera and record license numbers. I have another alarm that will burst the eardrums of anybody who enters the camper while I'm gone."

"Don't attract too much attention taking photographs. A good description should be good."

"I'll be careful. I have a right-angle mirror I attach to the front of the lens so I can point the camera one way and take a picture to the side."

She was proud of all of her stuff. I was impressed with the level of preparation. Obviously, Jenny shared Rocky's enjoyment of the gadgets of their profession. I needed to confer with him to see if he had any ideas for the rest of our project.

Rocky drove up. He proudly showed me the infrared motion detector. I watched for only a moment and then left them to the careful placement of the small black box in the rubble of construction waste. I met Patricia as she walked off the jetty.

"It gets spooky out there real fast," she said.

"Yes."

"Are we done?"

"Looks like Jenny is well prepared with a whole slew of spy equipment. I think we can go get ourselves parked."

"Sam, thank you for getting her to do this. I'm glad Mary Elizabeth and Preacher are not taking this job. I can't imagine what this is costing you."

"Not that much. Rocky doesn't much like traffickers. It's worth it for the peace of mind."

Jenny wandered off toward the beach with her camera. Rocky waited for us. He said, "I think she's ready."

"I think she is more than ready. She's going to do good. We're leaving. Impress on her there is absolutely no need to confront anybody for anything out here."

"She knows. If a confrontation happens, it will be because somebody tries to break into the camper. She's well prepared for that, too."

Having seen the thoroughness of her preparation, I laughed to think what might happen to some beach trash who tried.

Everyone went their separate ways. Rocky walked down to the beach. Patricia and I headed back to my boat for another night of on the water surveillance.

And, surveil we did. That night. And the next night and the next night.

Patricia and I had companionable meals and a lot of great conversation. There were terrific, quiet moments when we lounged around and read or just sat watching the bay and passing tankers. What we didn't do was catch any glimpse of our quarry. The night vision binoculars made it a bit more interesting by allowing us to peer in a voyeuristic way at boaters passing by, unreal images in the green glow of the night vision screen.

There was a moment, right after dark on Wednesday, our third night of sitting there, when the low throated rumble of engines from a powerboat rolled across the water. There were three offshore powerboats coming in from the Gulf, not our smuggler going offshore. Using the night vision device, I could see the girls on the boats putting on their bikini tops.

On Thursday night I took Patricia to eat in Galveston at a seafood place over the water on the Strand. We were back on the boat and anchored at our spot off Bolivar in time to watch the sun go down. There was a nice breeze blowing hard enough off the bay to chase bugs away and I left the mosquito net rolled up. Patricia took a call from Mary Elizabeth and talked for some time.

A lot of their conversation concerned the fun day at Six Flags. At the end of the call, Patricia responded to something said by Mary Elizabeth, "No. We haven't seen or heard anything we think is him. And, trust me, you will be impressed when you see exactly how he has the jetty being watched." She was quiet for a moment. "No. Trust me. It is being done much better and much safer than the two of you could have done.

"Yes, okay. We'll see you tomorrow night. Good-bye."

"How are they?"

"Sounds like they had a lot of fun."

"But she can't wait to get back here and join the hunt, can she?"

Patricia laughed. We were sitting next to each other facing the setting sun, and she leaned toward me, bumping shoulders. She stayed pressing against me and said, "You've got that right. There is absolutely nothing she can do, but she really, really wants to do something."

"I just don't know what else we can have her do. We're still a couple of weeks from the arrival of the *Soliez*. I guess she could come sit on the boat with us, but that doesn't equate to getting anything done, does it?"

"No. Plus, she would add nothing to what we're doing, and you know what, I'm kind of enjoying being out here, just you and me."

I gave her a shoulder bump.

She continued, "I think we're doing all we can, but we don't have to sit here and talk about it. I love her dearly, but if she was here, we'd be talking about it. Guaranteed."

"Yes. It has been nice. I like somebody who enjoys reading. It means I can read, too."

"I know exactly what you mean, but, speaking of the case, how long do you think we'll sit out here?"

"I've been thinking about that. We know this is a long-shot. We're counting on the bad guy having a smuggling job. Even then his timing will depend on when whatever ship he's taking stuff off of shows up. We're coming up on the weekend, and the bays will get busy with recreational boaters. I think he'll skip smuggling on the weekend if he can."

"But we should stay out here anyway, shouldn't we?"

"Yes. As long as we don't have anything else to do. Jenny is doing a great job of getting license plates and photos of folks. I'm more excited about what she might observe than what we might see or hear. She might actually come up with the thing that will lead us where we need to go."

We continued to sit quiet and close, so close that if we both breathed just right, in the same rhythm, her shoulder touched mine. It happened more and more. There was a growing awareness of each other. I felt it. I knew she felt it, too. There were signs, eye contact, little touches exceeding random chance in number. We communicated without words.

No, I did not want to stop our surveillance, and we didn't need any company on the boat. I could objectively analyze what was going on between us. We were male and female in secluded proximity, senses and emotions heightened by tension. Our excitement increased the closer we got to a conclusion of our quest. It was not a good idea to seek an outlet for all that tension in an emotional entanglement. But having an objective awareness of that didn't override the primeval instincts. That meant I needed to get some sleep before I said or did something awkward.

"Okay." I took a deep breath. Patricia turned to look at me.

I said, "I guess it is time for sleep if we're going to get up at midnight and listen for him."

"Yes. I guess so. This is nice. I hate to agree, but you're right. Are we sleeping out here, again?"

"Nice night. Might as well. I'll drop the bug net."

"I'll get the stuff."

We stood. She turned and, standing close to me, said, "I really appreciate what you're doing and for how you're keeping Mary Elizabeth off the front line. Thanks."

With that, she put her hands on my shoulders, stood on her tiptoes and kissed me. It was mostly on the cheek, but she did catch the corner of my mouth. It was a surprise. Before I could respond with any meaning, she'd turned and gone below to retrieve our bedding.

We slept, getting up to check radar alarms. We watched and listened and morning came. We met Jenny over coffee at the marina where she handed over a thumb drive with a spreadsheet of vehicles parking at the jetty, their make, their license number, a description of the vehicle and driver, times of arrival and departure, and a number referencing the photographs she made of the vehicle and drivers. The spreadsheet included a pivot table making it possible to sort the data in any number of ways making it easy to check for more than one visit to the jetty by a particular car or truck.

I asked Jenny, "Nobody is getting suspicious of you being parked there every night?"

"I don't even think they notice. Just to make sure, I got there early one night, went in the store and bought some snacks. I talked to the two guys working there. They now think I'm a marine biology student at A&M doing some month long research project that requires me to get up all night long to record data. I labeled some bottles with some meaningless numbers and put water in them from the ocean. Plus, I have a microscope. I'm good."

I laughed. "You are good. If I have any money left at the end of this thing, I'll make sure you get a bonus."

With the data Jenny Mills collected, we could make charts and graphs of the arrival and departure times of vehicles visiting the jetty broken down by vehicle make and model. I did it once when bored and actually combined a graph of arrival and departure times with a chart I grabbed off the internet showing predicted tide levels at the jetty. There was a correlation and, like so many collections of as much data as could be accumulated, it was all useless. We could do nothing more than sit and wait for our guy to show up, and we had to have the luck to be there and to notice.

We did it again on Friday. Activity increased with the arrival of the weekend. The numbers in Jenny's spreadsheet more than doubled. There were a greater number of the noisy off-shore power boats. I watched for the bad guy, and I watched for my friend Leeland. I did not see either.

We were in place again on Saturday night.

Early on Saturday night Patricia and I shared our patch of water with a young man in a beat-up aluminum skiff. He looked to be fifteen or sixteen years old. He eyed us warily and I waved at him. He knew some kind of secret because he anchored and immediately started catching fish at a pace that made me long for a good fishing trip. It didn't take long until he was catching good-looking speckled trout and releasing them back into the water. He had reached his daily limit, but he was still having a good time.

I asked Patricia, "How about some of the freshest seafood you could ask for?"

"Sure."

I gave one short blast on the horn. When the boy looked over, I waved, signaling him to make his way over to us. He started up his old, but clean and polished, outboard motor and came alongside, skillfully holding his boat a couple of feet away.

"Yes, sir?" he said.

"Looks like you're having a pretty good day."

"Yes, sir. They come through here about this time."

He was deeply tanned. His inexpensive fishing equipment, like his old boat, was well cared for. I could tell he was a denizen of the bay. He obviously knew the rhythms of the tides and the fish inhabiting the bays. When he spoke about the fish coming through at "this time," he was not talking about the time on the clock. He was talking about a multidimensional time involving the seasons, the tidal flow, the feeding habits of the fish, and the weather. I suspected he might occasionally have trouble getting to school on time, but out here on the water, he understood the ancient and nonadjustable clock of the earth.

"How would you like to sell me a couple of your specs? Looks like you wouldn't have any trouble replacing them."

"Well, sir, it would be illegal for me to sell you my game fish and then catch more."

"Yep, but here's how I see it. You've got me wanting some freshly grilled fish. If I have to pull up anchor and go buy me some bait shrimp, it's going to cost me at least twenty dollars. Plus, by the time I get back, they will probably be gone."

"Yes, sir."

"I'm just giving you two off my daily limit and neither of us is going to tell."

His eyes flicked to Patricia in her shorts and bikini top.

He shrugged and said, "Sure."

I gave him a twenty, and he gave me two of his best eating size fish. He went back to his spot. In the time it took me to clean the fish, he'd replaced them in his fish box. He waved and motored off.

I hung the grill over the side and grilled the fish. We agreed one glass of white wine would not impair us to the point we would neglect our job. It was a good meal.

After the sun set, that night became something much different than the other nights we'd spent out there on the edge of the bay.

CHAPTER TEN

PATRICIA AND I SAT SIDE by side facing the channel and watched the sun go down. The lights of Galveston slowly became more prominent. The ferries plying their route between Galveston and Bolivar were lit by their deck lights. The night sounds began to come to us over the water. The sounds of marine engines and fish flipping on the surface became more noticeable.

All the offshore powerboats we heard were heading in from the sea. I scoped them all with our night vision equipment confirming they were all pleasure boaters. Their sun warmed passengers would continue partying in clubs on shore.

We'd been sleeping early in the evening to be more alert in the early morning hours during which I expected the smuggler made his runs, but that night neither of us suggested we go to bed. We talked again of inconsequential things. Until she turned to me and put her hand on my arm.

"It is really nice out here. I wish we could enjoy the simplicity of it without the ugliness we're waiting for."

"Yes." I put my hand over hers. She shifted her fingers to intertwine with mine.

I looked closely at her eyes. She did not blink, and the corners of her eyes moved as she smiled.

I looked at her lips and watched them form the word "Yes," said without sound.

We leaned toward each other. I heard her take a deep breath. I watched her eyes close. I moved a hand to her neck, and we kissed. The first was kind of quick, but the second was longer.

She said, "About time. I was starting to wonder what I'd have to do."

The third and forth kisses kind of melded together as we adjusted to get closer until, finally, she leaned across my lap, supported by one of my arms, my hand holding her shoulder while my other hand was on the bare skin of her side, feeling her move with each breath.

We finally paused. I said, "I hope this isn't just a reaction to the heightened emotions of our ongoing project."

She put her hand behind my head and pulled me closer until the tips of our noses touched. "What if it is?"

I quit worrying about motives.

We moved the cushions to the deck and retrieved the linens from the cabin. There, on the deck of my boat, our clothes in a heap, we shared the ancient, familiar explorations that are new every time.

The image from that night I will always remember is Patricia, eyes closed, her face and breasts lit by the soft light of the moon as she arched her back beneath my touch, her mouth gently curved with a beautiful smile.

We slept less that night than the nights before. We had too many things to learn about each other. We still checked each radar alert and once again, we saw nothing suspicious.

The next morning we were not embarrassed with each other. We laughed more. We touched more.

We'd made a date to meet Jenny Mills for breakfast where she handed over the thumb drive with her updated spreadsheet and photos. We transferred it to my laptop right there at the table.

"There were more people than usual last night," she said.

"How are you holding up?" I asked.

"I'm actually having a good time. It gets peaceful out there at night and it's not been difficult to get what you need. How much longer do you think?"

"Well, if we don't get anything before about Wednesday, I don't think we'll keep watching from the boat. The ship we're interested in is due in a couple of weeks, and we'll have to start watching the highway soon. I'll talk to Rocky. We might let you take a break and then start watching again in the week it is due to get here."

"It's no problem." She yawned. "As long as I can keep napping. I think Rocky is testing me to see if I can stick with something he thinks would be so boring I'd want to quit. That is not going to happen. Besides, this is about that girl's sister, right? The girl at your house the other day?"

"Yes."

She was quiet for a moment. "Then I want to help you catch the guy."

"Okay, then. We're meeting at my house this afternoon. I'll let them know what I think we should do. We'll see if somebody has a different idea."

We parted. Patricia and I rode back to my house for a nap. This time there was a difference. We both curled up in my bed to take our morning nap. We expected everybody at one in the afternoon. We were more exhausted than usual for some wonderful reasons. All we did was nap, but it was nice to curl up spoon fashion to do so.

We were awakened by a "Praise the Lord, I found them both."

Preacher had a key to my house. It was a quarter to one. He'd come to my bedroom to wake me up while Mary Elizabeth went to the guest bedroom to get Patricia. We untangled and sat up in bed. Preacher stood there grinning. Softly, he said, "I'll knock next time."

"We'll be out in a second," I said.

"Take your time." He closed the door.

I looked at Patricia, relieved to see she was almost laughing. "Well," I said, "I guess our secret is shared."

She shrugged. "It's okay. I'm a big girl. I haven't been a nun for years."

"What's Mary Elizabeth going to say?"

"Doesn't matter. If she has objections, she'll have to pray for me. And I'm sure she will, officially. She knows I'm not a virgin. Unofficially, and even though she will not admit it, she'll approve. I think."

We joined Preacher, Mary Elizabeth, and Mina in my living room. Mary Elizabeth said, "Well, I guess the two of you skipped church this morning."

I turned to get coffee as Patricia said, "Not my biggest sin of the weekend."

Yes. Our secret was out.

I sat next to Patricia on the sofa. Preacher sported a fatuous grin. Mary Elizabeth was not smiling and wasn't frowning. She was composed.

"Okay," I said, "this is where we are. We have heard nothing and seen nothing we think might be our guy. Our investigator sitting at the jetty is doing a superb job. We have a list of vehicles and their license plates. We have photos of the vehicles and the people who arrive and go. Like any collection of data, we might find something in there if we ever get a starting point."

"Are you watching carefully?" asked Mary Elizabeth.

"Yes. We check out every boat that might be our guy. All night long. We have radar. We have night vision goggles, and we listen. We might miss him, but not because we're not paying attention."

Patricia added, "Mary Elizabeth, we have not quit

paying close attention to what's going on out there. I promise."

Mary Elizabeth nodded. And, finally, she smiled. "Good," she said.

"What next?" Preacher asked.

"Unless somebody has a better idea, I say we keep watching for a few days. Who knows? Maybe we'll see or hear something. I am actually more excited about all the data being collected by Jenny at the jetty. I'll talk to her boss, but I want to have her continue until we know the *Soliez* has arrived. Even if we miss everything else, if we're right that the smugglers always post a lookout at the boat cut, chances are excellent she'll have his license tag and probably a photograph of him.

"I'll keep tracking the ship. Those ships travel about four hundred miles a day. I've thought about it and maybe our guy goes offshore the night before he plans to rendezvous with the ship. That way he can get out of the bay in the dark. He's safer out on the open water. The next night the ship would be that much closer and he could make most of his run to the ship in the daylight and meet them far enough out to limit the risk of attention from the Coast Guard."

"So what? Keep watching until the ship arrives?" Preacher asked.

"No. We keep Jenny at the jetty until it arrives, but we need to decide where we're going to sit and watch for the van. Unless I can find better information somewhere, we can't be sure of exactly when the ship will arrive. We can't be sure about the exact date he'll pick up the girls, so we need to watch the highway sooner than I actually expect him. Last time I checked the *Soliez* is due to arrive in Houston one week from today. We'll spend another three nights listening for him on the bay and then Preacher and I will drive up and pick out a few places to watch for the van."

Mary Elisabeth said, "I want to be with you when you watch for the van."

"No," I said. "I told you, I will not play if you insist on doing that."

"But ... "

"No, Mary Elizabeth," Patricia said. "They are perfectly capable of doing what needs to be done. You need to stay with Mina."

Mary Elizabeth sat back in her chair.

"Preacher," I asked, "have you been practicing up on your Ukrainian?"

"Absolutely." He rattled off a couple of sentences I couldn't understand. Mina cracked up laughing and hit him on the shoulder.

"Okay. Sounds good to me. I'll rustle up some sandwiches."

Preacher followed me into the kitchen, took a bag of carrots out of my refrigerator, and said, "I'm going to take Mina and feed some goats. So, you and Patricia?"

"Private. Not going to talk about it."

"I respect that. But this thing? It's a good thing. God bless you both."

Like I said, my kind of minister. He left the kitchen. I put sandwich fixings on a platter, grabbed a bag of chips and took them out to the porch. Mary Elizabeth and Patricia were leaning against the porch rail talking quietly. Mina and Preacher were the center of attention of a bunch of goats at the fence. I whistled to get their attention and waved the two of them over.

After lunch, I said, "You are all welcome to hang out here, but I still need a couple of hours of sleep."

"Me, too." Saying that Patricia stood and walked straight to my bedroom. That earned an indecipherable look from Mary Elizabeth.

Preacher slapped his hands on his knees and said, "We'll go fish off your boardwalk. Maybe catch some crabs for dinner."

"Okay," I said, "you know where the stuff is, and you know the limits. Don't worry about waking me up. I'll set an alarm."

This time, I locked the door to the bedroom behind me. In the bathroom off my bedroom, the shower was running. My house is old and has a wonderfully large, hand tiled shower. I joined Patricia there.

She said, "Thought you'd never get here." And she kissed me.

There were many fine things in life, but right up there at the top of the finest things was a lover, naked in the shower, slippery and warm.

Later, we lay face to face under the sheets. From a few inches away I asked her, "So, what did Mary Elizabeth have to say to you."

"She said that she could not condone sex outside of marriage, but that if I was going to indulge, I'd picked a good man."

We kissed and we caressed. Her hand slipped low between us. She raised her eyebrows and said, "Seriously? I thought you were tired."

"I am tired, but there are parts of me that did not get the message."

"Well, save it for later. I'm tired, too. Hold me."

She turned her back to me, and we snuggled close. She pulled my arm between her breasts and held my hand with both of hers. Her hips made one teasing movement before she fell asleep. We slept for a couple of hours.

Preacher and Mina caught several sand trout. Patricia and I left the other three at my house preparing their fish for dinner. We grabbed take-out on the way to the marina. Although we certainly spent some of our time with each other in some new ways, once again we spent the night waiting and listening and watching for a quarry who never appeared.

Jenny surprised us the next morning at breakfast when she arrived excitedly, and said, "Was that him? Did you hear that boat early this morning? Did you see him?"

"What? You heard something?"

"Yeah, about three-thirty or so, a souped-up powerboat going out."

"No. I guess I was asleep."

Patricia glanced at me. Did our newly enjoyed physical activities make us miss what we were out there for?

"When we have to sleep, we rely on the radar alarm. Maybe it couldn't pick him up. It's caught others, but maybe the boat you heard had too low of a profile. Maybe he actually comes through the channel between Galveston and Pelican Island. That would put him east of us. No. Too easy to see there. Damn. Damn. Damn."

Jenny said, "I didn't hear him come back, though."

"My best guess is he's making about an eight hour round trip. I think he spends the day on the Gulf. We'll be extra vigilant tonight. If it was him, maybe we'll get lucky when he returns."

I added Jenny's data to the collection.

We didn't see any of the others that entire day. Back at my place we napped, we had a light lunch and went back to bed. Eventually, we tried to sleep some more. We were determined to be vigilant that night.

As we settled in on the boat that evening, I called Jenny. "You call me if you hear a boat tonight. Just in case."

"You got it."

We sat and we waited. Talking quietly. Kissing with restraint and fooling around only a little. We stayed alert.

At midnight I turned on the exhaust blowers. According to my boat's manual, they're designed to run for hours with no issue. I wanted to be ready to start up the boat instantly. We didn't sleep that night.

Shortly before three in the morning, my cell phone rang. Before I could get up and cross to where it sat on the cockpit table I heard the distant rumble of a powerful engine. It was a ways off, a boat coming in between the jetties.

"What do I do?" Patricia said.

I tossed her the phone. "Tell her we hear it, too."

"I'll get ready." I started the boat. I hit the switch to raise the anchor. I got the night vision goggles. I went up top to swing the *Star* around to face into the bay. I kept my hands on the throttles, adjusting as necessary to hold her steady.

Patricia joined me and said, "She said she'd keep an extra sharp eye out for folks coming off the jetty. What do I do?"

"Not much to do except watch for him. If he passes, we'll follow as long as we can. Maybe we'll be able to tell which way he turns. I don't think it will be wise to follow so close that he sees us. We'll just do what we can."

Adrenaline kicked in. I checked the radar. I listened carefully. I scanned the channel leading to the sea through the night vision goggles.

Suddenly, while still some distance off, the rumble of the engines powered down. I lowered the goggles, straining to listen.

"Did he stop?" Patricia asked.

"There is no place for him to stop. I'm pretty sure he's in the channel. I don't know what's up. Maybe he's riding quiet, letting another boat get past or something. I'm going to shut the engines off for a moment, see if we can hear anything."

I powered down and strained to listen but heard nothing that might be the boat for which we were waiting. The *Star* started to turn and take the slap of waves on her side. I started up again and moved slowly parallel to the channel, steering with one hand and holding the goggles with the other to watch to our port side.

Patricia said, "Is that him?"

I looked where she pointed. There were running lights of a boat coming down the channel. The boat wasn't moving as fast as I would expect and there was no engine noise. I put the goggles on the boat. It was hard to make out at first. In the shimmering green of the screen on the goggles, I could see a boat of some sort. At the angle it approached I could see a low profile and an operator standing in the glow of cockpit lights. I thought I could make out a couple of fishing rods sticking up at the back of the boat.

"It looks like a fishing boat, but it's kind of strange."

I continued to watch the boat, increasing our speed a little as it got to a point off our side. It was some distance away, but I could make out enough of its shape to see it didn't look like a normal fishing boat. It was too low, its bow too long.

"It doesn't sound like one of those boats, does it?" Patricia said.

"No."

I continued to watch and suddenly realized that the driver of the boat was looking at us. He was indistinct, but I had the impression of his arm raised just like mine, holding glasses on us as I held them on him.

I looked closer at the profile of his boat and realized it could be nothing other than a low slung powerboat. It could be him.

"He must have mufflers." The boat I watched picked up speed, surging ahead of us. "He must have slowed in the channel and connected his mufflers. That's why the sound died off."

I turned on my running lights and lowered my night vision goggles. I could see his running lights without the night vision. If he was watching us and we continued without running lights and he could see me as I could see him, he'd know something was up.

I angled toward the channel. Any boat would be expected to do so. I punched us up to a speed I would usually never run in the dark, but he continued to outpace us.

"Watch him close," I said. "We will not be able to keep up with him. He knows somebody is back here and, if he's our smuggler, he will not be waiting for us to catch up."

Patricia braced herself. I glanced at my speedometer. We were traveling a foolish thirty miles an hour. I started remembering things I've seen floating in the bays. Things like water-logged tree trunks that had floated down the river, barely visible during the day and impossible to see at night. After a good storm, I've seen huge steel propane tanks in the water. I turned on the spotlights on either side of my bow, lighting the forty or fifty feet in front of us.

"I think he's turning," she said.

Sure enough. I could just make out a green bow light starting to separate from the white light on his stern. That meant he was turning to the right of our course. Then, the lights went out.

I immediately slowed down. "I think we made him nervous."

"Do you think he knows we were watching for him?"

"Nah. No way he could know that. I'm sure he was just taking a precaution. There are always boats out at night. I was running foolishly fast, but there are a lot of fools out here driving boats. He is wary."

"So, where is he headed?"

I shook my head. "I have no idea. He could be angling to an approach into Trinity Bay that would take him closer to shore, just in case somebody had radar on him, trying to lose himself in the clutter on shore. He's not too far north. He could be headed into East Bay."

I hadn't paid any attention to my radar once we were watching him, but a glance at it now revealed no boat.

"Well, what do we do now?"

"Even if that wasn't him, we learned we're not going to get close to anybody coming in who doesn't want company. I'm calling our surveillance off. We either saw him or we didn't. The most important thing now will be to see Jenny's info and photos."

I called Jenny and she answered quickly. "That might have been him," I said. "Are there vehicles there?"

"Actually, there aren't any. Some guy walked down the road earlier tonight and went out on the jetty. I got a crappy photo of that guy once he got under the streetlight. He has not come back, yet. I'll try to get a better picture of him when he comes back."

"Good. I think he's our guy. See what you can do. Safely. We're headed to the marina. See you at breakfast."

"Did she see anything?" Patricia asked.

"Maybe. Who knows what we're all seeing. Maybe it will all tie together somehow at some point."

Jenny arrived at our breakfast meeting and we all crammed into one bench with her laptop taking center stage.

"Here's the guy," she said.

She had a decent photograph of a man just at the end of the jetty. It was low light, but she'd taken it just as he walked into the brightest pool of light from the streetlight on the side of the bait stand.

"This isn't from your truck."

"No. I hunkered down in the trash where I had the best view. Don't worry I was careful and quiet."

The man looked like somebody who had been fishing. He carried a couple of rods, a net, and a pretty big tackle box. He was dressed in what looked like faded khakis and a shirt of the same color. He was thin, wearing a hat that somewhat shadowed his face, but it looked like he had a scruffy beard. It was hard to get a good idea of his age, but my impression was that he was not a real young guy. He looked like so many of the old guys who populate the coast.

"Awfully big tackle box for somebody fishing very far out on the jetties. I wouldn't want to carry it out that far."

Jenny said, "That's what I thought based on what I've seen most people take out there. You will also notice there is no evidence of any fish."

I looked at the time stamp on the photo. "No wonder. He's coming in about the time he ought to be fishing the tidal flow if he wanted to catch any fish."

She turned the laptop her way and said, "Like I said, he didn't come in a vehicle. He came walking up the road. After he'd gone out on the jetty, I walked the road all the way to the highway and there wasn't a car parked anywhere.

I tried to follow him when he walked back up the road, but I was too careful. I followed Rocky's orders to not get close. I might have heard a car stop and pick him up, but I wasn't close enough to see anything."

I sat back. Patricia squeezed my thigh. I took a deep breath. It had to be. We'd figured out these guys.

"Jenny. You earned a bonus. Out of everything everybody is doing, you are the one getting things done."

"Just doing my job, but you might mention that to Rocky." She handed me the thumb drive. "You want me to keep watching don't you?"

"Yes, but you ought to take a break if you want. This has to be the guy and they don't do this every night."

"But, we don't know for sure. I'd just as soon stay on it as long as you're chasing them. I'd hate to make an assumption and miss something. Unless you're trying to save some money. Maybe Rocky will cut you a deal. I'll talk to him."

"No. It's not that. And you're right. We're not going to sit out there on the boat anymore because we proved we're not going to be able to do much anyway. Not near as much as you're doing. He saw us. I don't want to alert him. Besides, we have to start getting ready for the next part."

We left without having breakfast. We went back to the boat and called Mary Elizabeth. As always, she immediately asked if we saw anything.

"I think so. But even if it was a false alarm, we're not going to sit out there on the boat anymore. Patricia is going to drive my car back to my place and I'm bringing the boat."

"So, we meet at your house, and you give us an update?"

"Yes. Let's say around noon. We'll tell you what we have, and Preacher and I need to plan our next step."

While taking my boat back to its usual home, I realized it had been a while since I'd thought about the plans I'd made with Jason to only pretend a diligent effort and create an excuse to call off the rescue mission.

CHAPTER ELEVEN

At the house, Patricia and I went to bed. Neither of us had slept during the night, and we were asleep in moments. I tried to ignore the knocking on the bedroom door that woke me up. Patricia moved closer to me when I raised to look at the clock, but she didn't wake up.

I walked over to the door and trying to not wake her up, said quietly, "I said noon. It is eleven-thirty."

It was Preacher knocking on the door. "We're here. Just wanted to let you know. We brought food."

"Fine, we'll be out in a bit."

I sat on the bed and shook Patricia's shoulder. She pulled the sheet over her head, peeked out at me and said, "Already?"

"They're early. Stay asleep if you want, but if I don't go out I'm afraid they'll all end up in here with us."

She groaned. "I'll be out in a minute. You shower first."

I did and joined Preacher, Mary Elizabeth, and Mina in the living room. There were sandwiches from Clara's on the table.

Mary Elizabeth couldn't wait. "What did you see?"

I was a little put out that she'd seen fit to interrupt our sleep earlier than requested. "Let's wait for Patricia. She'll be out in a moment. Give me a sandwich."

Patricia joined us. After she was hugged into the room by Preacher and Mary Elizabeth, I told the story of our night. I showed them the photos taken by Jenny. Mina did not recognize the man. I explained how Jenny did not find his vehicle.

Mary Elizabeth asked, "What next?"

"Preacher and I are going to find some places for us to sit and watch for the van. We really can't do anything just watching for the boat. Last night proved we can't follow him on the water by ourselves."

"Aren't we all going to watch for the van?"

"That's a part of what we'll decide. We'll scope it out and decide whether it will really help to have watchers at more than one place."

"I want to help."

"Mary Elizabeth, none of this would have happened without you. You've done more than one person's share. You sucked me into doing more than I ever thought I'd do."

"I know. I know. It's just that we're so close."

"Yes. And we continue methodically and safely. Our chances of success are still very slim, and the whole thing is very dangerous. You have to trust your troops."

"I do. I trust you."

Patricia moved over, sat down next to Mary Elizabeth, put her arm around her shoulder and said, "Mary Elizabeth, listen to Sam. If he needs you to do something, he'll tell you. Don't distract him. We've put him in a very risky situation, and he's been nothing but the best."

"Yes. I know. Thank you, Sam."

"Yes, thank you, Sam." Mina surprised everyone by saying that. She had tears tracking down both sides of her face. Mary Elizabeth turned to put her arms around her.

The emotions had everybody on edge. Obviously, Mina felt it. More and more, the laid-back Preacher moved to the edge of his chair, one leg bouncing slightly. Mary Elizabeth acted like there was a finish line in sight. I worried about how she would react when we failed, the most likely outcome.

I took a deep breath, slapped my hands on my knees,

and said, "Okay. Next step. Preacher, we're going to take a long drive. In fact, just so you all know, we will probably spend the next couple of nights on the road somewhere."

Patricia followed me into my room. She said, "I'd really like to go with you, keep up with what's going on and spend time with you, but I think I'd better stay here with Mary Elizabeth."

"Yeah. I agree. But as long as we're on the topic of long drives, when this is over we need to take a nice long trip somewhere. Maybe on the boat."

"I'd like that."

We kissed and went out to face the crowd.

Before Preacher and I left, I checked the internet one more time. The *Soliez* was still reported to have an estimated arrival date in ten days. It would be within range of the smuggler sometime before that. We needed to start watching the highway soon. That meant some more long nights. The nights would not be near as much fun with Preacher as they'd been with Patricia.

I packed a small bag, and Preacher and I drove off. We stopped by his storefront church where it took him less than two minutes to come back to the car with a backpack.

As he settled into his seat, he said, "So, what are we looking for?"

"We need to find a few places with good access on and off the interstate where we have a good view of oncoming traffic. Hopefully, somewhere there's some light on the oncoming traffic. I think we need three or four places because we're going to start a watch that I expect will last several days. We don't want to attract too much attention. We'll find a few places up north, past the point where all the major arteries feed into forty-five."

Over two days and two nights, spending the nights in a

cheap motel in Huntsville, we chose three locations from which we could watch the highway at night and not attract too much attention. We tested each possibility to see how fast we could get on the highway. We looked at how crowded each was. We would carry clipboards and count trucks. If anybody asked us what we were doing, we'd be doing a study of trucks on the road at night. If they asked for whom, it would be for a client and confidential.

After the second night on the road, we drove back to my place and met with the others. Preacher called some member of his flock to watch over his church. He and I gathered what we thought we'd need and drove back north. We napped that afternoon in our cheap motel room. I called Jenny and told her what we were doing. She would call if she heard a power boat or if she saw the man we thought was the look-out. That night, we started watching the highway. The reported location and travel time of the ship had it arriving at the Houston Ship Channel in a week. If all our theories were correct, the week ahead would define our success or failure.

We started the drudgery of sitting and watching for a vehicle I didn't expect to see. I expected we would deal with disappointing failure. Mary Elizabeth would take Mina somewhere. Patricia and I would discuss the possibilities of us.

Sunday night Preacher and I sat and watched and saw nothing. Early Monday morning, while driving back to the motel, Jenny called. She didn't even say hello.

"I saw him, Sam. The same man without a truck. He was here last night. He just left."

"Did you hear anything?"

"No. I didn't hear a boat, not this time."

"Thanks. Good job."

"I'll keep watching, just in case we're wrong about him."

"Okay. It will be over soon, one way or another."

I called and talked to Mary Elizabeth and Patricia. I told them about Jenny seeing the man. Preacher and I slept. We got up. We stocked up on snacks and headed back to our favorite vantage point over the highway. I didn't feel tired that night. Expectation kept me wired. But, nothing. We stayed a little longer. It was a bright Tuesday morning before we went back to our motel. This time, Patricia called me.

"Sam, I'm worried about Mary Elizabeth. She is spending her days alone on the beach. This is really getting to her. Is there anything I can tell her? Something I can give her to do?"

"No. We're just sitting and watching."

"But Jenny saw that man."

"Who may or may not be one of the bad guys. If it's going to happen, it will be in the next few days, but the chances of us doing anything is practically zero. You know that. I suspect she does, too."

"Okay. I know. And Sam, I really miss you."

"I miss you. We'll drive down there, try to assure her we're doing everything possible and you and I can have lunch."

"Okay." She paused for a moment. "And, maybe, we can take a nap together."

I laughed. "Yes."

Preacher and I made the drive south.

Mary Elizabeth looked haunted, her despair obviously growing and showing on her face as dark circles under her eyes, deepening lines around her mouth etching her stress.

We gathered at my house for lunch and talked

generally about what we were doing. After we ate and talked, I walked out to the shop to check on Joshua and let him know I'd be back to work soon. He was busy building the grills we sold online and through a few special retailers.

Mary Elizabeth met me as I came out of the shop.

"Sam, please be honest with me. What chance do we have of saving Zoio?"

"I don't know. We've done more and learned more than I expected. The ball is rolling. All we can do is stick with our plan. If it doesn't happen this week, I don't think we'll succeed."

"I should have done more to get the police involved, shouldn't I?"

"I don't know."

She started to silently cry.

Once we implemented Jason's plan of failure, went to the authorities with everything we could, and found ways to push them to act, Mary Elizabeth's healing could start. I hoped the authorities would be able to save Zoio. We'd worry later about what to do with her if that happened.

My nap with Patricia turned out to be just that, a nap. What we were doing messed up my days and nights and I had to sleep. It was, however, very nice to do so while holding her.

Preacher continued his nap on the way back north that afternoon. By ten we were sitting beside the highway, clipboards in hand, counting trucks.

Tuesday night. Nothing.

Wednesday night. Nothing.

On Thursday night Preacher and I sat on a corner at an overpass watching the interstate. If the man Jenny saw was the lookout for the boat, it was time. We were getting a lot of sleep during the days, and we were excited because of

Jenny's call, but night was still difficult. The darkness, the endless stream of traffic lights, and the rhythmic noise of traffic could hypnotize a person into a stupor if not careful.

We stayed alert on coffee and conversation. I spent a lot of time uselessly trying to learn something about Preacher's past. He could deflect, ignore, and redirect better than a politician. Despite the strength of our friendship, I learned nothing about his past in our nights of forced closeness. The only thing interrupting our diligence were the two regular phone calls each night from Mary Elizabeth seeking updates.

Occasionally, Preacher or I would stretch, lifting our butt up off the seat trying to relieve the pain of just sitting for hours.

There came a moment when we weren't talking. He was softly reciting the Ukrainian phrases he'd been taught by Mina. I was thinking. How many more nights would we have to watch and wait before we could declare failure and end the heartbreaking charade? I could tell from our phone conversations that Mary Elizabeth withdrew a bit more every day. She spoke less and with less spirit.

From our vantage point, we could discern the shape of vehicles some distance away. As they moved under the overpass on which we sat, they were easy to see because of the sodium vapor streetlights at our location. For the last several nights, I'd watched dozens of vans, waiting for them to get close enough to discern their color and markings. Three times I'd jumped out of the truck and ran to the other side of the overpass with binoculars to scope out a van that happened to pass under us at the side of a truck blocking our view.

That night two vans came along about the same time. It didn't take long to realize that the one in the left lane of the highway was white. The other was in an inside lane, being passed by most other vehicles. Of course, smugglers would be driving close enough to the speed limit to not be stopped. I sat forward watching closely. I realized it was an ugly brown.

Shortly before it went under the underpass, I saw the cross on its side.

I said, "Oh my God. There it is."

At the same time, Preacher said, "That's it. That's it."

I started my truck, my mind racing. I knew what Jason would say we should do, let the van go. Bring closure by failure. Keep everybody safe. Zoio might have just passed us fifty feet away. Should I do the safe thing and let the van lose us? Perhaps Jason would have changed his mind if he'd been sitting in the truck with us.

I drove over the curb and down the ramp, moving to the left on the highway to catch up with the van. Preacher called on the cell phone to tell the others we'd found the van. I could hear the exclamations of an excited Mary Elizabeth. He finally got a word in. "Yes. Of course. We will call you as soon as something happens. It may be a while. Don't worry. We have to catch up with them and follow them for a while. Maybe a long while." He paused to listen to her. "Yes," he said, "we have a full tank of gas."

The rational part of me hoped we'd never catch up with the van, but a part of me thought we were smart enough and lucky enough to pull this off.

I stayed in the outside lane. At two in the morning, traffic thinned. I pushed the truck faster, halfway thinking a traffic stop would be a good idea.

"Samuel," Preacher said, "we've got time and space. It would not be good to be stopped for speeding."

"Just watch for them. They could pull off at any time."

I made calculations in my head while scanning the vehicles in front of us. We got on the highway and up to speed in about a minute. That put them close to a mile ahead of us. If they were driving the speed limit and I drove ten percent faster than the speed limit, how long would it take to catch them? I had no idea. My mind could not concentrate on that problem while I looked for the van in the traffic ahead.

We chased them, watching carefully on the highway out of Conroe. We passed the statue of Houston. Traffic condensed, becoming crowded as we approached Huntsville. Preacher and I talked little, each watching diligently for the van. It could have left the highway at any of several exits we passed as we approached and skirted Huntsville. Fast-food restaurants and service stations crowded those exits. During those long hours sitting and waiting, I should have spent some time with a calculator to estimate how long it should take us to catch them. Next time, I thought.

We planned to drive north until sure we should have seen them. Then, turn around and keep watch going the other way. That would be Jason's primary plan, augmented with the hope we never saw the van. I kept telling myself that was the best plan. But always in my mind was the vision of Mary Elizabeth, her compassionate eyes, her drive, her refusal to back down, her everything about seeking to save at least one more girl. And Mina, the hell she'd survived, the beatings and risks she'd taken to save her sister.

North of Huntsville it got darker, the highway bordered by the dark of the forest. Possible stopping places were farther apart. According to what Mina told us, they drove for a while after passing the statue of Sam Houston before stopping for food and a bathroom break.

My mind spun ceaselessly with all the variables.

Preacher seemed to be more focused.

"There they are," he said quietly, leaning forward peering over the dashboard.

The van appeared quickly out of the dark. We were driving faster than it and quickly closing the distance between us.

I couldn't slow suddenly. A wary driver might notice. Or, worse, somebody driving behind, riding shotgun, might notice. We'd passed a lot of vehicles without paying attention. I checked the rear view mirror. There were several headlights behind us, any of which could be bad news.

I read off the license plate, and Preacher wrote it down.

"Stolen plate," I said.

"Most likely."

I maintained my speed, slowing slightly as we passed the van. I suddenly noticed my handgun pressing heavy against my hip. On the side of the van in light brown letters was a cross and "Church of Hope." Underneath that, in smaller letters, it said "Youth Outreach." Youth Outreach. That really pissed me off.

"Don't stare," I told Preacher.

The van slowed as we passed. Nothing, not even a shadow, could be seen behind the tinted windows at the back of the van. I imagined them, the nervous, scared girls peering out, too excited to sleep, trying to see all they could of the promise land.

The driver happened to be looking at her cell phone in the brief moment I glanced over. In the dim glow of the phone, I saw a lady, blonde hair trailing out from under a ball cap. She wore a shiny, pink jacket. Then, we were past.

"What now?" Preacher asked.

"Let's think. We're far enough ahead. She won't notice. Turn around, see if you can find a way to recognize her headlights so we can watch her from the front for a while."

He turned. After a moment he said, "Yeah, okay, I think we're good. Her left headlight is not as bright as the one on the right. Maybe it's aimed differently or something. That's the best I can do."

"Keep your eye on the van. Don't lose it. We'll find a way to get back behind her. Watch for another vehicle traveling with her. There are not many places to stop, but if she pulls off somewhere, you tell me. I'll jump the median and go back."

I peered into the darkness ahead, looking for a place to get off the highway and get back behind the van without attracting her attention. Preacher stared into the stream of headlights behind us.

My mind could not settle on one single thing to think about. I felt the weight of my gun and the quick beating of my heart. I'd been breathing shallow and took two big breaths. Our plan had worked to perfection. That's the moment I decided the thing might go the way we'd planned. Perhaps Jason was mistaken. Maybe our plan was good. Maybe we could snatch one or all the girls safely. The smugglers were too complacent, too arrogant about their safety and abilities. I doubted they had heard of Mina's escape or her sister.

One more deep breath and I decided we could do this thing.

We led the van through the night. Finally, a sign for a service station at the upcoming intersection invited us with its promise of easy off and on highway access. I slowed and signaled my exit from the highway. Just as we stopped at the stop sign at the top of the overpass, I watched the van continue past on the highway below us. I drove through the intersection and took the ramp back to the highway. This time, we got on the highway not very far behind the van. Easy off, easy on.

We passed Madisonville and Centerville. I thought for sure they would stop somewhere at Centerville with its myriad of service stations and small cafes. Barbecue is the thing in Centerville and some establishments advertise twenty-four-hour service. But she kept going.

Much farther and we would encounter more traffic headed for Dallas. If we got the chance to do this thing, I wanted it in as public a place as possible, but one that still gave us room to maneuver without interference and a chance to get away to someplace we could hole up without the authorities becoming aware of Zoio.

In the end, of course, we couldn't control where she stopped the van, but it looked as ideal as it could get for us.

It was a truck stop. Not one of the giant ones, but large enough to have a food counter, separate areas for fueling cars and trucks, and a broad expanse of dirt lot in the back where tractor-trailer rigs could park. When the van's turn signal started blinking, I caught myself breathing in time with the flashing light. I glanced over at Preacher. He leaned forward, his hands on the dash, his eyes wide. He started repeating the phrases we'd practiced over and over in Ukrainian: "Zoio, your sister sent us. You are in danger. Come with us now. Here is her picture. Here is a message from her. Come quick. Fast. Danger. Bad men. They have lied to you."

I exited without signaling, the confidence I'd felt back on the highway drained quickly, replaced with an adrenaline-charged surge of fear. But we had a plan. It is why soldiers drill before battle. Action must supersede fear and spur of the moment thinking. I nodded my head quietly in time with the cadence of the foreign phrases being repeated over and over by Preacher.

The food counter, at the end of the building closest to the highway, had its own entrance. I turned into the parking lot of the truck stop just in time to see the van turn into the dirt lot behind the building.

According to what Mina told us, the girls in the van would not be getting food, but those who needed to use the restroom would go in groups of two or three under the watchful eye of the driver. That would be our opportunity.

I assumed the driver would lock and unlock the door with each group. We planned to move when the driver had the door unlocked instead of trying to get the doors open somehow while she was gone. We would go when she returned for the first time. She might make only one trip. The best thing would be for Zoio to be in that first group.

She wasn't.

I drove into the parking lot a few seconds behind the van. The van parked close to the end of the dirt lot closest to the highway. As we turned into the lot, the driver stood at the side door of the van where two of the girls were climbing out. The driver was in jeans and a pink satin jacket. I slowed to see if one of the girls getting out was Zoio.

"Get ready Preacher. If Zoio gets off the van we're going to stop and go for her now."

"Okay. I'm ready." He put one hand on the door handle and started running through the Ukrainian phrases. I shifted the pistol on my hip.

"She's not there," he said.

"No, we'll park close and as soon as she comes back and opens that door, we move."

"Okay. God be with us."

"Amen."

I pulled in next to the van with maybe fifteen feet

separating our vehicles.

The lady walked the girls toward the restaurant. I peered at the van, but the windows were dark and the light was poor. I saw only shadowy images moving behind the tinted glass.

A huge pick-up truck rumbled into the parking lot and drove to the far end. A car pulled in. It, too, drove down to the better-lighted end of the lot. I concentrated on the van and didn't pay a lot of attention to those other cars. I gave them a quick look to see if anybody walked toward us. I saw nobody.

The lady and the girls came around the side of the building headed toward the van. As she put the key in the door of the van, I opened my door and heard Preacher do the same.

She slid the door back.

We quickly covered the space between the vehicles. I pushed passed the lady who stumbled and said, "Hey."

I grabbed the door to hold it open and Preacher leaned into the van speaking loudly in Ukrainian, calling Zoio's name and repeating over and over the phrases he'd memorized."

I leaned in and there she was, sitting in the back row, a startled look on her face. She half rose from her seat and started to say something when Preacher made a noise and fell to the ground.

I turned to see what happened. There was a looming shape of a man who quickly moved behind me and grabbed me roughly by the hair. His breath smelled of cinnamon. Before I could form a cry or a thought he touched a Taser to my neck. There was a cracking noise and, in my ears, the sound of a waterfall. My entire body clenched in pain, stopped working and collapsed.

Later, I pieced together memories of what followed. Someone kicked Preacher where he lay on the ground. Somebody dragged me to the front of the vehicle and zapped me with the Taser again. He kicked me. In the stomach, in the ribs, and in the head. He called me a stupid motherfucker. I'd have tucked myself into a ball for protection, but the shock from the Taser turned me to jelly.

A kick to my head put me out cold.

I lay there unconscious for some time. Eventually, I thought I was laying on a beach at the edge of the ocean.

Pain removed the illusion I was on a beach. The water I lay in was not the ocean. It was a fetid pool of water, stagnate and smelling of vomit.

I vomited causing excruciating pain in my head until I sunk again into a dark miasma of unconsciousness.

Finally, Preacher crouched beside me. His voice, cracking and distorted, came from a distance place. "Sam. Sam. Get up. We have to move. We have to get out of here."

He pulled me. I tried to speak, but couldn't. He pulled harder lifting me to my knees. I gagged.

I saw my truck and made a crabbing motion toward it. Somehow, Preacher was able to stand. He pulled me half erect and dragged us both toward the truck.

Someone came out the back door of the cafe and threw a bucket of water out. I saw a halo of light around him. I'm sure he thought we were a couple of drunks. The halo disappeared as he went back inside, closing the door.

We did need to move. That much I knew. I wasn't exactly sure why, or where, but we needed to go.

Preacher dragged me to the passenger side of the truck and, holding me up with a shoulder, opened the door. He wrangled me into the truck where I faded once again into darkness.

I knew when he got in and started the truck, but I could not speak. I could not even turn my head to look at him.

I faded in and out, occasionally aware of lights passing on the highway. My head and neck hurt. My ribs hurt. My gut hurt. My legs were tingling with pain. My ears buzzed with static. My brain tried to connect coherent thoughts, but it was easier to sleep.

Occasionally, Preacher would yell at me, and I'd make a noise at him. Words didn't quite gel, but I made it clear that, despite the pain, I still lived.

I remember little about the drive back to the coast. There were other things we should have done, but my brain failed to work. It was busy trying to restore the connections necessary to function. It was easy to slip into a stupor and let Preacher drive.

Memories of the drive consist primarily of highway lights flashing as they passed over my eyelids and, at one point, Preacher saying, "Oh, man. We fucked up."

I tried to agree, but my voice was little more than a raspy croak. After that, nothing but gray moments and gray movements. I rested in my semi-consciousness.

THINGS RETURNED. First, the scent of lavender, soft as rain and a thin illusion of comfort in the blood-red pain enveloping my body. Then, more darkness, only to half-waken, confused by memories that could not be real.

I struggled with a memory of sand and the sea beneath my cheek. Had I been lying on the beach?

There were rustling and voices I could not understand. The voices sounded electronic and faint as if coming from far off broadcasts half tuned in on an old radio, with multiple signals overlapped and interfering with each other.

I swallowed. My throat hurt with the burn of acid. The memory of the puke smell of rotting garbage and waste overwhelmed any thought that I'd been on a beach. I had been laying in filth. But, when? At a time when the sound of a rushing surf dissolved into the grinding clatter of a diesel truck.

Trucks. Imaginary beach sand had been grit from the parking lot they'd dragged me across. Back behind the truck stop. It hurt. I jumped. Hands held my shoulders, seeking to soothe. But why? Who?

Cinnamon. I remembered the taste of the greasy, fetid water pooled in a ditch behind the truck stop. And yet, the strongest impression in my memory was the incongruent scent of cinnamon. Once again hands held me still on a lavender cloud and something cool pressed on my head and I remembered the disastrous rescue. Painfully, I opened my eyes.

Apparitions hovered, quivering in blurred shapes, merging and separating, slowly resolving into three distinct shapes. I blinked to clear the water from my eyes. One of the shapes harrumphed and said, "Here he comes. Looks like he'll live, but you should still take him to a hospital."

"He'll be fine doctor. We'll watch him." I recognized the voice of my next door neighbor Joanne.

"Hi, Jo. Hi, Doc. Where's Preacher?" It did not come out smooth. My voice rasped. I tried to sit up through the pain in my head. Fully awake, the dreaming parts faded away and I remembered what had happened. The dreams while becoming conscious were bad. The reality was a nightmare worse in every possible way.

My cell phone rang. Jo picked it up from the nightstand and handed it to me. The caller ID advised of an unknown caller. Jo said, "Preacher said he'd call. Maybe that's him."

I answered with a creaky hello, and the nightmare got worse. It was the man with cinnamon on his breath.

"Hello, counselor. I have your number. Tell the nun to give me back my whore or I kill the girl."

CHAPTER TWELVE

IN THE FOG, I FELT for my pistol only to find I was
without pants.

Joanne said, "We took your clothes off, so the doctor
could examine you."

"My gun?"

"No. You had a holster, but it didn't have a gun in it."

I struggled to sit upright. She put her hand on my
shoulder to help. Her eyes were sensitive. I knew she had
questions. Questions I could not answer.

"Thanks, Jo. Preacher and I had a run in with some bad
people. Where is he?"

"I don't know. He dropped you off and hung around
until the doctor got here. He didn't look a whole lot better
than you other than the fact that he could walk and talk. He
borrowed our phone and made some calls. When Doc got
here, he told us he had to go take care of some things and to
let you know he'd call as soon as he got a chance."

I nodded. I squeezed my head in both my hands to try
to stop the pain.

"The doctor was reluctant to give you any kind of pain
pill because you need x-rays and a cat scan."

I shook my head. I did not want to go to a hospital.

"Sam, you need to go to the hospital, but Preacher was
adamant. He said there were things he couldn't tell us." She
paused, but I wasn't ready to fill in any blanks. "You're a big
boy, and we're not your moms, but Maude and I are really
worried about you."

"I'll go if I really think I should, but things are clearing
up. It just hurts from being kicked and because I was

shocked. Literally shocked."

She sat still, not asking questions in her quiet way. Maude and Joanne are big on people minding their own business. Finally, she nodded, put her hand on my knee and stood up. "Sam, we've done what we can. Doc checked you over. Don't piss me off by dying."

"I need my clothes."

"I'll get them. Maude ran them through the wash to wash away some of your blood and other crap. I'll see if they're ready."

I used the phone to call Mary Elizabeth.

"Sam. Preacher called. Are you okay?"

"Not really. Things went bad. Where are you?"

"Preacher told us things went bad."

Suddenly what the man on the phone said struck me. I had to get my brain back in gear. How did he know there was a nun involved? Where did that come from?

"Mary Elizabeth. Listen. The guys who attacked us were making sure nobody got to Zoio. Somehow or another they know there's a nun involved."

"What?"

"Yeah, I know. This thing is deeper than we thought. You need to get somewhere and take Mina and Patricia with you. Jason needs to be warned. I don't know what they know or how they know it, but you have got to get out of sight."

"What's going on?" She was crying.

"I don't know. I'm sorry. We missed something or made some fundamental mistakes somewhere. We have got to protect you and Mina and try to figure out what's going on. Mary Elizabeth, I cannot avoid going to authorities. I'm sorry, but I've got to tell them what's going on."

"Do you think there's any chance they could save Zoio at this point?"

I looked at the clock. It had been hours. "No. Maybe if we'd reported it immediately. But, frankly, I was non-functioning. The bad guys know, and they know for sure. They've had plenty of time to disappear. I don't know what to do next."

"Then, please, not yet. Don't tell anybody. I'll take Mina, and we'll get out of sight. We have to think this through."

"We'll get you somewhere. Where's Preacher?"

"I don't know. He came by here and told us you were both attacked when you tried to get to Zoio. He said he had to leave, but I should wait for a call. He left. I don't know where he was going or where he is. Sam, what are we going to do?"

"I don't know. First, we have to get you safe. Do you have any cash? Enough for a hotel room?"

"Yes. Or I can get it."

Slowly my mind started to function. "No. Wait. I can take care of the hotel room. Here's what we're going to do. I know somebody at the Gulf Grand Hotel. I'm going to call and tell them I need a room under a completely false name for a client who needs protection. The three of you get ready. I'm going to make that call. I'll call you back."

"Hold on, Patricia wants to talk to you."

"Sam, are you okay?"

"Sort of. It wasn't fun. Right now, I have to get all of you somewhere. I've told Mary Elizabeth. I'm going to get you all a room. You make sure they get there and stay out of sight."

"Okay. When can I see you?"

"I'll come to the hotel as soon as I can."

"Okay, then. I'll make sure we get there. Bye."

I didn't feel like I should honor Mary Elizabeth's

request to keep quiet. The thing had blown up and was way bigger than I'd thought. I'd probably get in trouble, but Zoio's only chance was to get someone with competence involved. I also needed to think about my obligations as the lawyer for Mary Elizabeth and Mina.

I needed to get myself together, and I needed to find Preacher.

Joanne brought my clothes in. Maude stood in the doorway. Joanne said, "I heard a little of that. I don't know what's going on. I don't think I want to know what's going on, but are we safe?"

"You are not in any kind of danger."

Suddenly, I thought, what if we were followed when we limped back to the island? My breathing shortened as I thought about the possibility of that man waiting for me just outside. Perspiration broke out on my head.

Joanne's nursing instincts kicked in. She put a hand on my forehead and asked, "Are you okay? Your paleness just got paler. Is something happening?"

"No. I'm fine. Just queasy I guess. I'm feeling better every moment."

"Sam. You tell me the truth. Do I need to get Maude out of here?"

I thought for a moment, feeling the pressure of her intense stare. Could I make any kind of judgment about the safety of anybody? I wasn't doing very well in that area.

"Jo, some very bad people have kidnapped a girl. There are complicated reasons why we did not want to go to the authorities. Preacher and I tried to get her back. It didn't work. They were waiting for us with Tasers and boots. You are not connected. You should be okay."

She looked at me for several seconds and then nodded her trust.

"But," I said, "I really don't want to run into this guy again. If you see any strangers coming onto my place, feel free to call the sheriff."

She nodded again.

"Jo. Go. I need to make a phone call. Let me get washed up and dressed in private."

She nodded again and left with Maude, shutting the door behind them.

My head hurt like I'd been poleaxed. My gut hurt like it had been hit by a baseball bat. My shoulders ached and felt numb at the same time like I'd been throwing bales of hay all day. Things still shimmered and sparkled, swimming in and out of focus when I looked at them. If I paid too much attention to anything too long I got nauseous. I wanted to shake my head to clear it so I could get to work, but I knew what that would feel like. I moved slowly and carefully.

I looked at the time. Late enough. I called a direct line to an office at the Gulf Grand Hotel. Dialing from memory, I was relieved my brain could come up with the number.

I got it right. She answered.

"Gulf Grand Hotel, Guest Relations, Cecilia Harrigan speaking. How may I help you?"

"Cecilia. This is Sam. I need a favor."

"Sam. I'm glad you called." She lowered her voice. "I've missed you. Of course, anything. Are you okay?"

She was concerned because, although we were lovers, the nature of our relationship had bright-line boundaries and me calling her at work was way outside those boundaries.

"Cecilia. I miss you, too. I need a huge favor." I would have to think later about the effect of my new relationship with Patricia on my relationship with Cecilia. Cecilia would, as she had in the past, fade into the background if I was in a serious relationship.

"What? Anything."

"I have some clients who are in trouble. It's not with the law. They've done nothing wrong, but I need to hide them for a while and keep them completely incognito. Can I get a room, keep it under a fake name and make sure their privacy is rock solid secure? I'll be paying."

"Sure. I can take care of it. Tell me what you need."

"I need a room for three ladies. Put it under the name of Joshua Slocum."

"No problem. I can take care of that. What else?"

"That will do for now. Is there a way we can keep my name and credit card info out of the record, but still make sure they can order room service if needed?"

"Absolutely. I can refer everything to Guest Relations. We do it for certain guests all the time. Nobody will think it strange. I doubt if anybody will even ask me about it, but I can explain it if they do. How long will they need the room?"

"I don't know. Maybe a couple of days, maybe a week. I'm trying to figure out how to keep them safe in the long term."

"Okay. I'll make the arrangement. I'll get you a nice discount, but if you want to avoid questions at my end, I'll have to pay the bill at least weekly."

"Hopefully, it won't even be that long, but if it is, I'll get you the money."

"Okay. Have them call me, and I'll meet them in the lobby. I'll make sure they have their privacy."

"The person calling you will be either Mary Elizabeth Kincaid or Patricia Carr. Just so you know they're not going to be a problem, Mary Elizabeth is a nun and Patricia used to be a nun. They'll have a teenage girl with them who we are protecting from some bad people. You cannot breathe a word of any of that to anybody."

"I didn't even make a note. I'll wait for them to call. Will it be soon?"

"As soon as I can get them there. Hopefully within the hour. And, Cecilia, thank you."

"Sam ... ?"

"Yes, me, too. Hopefully soon, but I have to take care of this problem."

"Okay. By the way, who is Joshua Slocum?"

"He was the first person to sail around the world by himself."

"Ah. Bye, my friend."

My friend. My very special friend. How nice it would have been to spend the afternoon with her in the darkness of my bedroom without the intrusion of evil men with boots.

I called Mary Elizabeth and told her what to do.

I called Joshua Bell and told him to take a paid vacation until I called him. I told him I would be working on a case full-time. He took the news in his happy-go-lucky way.

I sat for a moment, trying to not move my head, concentrating to dredge from my still muddled brain what I should do next. The phone rang. The caller I.D. said LCSD. We'd tried to snatch Zoio in Leon County. LCSD undoubtedly stood for Leon County Sheriff's Department. I had a bad feeling as I answered.

"Are you Samuel Locke the attorney?"

"Yes."

"This is Deputy Sheriff James Collins, Leon County Sheriff's Department. Do you know the man who calls himself Preacher?"

"Yes." I stood up ignoring what it felt like to do so.

"Are you his lawyer?"

"Yes." I'd not really thought about it before, but I became his lawyer right at that moment, hoping it was the right thing to do. "What's going on?"

"Well, I don't know exactly. He called to report something about a kidnapping and an assault. I started to ask him some questions, and he told me he needed to talk to his lawyer. You. I'm hoping you can tell me what's going on."

"Obviously, I need to talk to him. He doesn't have a phone. Did he leave a number?"

"No. He called, asked to speak to us, said what he said about whatever it is he's talking about and then said he needed to talk to you. Caller ID said Clara's B&G."

"Okay. I'll find him and call you back."

"Please do."

I thought for a moment. Even though I didn't know exactly what Preacher had told them, I said, "Deputy, I know Preacher is a little quirky, but I'd believe whatever he told you if I were you and act on it."

"We are."

Dammit, I thought. I had no idea what Preacher had told them. I had no idea what half-ass plan he had making me his lawyer.

I fell back on the fact that lawyers routinely don't talk to cops about their clients. "I really need to talk to him. I'll call you as soon as I can."

"Do you have any idea what he was talking about?"

I wrestled with my brain, not sure I could trust it to make good decisions. Memories, images, and dream-like sensations flickered in my mind making it hard to rationally think about what I should do. I decided too much time had passed to let another hour make much difference. If Preacher had said something, anything I might add could confuse the issue so much it would actually cause more harm than good. I had to see him. I was sure he'd given them basic facts, described the van, gave them the license plate, and told them the time we caught up with the van. That was enough for them to do what they need to do.

I took a deep breath. "I need to talk to him. It might take me a while to find him."

There was a long pause during which I am sure Deputy Collins thought about Preacher, lawyers who are intentionally oblique, and whatever story Preacher had told.

"Fine. If what he told me was true, I hope you're not holding anything back. It sounds like he knows more than he was saying. If there was a kidnapping, you would be foolish if you do not tell us everything you can."

"I'm his lawyer. You know what that means. I have to talk to my client."

"Fine. If you don't mind, come in and say hi to me one of these days."

He was frustrated with me, but I'm sure he was used to being irritated by lawyers. He hung up the phone abruptly without another word.

I stood in front of the bathroom mirror assessing my appearance. My torso looked bruised and battered. I didn't want to think what it would look like in a day or two. I couldn't even see a lot of it because the doctor had wrapped my chest tightly in a flexible bandage. Ribs hurt with every breath and were likely cracked or broken.

My legs looked just as battered with dark, mottled, purplish red bruises. The tibia on my left leg hurt bad and had a lump on it. High up on that leg a bruise actually showed the imprint of the tread on the boots of my assailant. He'd stomped on me.

I thanked my lucky stars I could move at all. I would take a photograph of my body later. It might be helpful if the powers that be prosecuted someone besides Preacher and me.

It was hard to see the lump on the back quarter of my head but not the related bruise on the side of my neck. There were abrasions on the back of my shoulders and head contributing their own burning pain. At some point, he dragged me across the parking lot.

All things considered, it was good to be alive. Literally. I nodded my head in thanks to the genetics that gave me strong bones and confirmed that it really hurt my neck to move my head.

If I moved slow and didn't wince, I should be able to avoid questions. Except for my eyes. The whites of my eyes were bloody pink and not likely to be helped much by eye-drops.

I dressed slowly. Jo knocked on the door and stuck her head into the room. "Preacher is coming up the drive."

"We'll get out of your hair and go back over to my place."

Jo nodded with a grim expression and started to close the door. She opened it back up, gave me a stern look, started to say something, but just shook her head and closed the door.

My recently acquired client, Preacher, sat on a chair in the living room. Jo and Maude were on the sofa. I said, "Thank you ladies. We'll get out of here and leave you in peace." I directed Preacher to the front door with a move of my head. Outside, he tossed me the keys and climbed into the passenger side of my vehicle.

As I started the truck, I said, "Well, I got a call from the sheriff."

"We agreed we needed to tell them what was going on," he said. "Both of us don't need to get in trouble, so I called them and told them what happened. I just left you out of it. I told them I'd received information in confidence as a minister about a girl being smuggled into this country to work as a prostitute. I gave them Zoio's name, but I didn't tell them about her sister or about Mary Elizabeth or anybody else. I told them I found and followed the van. I described the van and gave them the license plate. I told them I tried to intervene and got beat up and called them as soon as I could function. I avoided questions by insisting they needed to get to work. Maybe it won't help, but maybe they'll start a search. Oh, I also told them I had no phone, but that you are my lawyer."

"What else?"

"Nothing."

"What exactly did you tell them about the people who assaulted you?"

"Nothing. I told them I was hit over the head from behind and never saw who did it. That's the truth. I told them I saw a lady driving the van. I said she looked to be in her mid-thirties and blonde, not likely naturally. Other than that I could not give them a good description."

"Did you tell them where it happened?"

"Exactly. Oh, I also gave them my driver's license number, so they would know I was for real."

That gave me pause. I just stared at him for several moments. "You have a driver's license?"

"Yes."

"I didn't know that."

He shrugged.

"Can I see it?"

He pulled it out of his back pocket and handed it to me. Sure enough, at some point, he'd legally changed his name. The name on his license was A. Preacher. The address on the license was the address of his store-front church.

"What did you tell him about the gun?"

Preacher's eyes went wide. "I forgot all about the gun. I guess they took it, huh?"

"It's missing. Yes."

"I guess it's good I forgot that."

Just as I pulled into the drive in front of my house, Mary Elizabeth called. "Sam. We're here. At the hotel. When can you come to see us?"

"In a bit. Order room service or something and Preacher and I will be there in a couple of hours."

"Sam, what are we going to do?" Her voice pitched high and brittle. It sounded like she was on the verge of falling apart.

"Eat something. We'll try to think better this time around. We'll see you soon."

"Okay. Good-bye."

Preacher said, "We could go eat with them."

"No. I need to think. Let's go to Clara's."

He was quiet on the drive to Clara's, not offering one optimistic platitude. The only thing he said was, "Sam, I'd appreciate it if you kept it quiet about me having a driver's license."

I nodded.

At Clara's, we each had lots of dark, rich coffee and shrimp and egg breakfast burritos, Cajun style. I thought the coffee and spicy breakfast went a long way to making me feel better until I tried to stand up. My body was stiffer than it had been before. I groaned and moved slowly.

Luckily, they'd not taken my credit cards. I could pay for breakfast. Clara put a few extra dollars on the card and gave me the cash.

"Bad?" Preacher asked.

"It is what it is. I think I'll live. There is less and less blood when I pee. We might as well go see them. You?"

"About the same."

We drove toward the Gulf Grand. Somewhere during that drive, I merged the anger at being taken so easily and the beating I'd suffered into the anger at what was happening to Zoio and the other shadowed figures in that van. We'd inserted ourselves deeper into the darkness and paid a price. But, with that price, I purchased a greater resolve. We were in a defensive position for the moment. I would find a way to re-enter the battle in my own way and from a position of strength.

I hit the steering wheel with both palms. Preacher looked over at me, nodded his head, and said, "What do we do next, Sam?"

"We go after them smarter. They kicked our ass, but they did it stupidly. We may have been naive then, but now, we are smarter than we were. They made some mistakes."

"What do you mean?"

"They had us incapacitated from the start when they hit us with the Taser. They took too much time to beat on us. They should have left much quicker. The beating went on too long. He took pleasure in it. Like a bully. Once we were down and he had my identity from my wallet they should have gone. Dumped the van. Done something to hide. They probably did that, but they shouldn't have taken the time they did to play with us."

"Okay. I think I see what you mean."

I continued to think out loud. "In fact, from a strictly

business point of view, if he was going to go as far as he did, he should have just killed us. I'm pretty sure he has that capability."

"Well, I'm glad they skipped that part. You keep saying he, but there were at least two of them."

"But only one of them is in charge. He's the one who guided the brutality and made the decisions. He would not work well unless he is the top dog. I bet he bullies whoever he has working with him."

"And you're saying he should have just killed us."

"Yes."

"Maybe he was worried about us being cops."

"If we'd been cops, there would have been a dozen of us wearing a lot of Kevlar."

"So, what do we do now that we're so much smarter?"

"He called me. It's not over. He'll be able to find me. You're pretty distinctive. It won't be hard for him to find you. He wants Mina. He'll be after us. We're his ticket to her. He knows we didn't involve law enforcement or they'd have been there. He's can't be sure we have Mina, but he'll work to find out."

"You're not reassuring me very much."

"We know stuff, too. We have a license plate, probably stolen, but it is something. We've seen the van. We've seen the woman driving the van. We know things about them. We've probably seen his lookout." That gave me pause. "We need to call Jenny right now and tell her to not go back to the jetty. Just in case."

"We don't have their names and addresses like he has for you."

"No, but we have a couple of threads. We're going to start tugging on them. You created a little official heat when you talked to the Sheriff. We'll run down the license plate, too."

"What about Mary Elizabeth? How did he know she was a nun?"

"Excellent question. Somebody's been hunting. That had to have started in Chicago. Too bad, but good to know. Plus, whoever has been looking for them created some kind of tracks. We can look for those."

We approached the Seawall, getting closer to the Gulf Grand Hotel. My mind was obviously starting to work again. I thought about the threads we had and how to do the tugging without getting anybody killed.

I said, "Our first obligation is to keep everybody on our side safe."

I realized the bad guys knew some things. They, too, had threads to tug. I needed to take my own advice. I checked my rear view mirror. There was no way to tell if any of the vehicles in the mirror were following us. I slowed and took one of the roads away from the beach and toward the bay. Preacher looked over at me and immediately understood. He turned to watch behind us.

We were the only car on the road, and nobody followed us. I skirted the airport and drove into Galveston on Stewart Road. Nobody followed us. Preacher kept a diligent watch all the way through the city. I parked on the street a couple of blocks north and east of the hotel. We walked from there. I decided I needed to get a different vehicle. Get away from anything traceable to me. I looked over at Preacher.

"You need to change what you wear for a while. And cut your hair. You stand out."

He looked at his loud Hawaiian shirt, gave a grim smile, nodded, and said, "We need to go undercover."

"Yes."

"I'm glad you've decided to go head to head with them."

"I've decided to find the girl. I'd just as soon not have another head to head with those guys."

Walking toward the hotel, I called Mary Elizabeth. They were in room 505. I parted with Preacher in the lobby sending him up to the room, telling him I had to take care of arrangements with the hotel.

I asked the concierge if Ms. Harrigan was available to speak with Mr. Slocum. He made a call and directed me to a hallway just past the main desk. By the time I got there, Cecilia stood in the doorway of her office. It was the first time I'd ever visited her at work. Her office was a place outside of our world, but this was business.

She greeted me with a firm, businesslike handshake that did not linger, a subtle smile that did, and a "Hello Mr. Slocum. Nice to meet you." I saw that she noticed my eyes and their burst capillaries.

"Ms. Harrigan."

"Cecilia, please."

She ushered me in, closing the door behind us and stood close, much closer than businesslike, looking up at me, her eyes luminous. I breathed her in, realizing she wore a scent different than she wore when she visited my house.

"What is wrong with your eyes?"

She deserved the real answer. "You know those bad guys after my client? I had a run in with them. It didn't turn out well."

"Sam. Are you okay?"

"Yes. I'm just beat up a bit. I have some bruises, but I've seen a doctor. This just goes to show you why I don't want anybody finding my clients. Thank you for hiding them."

She did not step away and continued to look closely at

me, finally taking a deep breath. "No problem."

"I know I can trust you to keep them incognito. They know not to let anybody know they are staying here. There won't be any trouble." She nodded. Coming to her place of business was well outside the boundaries of our relationship. I was very aware of how close she stood to me. I said, "I know it is a little strange for me to be here."

"Yes, and I'm going to break a rule one time." She grabbed my shirt, pulled me close and kissed me nicely. Stepping back, she took a deep breath and moved behind her desk. "Now, Mr. Slocum, how can I help you."

"I want to thank you for making arrangements for my clients. I didn't bring enough cash, but I'll return and pay for their room."

"It's no problem. You can pay at the end of the week if you'd like. Make sure they know they can call me if I can help them in any way."

"Thanks. Again, it is important they stay incognito. Nobody knows they're here, and we really need to keep it that way."

"That's obvious. I put their room in the name of Customer Relations. I checked them in. Jennifer Lopez stayed here for a weekend once and nobody found out. It's part of my job. They should be fine."

"Okay. Thanks again." She showed me out the door.

I went up to their room.

There were greetings and hugs and sympathetic exclamations about the beatings. I told my version of the story about what happened. It was a nice room with a sofa big enough for the three ladies to sit side by side and stare at me while I told the story. Preacher sprawled on one of the beds.

When I finished telling the story, there were a few

more expressions of sympathy, then, Mary Elizabeth said, "What do we do now? Do you think the police will do anything with what Preacher told them? Are the police coming after us?"

"What we do now is regroup and plan our next step to get Zoio away from them."

She nodded. She had an arm around Mina and hugged her, pulling her closer to her side. "What about the police?"

"I think they'll go to the truck stop and find that nobody there saw a thing. I think they'll run the license plate and find it stolen. I'll get another phone call. They may want Preacher and me to talk to them. We'll make a decision about that when it happens. You and Preacher and Mina are my clients, and I have to maintain the confidentiality of what you've told me about past events."

She nodded again, and said, "And what do we do next?"

"We think about what we know. I've told Preacher how they've made some mistakes. We'll try to find a way to capitalize on those. There's one extremely important thing that needs to be addressed. I had business cards with me and my driver's license, but both have only a post office box as the address. He will be able to find my place, though." I looked at Preacher.

He said, "The only thing I had with my address was safe in my shoe."

"He called me." I looked at Mary Elizabeth. "He mentioned the fact that a nun is involved."

She sat back and her forehead furrowed. "You said that earlier. How would he know that?"

"Good question. We had nothing with us that revealed that. Either you attracted attention somehow, and it got back to them or they're looking for Mina in Chicago and found out there somehow. I think it most likely that the guys who attacked us are merely transporters. After we made our try, he probably called whoever he delivers to at the other end and they had a discussion. But how did anybody find out? That's what we need to know."

Mary Elizabeth spoke quietly, "I talked to the FBI, but only over the phone. I didn't mention my name or that I am a nun. I talked to somebody at the Coast Guard, but it was the same thing, no mention of my name or that I'm a nun."

"You have to think hard and make a list of anybody else down here who knows who you are, whether or not they know what you're doing. We need to call Jason. Find out if they might have learned Mina was at The Beacon."

Patricia said, "I'll call him."

Preacher asked, "What else?"

"I'm going to find out about the license plate. I'm going to try to find his boat."

"What can I do?" asked Mary Elizabeth.

"Stay safe. Are you okay here?"

"Yes. This is terrific. They're being so nice."

"I hate to say it but I think you should just stick here for a little while. Order room service. Don't go out for anything. Is there anything you need?"

"If we have to stay here, you might get us some drawing pads and some colored pencils. Give us something to pass the time."

"I'll do that. Mina, when you draw, think back carefully about the woman driving the van and come up with the best possible picture of her."

Mina, wide-eyed, nodded her head solemnly. Tears welled up in her eyes. "Did you see my sister?"

"Yes. I saw her." I hesitated, but knowing circumstances had made Mina as adult as the rest of us, I told her the truth. "She started to come to me when I was attacked. I am so sorry."

She nodded. A huge, crystalline tear rolled from her eye and down her cheek. She nestled closer to Mary Elizabeth who stroked her hair. I did not mention my hope that nobody made Zoio pay the price for our bungled rescue.

I said, "I'll go buy you some art supplies, and then I'm going to my place. There are things I need to do, and I need time alone to think about everything. You all need to do the same. Any detail about this whole experience you can think of, no matter if you think it is important or not, write it down. Also, I have to get ready for a trial next week. I'll be in court a couple of days. I'll skip that only in extraordinary circumstances."

Preacher stood up. "I'm going with you, so I can buy something different to wear."

Patricia followed us to the door and said, "I'll call Jason from here, but when you come back with their art supplies, I'm going with you. I will go stark raving mad if I have to stay cooped up here. I won't interfere with your thinking, but I cannot just stay in this room." She looked back to where Mary Elizabeth talked softly to Mina. "They'll be fine. They don't need me. They're not going anywhere and can draw to their heart's content. I would have nothing to do."

"Sure." She hugged me.

I called Rocky while we walked to the car and told him briefly about our run in and that Jenny needed to stay away from the jetty. Preacher and I drove to a Target. He picked up three pairs of khaki pants, three button down shirts, some socks, a pair of tennis shoes and a cap. I paid for it all along with two thick sketch pads and two twenty-four count sets of sketching pencils.

I started back to the hotel but had an idea. I pulled off the road, told Preacher I knew where I could get a different vehicle and called one of my clients, Larry Peters. Larry has three ex-wives, seven children scattered among the three, and runs a pretty nice used car lot. He keeps a running tab with me for his personal and business legal expenses. He agreed to let me have a reliable Ford Explorer and to store my Land Rover on his back lot for five hundred dollars a week off of what he owed me, no documentation required. I told him a story about an angry and dangerous ex-spouse of another client looking for me. He is very familiar with angry ex-spouses and promised to keep his mouth shut about our deal. His lot was just over the bridge on the mainland. Preacher called the ladies and told them we'd be a little longer than expected. We made the vehicle trade without any problems.

On the way back to the hotel I stopped at a branch of my bank and got two thousand dollars, glad that the Scamp Boat check was in my account.

At the hotel, Preacher headed to the room with the drawing supplies. I went to Cecilia's office and gave her a thousand dollars to draw on for the room charges, telling her to let me know if she needed more. We were all business.

Preacher and Patricia came back down the elevator. Preacher said that Mary Elizabeth and Mina were working on getting the best possible drawing of the van's driver. Patricia said she'd left a message for Jason, and he'd be calling her back.

Despite her protestations that she had much shorter legs, Preacher insisted Patricia ride in the front seat on the way back to my house.

CHAPTER THIRTEEN

It surprised me to find Joshua's truck parked at my place. He came out of the shop holding a broom. I said, "Joshua, I told you not to bother coming in for a while."

"I know, but I didn't have anything else to do and thought I'd sweep up the shop a bit."

I sent Preacher and Patricia to the house and walked with Joshua into the shop.

"Look," I said, "I've got a client who's in a lot of trouble and some bad people are looking for her."

"That girl from the other day?"

"Yep."

He looked intently at my face and my eyes which had not lost their pink. "Looks like maybe you found them."

"Yes."

"Looks like it wouldn't hurt to have some backup hanging around."

"Thanks, but I don't intend to be around much. I really don't want another run-in with them, and you do not need to be here if they show up. Joshua, these guys are really, really dangerous."

He was quiet for a moment. "I guess we should have finished working on that alarm system."

We'd been planning to do something so that if anybody drove through the gate, we would get an alert in the shop. "Yeah, wouldn't hurt."

"Let me do it. We have the wire and conduit. Let me work on putting the system in."

"Yes. You're right. Can't hurt. Go ahead. But these guys sandbagged Preacher and me before we saw them. I don't know how many of them there are, but there are at least two. I do not know what they look like or what they're driving. We need to keep the gate locked, and our eyes open. If something happens, your only job is to get out of here and call the cops. Here's a couple of hundred dollars if you need to buy anything to get the job done. If you think you need more than that come talk to me."

I handed him the cash. He nodded, turned into the workshop with purpose, and I went into the house.

Inside, Preacher stretched out on the couch and headed for a nap. Patricia was on the phone. It was obvious from her side of the conversation that she was talking to Jason. There was urgency in their discussion. She said, "Yes, here he is" and handed me the phone, with a shrug and a grim smile.

He was angry. "I thought we had a plan."

"It looked easy. I was wrong."

"And now you've brought more danger."

"Wait a minute. No. At worse, we created a great excuse to walk away like you want. Meanwhile, we learned something that we did not know before. I'm sure Patricia told you. We know now that somebody knows that Mina is with a nun. I'm sure it didn't come from here, so it is likely they traced her to the Beacon. I think knowing that is a very good thing and makes us more wary in a good way. What do you know about that?"

He was quiet for a few seconds. "Okay. Yeah. You're right. It is good to know. Do you have them safe?"

"Yes. Nobody can find them where they are, and they're not going to move."

"Good. And no. I have no idea how he could have discovered Mina is with a nun. I will see if I can find out."

"Be very careful. Preacher and I have experienced their viciousness. Trust me, you do not want to attract their attention."

"I guess we already have. Damn. Okay. I'll be careful and let you know if I find out anything. What are you planning to do next?"

He didn't sound happy. I couldn't expect him to think much of my abilities. "I don't know, yet. We're regrouping. We're thinking. I'm going to keep everybody safe. There may be nothing we can do. We've told law enforcement as much as we could. Maybe we wait until I can consult with the specialists again."

I told him a shortened version of everything that happened and once again, exhorted him to be very careful. The last thing he said was something about having to go to one of his supporters about coming up with the funds to increase security. We promised to keep each other updated.

I handed Patricia her phone. She asked me, "Is there something I can do?"

"Can't think of a thing. I'm going to sit on the pier. Try to concentrate. Help yourself to the fridge or anything else you need. It may not be any more interesting around here than it would have been back at the hotel."

"I'll find something to do. Do you mind if I walk down there with you? I won't bother you, but there's something I want to say. I'll come right back here."

"Sure."

Outside, Joshua, whistling as usual, carried conduit laying it beside the drive. He waved and shouted, "Hey, Sam, do you mind if I go rent a Ditch Witch once I get this strung to the gate?"

"No. Get what you need. Let me know if you need more cash." He went back to work.

Patricia and I walked the boardwalk toward the pier. "Sam. I heard what you said to Jason. You were right, you know, you have not put Mary Elizabeth and Mina in any more danger than Mary Elizabeth had already created. In fact, as you said, it's good to know that they knew a nun is involved. Scary, but something we needed to know."

"I know."

"You seem to be thinking you've done something wrong."

I glanced out over the bay, looking across the horizon and not seeing a thing other than Zoio in the back of that van starting to rise, starting to come to me. Starting to come to safety. I looked at Patricia. She was softer looking than she'd been that day we first met, her eyes sympathetic instead of wary, her half smile not at all like the thin, tight line it had been that day.

"Your hair looks good. I like it better than that first day we met."

It took her a moment to process what I'd said. She frowned in confusion, then, she shook her head and laughed. "Yes. Yes, it is nicer. I must have looked terrible to you that first day." She'd read my mind.

"Not terrible. Militant maybe. But not terrible."

"I'm sorry about that. But it's related to what I want to say to you. Jason and I were at your place only reluctantly. We both just wanted to have the problem disappear. We both just wanted Mary Elizabeth to move on, not create a problem."

I nodded. "Might have been a good idea."

"No," she said. "She won't stop. I know Jason is not happy with us, but I want you to know what I thought when we met."

We reached the end of the boardwalk. I waited for her to continue.

"I was worried about Mary Elizabeth and Mina back

then. Desperately worried. She was seeking to do dangerous things and wasn't going to stop. I didn't think Preacher was really helping things. He is ... "

"Strange," I said.

She smiled. "Yes. And way too optimistic, I thought. I've lost a lot of faith in the intervention of God. Anyway, he suggested we talk to you, and I expected you to be a flake."

I laughed. "I might have lived up to your expectation."

"No. You were not at all what I expected. We entered your shop and there you were standing in front of that beautiful thing you'd created. You were obviously very competent. The more we talked the more that became apparent. You immediately recognized the statue in Mina's drawing. You took command. You put us on your boat, and you became our captain. You took us straight to the jetty and everything became much more real. I knew you were testing Mary Elizabeth, trying to convince her of the impossibility of what she'd started. But at the same time, you were solving the problem. You were calculating what needed to be done."

I looked at her, but she just stared out over the bay. There was a blush on her cheeks and tears in eyes, showing surprising and unexpected emotion. I kept quiet.

"You were processing things so quickly. You found those people. You accomplished things in a few days I would have thought impossible."

"Patricia ... "

"No. Just listen. You are thinking you have made some kind of huge mistake. But you haven't. You've not made one mistake."

"That's not what my ribs are telling me."

She looked at me then. "Shut up. Your ribs hurt because you were willing to do things that needed doing when they needed to be done. It is not a benign evil you have engaged. You tried. You survived. I can see your mind working. You are going to carefully calculate the next step. You are going to do something, and you will do it with extreme competence. I don't think the bad guy has a chance."

"Yes, he does."

Now we were looking straight at each other. "You know what," she said, "we may not get to Zoio. She may be beyond our grasp. If so, it is not your fault. But I bet you find the guy who beat on you. I bet you win that part of the battle. I bet he goes to jail."

She hugged me and said, "Anyway, that's what I wanted to say. It probably doesn't make sense."

She leaned away from me but still had her hands on my shoulders. Mine were on her waist.

"You did have a lot to say."

She laughed a little. "I'll go, let you think."

She walked back up the boardwalk. My mind was a jumble of images, everything from what had just happened to the other things we'd done, hiding in the hotel, Joshua putting in an alarm system. I thought about Preacher actually wearing khakis and a tucked in shirt.

Thinking about Preacher's garb caused some circuits in my brain to connect. The girl's pink satin jacket. I'd seen that jacket somewhere before. Where? Pink satin. A pink satin jacket on a girl. Where? When? I closed my eyes trying to picture a very dim memory.

Bingo. Something about the jacket was familiar. I'd seen one like it in the past. I was short on details, but I'd remembered one important thing.

I walked quickly back to the house. Patricia was sitting on the porch. "So soon?" she asked.

"I've got something."

"What?"

"About the driver. It's not much, but it is something. I need to call and see if Mina has come up with a drawing of the lady."

She followed me into the house where I called Mary Elizabeth's cell. She answered immediately.

"Mary Elizabeth. I've thought of something. Was Mina able to come up with a drawing of the van's driver?"

"Hold on. Let me go somewhere private." I heard her tell Mina she'd be right back.

"We've worked on one, yes. I don't know how good it is. The best one is in profile. What have you thought of?"

"It's slim, but she had a distinctive jacket. I'm going to try to trace it. I need the best drawing of the driver Mina can do."

She was silent for a moment. "We really don't have much at all, do we?"

I knew more about the jacket but didn't want to create more false hope. "We have more details than we did a week ago. We really do. You have no idea how much I regret not being better prepared than we were, but I am determined to find Zoio. I promise you I will not quit."

"Thank you. I trust you. I know it is not your fault."

We hung up. I knew on one level our joint fiasco was not my fault, but I had been so close to Zoio. I'd seen her. I'd looked into her eyes. She'd looked at me and started to me, her eyes never leaving mine until I was attacked. She did look like Mina. I got so close and I'd messed up. This could have been over if we'd been just a bit better prepared, if we'd done just a couple of things better. No matter the truth about fault, I knew I would be haunted forever by what was a monumental failure and the look of confused fear in her eyes. Her personal hell might have been made worse by what

I'd done.

Patricia touched my arm. "Sam, what are you on to. I can tell it is something."

"The jacket. I need to make a call."

I didn't take the time to look up the number in my records, I called information and asked for the phone number for the office of Gregory Maines. I've known Greg since high school. He'd been a year behind me in law school. Greg went to work for a firm doing commercial bankruptcies. Houston is the largest city in Texas and one of the largest cities in the country. It is known for its clusters of big city skylines featuring architectural masterpieces funded by oil and gas companies and big banks. Houston takes pride in its fast-paced business atmosphere and its entrepreneurial spirit. Entrepreneurial spirit creates a large number of bankruptcies. Houston is also known for its topless clubs.

The first topless club business to be listed on a stock exchange got its start in Houston. It is a thriving industry. One would think it is reasonably recession-proof, but one of Greg's early bankruptcy clients was the owner of the topless club Saffron.

Saffron's owner grew weary of the financial battles, being pursued by the IRS, the State of Texas seeking liquor taxes and all the other hassles of running such a business. I'm not sure exactly how he did it, but Greg ended up owning the business.

When he acquired the club it was what I'd call a mid-level club, not terribly seedy when measured against other such clubs, but not one in which you would find billionaires and Playboy models. Over the course of five years, Greg changed all of that, making the club one of those where celebrity models do appear and where a lot of big business expense account money gets spent. Annually, it ranks among the top three businesses in liquor sales in the state. Greg has done very well.

Greg maintained an office in a house in the Heights, but the only legal work he did was to represent the dancers who work in his club. A lady answered my call. I was pretty sure she was not a legal assistant.

"Hi. Greg's place. Whatcha need?"

"I need to talk to Greg. Is he there?"

"Yep. Hold on." She didn't actually put me on hold. She just carried the phone with her. I heard her open a door and shout for Greg over the sound of music and several ladies laughing.

"Hi, this is Greg."

"Greg, Sam Locke. Hope I didn't interrupt anything important."

"Sam, buddy. You did. You interrupted a very important basketball game. The girls in the pink satin shorts are beating the girls in the baby blue satin shorts by three goals. Are you in town? Denise is the captain of the pink satin shorts and we are celebrating her second divorce and planning her third. We have tapped a keg, come on over and help me cheer them on."

"No. I wish I was in town, but I'm at my place. But, speaking of pink satin shorts, I have a question. Some time ago, somewhere, I saw a girl wearing a pink satin jacket with the name of a gentleman's club on the back. I cannot for the life of me remember the name of the club. I have a case going on where a witness I'm trying to find was seen wearing a pink satin jacket. Would you have any idea which club has jackets like that?"

"The Pink Cocktail. Stupid name. They try to market all sorts of stuff, but I don't think their pink jackets have gone over very well. The jackets have the name of the club and a champagne glass printed on the back. I can't imagine very many of their customers buying such a thing for the wife or girlfriend. Very few of their dancers would wear such a thing in public."

"That's it. Thank you." I remembered where I'd seen the jacket before. I'd caught a brief glimpse of someone wearing the jacket at a massive New Year's Eve celebration in downtown Houston a couple of years earlier.

The girl wearing the jacket had been holding sparklers in each hand while sitting on the shoulders of a very large man running through the crowd leading a couple of policemen in pursuit. It was memorable.

I didn't know if the jacket on the driver of the van was the same, but it sure seemed to be the same color and have the same trim. I had to be careful not to create memories of things that didn't really exist, but it was something, and we didn't have much. We needed as many somethings as we could find.

What else did we have? The license plate. It used to be easy to get the registered owner of a vehicle's license plate, but no longer. I called my go-to person.

"Sherwood, Thomas, and Cain, this is Rosalyn Myers."

"Rosalyn, this is Samuel Locke. How are you doing?"

"Mr. Locke, I'm doing fine. What can I do for you today?"

"I need to get some information I'm not supposed to be able to get, and I don't know where else to turn."

"Ah. So you're thinking I might be able to do your dirty deed?"

"Not personally, of course, but you do have magical ways."

"Tell me what you need. I'll tell you if I have any interest in helping you."

"I need to find out who owns a car. I have the license plate. It is probably stolen, but it wouldn't hurt to know the owner and from where it was stolen."

"I hesitate to ask, but why?"

"The plate was on a vehicle involved in the immigration matter I'm trying to handle."

"I see. I'm sure there are ways to get the information. Give me time to make some inquiries."

"Discreetly."

"Of course. Discreet inquiries. Nothing less in this business."

I gave her the number and said, "Thank you. I owe you."

"Yes. Yes, you do. Perhaps someday you will tell me the story of this case over lunch."

"Absolutely. If and when it gets resolved."

"Is there anything else we can do for you?"

"No. Thank you."

What else? I didn't want to call the sheriff and ask if anything had come of Preacher's thin report. I assumed if anything happened we'd hear about it.

I turned from the phone. Patricia was standing there looking at me. I explained to her about the pink jacket, ending my explanation by saying, "Slim, I know, but more than we had. She was wearing it when Mina was taken and she was wearing it when we saw her. It is distinctive and something more than we had before. She is probably a topless dancer. If so she has an adult entertainer's license. I'm not sure how to get the information about her license, but it could give us enough information to lead us to her."

Patricia nodded. "If she has such a thing, I'm sure you are resourceful enough to get the information."

Suddenly, I felt weary. The beating, the stress, the

day—they all were taking toll. I needed to rest. There was the urge to push ahead, try to find the girl that night, but I knew there nothing could be done right then. The driver of the van had to be on the road somewhere. I wouldn't be able to find her right then.

Patricia noticed something. "What's wrong?"

"The day just caught up with me. I'm tired."

"Is there anything you absolutely have to do tonight?"

"No. Nothing that will really help. I'm going to try to sleep. I guess I could drive you back to the hotel."

"No. I'm staying here, with you."

Joshua knocked and opened the door. "Sam, it may be nothing, but I think there's a pick-up truck that's driven past the gate at least three times."

Adrenalin kicked in. I breathed deep. "What exactly did you see?"

"Normally I would not have even noticed, but I guess you have me on alert. I really only saw it once, and it was just a flash of a pick-up passing the gate. I can't even tell you what model. It was a dark color, maybe black. I wasn't that close. It was loud, souped up. I realized I'd heard what sounded like the same exhaust a couple of times before the last drive by."

There had been a big noisy pick-up pull into the parking lot just before we made our rescue attempt. It could be the same truck. At the time I'd been focused narrowly on what we were doing. I did not remember what the truck looked like. He had my name. It wouldn't be hard to find where I lived. I squeezed my forehead. Think Sam. Think.

"Sam," Joshua said, "I don't know what's going on, but if you need some help ... "

"We are involved in something with a dangerous person. He's trying to find the girl that was here a while back. We had a run in with him and a friend that did not turn out well for our side. You do not need to become another target. Did he see you?"

"I wasn't close to the gate when I heard him drive by. I wouldn't have even noticed, but I don't usually hear that kind of exhaust noise three or four times in a row like that."

"If you notice the pick-up again, and you're close enough, try to get a license plate but do not, and I really mean do not, let anybody notice that you have a particular interest in the truck."

He nodded. "If it's all the same to you, Sam, I think I'll sleep in the shop tonight."

I thought about things. I didn't think anybody would do anything other than watch and wait. He couldn't know where Mina was staying. Surely there wouldn't be a full frontal assault on my home. "Okay, Josh. Thanks. I'll tell you what I can about exactly what's going on later. Right now, just know that we're going to lock the gate tonight and I expect no visitors. I don't think it is going to happen, but if somebody shows up your job is to stay out of sight and call nine-eleven."

"Okay."

"I'm serious. Nothing but a phone call and then you hide."

"Got it. Really."

"Okay, then."

He nodded and went outside. I watched him through the door.

From behind me, Patricia said, "You have good friends."

I nodded. Joshua pulled a shotgun out from behind the seat of his truck and took it into the shop. I couldn't think of a reason to tell him it was not necessary. In a moment he drove his truck down the long driveway and locked the gate. Then he went back to work on our warning system. I stood and watched him for a while trying to think of what else we should do.

I turned around to find Preacher awake and sitting quietly on the couch. Patricia stood with her arms crossed leaning against the doorway to the kitchen. I smiled at the way they were staring at me and said, "Well, troops, anybody for dinner?"

Preacher said, "I know where stuff is. I'll make fish tacos."

"Okay. Make enough for Joshua, too." He went to the kitchen.

Patricia said, "I'll call and let Mary Elizabeth know I'm staying here for the night."

"Tell her I'll be there in the morning to pick up the sketch they made."

I walked out to where Joshua was pulling a length of wire through the conduit. He said, "You know what? I think we need to somehow wire up the pier and boardwalk, too. I'll figure out something for that."

"Good idea. Come on in for some fish tacos. And Joshua, thanks."

He walked with me to the porch. Just as we reached the door, we heard the loud rumble of a truck crescendo and fade away on the highway. We both turned, but from that distance, all you see are the quick flash of the lights of vehicles passing.

Once we were in bed that night, Patricia said, "Sam, make love with me. Slow. Keep your eyes closed. Don't say a word. Just lose yourself in us."

My body ached from the beating, but I did as she asked and was better for it.

Chapter Fourteen

The next morning was another beautiful day, but the gentleness of the predawn weather did not soothe the remains of the day before. I ached from the beating. Thoughts woke me up in the dark after midnight and did not fade. The gentle breathing of Patricia next to me created an aching wish to take her on a long cruise, but I knew that would be impossible until we'd resolved the dark thing consuming us all. Reluctant or not, I was engaged in a battle from which I could not hide.

First item on the battle plan, coffee. Trying not to wake her, I slipped on a t-shirt and a pair of jeans. I tried to be quiet on the way to the kitchen. Preacher snored on the sofa. I leaned with my hands on the edge of the kitchen counter watching the pot fill with coffee, thinking about the next thing to do.

I took my coffee to the porch. There was a rustle of movement inside the house. Patricia, carrying a cup of coffee, came outside wearing the t-shirt she'd borrowed the night before.

"Good morning," she said.

"Morning."

"You look deep in thought."

"Just thinking about the next thing to do."

"Ah, what's the plan?"

"That's the problem. There is no plan. We're stumbling in the dark, and it's only getting more dangerous."

She was quiet, sipping coffee and looking out over the dark toward the bay.

"But I guess I have to go after the best clue. The girl

driving the van. I'm going to go pick up the drawing from Mary Elizabeth and see if I can find her. Hopefully, she won't be with the man."

"How are you going to do that? She knows you. Maybe I should do what needs to be done."

"Probably not a good idea. You saw what happened to me. Besides, you'd have to visit a topless club or two. In fact, I just decided. I'm going to call Rocky and see if he can do it."

"Good idea."

The sun was coming up.

"Let's go," I said. "You should probably put on some pants."

"I guess the excitement of a new romance has faded."

She went inside. Joshua came out of the workshop and I waved my coffee cup at him and pointed toward the house. He nodded and walked toward me.

"I should be able to finish wiring the gate today. I have an idea about the boardwalk. I'll get it wired, too."

"You need any money?"

"Maybe not. Can I use the shop's credit card if necessary?"

"Sure. And, I've been thinking. You're doing great work, but why don't you put some of that portable fencing up and borrow five or six goats from the ladies next door? There's not a better intrusion alarm in the world."

He nodded at that. "Good idea. I'll ask to borrow some noisy ones. Should be fun getting them over here."

Patricia was ready. Preacher, up and drinking a Dr Pepper, wanted to go. Joshua joined us in my borrowed car, and the four of us drove down the driveway toward the gate. I thought about the fact that the bad guys had my address. I made plans accordingly. Joshua jumped out at the gate.

I rolled down the window and said, "Joshua, the guys who beat me up know my address. You be careful. If somebody shows up, you hide. If for some reason you can't hide, you just work here and you know nothing. Keep the gate locked."

He saluted.

Joshua unlocked and opened the gate for us. I turned right onto the highway.

"Where are we going?" Preacher asked. "Aren't we going to get the drawing from the ladies?"

"Yes, but we're on high alert. He has my address. If he's really trying to find Mina, he may be watching and trying to follow. We're going to take the long way. It'll take us an hour or so to cut back across the mainland, but it will give us a chance to watch our back and lose anybody trying to follow."

Preacher, in the back seat, swung his legs up and leaned against the door, turning to watch behind us. I watched for anybody parked in any of the little roads cutting through to the beach and bay. I decided to trade cars again. If I did that as much as possible, maybe it would be safer.

Patricia called Mary Elizabeth and told her to expect us in an hour or so. Preacher kept a vigilant watch to our rear. My brain was on overload trying to watch for the enemy while thinking about the best way to find the lady in the pink satin jacket and more confounding, what to do if I did find her.

I called Rocky.

"Hey, Rocky. Do you have the time to do a job? I need to try to find a topless dancer or get a lead on her if she's no longer dancing."

"Sure. What do we know?"

"What we know is that she may be wearing a pink satin

jacket from that topless place, the Pink Cocktail. Three of us have seen her and I'm headed to pick up a sketch of what she looks like."

"Okay. At least we have a place to get started. Where do I get a copy of the sketch?"

"Meet me at room five-oh-five at the Gulf Grand in about an hour, but call me on my cell and make sure I'm there before you go to the room."

"Okay. An hour. I'll see you then."

"Okay, and hey, Rocky?"

"Yeah?"

"Genevieve did a great job. She deserves a bonus."

"You pay extra. I'll make sure she gets it."

There were no cars directly behind us as we stopped to pay the toll at the bridge over the San Luis Pass. We drove the length of Follets Island and over the bridge to the mainland at the Intracoastal Waterway seeing nothing suspicious. I took some small roads through fields of cattle and a few light industrial areas. I drove us through the Brazoria Wildlife Refuge. For long stretches, there were no vehicles at all behind us.

At the town of Hitchcock, I was sure nobody was following us and got on Highway 6. It merges with Interstate 45 on the way to Galveston Island.

I stopped at Larry Peter's car lot. He wasn't there, but the guy who worked for him was willing to call him at home. Larry told him I could trade the vehicle I was driving for anything without a pending sale.

He had a white Honda Accord in good shape that was perfect. When I took the mandatory class to get a license to carry a concealed weapon, the instructor was an intense man. He taught that using a deadly weapon in self-defense should be the last resort. He preached the benefits of living a stealth lifestyle. He told the class that the Honda Accord was the most popular car in the country and white the most popular color. Drive it for the most anonymity, he said. And don't adorn it with any kind of bumper sticker. Laminate any mandatory parking stickers and stick them on the windshield only when necessary. Don't get personalized tags. He had lots of advice. At the time I was amused and considered him somewhat nutty. He no longer seemed so nutty.

I drove stealthily into Galveston. I hoped changing cars was overkill, but it couldn't hurt to take an extreme approach in every way I could.

I didn't want Patricia to be seen with either Preacher or me. The bad guys had not seen her. I dropped her right at the front door of the hotel while Preacher hunkered down in the back seat. I was sure we weren't being followed, but I felt better about doing that than letting her walk even a couple of blocks in public.

I dropped Preacher off a couple of blocks away at a convenience store and told him to be watchful without appearing strange as he walked back to the hotel.

I drove four blocks away, parked, and walked back to the hotel, going in a back door from the parking lot. The lobby was quiet, and the hallway with the elevators was empty.

Paranoia was exhausting.

I called on the way up. Mary Elizabeth opened the door to their room when I knocked. Preacher was sitting on the edge of the bed in animated conversation with Mina looking through a drawing pad with her. Patricia was leaning against the window.

"Do you have a drawing of the driver?" I asked.

"Yes. I have the best she could do. It is a profile. I don't know if it will help much." She spread a sheet of drawing paper on a table. It had few details, but I could tell it was the lady I'd seen whip around in surprise when I pushed her out of the way before I was yanked from behind.

Mina looked at us. I nodded at her. "I agree. Good job. It's the same lady I saw." Mina nodded once, smiling grimly, her eyes red-rimmed from crying.

"Will it help?" Mary Elizabeth asked.

Quietly, I said, "I don't know. I saw her. I don't know if anybody else can identify her. Let's try something. This is a good profile. Can you try drawing what she might look like face on? Maybe I can help. I did see her for a moment."

"I'll try." We sat down at the table. She turned to a fresh page in a drawing pad. She studied the profile and sketched the outline of a face.

"Her cheeks are a little fuller, but she had a pointy little chin. I think." She nodded and with strokes of her pencil made changes to the outline of the face.

I closed my eyes and tried to picture the lady. Her mouth had been opening, and she made a yelp as I shoved her. I thought about her and made some suggestions. Maybe her eyes were a little farther apart and her nose a little smaller. We were at it for a while until we had what I considered the best possible picture.

"I think that's it, Sam." I was surprised at Preacher standing close, peering over my shoulder. Mina, next to him, nodded her agreement.

"Well," I said, "I think it is the best we're going to get. We'll go with it."

Mary Elizabeth asked, "What are you going to do with it?"

My phone rang. "That's probably our private investigator now."

It was. In a few minutes, he was in the room. I gave him the sketch and walked him back to the elevator impressing on him just how viciously we'd been assaulted and implored him to not attract any attention.

"The best way to get info from dancers, bartenders, and bouncers is with cash. That's okay, right?"

"Yes. Spend what you need to spend. Put it on the bill."

"Oh, I will. I told Jenny what you said. She stuck it out, didn't she?"

"Yes."

"I told her I was going to go look for a dancer and she offered to go undercover as a dancer if needed."

I laughed.

He said, "My wife would shoot me. We're not going to try that."

"I don't think that will be necessary."

"But if we have to, she can be a waitress."

"I wouldn't want her close to these guys. You need to be careful, too."

"Discretion can take longer. Do we have an operational time frame?"

"I'm getting the license plate info off the van they drove. We've got a photo of the guy from the jetty. We have other threads to follow. On top of it all, we have a scared girl in considerable danger. We need to move as fast as we can without getting killed."

"Okay. All due haste. I'll get on it tonight. Saturday will make it nicely crowded and a lot of dancers will be working. Plenty of people to give your money to."

"Thanks. Just so you know, I've got a trial that might last two or three days starting Wednesday. I might be hard to reach during the day. I'll check in here and with Patricia for messages. If you need to call here, the room is in the name of Joshua Slocum." I gave him Patricia's cell phone number.

He left with a salute and an "Aye, aye, Captain Slocum."

Patricia decided to spend the night with Mary Elizabeth and Mina. Preacher went to my house with me.

Exhausted, I went to bed early that night and slept and dreamed and woke to haunted visions of Zoio, so small, so vulnerable, rising half out of her seat with a look of confusion and fear, starting toward me in that van. I started to picture what might be happening to her at that very moment. I shoved that vision back into the dark.

Sunday morning, I resisted the urge to call Rocky. I knew he would get any information to me as fast as possible. I made breakfast for Preacher, Joshua, and myself. Joshua had completed the wiring for an alarm on the gate and was doing something out on the boardwalk to put an alarm there.

I rested and treated my still aching body to a couple of hot showers. Joanne called. She and Maude brought over a pot of their homemade chicken soup with goat cheese. I talked to Patricia on the phone a couple of times. At the hotel they were mostly watching television. I could tell from our conversation that she was running interference between an anxious Mary Elizabeth and me.

In the afternoon, I pulled out my client files for Dr. Enrique Espoza, whose hearing in family court was scheduled the coming Wednesday.

Preacher, Joshua, and I fished off the pier that night and didn't talk much.

I couldn't resist and called Rocky on Monday. He reported he was going to make inquiries at some more topless clubs that afternoon. He said he got one maybe recognition from a bartender on Saturday. There are hierarchies in the topless dancing world. Dancers of a certain age who are determined to keep dancing eventually move from the crowded evenings where they can make the big bucks to slower afternoon shifts. Rocky was going to work the afternoon shift.

Joshua finished up the alarm systems incorporating a direct contact switch, an electric eye beam, and a pressure switch at the front gate. He had taken up two six foot sections of the boards on the boardwalk and remounted them on springs that would activate pressure switches. He liked to tinker and had everything wired into two boxes, one in the shop and one in the house. One or both would sound an alarm. It made different sounds depending on whether it was coming from the gate or the boardwalk. Everything was wired into a transformer in the shop, and the transformer was backed up by a couple of marine batteries. I increased Joshua's Christmas bonus in my head.

He backed up his elaborate alarm system by erecting portable fence sections around a shallow stock tank filled with water and a feed trough. At some cost to his dignity, he moved several of the goats from next door into the enclosure. Maude pointed out the ones she thought were most vocal. They made significant noise while he was getting them into their temporary home and would undoubtedly wake up anybody in the house if a visitor walked up at night. My two lawn mowing goats, Briggs and Stratton, joined in the cacophony.

On Monday night, I had dinner at the hotel with the ladies. Patricia and I agreed she would drive to my place on Thursday afternoon, when my court hearing should be over, and we would have some time alone. Rocky kept working.

On Tuesday I met with my client Dr. Espoza to prepare for his hearing. He wanted to take his kids home to his parents' place in Brazil during the summer and his ex-wife had filed to stop him. The man makes a million dollars a year doing plastic surgery in Houston, owns a huge house, a boat, and has a very attractive young girlfriend. His ex claimed there was a big risk he would not return the children to the states. I thought her complaint was mainly about that attractive young girlfriend getting to enjoy the boat. I expected to win in court. As irritating as it was to have to spend the time in a courtroom, at least I was being well paid.

The hearing began Wednesday afternoon and carried over to Thursday as the wife's lawyer put two or three witnesses on the stand talking about things we'd already covered. Judge Wilson is easy going and gave them all the time they wanted. The wife's lawyer tried to introduce a letter from the children's pediatrician asserting it would be emotionally bad for them to leave the country. It was bogus, and the pediatrician didn't show up in court so it went out on a hearsay objection.

Late in the morning on Thursday, we got started again. I started putting on our case shortly before lunch. I finished by four in the afternoon. After we spent about forty-five minutes on the hard benches in the courtroom, the judge decided in our favor. Dr. Espoza was free to take his kids to visit their grandparents.

I had messages from Patricia and Rocky on my phone. I had several excited messages from Mary Elizabeth. In his message, Rocky said he had some good information. I called him and left a message on his voice mail. I called Patricia. She'd taken a break from the hotel and gone to my house.

Rocky called and said, "I think I found her. I got word

she's dancing the afternoon shift at a place called Bucks and Bunnies on the south freeway. I think her name is Charlene Coster, but she dances under the name Dee Dee. That's a name I got from a bartender and a dancer who saw the drawing. The dancer said Dee Dee is dancing at Bucks. I went down there but didn't see her. I asked a dancer if Dee Dee was there today and she said she hadn't seen her. I didn't want to press. I wasn't sure what you'd want to do."

"Okay. I'm done here. Let's plan on going there tomorrow afternoon. I'll be thinking about what I want to do if she's there and if it is her."

Patricia called me back. "Sam, I keep calling the hotel and Mary Elizabeth's cell, but she's not answering. I'm worried."

"Let me call the hotel. Maybe they went to eat or something."

I tried the hotel but got nothing. Cecilia had left work. I called the concierge, but he was good and followed his instructions regarding the privacy of the guests in room 505. He would give me absolutely no information about the room or its occupants.

I picked up Patricia and we drove as quickly as possible to the hotel. She kept trying to get Mary Elizabeth on the phone. We used Patricia's key card to find the room empty.

"Oh my God, Sam. Where is she? What do we do?"

"I don't know. Maybe they're downstairs or something."

"No. She has been so good about staying here."

"Is all their stuff here?"

We looked around. Clothes were in the dresser. The television was on.

Patricia finally noticed and said, "The drawing pads are gone. That's the only thing not here. Sam, I'm scared.

What's going on?"

I shook my head and sat on the bed. "I have no idea. Maybe they're just out on the Seawall drawing."

"No. She would have told us. I know she would have."

A cold thought wrapped a tight grip around me. Rocky had called her trying to leave me a message. What if he'd told her what he'd discovered? Mary Elizabeth had been acting more and more skittish. More anxious. More excited about wanting to do something. She'd left me several messages about Rocky calling. What if she'd gone to see Dee Dee herself. But surely she would not have taken Mina.

I called Rocky.

"What's up Sam?"

"When you left a message with Mary Elizabeth for me at the hotel, did you tell her where to find Dee Dee?"

"Yeah, is that a problem? She kept pressing and pressing. I wanted to assure her that you and I were on the job and knew what we were doing. Surely she didn't try to find her?"

"I don't know. She and the girl are not here at the hotel. I have no idea where she is."

"Damn. I'm supposed to be staking out a wayward wife tonight, but this could be bad. Do you want me to go back to Bucks? See if I can find out anything?"

"Yes. I think we have to. I'll call you if she shows up, but if she went there we need to know."

"Okay. I'll get Genevieve to cover the cheating wife. She can probably handle it. Damn."

"Yeah."

Should I call the police? I still had client confidences to keep if she and Mina were just out walking. If she was missing, she'd been gone less than half a day. The cops would not get too excited about that, even with our disjointed story. Their focus would be on all of us for taking things into our own hands. Not that I would care, but I didn't expect any positive action. Not yet. As hard as it was, we needed to wait. See if Rocky learned anything. See if she showed up.

While I was on the phone with Rocky, Patricia tried her cell.

"Sam," she said, "it went straight to voicemail."

"Maybe her battery ran down."

"I'm scared. We have to do something."

I paced, pretending to think. Preacher called me from Clara's Cafe.

"Preacher, are Mary Elizabeth and Mina with you?"

"No. I was calling to find out what we're going to do next. I tried her cell, but it didn't work so I called you. What's up? You can't find her?"

"No. Patricia and I are at the hotel, but they're not here. I'm getting worried because Rocky left a message about where we could probably find that lady driving the van. I'm afraid Mary Elizabeth might have tried to take matters into her own hands."

"But, not with Mina, surely."

"I know. Maybe she stashed her. Rocky got a line on where the lady was dancing. He went there but didn't see the dancer. I hoped she wasn't there if Mary Elizabeth went looking for her."

"What are we going to do?"

"I have no idea. We need to find her. That's the bottom line."

"Let me find a ride, and I'll meet you at the hotel."

"I'll leave a message for you at the desk if we leave for any reason."

But we had no place to go. I was hoping the only

necessary thing to do was to sit there and wait for Mary Elizabeth to show up. But I couldn't risk it. There was too much at risk. I had to call the police. There was one call I had to make first, though.

I called the concierge and convinced him to call Cecelia Harrigan at home and have her call me in the room. He did and she did.

"Hello, this is Cecelia Harrigan, is there a problem?"

"Ms. Harrigan, my client has disappeared from the room and I have no choice but to call the police."

"Of course, I understand." She sounded most professional. "I will be in my office in fifteen minutes just in case I'm needed. Thank you for calling."

It took longer than fifteen minutes to get law enforcement interested. As I predicted, Galveston Police wanted me to call back after she'd been missing twenty-four hours. I explained the unique things about this case, two missing girls, trafficking, assault. Finally, the voice on the phone told me to stay in the room and somebody would be there. Eventually.

I made another call. The voice on the phone at the FBI got more interested when I mentioned the girls being brought in as prostitutes, but ended up saying my message would be passed along to the trafficking task force, but the agency would most likely await the call of local law enforcement.

While I made those calls, Patricia called Jason to let him know what was going on. I could hear her absorbing his call, shielding me from a very angry conversation he wanted to have with me. She told him to email the best photo of Mary Elizabeth he could find. I had prints of the photos we'd made of Mina.

Cecelia called to say she was in her office if needed. She

agreed to print several copies of the photo Jason was sending.

Preacher arrived. I sent Patricia to hang out in the lobby, just in case. If we were overreacting and Mary Elizabeth and Mina showed up while police were in the room, she could intercept and have her call instead of show up. That way we might still be able to protect Mina from being taken into protective custody by the government.

She did not show up by the time the Galveston Police arrived, two uniform officers followed by a Detective.

CHAPTER FIFTEEN

As Mary Elizabeth's attorney, I told Detective Anthony Monroe that Sister Mary Elizabeth, a nun and social worker, and Preacher, a minister, had tried to find and save a girl from Ukraine, Zoio Verenka, who had arrived in this country illegally.

Mary Elizabeth learned somehow the girl would be on a van marked "Church of Hope." I said Preacher tried to take the girl off the van and was beat for his trouble. In response to their questions, I told them, yes, Preacher, had reported the event to the police.

I told them Mary Elizabeth went to law enforcement but had not found anyone who could help her.

I said that Mary Elizabeth had information that a Charlene Coster, who danced at Bucks and Bunnies, might have been driving the van. I said that perhaps she went there to talk to Coster, but I didn't know for sure. I gave them the license plate number Preacher had seen on the van.

I parried questions. I didn't have a lot more to help them except a hazy photograph of a man on the jetty who might or might not be involved. I held back on that. I didn't think it would help and having it would create a lot of very distracting knots. Rocky had a copy and was going to his sources in law enforcement to see if anybody recognized the man.

I gave them the photos of Mina and Mary Elizabeth. In response to a question, I told Detective Monroe that, given the circumstances, I thought broadcasting an Amber Alert for Mina would be dangerous. He told me they, the officials, would make that decision.

Preacher confirmed what I had said. Eventually, Detective Monroe chased us out of the room telling us to stay close in case more questions arose. I gave him my cell phone and told him to call me if more questions arose.

On the way out, I stopped by Cecilia's office. "Thanks," I told her, "for everything you've done. I apologize for this mess."

She shook her head. "It's not your fault. I just hope your client is okay."

I nodded. "I told them I'd booked the room, so if it comes up with the police or your bosses, I don't have a problem with you confirming that."

"It won't be a problem." She didn't get up from behind her desk, but she said, "Call me when you get a chance."

I nodded and left to collect the others. We drove back to my place.

It was quiet there. We talked about things, but had nothing to say. Patricia called Jason telling him we knew nothing new and I was not available. I was dealing with the police. I knew Jason was livid with my betrayal of the plan he thought we'd had.

The afternoon passed. Eventually, we went to bed.

Around noon the next day, they found Mary Elizabeth's body washed ashore on East Beach, right by the south jetty.

CHAPTER SIXTEEN

I GOT THE CALL FROM DETECTIVE MONROE. He told me they'd found her and to come see him. Somebody had to officially identify the body. I left Patricia and Preacher clinging to each other in tears. I met Monroe and identified Mary Elizabeth from a photograph of her from the shoulders up laying on a steel table. The sea and its creatures are quick to consume things within its embrace, but I could officially confirm it was her. The weight of her death was heavier than anything I'd ever experienced.

Detective Monroe asked me more questions. I assured him that Preacher was with me all afternoon. I guess that did one of two things. It alibied Preacher or made the two of us joint suspects. He let me in on one important piece of information. I think he wanted to watch my reaction and, perhaps, shake my confidence in Preacher. The license plate Preacher reported was not stolen. It belonged on a van owned by the Church of Hope in Chambers County. The Leon County Sheriff failed to share that with me when he'd called.

I asked about the van. Monroe said, "The Church of Hope is not well-organized. They canceled their youth outreach program. Probably because the church has no youth. The van was donated to the church. The preacher thought the van was parked in a lot behind one of his parishioner's business, a junk dealer. The junk dealer's lot is not fenced. He said he had no idea the van was missing. So far, I believe him."

I drove back to my house. Patricia had talked to Jason. She told me I should not call him until later.

We were sitting around the house that evening watching the news. It cut to a reporter standing on East Beach I turned up the sound thinking it would be another report on Mary Elizabeth's death.

The reporter said, "Another body was discovered here on the beach this afternoon just a few miles from where the body of Mary Kincaid was discovered this morning. The remains have been identified as Charlene Coster, a resident of Houston. Officials are not saying whether they think her death is related to the death of Kincaid. Coster has an arrest record for public indecency and prostitution."

The bad guy was cutting threads and covering his tracks. We did not have much time to find him, but I certainly intended to try.

The cops had a professional interest in finding the killer of Mary Elizabeth and Charlene Coster. I'm sure some of them had a personal outrage at anybody taking the life of another, but I had something else. I knew Mary Elizabeth Kincaid. I knew her unselfish compassion, her gentleness, and her overall goodness. I knew her quiet outrage at what was happening to Mina and Zoio and others like them. I'd come to share her frustration at the great weight of a complicated world in which an individual, victimized by a dark evil, can be lost.

Mary Elizabeth told me she constantly prayed to understand that world. I didn't understand the world, but I wanted to do something other than pray about it. I wanted to find the person who'd killed her.

I'd cried and there would be more tears, but on Saturday, the day after they found Mary Elizabeth and Charlene Coster, I refused to cry. Patricia got up with me. We woke Preacher when we went into the kitchen to make coffee. We all sat on the porch.

"What are we going to do?" Patricia asked.

"I plan to find that son of a bitch."

Preacher said, "Amen. How?"

"We try to follow any slim thread we have left. He's erasing them as fast as he can. I think he's getting ready to either run or lay low for a while. I'm sure if he can get to us he's going to erase us as well."

Patricia made a noise and grabbed my hand.

"That's why you're getting out of here. Let's face it, we don't know what he was able to find out from Mary Elizabeth before he killed her. He may know about you. You will get out of here."

"I want to stay with you."

I shook my head. "No. If worse comes to worst, you will need to be able to tell somebody what we were doing. We'll keep you posted."

Preacher said, "He's right. Besides two of us can move faster than three of us if we have to."

I looked at him. "One of us could move even faster."

"Forget it. No way."

I nodded. I knew he wouldn't agree, and I really did not want to be alone.

"Where am I going to go?" asked Patricia.

"You go back to Chicago with Mary Elizabeth. You go to her funeral. You find somebody you can trust absolutely, somebody not related to The Beacon. You get them to rent you a room, and you stay there incognito. I think it should be somewhere other than Chicago." She started to say something and I raised a hand to stop her. "You have to do this for me. I have to know you're safe. We will talk, but I don't even want to know exactly where you are."

A tear coursed down her cheek. "We'll talk about it later," she said. "I am afraid for you, too, you know."

"We need to be afraid. Fear will make us smarter. So far we have not been as smart as we should be."

She squeezed my hand and did not let go.

Preacher said, "Okay. What do we know? We know a little about his boat. We might know something about his truck. We know about the van they used and where they got it. We know about the man on the jetty. We know where the girl used to work. Do we go back to that strip club, try to find out more about her?"

"No. He's erased that connection. We can assume the police with their greater manpower are trying to find people connected to her. Maybe they'll get to him that way."

"I want him first."

"No. We don't. We have no idea what we'd do with him if we got him first. Other than turning him in."

Preacher looked like he wanted to say something more about what he'd do if we got to the guy, but he and I were not equipped to do anything other than turn him in.

"What are you thinking?"

"I think the van is gone, just like the girl. We have nothing on the man at the jetty other than a dark photograph. For all we know he is an innocent fisherman. If we run across him, great, but I cannot think of a way to find him. Rocky will get more information about him if it can be found. The only thread I can think of is the boat. He keeps it somewhere. We're going to go look for his hole."

Preacher nodded. "The plan?"

"Tedious. We travel all the way around East Bay and Trinity Bay in a boat. We video every single boathouse and dock. We video every structure that might have a place to hide that boat. If we see something, we find a way to check it out."

"I'm ready to go."

"We'll start in the morning. We'll pretend to be just a couple of guys fishing. Nothing we can do tonight. I'll call Rocky, see if he has a video camera I can mount on a boat. We'll cruise slowly by every structure and turn it on as we pass. That way we can study it in detail later. We'll record the GPS coordinates every time we turn on the camera, just in case we need to go back and look closer at something."

Patricia asked, "How long will it take you?"

"It is a long shoreline. It could take two or three days to make it all the way around. Then, when we don't find anything, I guess we'll do the same thing in Galveston Bay and West Bay. I'm pretty sure he's in the East Bay or Trinity, but, right now, I can't think of anything else to do."

"What about the girls," she asked.

"Our best bet is to get our hands on him. Let him make a deal with the powers that be to give up somebody up the chain. If he won't or doesn't have good info, or if we simply can't find him, then I'm going to Chicago and we'll see what we can do there. Can either of you think of something else we can do?"

Both shook their heads. We had very little string left to pull. He was aggressively covering his tracks. He had to be going into hiding. I felt less hope than on the day I first met Mary Elizabeth.

I called Rocky and asked him about a video camera to mount to the boat.

"I've got just the thing."

"I want to rent it for the next few days."

"Forget renting. In fact, you can forget getting any bill from me. I got those ladies killed, I want in on the hunt. In fact, I'll go with you to video."

"Thanks. It's not your fault, though. I know you know that, but I know how you feel. Preacher and I will make the video. The more crowded the boat the more it will attract attention. If you can think of something else to do, great, but right now I don't know what."

"I'll try to stay plugged in with the police. They're acting all pissed off at us right now, but they know we can do things they could not or would not do. I think I can find somebody who will keep me up to date on their investigation. The picture of the guy at the jetty is being passed around but so far, nobody recognizes him. I'll take it to the jetty and see if one of the regulars down there has seen him."

"Good idea."

We made arrangements to meet for me to get the camera.

I called Joshua and told him to stay away from my place until further notice.

I didn't want Patricia back at the Gulf Grand Hotel. I sat thinking, my fingers tapping a rhythm against the phone.

"What is it?" Patricia asked.

"We all need to go somewhere. You can't go back to the Gulf Grand. I'm thinking."

Preacher surprised me again. He said, "Don't you ever tell anybody, but I have a real California driver's license in another name. We can use it to get a room."

That's how I booked a cabin at the San Luis Pass County Park in the name of Caleb Tangley, the name on Preacher's second driver's license. It might even be his real name. We packed the car with stuff to take there. It was still daylight making it easier to watch for somebody following. I crossed the bridge and drove slow in the Saturday night traffic pulling into beach roads occasionally to let cars get past. I bought some tacos to go at Clara's and drove back toward the pass on the beach. We were not followed. The park is right on the tip of Folletts Island in the shadow of the toll bridge. I gave Preacher a wad of cash and he checked in. I left him and Patricia eating tacos in the cabin.

Back on Galveston Island, I stopped by my place and picked up my Mossberg Mariner shotgun and a box of shells. I called Benjamin Marsh at the Sol de Mer Marina and told him what I needed. By the time I got to the marina, he had one of the marina's center console fishing boats on a trailer behind one of the Sol de Mer pickup trucks.

When I took the shotgun out of the trunk and moved it to the boat Benjamin said, "Going fishing?"

I nodded, tossed him the keys to my borrowed car and said, "Watch my car. I'll be back in two or three days."

He nodded. "There's ice on board and frozen bait. You'll need to replenish the ice tomorrow."

I met Rocky in a parking lot, and we rigged the camera mount on the chrome bar over the windshield of the boat while he gave me instructions about using the camera. He gave me spare batteries, a battery charger, and an inverter, so I could use the charger with the boat battery. Mounted, the camera faced starboard. I could monitor what it captured on the screen of a laptop that fit in the boat's console. The small video camera nestled in next to the depth finder and GPS monitor. It looked, I hoped, like another piece of marine electronics. I drove back to the cabin where Preacher and Patricia were pretending to watch television.

We shot some video to try out the camera. "Cool," Preacher said.

"We'll motor past every structure on the bay and record the GPS coordinates every time we start the video. Hopefully, we'll see something, but we'll have the video to review if needed."

Patricia asked, "Can you upload it to the internet from the boat?"

"Occasionally. When we can get access. My cell phone will connect to the laptop and send data, and some of the places on the bay have Wi-Fi I can access. Good idea. We'll do it as we can. I'll send it to my Google drive, and you can start looking at it if you want. It will be deadly boring, but who knows, maybe you'll see something we miss." Besides, I thought, if we get ourselves killed the video might be a pretty good clue as to where and when and maybe by whom.

"Good. I won't feel so useless."

I removed the camera and all the other electronics from their mounts and handed them down to Preacher to take into the cabin. As he dumped it all on the kitchen counter he said, "The boat has one of those mosquito net cover things, right? I think I better sleep in the boat tonight just to be sure nobody steals anything."

"It does, but it will be safe enough."

"Shut up, Sam," Patricia said. "Thank you, Preacher. I'll have coffee for you early in the morning."

"Just let me grab a quick shower, and I'll get out of your way."

I was no dummy. I didn't argue. "We'll leave real early."

"I'll be ready."

As he showered Patricia put her arms around me. "As soon as he's out of here, you and I will take a shower. It's small, but we'll make do." We kissed. "I am nervous and scared and full of energy to get something done. I want to go with you."

"No. We might not always have cell service, and somebody needs to sit by a phone in case somebody calls. Besides, I like your idea of reviewing the video. You can get started doing that."

"I knew you'd say no. That's why I plan to dissipate some nervous energy in other ways. Unless you're too tired."

Preacher, freshly showered, took a couple of pillows off one of the beds and went outside to sleep. Patricia and I took a shower together. She was correct. It was small, but we didn't need much room.

After the shower, we didn't talk much. I think we humans have genetically programmed responses to great loss and tragedy. There was often laughter at funerals, a life-affirming reaction of those still alive. And there were physical urges that seemed out of place. Perhaps it was a prehistoric method of assuring life goes on following death. Or perhaps we achieved an emotional balance that kept us from going insane from sorrow by engaging in the ancient, soul-satisfying act between two people. I don't know why it happened but it happened that night and it was good.

Patricia and I fell naked into bed. We did not talk or laugh as much as we had in the past. Patricia pushed me flat and leaned over to kiss me, my lips, my neck, and down my chest. I felt the exquisite touch of her hair and breasts as she moved down my body. I pulled her hips to me, and we consumed each other with a fervor that had no room for words. Later, she swung a leg over me, took me in her hand and centered herself over me. We joined easily in slippery heat. She braced her hands on my chest.

My memory of her that night will always be her astride me, shiny with perspiration, her head thrown back, her eyes closed as she undulated in the instinctive rhythms until once again, we peaked. We slept naked and intertwined until the alarm on my phone sounded at five.

By the time I went outside, Preacher had stowed the mosquito netting and wiped condensation off the boat. Patricia made coffee and filled two thermoses for us. I put the electronics, including the video camera, in their brackets on the boat. I checked the charge on the boat's batteries, stowed a couple of gas cans, and did the other things necessary to get the boat ready for the water.

Others were stirring. I could hear the quiet sounds of people getting up and around, getting boats ready for a day of fishing. An old man and a rambunctious young girl carrying fishing rods walked past and greeted us quietly on the way to the park's fishing pier, a carefree counterpoint to our grim task.

A brisk breeze helped with the humidity. I flipped on the boats radio and tuned to the marine weather report. It was not expected to be too hot and no rain was in sight, a good thing for our plans to video. There was no moon. Pink and yellow rimmed the horizon to the east as we put the boat in the water.

Preacher held the boat at the launch while I parked the pickup back by the cabin. I put my arms around Patricia's waist and said, "Don't leave here. You have plenty of food. Walk up to that little store if you need something. I'm sorry if it gets boring, but I need to know you're here. I'll call and you can call. Just don't get worried if I don't answer, there are some cellular dead spots out there."

"I will be right here. You two be careful. And, Sam, if you see something, don't do anything dangerous, not today. Just find where he hides. Don't go knocking on his door."

"You got it." We kissed and I walked to where Preacher held the boat.

After a stop at the marina at Sol de Mer to fill the extra gas cans and for breakfast sandwiches, we made our way to where East Bay begins. Because the camera pointed to the right of the boat, I started on the Gulf side of the bay, going down the Intracoastal Waterway.

The Waterway is on the bay side of Bolivar Peninsula. There were no houses to our left. We cruised through each dredged out, back-water inlet with any kind of structure, videoing everything.

Using the GPS system I'd record the latitude and longitude at each place we started the camera. I didn't think there was any way our quarry would be holed up off the narrow Waterway, but we covered every inch. It took a while. There was less to video than there would have been a few years earlier. The last hurricane destroyed a lot of houses on Bolivar Peninsula that had not been rebuilt.

It took a while, but we traveled the length of the East Bay in the Waterway. We passed Rollover Pass and motored through a few of the canals lined with houses off the Waterway beyond the end of the Bay, even though I didn't think it likely he'd be that far down.

I could have kept going to Louisiana, but after we surveyed a few of those canals off the Intracoastal, I turned back toward the bay. We saw nothing I considered likely housing for the boat we sought. I noted a couple of boathouses that looked large enough, but they were in populated areas.

As cover, we trailed fishing lines as we motored slowly through the canals. We caught four speckled trout and put a couple in the iced down fish box. I talked to Patricia a few times throughout the morning reporting our lack of progress.

We went to the Stingaree Marina for lunch. I tapped into their Wi-Fi and uploaded the videos we'd made to my storage space on Google. I sent Patricia an email giving her access and invited her to start looking to see if she could see anything of interest.

It took a while for the videos to upload. When the

upload finished, Preacher and I loaded up, left the Waterway, and headed across the bay to continue our search on its north side. A lot of that side of the bay is part of two wildlife refuges and there are no houses there, but there are several other places with houses, some isolated and others in groups.

People with a place on the north side of East Bay are not there for the view. There is no real beach and few amenities. I was sure several of the owners of houses we motored by and captured on our camera want to be left alone. I believed if he was hiding out on East Bay, he would be somewhere on the north side. But we saw nothing particularly suspicious.

There were a few enclosed boat houses big enough to hold his boat and I noted their locations, but I felt like I was grasping at straws. There were more inlets and cuts into shore than I'd ever noticed. Some were navigable and we cruised up them, flipping on the camera at every structure.

We saw a man pulling his boat up a makeshift boat ramp on a graveled beach in one of those many remote inlets. Perhaps I'd been wrong about him not putting it on a trailer. With an enclosed trailer, he could park almost anywhere. Mina, and the girls smuggled in with her, were taken off the boat in the dark and put straight into a room without windows. Maybe the boat motored away and pulled out of the water. Maybe our search was more hopeless than I'd been thinking.

We boxed another couple of fish before we reached Smith Point. That's where the East Bay ends and Trinity Bay starts. The Trinity shoreline stretches way north. Seeing the expanse of water reaching to the horizon of Trinity Bay added weight to my sense of futility.

"It's big, isn't it?" Preacher said.

"Yes."

"Do you think we've seen his place?"

"No."

"Do you think we will."

"No."

"What are we going to do?"

"I have no idea. But we're done for the day. I'm bug-eyed, hungry, and depressed. Let's get back to the cabin."

"Are we giving up on this plan?"

"No. It's the only plan we have. We'll do Trinity Bay tomorrow."

"And then?"

"Preacher, I have no idea. Something."

"We're going to get him. I know it."

I made a noise, shoved the throttles forward and swung hard to the west, running flat out toward our hide out at San Luis Pass. The bad guy was winning.

Back at the cabin, while Preacher showered, Patricia joined me as I cleaned the fish we'd caught.

"I watched all the video you sent, some of it more than once. Do you think there's something there?"

"No. If there is, I didn't see it."

"Are you going to keep trying?"

"Yes. There's nothing else to do. Unless somebody has a better idea."

"I'll watch them all again."

She rubbed my shoulders and hugged me from behind. I tossed fish guts into the water, and we walked back to the cabin. I fell asleep within ten minutes of getting out of the shower. It was not a dreamless sleep. I still felt the rocking of the boat.

CHAPTER SEVENTEEN

PREACHER AND I LEFT a somber Patricia and headed toward Trinity Bay. I thought about our quarry. We were after the man with cinnamon on his breath who had so soundly intervened when we tried to save Zoio. He beat Preacher and me senseless that night with single-minded purpose. Perhaps he was hiding. Perhaps he was lying low or getting ready to run, but if we were successful and our paths crossed, he would want to correct his earlier mistake. He would want to erase us.

We stopped at Sol de Mer to top off our fuel tanks and get something to eat. I didn't try to be efficient with our fuel, running the boat flat out toward Trinity Bay. Preacher stood beside me, hanging on to the console's handrail. He leaned over to be heard over the sound of the wind and the engines.

"I can't tell if you're getting more determined or more discouraged."

"Both I guess."

"Have faith."

I just shook my head.

"The police are on it," he said, "and we're on it. He'll be found."

"He might not be. He killed the girl who was working with him. We don't know his name or what he looks like. He obviously has no problems cutting connections. There are lots of ways he can disappear."

"Somebody somewhere knows him and what he does. You keep saying we're chasing threads. There are more threads out there. We'll find some more."

I looked at him and shrugged.

"Sam, it may take a lot longer than we want, but if the cops don't catch him, I know you won't quit and eventually you will find him. And you'll find the girls. No matter how long it takes. I want you to know I'm with you brother. Whatever it takes, whatever you have to do."

I nodded and pushed at the throttles. They had nothing else to give and neither did the day. We did the same thing as the day before, only over a longer shoreline. We videoed every house and boat house we could see. There were more isolated, ramshackle houses than I'd ever noticed. There were small bayous and channels I'd never noticed before. There were dirt roads running to gravel beaches where a man could easily drop and recover a boat.

Our search from the water only scratched the surface. I looked for signs in the slow-moving inlets for room to move the type of boat he had. I looked closely for tire tracks at places a vehicle could drive up to the bay with a trailer large enough to handle his boat.

We caught a few more fish that day, but we didn't finish our video survey. We quit before we got to the more populated side of the bay. Before the sun completely set, Preacher and I went back to our cabin on San Luis Pass. Patricia came with Preacher when he brought the truck and boat trailer to the ramp. She stayed with me as I cleaned the fish.

"Sam, Mary Elizabeth is being flown back to Chicago the day after tomorrow. I'm going on the plane to be with her and to be there for the funeral. I know you said you are not going, but I have to go."

"Yes. You do. I would go, but I know the man who killed her is getting ready to run or crawl into a hole. I'm going to stay here and keep doing what we're doing. Listen.

We don't know what he might have been able to get Mary Elizabeth to tell him or what he's been able to find out on his own. We don't know what the slimeballs in Chicago know. You keep being very careful. Don't go to the Beacon. Stay somewhere safe. In fact, I still think that after the funeral you ought to go somewhere other than here. Stay incognito with family or something."

"I will be careful, but I will be coming back here as soon as possible. We are not going to argue about that. How long are you going to stay here, in this cabin?"

"I don't know. I feel pretty safe here. It's easy for us to get around on the bays from here."

That night, I relaxed as much as I could with my mind constantly searching for a new idea. I grilled our fish. After dinner, I drove Preacher to his church. We were vigilant about not being seen. He'd posted a notice on the door of the church that there would be no services until further notice and that members of his church should go do some good works.

He has a mail slot where members of his congregation can leave him notes. There were a few there, people in need of food and an invitation to go surfing in Mexico. He insisted he had to go check on the hungry folks. He called the young lady serving as his assistant pastor of the moment to have her come pick him up. He disappeared into the church and returned with a wad of cash to buy some food. Some time ago I quit wondering about such things as where he gets money when necessary.

"You watch out Preacher. I don't want him seeing you and I really don't want him following you back to me."

"Don't worry. I know how to be careful. You get back and take care of Patricia. I'll be at the bait shop at the park in the morning ready to go when you are."

I left him there at his ramshackle church. I did take care of Patricia that night and she took care of me. Preacher was at the bait shop before sunrise the next day.

WE COMPLETED THE VIDEO SURVEY of Trinity Bay that day. We didn't keep any of the fish we caught. We made our video. We studied the shore, and we saw some possibilities, but I found myself discounting each one for one reason or another, usually the proximity of other houses.

We headed back toward San Luis Pass shortly after the peak high tide that evening. There was a cooling wind. Our boat split the smooth surface of the bay. Clouds to the west were entering a sunset glow. I wondered if I would ever again be able to completely enjoy such a gorgeous day, having now experienced the darkness beneath the serenity.

"You look dispirited," Preacher said.

"Yes. I don't think we found a thing. I don't know what to do next."

"Remember. You've said before that finding nothing teaches us something. We can get something out of this."

"I don't know what. The only thing I learned is there are a lot of crappy little houses on the bay and way more channels and bayous and canals creeping inland than I'd ever realized."

"See. That's something. Maybe we just learned we have more work to do, more places to look. Would it help to look from a car?"

"I don't know. Maybe. I think we're running out of time. So far he's safe. He's killing to make sure he stays that way. He's getting ready to hide deep or run. We may not catch up. He may already be gone."

"Maybe we should go to Chicago. Look for the girls."

I shook my head. "And start where? If the bad guys are

half smart, the girls are somewhere other than Chicago. I'm sure we haven't looked everywhere possible right here where we live. It's a whole lot less crowded here than on city streets somewhere, especially a city we do not know."

"Maybe we could put up some fliers, offer a reward for information."

"Yeah, I've thought about that. We could say an attorney is seeking a possible witness to an accident. I'm afraid that would just drive him deeper underground or chase him out of our area faster."

"Do you think he'd leave? He's got to be making a lot of money taking all these risks."

"I think he'll stay if he can find you and me and kill us. A reward poster will give him incentive to do that. Besides, I have no idea what his thoughts are on risk and reward. There are tons of other places on the coast he can set up his operation. Maybe he's not worried. As far as I can tell we're not real close to finding him. Coster was our best chance, and she's dead."

He was wily. All he'd failed to take into account was the memory of a very scared girl and the tenaciousness of a very obsessed nun. He'd solved those problems, too.

"I guess," I said, "we'll go back and watch all our video again. List the places we have to go look at closer."

I thought about all those channels, dirt roads, and hard packed shore that might give him a way to pull his boat out. We should have made a list of all those places, so we could give them a second look. Maybe we'd have to make another trip around the bay and look at those places closer. But even if we charted every such place, it got us nothing unless he just happened to be there when we came by.

"What about the guy on the jetty?" Preacher asked. "Maybe we should just sit and wait for him and follow him."

"Every night? Forever?"

"If we have to. You said the girl was our best connection, and she's gone. Maybe he'll be easier to find than this guy's hideout."

"Maybe."

We didn't talk much more on the way back to where we were staying. It was too difficult to talk over the engines and the wind. Besides, we didn't have a whole lot to say.

Patricia had food waiting. She was leaving the next afternoon to fly to Chicago on the same plane as Mary Elizabeth's body. The gloom that night was expansive. We ate quietly.

After dinner, we gathered around the computer to watch, once again, our video. I had a legal pad to make notes, a chart of the bays, and a map showing the coast around the bays. We started at the beginning. Every structure got a rating of one to four. A four meant not a possibility. A one meant closer to a possibility than most others. A two deserved a second look, and a three was not a definite no, but almost. We wrote the ratings on my legal pad, along with GPS locations, and we annotated the maps. I marked even the fours. It made me concentrate on the mind-numbing, probably futile effort to look one more time at our video.

I also marked all the channels I noticed leading inland from the bays. I knew we'd have to check them out better than we had. We'd taken the boat up only a few of the largest. More of them would accommodate a boat with a shallow draft. If he was pulling his boat out, we'd be looking for one accessed by a remote road. It would take us a long time to track down all those remote roads, but doing so had to be part of our search. That thought finally led me to a new idea.

Rocky is a pilot. He has an airplane. I called him.

"Hey, Sam. Anything?"

"No. But I have my next idea. You can help."

"How's that?"

"Can you shoot good video from your airplane?"

"Yep. I have a strut mount for the camera. I can watch and record on the laptop in the cabin. I've used it a few times looking for things. If I fly slow and low it is remarkably steady and clear. What are we after?"

"I need you to video the entire shoreline of East Bay and Trinity Bay. Low and slow is exactly what I need." I explained to him I wanted to be able to view an aerial view of what we had from the water and more importantly, I wanted to try and find the out of the way places a boat might be launched and retrieved. I told him I was grasping at straws, but straws were all we had.

"Got it," he said. "Jenny and I will do it tomorrow. She's learning to fly and will love the time while I handle the camera duties."

"Feel free to send me a bill for your time and your expenses."

"Nope. Told you. I'm a part of this. It's on me. I want to catch the bastard."

"Okay, thanks. I'll be taking Patricia to the airport tomorrow afternoon. Maybe we can get together after that."

"Just give me a call."

"Now, see," Preacher said after I hung up, "I told you the next idea would come to you. Good idea."

I shook my head. "Not really, but it's something."

I turned back to annotating my maps and notes from our video. Eventually, Patricia went to bed. When I caught myself having to rewind too much, I called it a night. Preacher sacked out on the sofa and I fell dead to sleep next to Patricia.

In the morning I drove to my place to check on it and pick up a few things Patricia had left there. Joshua's alarm system was in place and working. He was there feeding the goats and cleaning up their temporary pen. I decided to keep the goats for a while longer. I told Joshua not to dawdle and to not hang around too long. He came by boat in the morning and evening to check on the goats. He was careful. His shotgun leaned against the porch.

I felt reasonably comfortable and secure at the park. I gave Preacher some more money and told him to book us another three nights. I drove Patricia to Hobby Airport for her flight to Chicago. We ate lunch at the airport. I left her as she entered security.

I drove back to Galveston during the insane Houston rush hour. Finally, breaking free of the bumper to bumper traffic, I called Rocky. He had the video. We met, and he gave me a DVD, telling me he'd kept a copy and that Jenny was intently scouring it looking for anything. We talked only briefly. There wasn't much to say. Back at the cabin, I found Preacher once again looking at the videos we'd taken on the bay.

I stuck the DVD in the laptop, and we started reviewing the aerial video. It was excellent. They flew low and slow, with very little vibration marring the image. I realized I'd been admiring his video more than studying it and started it over. As I'd asked, he duplicated our route starting at the Intracoastal Waterway and working his way down Bolivar Peninsula on the Gulf side of the bay. They flew a little farther up the Waterway than we'd gone and then gone on to the other side of the bay.

Preacher and I watched the video intently. I tried to concentrate on the structures we'd videoed from the boat. I thought I'd go through it a second time and look at all those channels and roads we had not concentrated on. Not having anything specific to look for made it feel hopeless. In the end, it was easier than expected. What I thought hopeless, was not.

On the video, we were making our way down the north side of the bay flying west. We could see the houses and docks and boathouses on the bay. The aerial view highlighted the desolation of parts of that shoreline. In expanses of nothing, an isolated dirt track often led to a house or group of houses. Most had access to the bay by a pier or dock. A few sported a boat house out over the water. A few had buildings on shore that could hold a boat.

I almost let it past before it caught my eye.

"Wait," I said, "let me back up the video."

"What? What are you seeing?"

I looked closely at a structure out over the water. Square in shape it was built of dark, weathered wood. I froze the video. Given the perspective of our view, it was hard to tell, but it looked like two adjacent and covered shelters connected together. The connecting middle part is what caught my attention. A narrow part of the roof in the middle was lighter than the two sides. The wood was newer, not yet weathered.

"Look at that," I said. "Something has been added there. It looks like two smaller boat shelters have been joined together. That gives a larger covered space. I wonder why somebody did that."

"You're thinking in order to hide his larger boat?"

"Maybe. Could be. Or maybe he just repaired the roof or something. I'm grasping at straws, but at least it is something different. And look." I tapped the screen. "Here's a larger shed or whatever just on shore. Perhaps it has some bunk beds. Let's find this place on the other video."

I studied the image and found the location of the structure on the chart. I used my notes to find the location on the other video. Preacher leaned over my shoulder to look at the video we'd made from the boat.

"What is that?" he asked. "Looks like a couple of boats?"

I move the video forward and backward looking for the best angle.

"Yeah." I tapped the screen. There were two small, aluminum boats tied under separate roofs. The sides of the boathouses were open. I would have not paid it a second look from the water because it obviously did not hold the smuggler's boat. From the water, you didn't see that lighter strip of the roof that attracted my attention.

Each separate boat cover had a peaked roof. The open ends, where the boats entered, paralleled the shore. Our video captured a view of the back of the boats in the periphery of its vision as we approached. As we'd motored past, all the camera caught was the side of the boat closest to the bay. I almost dismissed it as a possibility, but I had nothing else to consider, so I froze the video and squinted, studying the details of the boat dock.

In the brief view we'd captured of the open ends of the two boat houses, they appeared to be separate. There was a space between them open to the sky as far back as I could see on the video, but the view receded into a darker shadow. What kept my attention was the fact that they were tall, with siding that came down for some way beneath the roof line.

"Look," I said, "it looks like enough space above those boats to hide the boat we're looking for if it is on a lift. That would explain why somebody added a roof on the back part."

"Yeah, I see what you mean. It looks like it could be just the kind of hole this vermin would hide in."

"And that building just on shore could be where the girls slept."

We could see a house a little further inland, partly obscured behind some kind of bushy growth. I put the aerial view back in and you could see the house and another outbuilding that looked big enough to be a three-car garage or a nice sized workshop or barn. The road from the property appeared to be crushed oyster shell up to a gate opening on to a one lane road. There was not a big pick-up or a van visible on the property, but I would have liked to be able to see inside that outbuilding.

I was starting to feel a tingle of anticipation.

"What do you think?" Preacher asked.

"Could be. I certainly think it is worthy of looking at closer. A place where he does more than just park his boat inside a covered boat house kind of fits what we know about him. He has a specially prepared boat. I'm sure he's equipped it with mufflers he can use when he wants. He used the deception of a church bus and he obviously had a plan in place to monitor and protect his cargo during transport. He likes the intricacies of the planning. He complicates things but in a way that is effective. An extra level of security for hiding his boat, like a lift that would tuck it away in the roof of that place, fits what I sense about him."

"So, what do we do?"

"First we drive back by that place in the boat and get a better look at it. I'm going to find out who owns the property. We'll scope it out from the road if we can safely. Then we'll decide our next step."

"I told you, Sam. I told you we would track down this

bastard."

"We don't know that we have. We may just be desperately latching on to the only thing we could find and it could be completely wrong."

"Bet it's not. And if it is, I bet you get him in the end. Let's go look at it, right now."

"No. It's too dark. We'll take the boat first thing in the morning. We'll come back, and I'll go to the courthouse and look up the property records. Maybe we'll go find that dirt road and see where it leads."

"Yes. We got him. And next, we'll get the girls."

I thought we might actually have a shot at tracking the smuggler. After all, even if what we'd found wasn't his place, he did operate somewhere around the bay. It angered and saddened me, but the girls were gone. Finding the smuggler and getting him arrested would be some small retribution for that sad fact. That was my thought anyway.

I talked to Patricia on the phone that night. Not wanting to raise any kind of false hope or useless fears, I did not tell her what we'd found and that we planned to scope it out in detail the next morning.

The next morning Preacher and I approached the boathouse about fifteen minutes after sunrise. I'd gone down the bay and turned around to approach from the east to get the best view inside the building. The boathouse's openings faced the east. Before we got close, I used binoculars to scope out the area. I saw no one on the dock and saw no movement around the house. If there was a vehicle parked there I didn't see it.

A flash of aluminum attracted my attention and adrenaline surged when I caught sight of an aluminum skiff on the water just off the dock. But each boat shed still sheltered an aluminum boat. It was just a lone fisherman drift fishing about twenty yards from the edge of the dock. He was reeling in what looked like a nice sized speckled trout. I slowed my approach.

"Must be some fishing structure right there. The tide is coming in right now and moving right at us. Let's swing around and drift by right where that guy is. Do not stare at the place."

Preacher said, "Gotcha" and slipped on a pair of wraparound sunglasses. He started getting our fishing poles ready.

I swung wide so as to not disturb the man fishing there and went some distance past the place. I lowered the trolling motor but let the tide push us slowly in the direction of the dock. The depth finder showed the hardness and rise of an oyster bed. Lots of shrimp and baitfish hang out in and around an oyster bed eating the stuff collected there. I've spent hours drifting over similar beds to catch the predators gathered for those morsels as the tidal flow pushes them across the oyster bed.

Usually, I would not encroach on another man's fishing in such a small area, but this morning was special. I rudely set up my drift. As I did, the other man fishing started his outboard and left the area swinging around to pass us as he traveled west, back toward Galveston. I hoped he'd caught his limit. I raised a hand in greeting and as an apology, but he ignored me. Can't say I blame him.

I wasn't there to fish, but I noted that it looked like a good spot to do so. The depth finder showed that the oyster bed grew thicker as we drifted toward the dock. Some distance from the dock it actually humped up in a mound and, if I'd really been fishing, the sides of that hump would be a good place to try and entice some speckled trout to rise from the depths and take my bait. I may have been there on a surveillance mission, but I cast a plastic shrimp so that it bounced over that hump and fell off the edge.

A spec took my lure just as we drifted in front of the dock. I used the strike as an opportunity to hold the boat in place while I reeled in the fish. I led the fish to the shore side of the boat and let it fight me a little. From behind my dark sunglasses, I looked carefully at the boat shed. From the direction our boat faced, our video camera looked out over the bay. I should have done a backward drift to get video.

I leaned over the side of the boat and, to express my appreciation for her assistance, let the fish go. I heard a door slam on shore. Keeping my face pointed away I saw a man, tall with short blond hair and dressed in a bright yellow jumpsuit, walking down the pathway toward the dock from the house. I'd seen enough.

"Reel in," I said, "let's get out of here."

Preacher stowed his rod and reel. I started the video camera and the boat. I swung off the oyster bed turning to head toward Galveston. I glanced over toward the dock, and the man was tending to something in the boat closest to us. He looked at us as we passed about fifty yards away. I didn't linger looking at him. I resisted the urge to wave. I'd look at him closer on our video. As I headed up the bay, I imagined a cinnamon scent.

Preacher stood next to me, staring straight ahead, not trying to talk over the sound of the engines. After we'd traveled a couple of miles, he reached over, grabbed my arm, and, with a grim expression, nodded. I slowed the boat to make talking easier.

"That was him, Sam. Praise God. You found that son of a bitch. I know it."

"Did you recognize him."

"Well, he was big enough. A part of what I remember is noticing how big he was just before he zapped me to the ground. Don't you agree we found him?"

"Maybe. Did you notice anything about that boathouse?"

"What did you see?"

"Starting several feet back from their doors, the two boat covers share a common roof. Could just be storage space, but it looks long enough to pull a nice sized boat up on a lift. Those walls come down low enough to hide a low to the water boat like we're looking for."

"It's the place. I know it's the place. I bet the girls spent the night in that little shed just on shore. What next? How do we get that bastard? How do we get him to tell us where to find the girls?"

The girls. If the man doing the smuggling had Mina, she was probably dead. I assumed he'd put her in the hands of the traffickers. I hoped he'd put her in the hands of the traffickers. At least she'd be alive. I tried to not think about the hell she would be enduring. They'd probably send her and her sister somewhere away from Chicago. At least they'd likely be together. After all, they could earn a premium by working together. If Mina wasn't dead, what must she be thinking about me and the colossal failure I'd caused?

"Sam, what next?"

"Next, I drop you off at the cabin. I'll take the boat to the marina and get my car. I'm going to the courthouse in Anahuac to pull the deed records and see who owns that property."

"I'll go with you."

"No. It's a one-man job. I want the thinking time. It'll take me a while. I'll drop you off somewhere else if you want."

"Take me to the park, but I need to do some things at my church. Hand me your phone."

Preacher called somebody named Rob and told him to meet him at the bait shop at the park.

"You call Clara's if you're going to do anything else," he said. "I'll keep checking there for messages. If you have nothing planned for tonight, I'll find someplace else to sleep. I need to touch base with a lot of my congregation."

I understood that. Without his attention and food, his congregation found it easy to drift away to parts unknown.

Anahuac is the county seat of Chambers County, the county where we found the possible hide-out of the smuggler. Anahuac is off Interstate 10 on the shores of Lake Anahuac and Trinity Bay. I left Preacher at the dock at the park where we were staying, took the boat back to Sol de Mer where I showered and changed, and drove the ninety miles to Anahuac. It took a couple of hours.

Using the maps in the deed records room of the County Clerk, I found the property on the bay. I filled out a request slip and got the volume containing its deed records. The owner of the property was a Gladys Hopper, widow of James Hopper. There was no lien on the property. I wasn't doing a title search and didn't bother to go back through time to track the succession of the title. I made a note of her name and the legal address of the property. I returned the book of records to the clerk with my thanks.

I had my laptop in the car and turned it on, but didn't pick up a Wi-Fi signal. I drove a block back to the small, one story county library I'd passed on the way to the courthouse. Like all good libraries, it had free Wi-Fi access. I logged my laptop in and did a search for Gladys Hopper in Chambers County. I found her obituary. It was short.

Gladys Hopper died in the winter six years before having been predeceased by her husband and two children. A memorial service was held at her church, The Church of Hope. I paused and sat back in my chair when I read that. It was a van belonging to The Church of Hope that Preacher and I chased through the night two weeks before.

The church was an unexpected connection. There was nothing in the deed records about someone inheriting the property, but that's not rare. As long as property taxes were paid and there were no nosy neighbors, there might not be official interest in who lived on the property. Perhaps the smuggler was a relative, perhaps not. If he was careful, it was a good way to live incognito. In my mind, we'd found the guy.

By the time I'd left the library, I'd also looked at a map on the internet and found the roads leading to the house on the bay. Its driveway was off what was a road so insignificant the map called it "unnamed road." The road ran several miles along the bay, looping between two county roads. I expected it to be well traveled by those with places along the shore and by fishermen and birdwatchers. I should be able to drive by without being noticed.

I took the two-lane road toward Smith Point out of Anahuac eventually turning left onto a very unimproved road, two tracks heading off through the marshy, coastal flats. My tires threw up a salt colored dust cloud. I slowed and considered whether being on the road was too noticeable, but eventually, I met an old salt pitted pickup pulling a dull aluminum boat bouncing on a rusty trailer. Each of us squeezed to the side leaving the tires of one side of our vehicles on a track of the road. He nodded in response when I raised a hand in greeting. There was more traffic. I decided I would be okay.

The road curved to the southeast to skirt the bay. I fell behind another pick-up truck. It had a kayak in the bed. I didn't try to pass and appreciated that he gave me an excuse to drive slow as we approached the property holding my interest.

A ditch oozing with mud and water bordered the property. A strong looking gate made out of two-inch steel pipe closed off the entrance to the property. It had two locks on the chain holding it closed. I glanced toward the house and saw nobody. I slowed a bit and studied the property as much as I could without coming to a stop. I could see only a corner of the house. It was hidden behind the barn-like structure we'd observed in the aerial video. Made of steel siding, that building looked relatively new. A double car garage door closed off one end. The fact that there was a roll of chicken wire, a riding lawnmower, a stack of lumber, and a cement mixer next to a pile of oyster shells at the side of the building made me think it was primarily a garage for parking vehicles instead of storage.

I breathed fast and shallow as I drove past. The sun dropped toward the horizon behind me. I followed the dusty trail of the road as it curved back to the north, ending up at another small, two-lane paved road. Suddenly, I felt very tired but started the long drive back to the cabin on Follets Island. When I'd driven a short way my cell phone found service and immediately beeped that I had a message. It was Patricia.

"Sam, this is Patricia. I tried to call you, but it went straight to your voicemail. The funeral is tomorrow, and I'll be coming back on Saturday. I'll let you know when. There's no real news up here, but Jason wants you to call. Call me as soon as you can, I don't care what time it is."

She didn't answer her phone, and I left a short hello it's

me message.

An unknown number called my cell phone. It was Preacher.

"So, what did you find out?

"Not much. The lady listed as the owner of that place has been dead for some time."

"Do you think it's the place?"

"Get this, the lady who used to own that property was a member of the Church of Hope."

"Okay. That's it. I have no doubts now. Do you?"

"I think it's the most likely we've found so far. Especially since it's the only possibility we've found."

"What next?"

"Sleep."

"Okay. Leave me a message at Clara's when you decide what we're going to do. I have to feed some people. I'll be around."

I lay in bed for a while asking myself what next. I still wasn't sure about the place we'd found on the bay. Maybe we were too desperate to find anything. I knew what I needed to do next. I needed a closer look at that boathouse.

CHAPTER EIGHTEEN

I GOT UP EARLY AND WENT to check on my place. As planned, the goats made a racket when I drove up. Putting feed out for her goats on the other side of the pasture, Joanne held up a hand to shield her eyes to look my way. I waved. She waved. I went into the shop to turn off the buzzing alarm. A vehicle with a loud exhaust drove by the gate. I looked but did not see the vehicle. I wondered if he was circling me like I was circling him.

I thought about calling Patricia, but chances were good she was still asleep. I knew I'd have to make an awkward call to Jason at some point. I didn't know what to tell either of them. Until I knew for sure about that place on the bay, I didn't want to bring it up, and if it wasn't the hideout of our quarry, I had nothing to tell them.

After I ate something, I called Patricia. We said we missed each other, and when she asked what I had planned, I told her we had lots of video to look at again but no firm leads. I told her Preacher and I would start checking out places that looked the most likely and then assess what we were doing.

"There has already been terrible waste. Don't do anything dangerous," she said.

"Safety of everybody remains my goal, even if it didn't work out so good last time."

"It wasn't your fault."

"I know that. At least not the actual events, but I did set in motion the things that resulted in what happened. I'll have to live with that."

"You sound bitter or something. Don't let your

emotions get you in trouble. Don't do something silly."

"No."

"I'll be there Saturday. I miss you."

"Yes. Me, too. I miss you. I wish this thing was over. I'll let you know if we turn up anything new."

We said a few things. I hung up and took a cup of coffee outside and considered what needed doing. Weighing heavily in my thoughts were Mina and Zoio, gone to who knew where, and Mary Elizabeth and Charlene Coster, both dead. I wanted no more lost souls on my conscious.

It was well and good to say what happened to them was not my fault, but I knew if I'd been a little smarter and a bit more careful, none of them would be gone. I was caught in a game beyond me. I would play out my part while I had a move to play. I owed it to the missing and the dead, but I absolutely wanted nobody else close to harm's way.

I checked the state of my bank account online, moved some money around, grabbed a fishing rod and a small box of tackle and put some other stuff in a bag. I drove through Galveston to Larry Peters' car lot and traded my undercover car for a pick-up truck.

I crossed the bridge to Galveston and went to a place where I rented a kayak. With the kayak in the back of the truck, I made the hour and a half drive around Trinity Bay to Smith Point. I calculated the boathouse of interest was six or seven miles down the shore from Smith Point.

I'd planned to kayak in during daylight, fish that oyster bed and see if I could see anything. But the more I thought about that the more it seemed like an unnecessary risk. Perhaps I was projecting my nervousness on the man I was after, but he had to be wary to some degree. I expected him to look closely at anybody approaching his place.

I remembered the man I saw when Preacher and I

motored past. I'd had the impression he was watching us closely. I remembered the ghostly green vision of the man on the boat Patricia and I saw late at night coming through the ship channel. That man watched us as we watched him. I did not want to spook that man. I decided a quick look at the boathouse under the cover of darkness would be the best thing to do.

The bays stretched to the horizon. The sun glinted off a line of boats fishing Hanna Reef to the south. I put a fishing line in the water and paddled east along the shallow shore. Occasionally, gulls would check my wake to see if I'd stirred up anything to eat. I caught and released a few fish. There were people wade fishing for a couple of hundred yards, but after that I was alone. There were few boats on this shoreline. I took my time.

I passed a few rickety docks and fishing piers. On one, a young man had his arm around a girl. Her head was on his shoulder. Her left leg was over his right, and their legs were swinging with a gentle beat. Their fishing poles lay on the deck behind them. They were having a most successful fishing day.

Eventually, I paddled around a bend to within sight of the boathouse I was there to see. I glanced at it for a short time but did not linger. I didn't see anybody around the boathouse nor did I want to. I turned around and paddled back around the bend. There was a dock there in about three feet of water. The young couple was far enough away and focused on other things. They did not notice me paddling into the shadows beneath the empty dock.

I tied up there and knocked down a few spider webs with my paddle. I arranged things the best I could and stretched out on the kayak to wait for darkness. I ate some salami and cheese. I thought about things. Occasionally, I heard the sound of a vehicle on the unnamed road and hoped one of them was the bad guy driving away from his house. I napped a little.

The sun dropped toward the horizon. I had my cell phone in a waterproof case and tied it to my belt. I clipped on a waterproof flashlight. I reapplied a healthy layer of mosquito repellent to every inch of exposed skin. I secured my fishing things and life jacket. I slid over the side of the kayak and into the water. The sticky mud on the bottom sucked at my feet.

I shuffled around the kayak, dragging my feet through the mud in what those of us who wade fish in the bays call the Texas Shuffle. The idea is to scare away any stingrays without stepping on them. A stingray spike in the leg would quickly end my day.

I waded up to the shoreline and set out on land toward the east. The tide was approaching its low point for the day and there were fewer and fewer people fishing on the bay. There was less than two feet difference between high and low tide, but the lower tide revealed more mud at the edge of the shore and the strong decaying smell of the bay bottom got stronger. I walked on a combination of the crunchy bay gravel of crushed shells and marsh mud that tried to suck the shoes off my feet. The land on this point is coastal prairie, a combination of marsh and low, scrubby, flat land. I moved slow, not wanting to get too close until dark. There was minimal cover.

I got close and walked into the bay to gain what cover was possible behind the slight rise on the shore. To my left, the flat land stretched to the distance. To the right, the flat bay stretched to a lonesome horizon. I felt small in that expanse of nothing.

I started to doubt what I was doing, wondering what I

expected to accomplish. As I crept closer to the bend beyond which would be the boathouses, I sunk lower into the water until I was creeping along with just my shoulders out of the water. It was slack tide. There should be no feeding sharks. I hoped.

I rounded the bend. There was still enough light to see the boathouse. It was quiet with no person in sight. I didn't want to approach until complete darkness. I crept onto shore, staying low. By laying on the muddy beach, I kept out of sight of the house above the boathouse. I listened for any noise indicating somebody was about. I heard nothing.

The slack tide meant the water did not move. My skin itched from salt and sand. Mosquitoes buzzed me constantly and started ignoring the remnants of the repellent I'd put on. I lay my arms across my face to keep the hundreds of mosquitoes off my face as much as possible. And listened. I waited for some time after sunset.

A bright moon meant it would not get pitch dark. I'd have preferred it completely dark but had to get my surveillance done. I wanted to confirm this was the guy. I needed to get enough information to get him arrested. If I convinced myself this was his place I would make sure there was probable cause to do a search. Whatever it took. That was the only way we were going to get any information about where to find Mina and Zoio. Every day meant the girls might be sucked so deep into the darkness we'd never find them.

I moved closer to the property staying some distance from shore in the deeper water. The oyster bed I'd noticed on the depth finder of my boat curved closer to shore. When I first encountered it I stumbled and fell to my knees. It cut me as I scrambled to get up.

I moved closer to shore to avoid the conglomerate of

hard, sharp edges. I continued doing the Texas Shuffle through the mud and what felt like loose clumps of oysters. I kept as much of my body as I could underwater until I was standing beneath the walkway between the shore and the dock with the boathouses. I crouched there, listening again to nothing.

I walked carefully on shore at the edge of the walkway. Staying in a shadow, I looked toward the house. Nothing was moving. About fifteen yards inland was the shed we thought might be where the girls slept. It was maybe twenty feet long. I could see one window close to the right end of the building. The rest was cinder block with no other windows. Beyond it was the house, a typical bay place with weathered siding, hurricane shutters on the windows, and a screened in porch. Beyond that was the second outbuilding. A light on a pole glowed there.

I squinted up at the ceiling of the boathouse closest to me, but shadowed darkness prevented me from seeing anything. I would have to get closer. The dark window in the building closest to the shore interested me. I wanted to see what, if anything, I could see in that window.

I climbed up on shore, navigating the sharp break up the bank by keeping a hand on the crusty piling. I stayed low and moved to put the main house out of sight. I crawled on hands and knees toward the small building, ready at the slightest need to run into the bay. I can hold my breath for over a minute under water. If I had to run I would try to lose myself in the bay. There was no place to hide onshore.

I made it to the building without seeing or hearing a thing. I was glad the bad guy didn't own a dog.

I pressed against the wall, listening for any sound and feeling for any vibration. There was nothing. Carefully, I stood just to the side of the window. I moved until one eye could see into the space. There was no light. There was no window visible on the other side of the building. I held my breath and pressed my flashlight up to the glass of the window. I flashed it on briefly, once, and ducked to listen for anybody noticing.

In the quick flash of light, I saw a workbench against the far wall with an assortment of tools scattered about. There were scuba tanks on the floor beneath the bench and absolutely nothing of interest.

I could summon no desire to try to get closer to the residence. I turned back to the boathouses. They were open on all sides except for a closet-sized enclosure in the corner closest to where the ramp from shore extended.

I crouched to get out of the sight of the main house. I glanced between the house and the walkway out to the boathouse. I had to either go back into the water and try to climb one of the crusty pilings or just walk the fifteen yards on the walkway. I looked again between the house and the boathouses out over the water. I sensed I was completely alone on the property.

The walkway was weathered wood with two or three newer boards evidencing repair. I put a foot on the walkway. Looking back over my shoulder with every step, I walked out to where I stood on the other side of that enclosed area, beneath the overhang of the roof of the boathouse.

The ceiling above the two boathouses dropped down, solid from about six feet from the front of the roofs. The wood in the ceiling was not as old as the rest of the structure. It was what looked like thick panels of siding. It looked like somebody had enclosed what had once been open storage among the rafters.

Down the center of the ceiling was a board an inch thick and eight inches wide. I saw no hinges of any sort, but the dimensions were such I could imagine the ceiling opening downward like barn doors with that eight-inch board covering the seam between the two sections.

I stood beneath a light on the side of the enclosed storage space. It was reasonable to think that the wiring for that light extended on up into the enclosed space to power a boat lift. On a lift could be the black boat of the smuggler.

I flashed the light briefly onto the ceiling above me. It appeared that the ceiling was scuffed in lines where it would rest against the support poles if lowered the way I thought it might be.

I tried the door to the enclosed storage area, and it opened. In the storeroom were six fifty-five gallon drums and the smell of gas. His offshore fuel supply? Running up the wall just inside the door was a ladder. Another quick flash of my light revealed an opening with a cover closing it off.

Still no noise or movement from the property. I had to look.

Slipping into the storage shed I let my flashlight dangle from its cord on my belt and using both hands I carefully climbed the ladder. I reached the top and pushed against the panel closing off the opening. It opened to the pitch black interior of the space above.

I reached down to get my flashlight. That's when I heard a clatter. I pulled my head out of the darkness and looked down just in time to see him and to watch him reach up, grab my feet and pull me off the ladder. He had short, bleached blonde hair and he was tall. He had small cold eyes and a look of rage.

I could not hang on. My head hit a rung of the ladder on the way to the floor, and I was half senseless after that. Probably a good thing. The pain from that collision of my head with the ladder obscured the pain of my head hitting the deck and the pummeling that followed. I heard him say one thing before I lost consciousness. I heard him say "stupid motherfucker."

I came to laying on the floor of the storage room on his dock. He'd used what felt like duct tape to bind my wrists behind my back and my ankles together. The tape wound around my head sealed my mouth tightly closed.

He flipped me over on my back. I'd have screamed my pain if I could have made a sound. My vision tunneled. I started to pass out again. I watched him bend over me with a knife. I thought he was about to gut me when he reached down and grabbed me at the waist. He lifted the waterproof bag in which I carried my cell phone and cut its lanyard with his knife. He dropped it to the deck and crushed it beneath a scuba tank. He took it outside. I never saw it again.

He noticed me awake. "Why couldn't you leave me alone? The whore is gone. That nosy bitch friend of yours is dead. You killed her. You stupid motherfucker."

He kicked me in the gut and the pain washed to my extremities. I fought to not throw up. If I retched behind the duct tape, I would suffocate.

Blood was running into my left eye from a cut on my head. He noticed. He ripped off a length of tape and pulled my head up by my hair. He pressed the tape on my head saying, "I don't need your blood around here."

He kicked me again. Taking me by the feet, he dragged me out of the storage closet and up the walkway. My head bounced painfully up to the walkway ramp and to the ground at the top. I couldn't move. He dragged me into the outbuilding I'd been looking in a few minutes before. Breathing heavily with what I guessed was more rage than exertion he stepped over me and unlocked the door to the back part of the shed. He dragged me in there and turned the light on. There were cots stacked against the wall. I'd found where Mina spent her first night in America.

He wrapped more duct tape around my legs from my ankles to my knees. He wrapped my arms from my wrists to my elbows. He wrapped more tape around my mouth. I expected him to wrap it around my nose and let me die. He clearly intended to kill me.

Leaving me on the floor, he stepped into the front part of the building and made a phone call. There was a rushing noise in my head, probably from a concussion I thought, but I could hear his side of the conversation.

"Get over here. We have a problem ... No. Tonight. Right now ... I'm not going to talk about it on the phone, but you get here as fast as you can ... I don't have time to talk about it. I have to go look for more trouble."

He hung up abruptly. I figured he'd called the man who helped him stomp Preacher and me behind the truck stop the night this whole thing got serious. He could go look for more trouble, but he wouldn't find it. I took care to make sure I was the only one who could mess up That meant nobody knew where to find me.

He looked at me and said, "You stupid motherfucker."

He closed the door, locking me into the darkness. I thought I would be dead that night. I struggled, but it was impossible to get free. I hurt. From the pain, I thought the straining to get free might cause a brain aneurysm. That would save him the trouble of killing me. I lay there in the dark thinking of the things that got me there and thinking of the things I would never enjoy again. The darkness consumed me.

Time became vague. I heard rustling in the front part

of the shed. The door opened once and the blonde haired man looked in at me and closed the door again. Every once in a while I heard him do something in the front part of the building.

Eventually, the other man arrived, and I heard the blonde haired man explain how he found me snooping around.

"How did he find you?" the new man said.

"I have no idea. The only thing I can think of is that bitch Charlene must have told somebody something. We're real lucky I noticed him creeping up here."

"What if the cops know where he is?"

"If they did, they'd be here."

"Somebody might know."

"That's why you're getting him out of here fast. Anybody shows up, he was never here. But, you've got to move your ass."

"Are you sure this is the best idea?"

"Yes. Unless you've suddenly got brilliant and can think of something else."

The man who'd just arrived started to whine a little. "This time, you need to do it. You come with me, but you do it."

"No, I have to stay here in case there's a problem. I have to get the boat ready to go offshore. Besides, you screwed up the last time and if you're going to be my partner you need to show me you can take care of the problem and do it right."

"I'll do it, but we need to get out of here. We've got enough money."

"I don't have all the money I planned on, but that stupid motherfucker in there makes it clear it's time to move on. Next week's job and we're gone."

"Okay. I'll do it. Help me get him in the car."

"You bet your ass you'll do it. Don't act like you're doing me a favor."

I resisted wriggling while they carried me to the guy's car. I pretended to be unconscious. Resisting would have been silly. The blonde guy should have killed me at the truck stop. He should haul me right out into the bay and kill me now. He was making it complicated, and complications might give me a chance. He was delegating my murder to his partner. It sounded like the partner botched the killing of Coster and Mary Elizabeth somehow.

"Lester, I'm not kidding. This time you do it like I told you. You get way offshore. This time you put his head in the water until he's dead. You untape him, you strip him, you weigh him down, and you sink him. Way out there somewhere. And don't do it where somebody on a drilling rig can watch. Then, you get back here and be on post on Monday night. I don't want to see you or talk to you. Just be there."

"Come on now. I'm not that dumb. You know I've done it right before. I'll be ready on Monday."

"You didn't do so good the last time. I'm just telling you, I really don't want this guy found. Ever. You've already cost me a bunch of money by screwing up so bad I have to get out of here before I am ready."

"It'll be fine. You have plenty of money. You can pay me a little less than we talked about."

They crammed me into the trunk of a car and stood there a moment. I was in a steel box built into the trunk. It stunk. It was used as a bait box or fish locker.

The blonde guy said, "You be careful. Don't you do something to get stopped by the cops. And I swear, Lester, you do it right this time. Understand? I do not want him floating to the beach."

"I'll take care of it. Trust me."

The blonde guy snorted. He slammed the trunk lid over me as he said, "Stupid motherfucker."

The trunk smelled like oil and fish guts. When he started driving, it was clear he needed new shocks.

It would have done me no good to try to get out of my bonds. The box I was in assured I could not kick out a taillight. I could, however, see the flash of his blinkers. He was driving as legal as he could, signaling every turn. After all, he did not want to get stopped by a cop.

I concentrated on trying to determine where he drove. Left out of the property and along the same dirt road I'd followed. Eventually, the right blinker came on and he drove on to pavement, undoubtedly the same road I'd followed from Anahuac to Smith Point. It wasn't terribly late. I heard other traffic. He stopped for a traffic signal in Anahuac.

I fought a weariness. I drifted, wanting to go to sleep. I wondered if I was getting any air in that fetid box. I wondered if something was broke in my head, slowly leaking to the point of a final seizure and oblivion. I decided it didn't really matter.

I knew when he got on the interstate heading west. That meant he was going to other side of Trinity Bay. I wasn't sure, but I felt like he got off almost as soon as he could on the other side of the bay's headwaters, right blinker to exit, left blinker to turn back under the highway. That meant he was headed toward Galveston.

From their discussion, it was clear he intended to dump me far out in the Gulf. He had to have a boat somewhere capable of going offshore. There were hundreds of places he could have a boat along the route I thought he was taking,

Baytown, Texas City, and any number of other places had marinas and boat storage. Maybe he had a boat on Galveston Island.

I stretched as much as I could. It hurt, but nothing like it did after the last beating they'd administered. My head hurt. My ears were ringing. I wanted to sink into a fog pressing from just under the surface of my consciousness, but I fought to stay aware. The pain where the blonde guy kicked me helped keep me awake.

Eventually, we made a series of turns for which I had no map in my head. We'd not gone far enough to get to Galveston. Plus, I would have heard more highway sounds if we'd crossed over the bridge to the island. There was the crunch of gravel. He slowed and finally stopped.

I kept my eyes half closed like I was only semi-conscious, but tried to see everything I could. I dug my fingernails into the crud in the bottom of the box I was in. If they recovered my body soon enough, maybe it would provide the crime lab a clue. It always did on television. I'd like to grab a big fistful of my captor's DNA right from his body, but that wasn't going to be possible unless things changed significantly.

He opened the trunk and leaned over me. He smelled of beer and body odor. He reached over to the side of the trunk and picked up a fish club, slipping its leather strap over his wrist.

"Now, you listen here. I'll use this club. There ain't nobody around and if I have to I'll club you right here."

What was I going to do? If there ever came a moment to resist, I would need my strength. There was no way I could do anything at that moment. I thought it likely I would get a ride out to sea and shoved over the side. But until that happened, I would wait for a circumstance with some possibility of success without being clubbed for the effort.

He grunted and strained to pull me up and out by my shoulders. That, at least, was something. My head wouldn't be falling to the pavement this time.

We were in a marina somewhere. I could hear the sounds boats make on the water, the slap of lines, the rustle of water on hulls. It didn't seem to be a place for pleasure boats. It was a Friday night, but there were no sounds of anybody having a party on a boat. I had no clue where we were.

The place was so deserted Lester didn't try to hide me as he dragged me across the parking lot and down a pier to where he pushed and shoved me over the side of a boat. He left me on the bottom of the boat, flipped on an exhaust fan, and went to untie the lines. I tried to fold myself and get to my knees, so I could go over the side. It was a bad option, but it was all I had. I got to my knees and leaned against the side of the boat. Unfortunately, I was against the port side of the boat, and that side was against the pier. There was no way to get into the water. I tried to push myself to the other side to go into the water, but he got to me and hit me across the spine with his fish club.

"Lay down, or I'll hurt you bad. Might as well make it easy on yourself. We get out there I'll make sure it don't hurt you none. You do something stupid, and I'll hurt you bad. I'll break every bone in your body before I toss you over." He hit me across the knees. I made a noise deep inside myself and broke out in a sweat. "I mean it. I'll break your kneecaps right here if I have to. Nobody saw us and I don't think you can scream loud enough to be heard. I'm willing to find out if you are."

He shoved me up against the starboard side of the boat.

He reached into a storage space on the port side and pulled out a canvass that he threw over me.

"You move," he said, "and I'll club your head."

He motored out of the protection of the marina and sped up in open water. Depending on where we were exactly I thought I had an hour or two before he got far enough out into the Gulf to throw me overboard. There were chains piled in one corner of his boat. I expected to be tied in those before I went over. Supposedly, drowning would be a relatively easy way to die.

He slowed. After a moment there was a different scent in the air. Over the musty smell of the canvass on top of me, I could smell seafood. We were close to somewhere frying seafood. I strained to listen for some clue of where we were.

I would forever remember the sound of the laughter of a lady I will never meet. It was loud enough to tumble over the water. There were nightclub sounds. I knew exactly where we were.

The boat was moving slowly next to the clubs and restaurants lining the channel at Kemah. It was a no-wake zone and well patrolled by the Coast Guard and the Sheriff's department. They arrested people for boating under the influence all the time.

Kemah was an entertainment district with theme restaurants and carnival rides. It had a boardwalk alongside the narrow channel between Galveston Bay and Clear Lake. His boat had been on Clear Lake. We were slowly headed for Galveston Bay. From the bay, he would go up the ship channel and out to sea.

This was my best chance at either survival or bringing attention to my murderer. We had to be almost through the channel. I slowly gathered my legs and twisted so my shoulder was against the side of the boat. I thought one time about the move I needed to make before it was time to actually do it. As Lester started to leave the channel and increase his speed, I pushed myself upright with my back to the side of the boat. I heard one exclamation from Lester as I pushed myself over the side of the boat. Lester, I thought, you should have tied me to the boat.

We were out of the channel, headed into the darkness of the bay and away from the view of partiers on the boardwalk. As I hit the water, I heard his boat power down. I took as big a breath as I could before I went under and wriggled like some kind of sea slug to push myself under the water. I propelled myself away from the boat. There were oyster beds there, and he could not follow far in the boat without tearing off his prop. If he had a gun and started shooting at me, it should be loud enough to attract the attention of those on shore.

My butt hit the oysters, and their edges cut my hands where they were tied behind me. I did my best to push against the reef and rub my wrists against the rock-hard edges of the oysters. I felt a gash open up down the side of my hand. I kept rubbing. Finally, I felt an oyster snag the tape.

If Lester was smart, he was anchored to the oysters and in the water coming after me. I had to be churning up the water.

Frantically, I sawed my wrist against the oysters, rubbing violently and trying to hang on to stay under the water. My lungs tightened, my body demanding a breath. I pulled and scraped and strained against the tape. I felt the tape part and loosen. I kept stretching my arms apart, blindly finding more snags to catch on the edges of the oyster bed.

My hands came free. My shoulders burned with pain

and my lungs demanded air, but I swam underwater like a mermaid, using my hands and kicking my taped together feet. I hoped I was swimming toward the jumble of rocks that line the shore beneath the Ferris wheel at the end of the Kemah boardwalk.

I had to come up for air. I stuck my head up and looked behind me. I could see Lester's boat. He was not coming after me. He was scanning the water looking for me. He held the club in one hand. I ducked back under the water and reached down trying to find an edge of the tape around my legs. The rising tide pushed me toward the rocks, bouncing me painfully across the oysters. It felt like I was being skinned.

I grabbed the oysters, finding places to hold that were a little less sharp. I dragged my legs back and forth trying to snag the tape. I stuck my head up again for a gulp of air and went back under without even looking back at the boat. I pulled at strings of tape. I pulled a half-inch wide strip loose and ripped it down and across and started unwinding tape from my legs. Two more breaths and I had several feet unwound. The effort exhausted me.

I kicked off the rest of the tape. My head pounded, my shoulder was on fire, and I'd swallowed salt water. The tide ground me against the rocks at the shore. I held on the best I could, stayed low, and watched Lester in his boat. Every time he started to look my way, I ducked under the water.

Lester was in trouble. The man who told him to kill me was going to be very angry. He'd been angry that Mary Elizabeth and Charlene Coster washed ashore. Lester had screwed up again.

I hoped Lester would decide I'd drowned. Even if I washed up and was found, that was a whole hell of a lot better than if Lester had to tell his partner I'd escaped. If he saw me on shore, his best bet would be to call the other man. I did not want to deal with either of them again. Not yet.

From their conversation, it was clear the two of them were about to run. If they thought I was alive and calling the cops that's what they'd do. The smuggler's boat had the range to get to somewhere on the coast of Mexico. They might even be able to work their way to the Caribbean. It was possible they'd disappear and with them the best chance of getting a line on the girls. So, I stayed in the water and let it batter me against the rocks, staying low and ducking under when necessary.

Lester attracted attention. It was a popular pastime to drive expensive boats through the Kemah channel. They would go out into the bay, turn around, come back through the channel, and then do the same thing the other way, enjoying being watched by those having fun on the boardwalk. The channel through the oyster reefs out of Kemah was narrow. The cruising line of boats was getting crowded behind Lester's boat. A horn sounded. Lester started up his boat and headed out to the bay.

He had to go out for some distance before he could turn around but would be coming back through the channel shortly. Fighting the current, half in and half out of the water, I worked my way to the edge of the boardwalk.

One very drunk girl leaning over the boardwalk railing saw me, waved, and said, "Hey, hi."

I found a place I could hold on to a piling and watch from the shadow of the boardwalk. Water funneled through the channel at a surprising rate. I hung on to the piling with both arms. I wrapped a leg around it. The friction burned. The cuts from the oyster bed became more painful.

In a few minutes Lester came back down the channel,

staring intently to port looking for any sign of me. The spill of light from the boardwalk lit the channel. He could not see me, but I could see him. I could see his boat well enough to memorize the registration number on its bow. Maybe he would come through the channel again to keep looking for me, but I had what I wanted. I needed to get out of the water and out of sight.

Chances were that Lester would tell his partner he'd done it right. Lester would be thinking that, with any luck, I would show up dead, but not before they were gone and he wouldn't have to deal with his partner's anger. Lester struck me as the kind of guy who often had to rely on luck to get by.

I went back to where I could painfully climb up the rocks to the amusement area. I attracted a lot of attention when I came dripping and limping over the edge. I walked as quickly as I could toward the parking lot. It didn't take long for a couple of security guards to find me. They were in an electric golf cart with lights flashing.

"Sir, are you okay?" one asked.

"Yes."

"What's going on?"

"I was on a boat with a group of people. One of the girls had a boyfriend I didn't know about. One of us had to leave. I chose me. I'm okay, but my cell phone is gone and I need to call somebody."

If I told them the truth Lester might be caught, but I wasn't so sure about the other guy. Lester would not know squat about the location of the girls. The other guy had to be cornered and ensnared in such a way that helping find the girls was his best option. I did not have the same faith in his partnership with Lester as did Lester.

I thought the other guy must have a lot of money

stashed somewhere, and he was primed to run. It wouldn't surprise me if he was already gone, leaving his buddy Lester behind. Besides, this was the second encounter I had with the other guy. Both times did not end well for me. I wanted a more personal piece of his undoing.

"Have you been drinking?"

"No. I'm stone sober. I just didn't expect to have to swim in from the bay. I got tangled up on the oysters. I'm okay. We'll all be friends next week. I promise."

They gave me a ride to a security office and pushed a phone my way.

Preacher had no phone, but I decided right then I would buy him one. Patricia was in Chicago. I looked at the clock. Clara's Bar and Grill was closed. I knew very few phone numbers by memory. I called Joanne and Maude.

"What?" Joanne answered.

"Joanne, it's Sam. I have a problem."

"Sam, now what? What's wrong?"

"It's a long story, but I ended up at Kemah without my car, my wallet, or my phone. I couldn't think of anybody's phone number but yours."

There were a rustle and whispers as she told Maude it was me on the phone, and they were going to have to drive to Kemah to pick me up.

"You need more friends with phones. What do you need?"

"Could you come to get me?"

"Do I need to bring a first aid kit?"

"That might be a good idea."

"Sam ... "

"What?"

"Never mind. We'll be there in about an hour. Where are you going to be?"

"Hold on." I asked the security guy where I could sit for an hour.

"Right here," he said, "or maybe outside so you can air out a little."

"Joanne, I'll be at the security office at Kemah."

"It's Maude, Sam, Joanne is getting dressed. We'll be there. Where's the security office?"

I told her.

"Okay, we'll be there shortly. Oh dear, Joanne is getting the first aid kit. What happened to you now?"

"Nothing deadly. See you soon."

I washed up as best I could in the security office. I did not ask for their first aid kit. I thought if I did, they'd have to fill out some kind of incident report. I didn't want to be documented. I hoped no flesh-eating bacteria were taking up residence in the web of cuts on my arms and face.

The ladies made good time, and in an hour we were headed back toward Galveston. Joanne didn't say much. She just threw the first aid kit in the back seat as I was getting in their car. Maude gave her a look and climbed in the back with me and tended to the publicly available wounds the best she could.

"The same guy?" asked Joanne.

"Yes."

"Learned your lesson yet?"

"I learn something new every time."

She noticed me looking toward the rear and said, "You think he's following?"

"No. I'm just being nervous. He thinks I'm dead."

"You look close to it."

We drove mostly in the quiet except for an occasional soothing sound from Maude. It wasn't hard to convince Joanne to drop me off at the park on the other side of the toll bridge. "No problem," she said, "I don't want you anywhere near us."

She left me on the road outside the entrance to the park. Preacher was sleeping on the sofa when I walked in.

He looked up blearily. I said, "You could have used the bed you know."

"Good God almighty. What happened to you."

"I ran into our friend, again. It's definitely his house."

"I told you to call me." He sat up. "What did you do? What's going on?"

I told him the story.

"So, you think he thinks you're dead?"

"Yeah, I don't think the man named Lester is going to want to piss him off by admitting what happened. Lester is going to hope I'm dead, and Lester is a weasel. He won't say a word. He really thinks the blonde guy is going to take him when he leaves, wherever he's going. I think Lester is going to find out what it means to be a loose end to this guy."

"Do we have a plan?"

"I have a plan, but I'm not sure you're going to want to go along with it."

"Try me."

I told him what I planned to do. He said, "I'll go along and pray for his soul."

I took a shower, scrubbing with anti-bacterial soap. It did not soothe. It hurt. I put ointment from the tube Joanne, and Maude left me on all the scratches and gouges. My ankles and forearms looked like I'd lost a fight with a hedge trimmer.

I sat gingerly in front of the computer. The Texas Parks and Wildlife Department's website allows anyone to do an owner search of boat registrations. The owner of the boat from which I'd jumped was Lester Hogan. Lester had what looked like an apartment address in Seabrook, a community on Clear Lake.

A quick search online revealed little about Lester Hogan. One bait shop's site listed him as a bait supplier. He'd put an ad on another site as available for hire for dock construction, pile driving, and above surface marine welding.

"Let's go get him," Preacher said.

"Tomorrow. I have to get some sleep. We'll stake out his place tomorrow. Meanwhile, we'll think of the best way to do this. A third time going bad will probably be the end of it for us."

Preacher rummaged in the first aid kit and said, "Ah ha. Bless you ladies. Here, take a couple of Vicodin."

CHAPTER NINETEEN

THE NEXT MORNING I bought a long distance calling card at the bait shop and parked myself in front of the pay phone in the parking lot. I called Larry Peters at his car lot telling him he needed to send a tow truck to pick up his vehicle at Smith Point. We negotiated a fee for that. I told him I'd be in to either pick up my car or borrow one of his.

I'd have to check for the kayak later. I would write it off and pay for it before going back and looking for it that day.

I called the marina and asked Ben Marsh to do me a favor with my boat. He agreed.

After some thought about what to say, I called Patricia.

"Listen," I said after we'd greeted each other, "I am going to ask you to do something and I seriously want you to agree."

"What's that? What's going on?"

"We found the bad guys for sure. I had another run-in with them."

"Oh, my God. Are you okay?"

"It wasn't fun, but I'm in better shape than last time."

"Tell me what happened and what you want me to do."

I gave her a sanitized version of my encounter and escape. Then, I said, "Patricia, I really need you to stay in Chicago for another few days. I think this part of this thing will be over within a week. We'll either have some info about the girls or we won't, but the bad guys will either be arrested or gone."

"Or, you'll be dead."

"No. The authorities will be the ones going after the

smuggler. I'm just going to point him out to them. If he's not caught soon, he'll be leaving the area, maybe the country, and we'll be starting over."

"Then why don't you want me there?"

"Because for the next couple of days Preacher and I will be completely out of touch. If the bad guy learns I'm still around, he will be desperate. I don't want to have to worry about you, and there's nothing you can do here."

There was a long pause.

"You better not be trying to protect me just because I'm a woman."

"That's not it. What we're going to do is find out when the smuggler is going out in the Gulf. Then, we're going to make sure the Coast Guard is ready. Then, we're going to stay out of sight until it's over.

"We almost know everything we need to know. We think we know when he's making his smuggling run, but we want to be sure. We know how we're going to do that. We'll be safe, but Preacher and I have to do that alone. I don't want anybody else here, male or female. Preacher and I can move, and we can hide quickly. The more people there are the harder that gets."

"Okay. I don't like it, but I trust you. When will it be safe for me to come down there?"

"By the end of next week. Then you can come down here unless we get enough information about where to find the girls. If that happens, I'll be up there or you can meet me wherever we're going to be looking for them."

"Promise?"

"Promise."

"Okay. It's easy enough to change my ticket. You keep me posted."

"When I can. Right now I don't even have a cell

phone."

"Get one."

"Yes, mam."

We said goodbye.

A grumpy Joanne picked Preacher and me up and loaned me the keys to their pick-up. Maude hugged us both and said, "Oh, dear."

We waited at the door of the Sprint store until it opened. I got a new cell phone for me and added another to my account for Preacher. The clerk told me if I'd bring in my old phone he'd transfer all the information to the new phone. I thanked him, but that was not going to be possible. Luckily, I backed up all my cell phone data online.

In the car, I told Preacher, "After this is over, I'll hold on to that for you. I don't want you letting everybody in your congregation using it to call home and use up all my talk time."

He gave me a look and a snort as he programmed the number of each phone into the other. On the way to Seabrook, I stopped by Larry Peters' car lot and borrowed another car, leaving the pick-up there. I gave Larry cash to pay the tow truck driver.

"I won't charge you for borrowing this car if you will promise to tell me what's going on," he said.

"Maybe someday."

Lester Hogan's place in Seabrook was a small apartment in a one-story line of small apartments in a building that might never have had a time when it was in good shape. Preacher and I could see Lester's place from the street as we drove past. I was willing to bet that the old Buick out front of his place had a fish box in the trunk. We followed the street to where it terminated at an industrial complex of some sort.

We stopped so Preacher could learn how to take a picture using his new phone. He got in the back seat and snapped a picture of the apartment building and car as we drove back down the street. I drove to where the street we were on intersected a main street. There wasn't much on the street Lester lived on, a non-branded gasoline station, a boarded-up office building, and a strip center. After surveying the length of the street, I returned to the strip center and parked in front of a laundromat.

"What now?" Preacher asked.

"We sit here and watch for him to leave. All day if we have to."

"No problem."

It was almost noon. We sat in the plastic chairs lined up in front of the laundromat's window. We sat there for hours while a few people came and went. Nobody paid us a bit of attention.

When we were alone, we discussed possible scenarios and what we would do depending on when and where we got to him. I wanted to do that as soon as possible, but if for some reason we didn't get to him that day or the next we'd go sit at the jetty. He'd told his partner he'd be where he was supposed to be. I assumed he meant the jetty. Having to get him at the jetty would mean a significant change in plans for him. I wanted him before then.

The vending machine in the laundromat didn't work. Preacher walked across the street to the gas station and brought back four bags of peanuts. That was lunch.

Lester pulled into the gas station a little after three. He put some gas in his car, but not much. We were ready to go when he left.

Lester didn't go far. He drove straight to a bar near his marina. We watched the door to the bar from our car parked at a spot at the end of the dirt parking lot. It was not as comfortable as the laundromat.

It was hot in the car. I sat in the back seat, stretched out low. Preacher did the same in the front. I was stiff and sore from my ordeal the night before. I would have enjoyed one of Clara's double-decked burgers. I had a bag of oranges, but I had plans for it later. We peed in empty water bottles.

Hogan exited the bar sometime after eight. He walked carefully, like somebody who'd had too much to drink. Preacher and I saw him at the same time and neither of us had to say a word. We'd turned off the dome light. I grabbed the Taser, made sure it was on full discharge, and got out of the car making very little sound. Preacher shifted over behind the steering wheel.

I would have enjoyed standing face to face with Lester Hogan to take him down, to let him see just who ushered him through the door to hell, but there's something to be said for a sneak attack. There would be plenty of time for us to get to know each other later.

I made my approach from the rear, quietly over the chalky surface of the parking lot, being careful not to bang against a car or kick a rock.

It took him a couple of tries to get his key in his car door. In that time I closed the last few yards. As my hand swept toward his neck he finally realized something was happening and started to turn my way. He was too late. With a sharp snap, the Taser did its job. Hogan fell, the only sound his crumpling to the dirt. He quivered spasmodically. The Taser had sapped him of the ability to do anything other than curl into a fetal position at my feet.

That was assault and battery on my part.

Preacher drove up next to where I stood over Hogan. There was a noise and I looked around. A couple of patrons were leaving the bar, but they turned to the parking lot on the other side of the building. I saw no one else, but I appreciated the need to get out of the area quickly.

Preacher and I tugged and pushed and struggled to cram Hogan into his Buick. Preacher went around and pulled him to the passenger side. I had a dozen plastic quick tie strips in my back pocket. I tilted him toward the door and pulled his arms behind his back. I put two of the sturdy plastic ties around his wrists, pulling the loose end tight. I hoped they weren't so tight they would cut off the flow of blood. I put three of the ties around his ankles.

That was false imprisonment on my part and kidnapping was not far off, but we'd finally won one.

I put the Taser within reach on top of the dashboard just in case. He stank of sweat and alcohol. He made a hiccuping kind of moaning noise. Other than an occasional twitchy spasm across his shoulders, he did not move.

I panicked for a moment when I realized I did not have his keys. They still hung from the door. I retrieved them, settled behind his steering wheel, slowed my breathing, started the car and left the parking lot, turning to head toward Galveston.

That was car theft. Oh well, there were other crimes ahead. Preacher followed in my car.

When I was a little way down the road from the bar, before I hit a main road, I pulled into the parking lot of some closed and dark business. Preacher stopped and brought the duct tape. I taped Hogan's mouth shut. I felt his hands. They were warm. They were getting blood. I decided to trust that his feet were okay. I wrapped some tape around his wrists and ankles for good measure.

We crossed the bridge over the Kemah Cut, the lights of the Kemah waterfront sparkled brightly on the channel. I remembered that lady's laugh from the night before. A few miles on the other side of Kemah, Hogan began to stir, twisting slowly at first and stretching. His eyes opened, pupils large, blinking away the sting of sweat. His head, pressed against the passenger door, twisted at an uncomfortable angle. He shifted to see who was driving.

I showed him the Taser and pressed the trigger to cause a miniature bolt of lightning to spark and crack between the contacts. "If you make a fuss, I will zap you again and hog tie you and throw you in that box in your trunk. It's not comfortable back there. Trust me, I know." He stared at me, eyes glazed by whiskey and sweat and fear.

Thirty minutes later I drove down the Texas City Dike. There were a few cars on the sand on the bay side of the jetty. A propane lantern cast a circle of light at one place on the channel side creating a pattern of black shadows in the cracks between the jumbled blocks of granite. A man sat there, holding a rod with a line arching down to the water. He smoked a cigar, raising it slowly, its tip glowing a bright red as he stared at nothing in the channel. He didn't expect to catch a fish, not at this time of slack tide with the sea calm and no tidal current. I envied his opportunity for contemplation.

The dike extends five miles into the bay. My destination was the boat ramp on the bay side a little more than halfway down the dike. There were five or six vehicles there with empty boat trailers strung behind but no boats other than mine. *The Lonely Star* sat still, secured to the bulkhead of the breakwater that shelters the ramp. I parked at one end of the lot, Preacher parked at the other.

Preacher got in the Buick with Hogan. He had the bag of oranges in hand. One of the kids from the marina came up from the cabin of the *Star* when I climbed aboard. He assured me he'd had no problems. I gave him a hundred-dollar bill and the keys to the car I'd borrowed from Peters. I pointed it out and told him to drive carefully. I flipped on the blowers and went back to where Preacher babysat Lester.

I said, "Help me get him on board, and you don't have to stick around. You know what I'm going to do. You shouldn't be a part of it."

"Your cause is just. I'll stick around. Besides, you need somebody to steer the boat. Not to mention you need somebody to back up your story later."

"Thanks."

He nodded. I opened the passenger door. Preacher looked down at the wide-eyed Lester Hogan and said, "Sinner, the time for your redemption is near." With that, he grasped Hogan by the shoulders and pulled him out of the car.

I took his feet and shortly we had him flat on the deck of the boat. I retrieved the Taser and my bag of oranges and locked the doors of his car. Preacher had the engines going as I untied the bow and then the stern, pushing away with my foot as I stepped aboard. With expertise that always makes me curious about the details of his past, Preacher turned the boat away from the bulkhead and toward the channel markers leading us the short distance to safe water away from the dike. The boat picked up speed as we headed down the channel toward the Gulf.

Mindful of my escape from his boat, I dragged Hogan down the steps to the cabin without untying his feet. "Don't make me use this." I touched the Taser hanging from my belt. I pushed and tugged until I could secure his wrists to the chrome pedestal base of the table with a couple of plastic ties. He continued to do the only thing he could. He stared at me.

"I don't necessarily want you to choke on vomit so I'm going to take the tape off your mouth. I don't want to talk to you, and I don't want you to talk to me. We'll do that later. Understand?" He nodded.

Without pause or mercy, I ripped the tape from his mouth. Little dots of blood appeared on his lips in places where skin stuck to the tape. He made a noise. "Shh, don't talk. I'm not going to kill you, but if you don't want to swim home, be quiet. Sober up." I left him there, going topside to join Preacher.

"Want to drive?" he asked.

"Not unless you want me to."

"I'm fine."

It was smooth on the water. I sat at the back of the boat by the bait table and the tackle cabinet. I took out some fish hooks, some pyramid weights, some wire, and some braided steel leaders. I went to work with pliers under the glow of the deck lights.

In an hour we were twenty miles into the Gulf. By then, I was at the helm, keeping a casual watch on the horizon and the radar screen. The GPS guided us to an abandoned drilling platform where we tied the boat. Preacher took a flotation cushion from the locker for a pillow and stretched out on the forward deck. I took one of the cushions and went below.

Hogan greeted me, "What the hell is going on?"

"Don't worry about it, Hogan. Get smart, and I give you greater odds at surviving than you gave me."

"Hey, that wasn't my idea ... "

"Shut up."

"My shoulders are killing me."

"Too bad."

"I really have to pee."

I cut the ties off his wrists and dragged him out from under the table. I opened the door to the head. He pushed himself to his hobbled feet and hopped into the head. When he was done, I made him get back on the floor. I attached his wrists to the table pedestal again.

He was at a most awkward angle on the floor, on his side beneath the table with his wrists against the table base. I pulled his head by his hair and put the cushion underneath him. "Sleep if you want. Tomorrow is going to be a busy day. If you want to think about anything, try to decide whether you want to live or die. It will be your choice."

He started to say something. "Shut up or I'll tape your mouth closed," I said. "Go to sleep."

I left him there. On my way out of the cabin, I flipped the switch that sets the entry alarm. I locked the door. I didn't think he would escape, but if he did I hoped the door alarm would wake me in time. I needed to sleep. Energy was draining out of me.

I checked the battery levels. I left the radar going. I filtered out the return from the drilling platform and set the alarm so that if a boat came within range of the radar it would let me know.

I checked on Preacher telling him to pray that the Coast Guard didn't come to check on us. I stretched out. The anchor lights were attracting fish. I heard the slap of water as fish broke the water beneath the lights. The boat was beginning to tug against a rising tide. The fenders rasped against the encrusted stanchions of the platform. I tried to turn off thoughts by looking at the rich field of stars. Finally, I slept.

The sun woke me. I'd slept longer than expected. Preacher was up, sitting on the bow with crossed legs, eyes closed, facing the sunrise. He heard me and stood up, saying,

"Coffee?"

"Yes. As soon as I check on our guest."

"I'll make the coffee."

We opened the cabin. Lester Hogan looked up with red-rimmed eyes, his face sallow. "What are you going to do to me?"

"Not sure yet. It's up to you."

"What do you mean?"

"First things first. We are forty miles from shore," I lied. "There's no reason you can't make it back to shore with us. I'll even drop you off at your car, but first, we're going to have a discussion."

"You can't do this."

"You want to call the cops?"

"Just tell me what you want."

"First, I'm going to let you loose for a moment so you can pee. Don't get smart. There are two of us. I have the Taser. Deal? If you pee on my boat or break any part of my boat, I'm going to hurt you. Understand?"

"Yeah. I understand. I probably can't even move after lying here all night."

"Try." I knelt behind him. I had one of the big knives, its leather loop around my wrist. I wanted him intimidated by everything I did. He'd had the night to let his imagination work. I was about to exceed the worst thing he could imagine. He limped into the head. "Leave the door open," I said.

I'd turned down the power on the Taser. When he walked out of the head, I touched it to him again and he crumpled to the deck. Preacher helped me drag him to the deck outside and do what I wanted to do.

Hogan might have been aware of what we were doing, but he lacked any ability to resist. By the time he could speak again, he was naked and sitting in the fish fighting chair, his arms tied and taped to the armrests, his ankles pulled back to either side of the chair, tied and taped to the circular footrest that runs all the way around the base of the chair. I'd tied his knees to the armrests leaving him uncomfortably exposed. I stood in front of him munching on an orange. Preacher was at the controls keeping us on a circular course around the platform where we'd spent the night. He watched for other boats.

I held a wedge of orange toward him. "Want some?"

His voice had lost all defiance. It cracked and wavered. "What are you going to do to me? What do you want?"

"Okay, here's what I want. I want to know who your partner is. I want to know why you killed Charlene Coster. I want to know why you killed Mary Elizabeth Kincaid. I want to know when and where your partner intends to make another smuggling run. Mostly I want to know where I can find the girls. I want you to tell me all that. I'll probably have some questions. Then, if you convince me you've told the truth, we'll take you back to your truck. Simple, isn't it?"

He stared at me, wide-eyed, his mouth opening and closing like a fish, but not making a sound. He made a croaking noise. "What are you talking about? I didn't kill nobody. I don't know what you're talking about. I don't know what he might have done."

"Lester, Lester, we both know you were going to kill me. You just lost your first opportunity to have a good day. I was afraid you'd pretend you didn't know what was going on, so I planned a little incentive. Sit back. Relax. We're going fishing."

He stared at me. "Are you some kind of crazy?"

I smiled at him, raising my eyebrows. "Just watch."

The marina kept plastic gallon buckets filled with the waste from cleaning fish. Holes were drilled around the sides of the buckets. When they filled them, they were wrapped tightly in several layers of heavy plastic wrap, sealing the holes. They were stored in a freezer. As requested, they'd put a couple on board at the marina.

I took one of those buckets from an ice chest, heavy with frozen fish heads and entrails. I unwrapped the plastic from around its side exposing the perforations, clipped a line to the handle, and threw it off the back of the boat. The chum inside would begin to melt and the bucket would leave an oily wake that is a dinner call to a myriad of fish. In accordance with the immutable laws of nature, the small fish come for the chum, big fish come for the small fish and bigger fish come for the big fish, right up the food chain all the way to the sharks. Sharks top out the food chain in these waters.

Hogan looked at me like he seriously thought I was crazy. I went about my business, letting the chum begin to work.

I used pyramid weights when fishing from the beach, wedges of lead designed to sink into the sand under the surf. For that day's fishing trip I'd designed another use. I'd used two of the big, barbed game hooks on each of three pyramid weights. The hooks are dangerous looking things with razor-sharp points curved two and a half inches from the shank. I'd wired them to the weight, wrapping the wire one way around the shank and then crossways across the weight between the hooks. I ended up with two hooks at an angle on each weight. The points pointed the same direction a couple of inches apart. The eyes of the two hooks were tied to several yards of sixty-pound test fishing line. On the other end of the line was another one of the hooks on a steel leader.

I held up one of my concoctions, showing it to Hogan. "A bit of tackle of my own design. Let's see if it works."

The oranges I had came in a mesh bag. I removed all but two of the oranges from the bag and tied it shut. I held it up for Hogan to see. "Remind you of anything?"

I tied the bag of oranges to a cleat on the side of the boat. Standing so Hogan couldn't see, I hooked each of the two wired together hooks deeply into the oranges in the bag. Stringing out the line, I went to the stern where I baited the hook on the other end with as much cut bait as I could fit on the hook. I put a float several feet from the hook. I tossed the baited hook well behind the boat, holding the line as it strung out behind the boat. The float kept the baited hook close to the streaming flow of chum.

I shouted up to Preacher at the helm, "We're fishing." He raised a hand, keeping the other on the wheel. He kept watching the horizon for other boats that might intrude on the solitude of our fishing.

There were several possibilities. The bait might be pecked off by something that never took the hook. It might be taken by a cobia, but the hook was probably too large. We were fishing for a shark. I did not want to be on the wrong side of the double hooks if anything took the bait. I moved to one of the seats behind Hogan. He twisted his head to try to see what I was doing. Preacher kept the boat in a gentle circle, keeping the float in the chum trail.

"Relax," I said, "let's see what we can catch." I squinted toward the sun. "Hopefully, we'll get done before you get a bad sunburn."

He did not seem to have anything to say. I sipped my coffee and settled back to watch the line curving over the transom.

It took a little while, but it was a shark that took the line. One moment we were sitting expectantly, and the next the line that curved into the sea zipped out of the water, strung tight. The two hooks embedded in the oranges pulled the sack of oranges parallel to the deck for a fraction of a second before the hooks exploded from the oranges in a burst of pulp. The hooks slammed against the transom and buried there, each barbed hook a solid inch into the side of my boat. One of them had an inch square of orange peel impaled. Bits of orange were strewn about the deck. The bag was ripped open and the two mangled oranges thudded to the deck. Hogan's eyes were rimmed in white as he stared at the oranges.

Before I could get to where the line strung tight in our wake, it broke. The shark would shake the hook loose from its tough mouth or it would dissolve. The shark, a single-minded feeding machine, probably never even knew it had been momentarily hooked. I pulled the line from the water.

"Wow," I said, running a finger over the two hooks embedded in my boat. "Look at that." I turned toward Hogan with what I hoped was a crazy grin. "You're up. You get the next one."

"What are you doing you ... "

"You know what I want." I moved behind him, pulled his head roughly to the headrest and wrapped it with four turns of tape so he couldn't move his head. I went to the tackle cabinet and pulled on a pair of gloves. I got the hooks and line I'd prepared just for him. He made a moaning noise as I lifted him, putting the two hooks between his legs beneath his scrotum.

"Don't do this you crazy son of a bitch."

"Be nice."

He twisted his neck trying, impossibly, to turn. "You

can't let him do this," he screamed.

"He's talking to you," I shouted at Preacher.

"Repent brother. Cleanse your soul by confessing your sins, and you shall be free," Preacher shouted over his shoulder. "And," he said after a pause, "you might save your balls. Hallelujah."

Hogan made a sputtering noise. I carried the coil of line to the stern and baited the hook.

"Stop. You're crazy. You can't do this."

I ignored him. To Preacher, I said, "You can stop here. We know we have some sharks." I turned my back to Hogan. He could not see that I tied the baited line in a slip knot to one of the hooks on the outside of the stern. The line attached to the hooks in his chair was separate and had nothing but a weight tied to the other end. The weight hung outside the boat to just below the hull. It kept a pulsating tension on the line that I'm sure was most uncomfortable to him, even though I'd filed the points off the hooks between his legs. I hoped he was more nervous than attentive.

"Make him stop," he screamed.

"Repent brother," Preacher shouted.

I stood just behind his shoulder and said, "Where are the girls?"

"Oh, man ... "

"Listen, the timing for this is kind of in the hands of you, God, and the creatures of the sea. If a shark takes that bait I don't think you'll be in any kind of shape to tell me what I want to know. It might not kill you, but I know I won't be able to take you back to shore in that kind of shape. Know what I mean? Oh, and it has been my experience that once you hook the first shark, the time it takes to get the second is considerably shorter."

"Okay, okay. Pull that bait in. Get this thing off me."

I moved the hooks from underneath him. I propped the hooks up on the bait table and pulled in the baited hook, coiling the line and laying it beside the double hooks. I turned to him.

"I don't know where the girls ended up. I didn't kill nobody. He did."

I was sure that last bit was a lie, but I let it pass.

"Hang on. I have an idea. If I untie you, will you be good? I don't want to have to zap you again. I'd like to get this on tape."

"You don't have to tape it. Don't do that. Just let me tell you what you want to know."

"No. We'll tape it. Keep in mind I am mad at you. You hurt me. And I know some things. After all, I found his place. If you don't tell me everything I want to know, or if you lie, I will zap you. I will tie you back to that chair, we will go fishing, and after I wash your blood off my boat, I'll figure out some other way to find out what I want to know. Preacher, take us back to the platform. Mr. Hogan has some things to share."

We waited until we were tied back up to the drilling platform before we untied him.

"Let me get dressed."

"No."

We sat at the table in the cabin, Lester Hogan on the bench against the wall and Preacher and me in the chairs on the other side of the table. I put a digital recorder between us and told him to start talking by giving us his name and the date.

"Man," he said, "Shaw will kill me."

"Shaw? What's his first name?"

"Ben."

"Shaw is going down one way or another. You don't have to worry about him. You have to worry about me, my patience, and the creatures of the deep."

He gave up. He was afraid of Shaw, but he had a short-term view of survival. I was the deranged devil he needed to deal with at that moment. I'm sure Hogan was planning which state or foreign country to move to next. Texas did not feel like the friendship state.

He swallowed and nodded. I started the tape recorder. In a shaky voice, he began. "My name is Lester Hogan."

He asked me the date, I told him, he repeated it and, with no further prodding from me, he told us the story.

Hogan did a good job once he started talking. He was, of course, most concerned with the immediate trouble in which he found himself. He thought I was crazy enough to do what I threatened to do. Preacher had extolled him to redeem himself in the eyes of God. I'm sure Hogan thought he was in the grips of a couple of madmen. He knew first-hand the viciousness of Shaw. If he was lucky enough to escape my clutches, I did not doubt he intended to disappear from this part of Texas.

"I didn't kill them women. I didn't know Ben was going to kill them. I was just doing what he told me to do. That woman from Chicago was causing trouble. She found Charlene. He figured you and her was the ones that tried to get the girls off the van that night. Y'all were going to ruin a good thing. I've never seen Ben so crazy mad."

"What good thing are we going to ruin?"

"Ben makes money. Ben makes a lot of money bringing things into Galveston off of ships. He was afraid she was going to mess that all up."

"What kind of things does he bring in?"

"People, girls mostly and, you know, drugs. Cocaine. I

think."

"For whom?"

"I don't know. Somebody he knew in New Orleans, I think. Whoever it is bought him that boat. He's real careful nobody sees it. He keeps it under wraps except at night. He just wanted to make a million dollars. Then we were going to go to an island somewhere and open up a dive shop."

Hogan was fibbing about who did the killing. I was sure he'd done it. I'd heard their conversation.

"How did Shaw pick you as his partner?"

"He's my nephew. We're family. We come from Louisiana. He got a job at the Glencannon Chemical Plant down here and called me to come down to help out in his . . . uh . . . side business."

"Tell me about killing Mary Elizabeth Kincaid and Coster."

"Charlene was dancing, you know. That woman somehow found out about her. She came snooping around wanting to talk to Charlene. Charlene convinced her to not cause a scene at the club and agreed to meet her when she got off work. Charlene called Ben, freaking out.

"We worked out a plan. I thought he was just going to scare her off, you know?"

The weasel was coming up with his story, trying to put it all on Shaw's back.

"Charley was kind of Ben's girlfriend off and on. She was there, that lady, sitting in the parking lot waiting for Charlene to come out. I drove Ben to the club. Charlene waited until Ben called her to tell her he was there. When Charley got in that lady's car, Ben climbed into the back. I followed them to Ben's place.

"Can I have some water?"

Preacher gave him a bottle. "Keep going."

"You're gonna kill me, aren't you?"

"Not if you keep talking into that recorder. You're peanuts to me. I want the girls and I want Shaw."

"Ben wanted to know about you. What you knew. What you planned to do. He wanted to know where the whore was. I know he'd talked to somebody after y'all tried to get the girls and they said they'd pay to get her back."

Preacher slapped the table and said, "Stop it. That little girl was a child. She was not a whore. Do not call her that."

Hogan nodded. "Sorry. I didn't mean nothing."

"Keep going," I said.

"Anyway, that lady wouldn't tell him nothing, even when he slapped her around a bit."

It was all I could do to keep myself from slapping Hogan around a bit. Preacher stirred and put a hand on my shoulder, squeezing once.

"Anyway, Ben was pacing and swearing. I've never seen him like that. Finally, I guess he slapped her a bit too hard and knocked her out. He found a hotel key in her pockets. It was in one of them envelopes with a room number written on it."

All our precautions, switching cars, hiding out and watching our back and Mary Elizabeth went off with her hotel key in her pocket in the envelope with the name of her hotel and room number. I should have never left her alone.

I'd known she was getting more and more anxious to do something. She took the message from Rocky about where to find Coster and blinded by something, her faith, her sad anger, something, she went off on her fool's errand, trying to do something while I was in trial. Another weight on me. I kept listening to Hogan's tale.

"Ben was some kind of mad. He knew who you were,

and he'd looked for you, but he couldn't find you. And this lady walks into the club where Charley was dancing. He couldn't figure out how you were finding out stuff. Charley started freaking out a little saying we were all gonna get caught and go to prison. Ben yelled at her to shut up. All of a sudden he upped and grabbed Charley by the head and slammed it against his toolbox knocking her out. I think that's probably what killed her, you know. Him doing that was a big surprise to me. Scared the bejesus out of me, you know. I thought he was going to kill all of us right then and there."

I was sure Hogan was right that Shaw decided at that moment he had to cut all ties, take his stash and disappear. I did not think his family relationship with Hogan would have saved Hogan. He needed Hogan to do a little more dirty work. He was super careful to keep his lair free of any actual killing.

From the conversation I'd overheard back when they had me in the trunk, I was sure Hogan was the one tasked with the actual killing and that Mary Elizabeth and Coster were not his first. Unlike Hogan, I didn't think Shaw was going to take him along to open the dive shop. Once he didn't need him to do his killing he was a dangerous loose end. Obviously, Hogan talked too easy when faced with pressure. If things had worked as Shaw planned, Hogan would probably have ended up being the first person Shaw actually killed himself.

"Hey, man," he said, "can I have something to eat?"

"No. Not yet. I offered you an orange earlier. You turned it down."

He started to get too comfortable. The longer we went without me threatening to rip off his testicles, the more his story would vary from the truth and in his favor. There was really only one thing I wanted to know.

"I take it he went to the hotel and got the girl. Where did he take her?"

"Yeah, he went and got her that night. I don't know where he took her. I wasn't there."

That might be true. Hogan was probably out on the Gulf killing and dumping bodies.

"You went with them when they transported girls. Where did you go."

"We'd go to Dallas and St. Louis and Chicago. Sometimes one city, sometimes a couple of them in one trip. We'd drop girls off in each city. We'd go to some warehouse somewhere, and there'd be guys there. They usually could talk to the girls in some language I didn't understand. Some would leave, and some would go on somewhere else."

"Who paid y'all?"

"I didn't get in to all that. We'd drop the girls off. Ben would sometimes go off with one of them and come back with a case. I guess it had the money in it."

"How much?"

"I don't know. He was saving most of it up for our dive business. He'd give me and Charlene five hundred dollars a trip. I know he liked dealing with the cocaine more than he did the girls. The girls were a pain in the ass, and we had to haul them across the country. The coke he dropped off somewhere in Houston. I think he made more money with the coke."

"How do we find the warehouses you took the girls to?"

"It changed all the time. I don't know. Charlene would drive the van, and we'd follow. Once we got somewhere, she'd have to follow us. Only Ben knew where to go. I never did."

"Try to remember something."

"I don't know. I really don't know Chicago. In Dallas it was usually someplace kind of close to the Cotton Bowl. We'd pass by there every once in a while. One of the warehouses in Dallas had walls painted green on the lower half and brown on the top. Other than that they all looked, you know, like warehouses, nothing special."

Great. A warehouse somewhere on the east side of Dallas. I didn't think he knew anything better than that.

"How about the guys who met you. Describe some of them."

"I stayed in the truck and never got a close look. They were all short dudes, shorter than average and like I said, they spoke some other language."

"When did you hear them speak to the girls?"

"You know, they'd open the door on the van. They'd have a sheet of paper with names on it, and they'd talk to the girls in the van, call out a couple by name."

"Concentrate. You can't think of anything about any of the ones you saw open the van? You must have looked at them."

"Really. Nothing special. I was always real nervous about then." He paused and looked up at the ceiling. "There was this one dude. In Dallas. One of the other guys patted one of the girls on the ass while she was getting out of the van. This dude came over and slammed him up against the van and screamed at him in that language they talked. He was mad. He had a weird scar. It ran around from back of his ear and up to his eye. It looked like somebody might have cut off his ear sometime."

"Which ear?"

"It would have been his left one."

"Okay. That's good. Was that in the warehouse with

the half brown wall?"

"Oh, hell, I don't remember."

"Okay. Anything else?"

"Not really. If I think of anything I'll tell you. I promise."

We talked some more. He didn't know Gladys Hopper, the listed owner of Shaw's property. He thought Shaw owned it. He talked about how smart Shaw was and how he modified the boat with a muffler to keep it quiet when necessary. He was proud of the place Shaw built to hide the boat in the top of the boathouses I'd discovered. Shaw actually had a written business plan for running his dive shop somewhere in the Caribbean. I think Hogan's vision of paradise was living in the Caribbean working on Shaw's dive boat.

For all his gabbing, Hogan never mentioned his role as look-out on the jetty, and I didn't ask about it. I knew it was him in the photos Jenny had taken. He was trying to tell his story and keep his involvement as small as possible.

Shaw had taken all the sketch pads in the hotel room. He must have seen the drawings made by Mina. He had to have felt the tightening noose, but he thought that rope had been cut by my demise. After all, police had not shown up at his doorstep.

"Sit still," I said. "I have to get a breath of fresh air."

The Gulf stretched around us horizon to horizon. There were boats, but they were all far away and looked insignificant in the surrounding sea. I felt small in the world.

Mary Elizabeth, a person with as good a heart as I could imagine, was dead. Mina and Zoio were out there somewhere in an unfathomable horror. I thought about having to live for the rest of my life imagining their fate, but never knowing for sure where they were or what was happening to them. In the end, Hogan and Shaw were just a couple of organisms as insignificant as me. I would help Shaw offload his coke if he could get me to the girls.

"That son of a bitch is lying about who killed Mary Elizabeth, isn't he?" Preacher said.

"Yeah, he is. I've got to decide what to do."

"You going to give him to the cops?"

"I was, but let me tell you what I'm thinking and see what you think. This guy Shaw uses Hogan to do his murder. He doesn't let it happen at his house. He is not living flashy. I don't think he's spending the money he's making. He's got a job at that plant for his living expenses. I think he really is saving up to open a dive shop somewhere. If nothing had happened, maybe he'd have taken Hogan with him. He likes having a flunky. He won't now. He's feeling the heat, and he plans to get out of here alone with nobody around who could put somebody on his tail.

"He thinks I'm dead. Shaw knows Hogan can do it right when he tries. He's killed for Shaw before. I don't know what went wrong with Mary Elizabeth and Coster. Maybe Hogan was too drunk to worry about getting them out far enough to disappear. Doesn't matter.

"Shaw is a planner. He has the money somewhere ready to run. That boat can get him there if he's careful. It's probably legitimately registered somewhere. He's a planner. He knows how and where he's going. A part of his plan is the money. He'll want as much as he can get without trouble, at least whatever the next run will pay. That's his problem. That and the guys who pay him. He has to do at least one more run and make one more chunk of change. Plus, he doesn't want to piss off the people he works for. He doesn't know it, but he's giving us one more chance."

"So, what are we going to do?

"I think we're going to let Lester go. I only care about getting to the girls. If we get balled up with the cops, it'll limit us. I'll find a way to let them know enough to get what they need. I'll hire a lawyer to represent us and talk to the cops. If I have to, I'll go in. Later. But if Shaw goes out like he did the time we know about, he's out there today. I don't want to spend the night in jail or spend a couple of days talking to law enforcement."

"He killed her. I hate to think that scumbag down below will get away."

"How long do you think it'll be before he's caught? Not long. He's a loser. If they get Shaw, you know he'll give him up. Besides, I don't really care about anything other than finding the girls. If we become involved as an official part of this thing, we're going to be limited in what we can do later. We'll be known. Maybe the guys who pay Shaw will come after us. They'll sure be aware of us. That would limit us. There's no statute of limitations on murder. We can give him up later. Hopefully, after we have the girls."

"Okay. That makes sense. I would be willing for Shaw and Hogan to have their damn dive shop if we can get Mina and Zoio safe."

"Me, too. There's another thing. Frankly, I'm tired of him kicking my ass. I want a part in bringing Shaw down. I don't want to be told to stay away or be locked up."

"What are you thinking?"

"I'm thinking we put the Coast Guard on Shaw anonymously and I take up Hogan's look-out job at the jetty. I'll make sure it doesn't help him. If he tries to come that way, I'll turn him around. If he still gets away, we know where he's going. We'll let them know about that. They'll get him. Then, once they catch him, we'll get all the info we have to them."

"Sounds good, with one change. You and I take over the look-out. I'm going with you."

I shrugged. "Sure."

"Now it's a smart idea."

"No. It is a foolish idea, but I want it. I want to be a part of it."

We went back below.

"Lester," I said, "I'm going to tell you what we're going to do, and I'm going to ask you some questions. First, you have to understand a couple of things."

His bloodshot eyes, no longer blurred by alcohol, focused on me with clarity. He needed a shave. He was keeping his legs pressed together to hide his nakedness. He nodded.

"Mary Elizabeth Kincaid was a very good friend of mine. She was a good and decent person who dedicated her life to taking care of other people. She was a nun. Did you know that?"

He blinked at that. "No, man, I didn't know that."

"She was. She believed in doing what was right with God. I am not a nun or a priest and I don't often go to church. I am unwilling to wait for God to punish the people who killed her."

"It was him. It was Shaw man. I'd never kill nobody, especially a nun."

I held up a hand to stop him. "Bottom line is this. I am upset about her death. I am so upset I would have left those hooks in your balls if you hadn't agreed to talk to me about it. I am so upset that if I catch you in any kind of lie, I am going to shoot you in the head and dump you overboard."

He blinked a lot at that, probably thinking about all the lies he'd already told me.

"I ain't lying to you, man."

"Nevertheless, we are not done. Answer this one. What is the schedule for Shaw's next smuggling trip?"

He swallowed. "What is today?"

"It's Sunday."

"He's already gone. He goes way out, hundreds of miles and spends the night out there. He'll pick up his load tomorrow and get back to his place in the dark tomorrow night."

"What's he bringing in this time?"

"A load of coke."

"Answer this next question carefully."

"Okay."

"Did you tell him I was dead?

"Yeah, man. I had to, you know. I didn't know if you drowned or not when you jumped out of my boat. I didn't see you. I figured you drowned. I had to tell him you were dead or ... "

He paused, probably thinking what would happen if Shaw knew he'd messed up again. Shaw would take him out. He didn't want to think about it, but he knew it.

"So, as far as he knows, he's safe?"

"Yeah."

I didn't ask him about his role in the smuggling. He'd have lied. I didn't really care. I didn't know if he kept quiet about it because he was trying to distance himself as much as possible. Maybe he was hoping Shaw would get away one more time and make the dive shop a reality. Paradise. If that was it, I would have to keep Hogan away from the jetty. If Shaw had reason to try to make a run through the cut, I'd stop him. If he didn't I'd have cops waiting for him.

I tried every which way to get more information that would help us look for the girls, but he just didn't have it.

Finally, I handed him an orange and motioned Preacher to follow me topside.

Once out of Hogan's hearing I said, "Change of plans."

"What?"

"You're going to have to keep Hogan out on the boat tomorrow night. We can't have him getting brave and warning off Shaw in any way. We don't want him going to do lookout duty at the cut. We don't want him calling Shaw, and we don't want to get caught with him on shore."

Preacher nodded. "Yes, I see what you mean. Okay. You'll go to the cut, and you will be careful, right?"

"Yes."

I went below to let Hogan loose to get dressed. I gave him another orange and one of the packaged sandwiches from the fridge on the boat.

"What are you going to do? You're letting me go, right? I did what you wanted. I have to get away, or Ben will kill me when he finds out."

"We're all going to spend the night out here. I'm going to shore tomorrow to take care of Ben. You're going to stay on the boat with my friend until I'm done. Eat. Pee. Then we'll go up top. You give me grief, I zap you and tie you up. If, at any time, the Coast Guard or a game warden wants to talk to us and you say one word, I will immediately explain what's going on and give them a copy of the recording. I'll tell them what you tried to do to me. I'll tell them you killed a nun. Got it?"

He just nodded.

We spent the rest of the day not doing much. I kept talking to Hogan looking for information that might get me to the girls. He convinced me he had no idea. He convinced me didn't know what happened with the cocaine.

I showed Preacher how to use the Taser, despite his

assurance he knew how.

Preacher and I slept on deck. Despite his assurances he would not try anything, I tied Hogan's wrists and ankles and tied his wrist to a chrome rail at the side of the sofa where he slept. I tied a line from his wrists to mine running it up and out to where I slept. I told him to tug me awake if he needed to get up during the night. I checked on him during the night and each time he was snoring.

We headed in well before daybreak. The sun wasn't up when I got off at the Texas City Dike where we'd left the cars. I drove to my place on Galveston. I had things to do.

CHAPTER TWENTY

ON THE WAY TO MY PLACE, once I got to the west end of Galveston Island, I drove down the beach looking for Max James. Five days a week Max worked at the big Dow plant. On the other two days and holidays, he fished on the beach, accompanied by his wife Shirley and his six children.

Occasionally, a group of solitary surf fishermen socialized. Typically it would be around a pot of gumbo or a grill. There were contributions of food and a considerable amount of beer. Max and Shirley were a part of the group I joined from time to time.

Max used to be a commercial fisherman of sorts. Back before the crackdown, he used gill nets to catch loads of fish he sold to area wholesalers and restaurants. It was not exactly a legal occupation and, at Shirley's request, Max went straight, getting a job at the Dow Chemical plant and confining his fishing to legal pursuits.

All six of the James children were a very well-behaved tribe of beach bums. Like their dad, they were sun-tanned brown with white teeth in a healthy grin in grimy faces. They would all stop whatever they were doing and looked at Max when he shouted "hey, you."

I found Max and his family about eight miles down the beach from my house. All of his children but the oldest were bedded down on blankets in the back of his pick-up. Shirley was tending a coffee pot on a propane burner. Twelve-year-old Max Junior and Max were at a bait table, cutting bait for the six surf rods fanning out from their section of the beach.

I stopped and got out of my truck. "Hey Max, Shirley."

He stopped cutting bait and wiped his hands on the

front of his t-shirt. "Hi, Sam. What's up?"

"I was wondering if I could borrow your flounder rig for a couple of days."

He looked at me with a raised eyebrow. "Sure, but it ain't time to go floundering."

"I know. I'm not going after flounder. I just need a shallow draft boat with lights to check on something."

"Well, sure, you know where it is. It don't have a motor on it." He went to the cab of his truck and got a key ring with about twenty keys. Pulling off a small brass key, he said, "Here's the key to the padlock on the trailer."

"It will take my little seven horsepower outboard, won't it?"

"Sure. No problem. The trailer has a two-inch ball." He asked no questions.

I accepted Shirley's offer of a cup of coffee and admired the three redfish and four black drum the James family had harvested since midnight. I left, telling him I would take care of his boat and return it sometime the next day. He waved me away. I hoped what I'd said about returning the boat would turn out to be true. I wondered if the kayak was still where I left it.

At my house, I picked up my small outboard motor and marine radio. The radio picks up all the bands of offshore traffic. I took one of my fully charged batteries and a clip-on cable to power the radio. At the last moment, I thought about the portable antennae.

Max's house was on the waterway at Surfside, just east of the big bridge to the mainland. Around and beneath Max's house was a clutter of the things that accumulate around a coastal home in which somebody lived full time.

Max's flounder rig was a flat-bottomed aluminum boat. He'd built a platform up on the bow on which he could stand and either pole his way through shallow water or use an electric, foot steered trolling motor. The stern of the boat was taken up by a square fish box. There was an extended boat mount where I could put my little outboard. I would have to sit in the fish box to steer.

When Max used the flounder rig, he went out in the dark and stood on the platform up front. In front of the fish box, he had a bank of batteries to power the powerful floodlights on poles on either side of the platform. The whole thing floated in less than eight inches of water even when loaded.

He would stand on the platform on the bow with gig in hand and move slowly across the shallow seabed. The lights would be pointed down into the water and when they lit up a flounder lying on the bottom, he'd gig it and in one fluid motion swing the fish over his head and into the fish box. Max James and his flounder rig were an efficient fishing machine.

The platform in the bow was large enough for both him and Shirley. One night, in the middle of a storm, he and I were drinking beer and eating tacos at some joint. He told me he decided to marry Shirley the moment he saw her cutting bait using her left hand. Max and Shirley could stand side by side on the fishing platform and neither would interfere with the others strike with the gig. It was a marriage made in heaven and blessed with many flounder and many children.

I needed the lights, but thought the low profile of the boat might come in handy as well. I was happy to see that Max had a trickle charger hooked up to the bank of batteries that powered the lights.

I hooked the boat up and headed back toward Galveston. My first stop was at a convenience store in

Surfside. I bought a foil-wrapped chocolate bar and a long distance calling card from a vending machine. I ate the chocolate and kept the wrapper.

I used the calling card at the pay phone in the parking lot. First, I called the Coast Guard. I put the foil over the mouthpiece. As soon as the phone was answered, and using my best imitation of Hogan's bayou influenced accent, I said, "My name is Lester Hogan. I know a guy named Ben Shaw, lives in a house on East Bay that used to belong to Gladys Hopper. He's got one of them offshore racing boats. He is bringing a big ol' load of cocaine up through Bolivar Roads tonight. Tell him to stop screwing other guys' girlfriends." The man who answered the phone was talking as I hung up.

I called Chambers County Crime Stoppers and gave them the same information. I even got the code number to collect my reward if one was awarded.

Back on Galveston Island, I drove to the Walmart just off the seawall and purchased four coiled cotton anchor lines. I bought two mushroom type anchors and four small, five-pronged grapnel anchors. I hoped the sea would not be running so rough that I would need more.

I went back to my place and called Patricia to tell her all was well and that we had the Coast Guard involved. We talked for a while. She told me to call Jason. I said I'd do it sometime the next day. I ate, checked the tide tables for the jetties, and took a nap the best I could before driving to the other end of Galveston Island.

The ferry deposited me on Bolivar Peninsula, and I drove to the north jetty. I turned at the bait shop where Jenny spent all those nights and drove down to the beach nestled between the jetty and the remains of the old Fort Jackson. It's a nice little stretch of sand protected by the breakwater at the foot of the Fort on one side and the jetty on the other. At the base of the jetty is a boat ramp where I could launch Max's small craft.

Waves crashed roughly along the length of the jetty, and I hoped the seas would lessen somewhat closer to the slack tide. Otherwise, I had an excellent chance of sinking Max's boat or piling it up on the rocks. I thought Shaw would wait until after midnight to make his run. I had a while to wait.

Down the beach, in the glow of a propane lantern, a black gentleman with two small boys was kept busy baiting the boys' hooks and keeping their lines untangled. His rod and reel leaned unused against his car. There was a quiet joy in their camaraderie, and even though I knew it wasn't likely, I hoped that man and his sons would always have such a peaceful and close relationship.

The light changed as the sun set. The waves in the gulf took on luminescence from the lower angle of the sun, the breaking sea a foamy white against the slick water of the waves. It would have been one of those peaceful moments in which Mary Elizabeth would have taken great delight. I would have liked to have shared it with Patricia. I wanted to get to the boat cut while there was still some daylight left.

I rigged the lines and anchors I'd bought. I wrapped a life vest around my radio and tucked it into the fish box. I left the spotlights lowered with their poles folded back along each side of the boat. I put my motor on the boat and pulled it off the trailer at the edge of the water so that just its rear half tried to float. I did not even try to back the trailer into the waves cresting on the beach. I left the front half of the boat on the beach tied to a rock. I parked and locked my truck on the beach and waded into the water to wrestle the boat around until the waves beat against the bow.

I pulled it deep enough to get the motor out of the sand and banged my shins climbing over the side. The ocean immediately tried to turn the boat sideways and tumble me overboard. Luckily, the little outboard started on the first pull, and I was able to keep from swamping the boat.

The boat struggled as I turned it away from the beach. The waves beat against its square bow. Water splashed into the boat with every wave. I worried I could not get the boat out to the cut, or be able to hold it there if I did. I hoped the sea would lessen.

I stayed well away from the rocks of the jetty. The boat was like a see-saw in the rhythmic rise and fall of its bow. It sounded like an aluminum drum as I pushed farther away from the beach. One old man on the jetty shook his head in bewilderment at me.

I made my way slowly down the length of the jetty. If I went too fast, the boat would spear its bow into the center of the waves and threaten to fill itself with water. I started thinking maybe I should have walked out and set up something on the jetty.

Eventually, my stomach feeling like I was riding a bucking horse, I approached the boat cut. At the cut, currents had swept a hole into the seabed, and the waves lessened in the deeper water. Plus, the currents swirling through the cut dissipated the water's energy, increasing the speed of the current, but smoothing out the waves. That current threatened to pull my little boat through the cut or into the rocks.

I backed off the power on the motor and let the boat be pushed toward the jetty. Luckily, there was no one around. Otherwise, they would have thought me foolishly in trouble and tried to help. I threw one of the grapnel hooks into the rocks where it found solid purchase in the crevices of the tumbled granite slabs. I played the line out as I twisted the throttle and moved the boat across to the other side of the cut.

I threaded the line of one of the other grapnel hooks through the eye of a mushroom anchor. That anchor would pull the line down out of the way of any passing boats. I hoped. I tossed that anchor into the middle of the cut and let the line run freely through my hands as it sank. When it settled, I twirled the grapnel anchor over my head and tossed it into the rocks of the jetty. It lodged there solidly.

I let that anchor line out slowly while pulling the other anchor line tight and moved my tiny craft back to a point just inside the cut. The waves there still rocked, but it actually smoothed enough that I was no longer worried about having to swim to the jetty. I tied off the anchor lines in a way that held me secure just off the rocks. I raised the spotlights and, with wet, aching arms, settled down to wait.

As the tide slowed, the waves calmed. After an hour or two, I did not have to keep one hand on each line ready to heave. No boats approached the cut from either side.

At midnight, the sea was calm. A couple of times I heard the rumble of off-shore power boats, but could not see if either of them was Shaw. I heard the sound of a big boat powering out to sea and eventually saw its lights out in the Gulf as it turned north. I could not, however, tell if it was a Coast Guard cutter. I had the radio on monitoring the channels on which I expected to hear any Coast Guard transmissions.

Using the anchor lines, I pulled out to the middle of the cut and tied the lines down so that the boat was held with its bow facing toward the Gulf through the cut. I fiddled with the radio, not wanting to miss any transmission. At some point, a helicopter roared overhead sounding to me like another Coast Guard craft.

Finally, on the off-shore hailing channel, I heard, "This is the United States Coast Guard calling the unidentified power boat on our starboard side. You will heave to and prepare to be boarded for a search. Please respond."

Bingo.

I heard no response.

"I repeat, this is the United States Coast Guard, heave to and prepare to be boarded." I raised my head to listen without the radio but could only hear wind and waves. "Attention unidentified power boat. You are ordered to stop and . . . damn." The transmission stopped. I assumed the chase was on.

I wondered how far away he was. If Shaw decided to use the boat cut, he would want to get to it fast enough to outrun the Coast Guard before they had time to marshal other forces. Soon, I heard the unmuffled roar of the twin engines on Shaw's powerboat.

I could not tell directions, but I assumed he was headed my way. The Coast Guard cutter would have to take the long way around. Shaw counted on the shortcut to allow him time to get safely ensconced in a hiding place in the bay system. It was a good plan, worthy of a wily coastal smuggler, except for me. He did not count on me.

I tied a line to the boat to hang on to and stood, peering into the darkness. He was, of course, running without lights. Offshore, every few seconds, I saw a light I assumed was the searching beam of the Coast Guard helicopter. I saw spotlights on the side of what had to be the cutter sweeping the ocean. At his speed and maneuverability, I expected Shaw to be able to dodge those lights. At some point, the captain on the cutter would figure out Shaw's plan and he would have to head to the channel, sending the Coast Guard miles out of the way.

The sound of the powerboat was definitely headed my way. My plan was to deny him use of the boat cut and turn him back out to the waiting arms of the Coast Guard. Or force him to the beach of Bolivar Peninsula to try to escape on foot. On his side of the jetty that would put him in an expanse of mud flats. Either option assured his capture.

I stood watching with my foot on the switch for Max's bank of lights. If I turned them on too soon, it would give him too much time to compensate. He might see enough of me to realize he could probably blow right over me with little consequence. I strained to see him.

I expected him to try to slow down, but the sound of his engines stayed constant. I'm sure he was wondering about Hogan. He had to be navigating solely by GPS and radar. I assumed he had practiced this maneuver. It took a certain amount of stupid courage to race toward a granite jetty at what must have been fifty miles per hour.

When I finally saw light reflecting off the spray of his bow, it surprised me how close he'd come. He was almost on top of me when I pressed the light switch with my foot.

I had the lights turned up as bright as possible and pointing straight into Shaw's face and his boat. They were blinding. The bright lights etched everything into sharp relief. I could see the hard sharp edge of the granite slabs of the jetty. The listing masts on the sunken shrimp boat forty yards from the cut loomed in the bright light. I could see his boat closer than it should be, its wake bright in the light.

I saw Shaw's startled face and his hand as it came up to shield his eyes. I did not think he would stop and prepared to dive whichever way looked safest.

His actions outstripped his ability to think. He swung

hard to port without slowing down.

I saw the broad bottom of his boat as he cut into the turn. I thought for a moment he might make it, but then, his propellers came out of the water. His boat slipped sideways at forty or fifty miles per hour. He had no control.

Shaw's boat crashed into the unforgiving mass of the jetty. I watched Shaw fly a short way down the length of the jetty, his mouth open in an unheard scream. The sound of the boat hitting the rocks was horrible. There was a whump and a flash as his gas tank ruptured and the fuel hit the heat of the engines. The only other sound I noticed was the wet sack sound of Shaw hitting the top of the jetty. A white cloud of cocaine blew into the air. I wondered for a moment if it would hurt the fish.

It had not been my intention to kill Shaw. I didn't want him dead. If he was dead, I had ruined our best chance to find Mina and Zoio.

I pulled my boat over to the jetty, bow first so the lights could shine down its length. The fire from his boat faded fast off to the side. I banged a knee once before I got solid purchase on the rocks. I got to where I could peer over the edge of the jetty. Shaw lay in a crumpled mess, folded into the rocks. His head was at an unnatural right angle from his body. He was beyond help.

"Stupid motherfucker," I said.

There was no reason for me to stick around. I motored back to the beach, put the boat on the trailer, and headed for the ferry. In the sky behind me, the spotlight of the Coast Guard helicopter approached the jetty.

CHAPTER TWENTY-ONE

IT WAS IN THE NEWS THE NEXT MORNING—*smuggler running from coast guard crashes into the jetty trying to escape through the boat cut.* Fishermen and sightseers were advised to stay away from the active crime scene.

I'd called Preacher the night before, told him it was over, that we'd talk onshore, and to drop off his passenger at his car. He dropped Hogan off at the Texas City Dike, I met him at the marina and filled him in on what happened.

"God rest his evil soul," he said. "What about the girls?"

"I don't know. I guess we'll get started looking for them."

The next morning I called Patricia and told her the smuggler tried to run and died in a crash. She told me she'd let me know what flight she was on to Houston.

I finally made the call to Jason. It went better than I expected. I told him about Shaw's death.

He said, "It's on CNN. I thought that might be the guy. Listen, I was furious at you for a while, but I want you to know I honestly know it wasn't your fault. Patricia filled me in on all of your precautions, and I don't know what you could have done differently."

"I'm probably coming up there soon. I want to look for the girls, and I have to start there."

"I don't know how you're going to find them, but I didn't expect you to find the smuggler and you did. Fast. And look how that turned out. You got him."

"I know, but it wasn't so good. I wanted him captured, so he'd help find the girls in exchange for a no death penalty plea deal."

"Come on up. I'll help as I best I can. We owe it to Mary Elizabeth."

"I'm pretty sure what happened here won't come back to bite you, but who knows what they'll be able to get Mina to tell them if they apply enough pressure. Be careful."

"We're doing what we can. I hate it, but we now have the services of an armed guard for a while."

I called Rocky and filled him in on what happened. He said it wasn't the best ending, but it certainly wasn't the worst possible. He was going to send Jenny to Dallas to visit some family for a while. Just in case.

Later in the day, the news reports identified the dead smuggler as Benjamin Shaw and announced that law enforcement officials were looking for his uncle, Lester Hogan. Hogan's driver's license photo was broadcast. Hogan knew I had the recording of his confession. I thought he would be found, but hoped he'd be quiet about his day and night at sea with me. If he didn't, I'd hire a lawyer.

Rocky called later in the evening. His sources told him that Gladys Hopper, the deceased owner of the house Shaw lived in, had been identified as Shaw's great aunt. And by the time the cops got there to search the house, it had been ransacked. Hogan must have driven straight there and done a hurried search for Shaw's money stash. I doubted he found it. Shaw was too careful to make it easy.

I hoped Hogan hadn't found it. I hoped law enforcement didn't find it. I wanted it, and I thought I knew where to find it. The search for the girls could take a long time and be very expensive. I needed the money for that. If I was right, I would have to move fast and at night before somebody else figured it out.

I'd never thought about where the money might be,

but my subconscious must have been chewing on the question. That morning an idea had urged me awake after only a couple of hours of sleep.

Shaw had a cement mixer, chicken wire, and a pile of oyster shells. When I'd walked through the dark water toward his boathouses, stumbling along the oyster bed just offshore from his place, I'd encountered a lot of oyster shells scattered loosely along the bottom. And there had been that lump in the oyster bed I'd observed on my depth finder the first time Preacher and I approached his place.

A stick of dynamite pushed into the oysters late at night might have done the scattering. An explosion under water in the oyster bed at night would not have been noticed by anybody. He could have cemented oyster shells over a frame of steel and chicken wire and replaced the hole opened by the explosion. If I was right, I would be glad he was smart enough not to have Hogan help sink his oyster vault.

Preacher and I were sitting on the deck of my boat drinking whiskey when I told him what I thought.

"You would be right to go get his money. You can use it to find the girls. What better use would there be for money so very dirty? I'm in."

"That's what I'm thinking." I'd quit tracking all the crimes I'd committed or planned to commit.

We needed to move fast. Shaw didn't live loud or spend a conspicuous amount of money. The law enforcement agencies involved in investigating Shaw's crimes and death had to be salivating over the prospect of getting their hands on his cash.

At twilight, once again, Preacher and I were fishing the shore of East Bay in Sol de Mer's center console fishing boat. Amazingly, the kayak I'd left under the dock was still there. We retrieved it and tied it on the front deck of our boat.

We began fishing the oyster bed. Our drift took us in front of Shaw's property. Crime scene tape circled Shaw's dock and boathouse. They'd opened the drop down doors I'd guessed were there. We saw a few people standing around the property. A news van was parked there, antennae extended. We drifted the oyster bed in front of his dock. A man in uniform came to the edge of the property and looked at us. I raised a hand in greeting and he nodded at me.

We boxed a couple of fish.

We circled and started our drift again. It was getting darker. When the depth finder showed the hump in the oyster bed, I slipped a float over the side to mark the location.

We boxed one fish on that drift.

The third time around it was so dark we could not see Shaw's boathouse. There was a glow of lights from the property. We anchored over the hump marked by my float. I slipped a scuba tank over the back of our boat and hooked it to the ladder. I looped the line on the marker float around a cleat and clipped a lead weight to the line.

"I'm going to go look. You keep a line in the water. Throw it way out there. I don't want you to hook me. If anybody gets curious about what you're doing, you drop that weight over the side and throw the float in the water. I'll check it before I come up if I can find it. If they get to you, tell them our prop fell off and I'm looking for it. Then, start thinking of who we can call to bail us out of jail."

I stripped down to shorts. To my belt, I clipped a mesh bag containing a knife, a small crowbar, a sturdy screwdriver, and a mallet. If nothing else, their weight would help me stay on the bottom. I had a flashlight looped around my wrist, but even with the light, seeing underwater was going to be a problem and spooky. I slipped quietly over the back of the boat. I could just stand on the oyster bed. I put on the tank and a dive mask and sank down into the water.

With the light, visibility was less than the length of my arm. Sand and stuff floated in the water. A scattering of mud minnows fled as I pulled myself along the oyster bed. At least this time I was wearing steel mesh fishing gloves. The hump was just under our bow. I examined it in the light. At first, it looked like the surrounding oyster bed. It rose over a length of about four feet and peaked at about two feet higher than the surrounding bed. I pulled myself to the mud and scattered shells at its side. There was an overhang there and a dark hole leading under the bed.

I scooped sand out of the narrow opening. It was a small opening. I wondered how, if this was his hole, Shaw could squeeze into that narrow space. But, I had to try. I took off the scuba tank and pushed it into the hole keeping the mouthpiece in my mouth.

I turned on my back and pulled myself into the darkness of the hole. I didn't move far before I could not feel anything overhead. I pulled my head and shoulders into the space and shined the flashlight around. I was in a murky chamber of some sort. I felt along the side to the top. I bumped into something floating.

I pushed the scuba tank to the side and pulled myself in until I could sit up, awkwardly bent at the waist with my legs still outside. In the murk, the flashlight beam reflected off a box of some sort wrapped in black plastic and tape. It had floats rigged so that it floated in an air space at the top of the chamber. I could feel and hear my heart beating.

I cut the floats off the box. It was still buoyant, but

easier to handle. It felt like a suitcase. I pushed and pulled until I got the rope I'd brought wrapped around it a couple of times. Shaw must have had a better system. I finally pulled myself completely into the cramped chamber. With my legs bent I could just fit. I am not claustrophobic, but I felt the pressure of the small space. I pushed my air tank down as far as I could toward my feet and wrestled the case to my side. I pushed and squirmed. Eventually, by laying on top of the case, I was able to turn it lengthwise and push it out the hole. I tried not to think about what would happen if it got permanently lodged there.

I kept the line to the case tight in my hand. Finally, it pushed free and I followed, gasping into my mouthpiece.

Preacher was fishing away. He helped me pull the case over the side of the boat. Exhausted, I could barely climb up the swim ladder.

We pulled up the anchor and headed home. The plastic wrapped package seemed awfully small.

It is amazing how many hundred-dollar bills would fit into an aluminum, five-inch thick Zero Halliburton case. That's what we found when we unwrapped all the plastic and tape back on board my boat. I popped the locks with the screwdriver and found stacks of hundred-dollar bills wrapped in bank bands. It was all very orderly.

"Lordy, lordy," Preacher said.

"Yes."

"Sam, don't you tell anybody about this."

I laughed. "I was about to tell you the exact same thing."

Each banded pack held one-hundred hundred dollar bills. That was ten thousand dollars per packet. There were eighty packets. Shaw needed another two hundred thousand dollars to reach his goal of a million dollars. Too bad.

I put the money back in the case, and we carried it to my place. I finally hid it inside a barbecue grill in the workshop. I turned on all the alarms and tried to sleep. I wondered how Shaw ever slept with that money out there in the bay.

CHAPTER TWENTY-TWO

THEY CAUGHT LESTER HOGAN just outside Baton Rouge. Rocky's sources told him that Hogan lawyered up quickly and kept his mouth shut. It looked like Shaw severing the ties to his crimes and me severing Shaw worked to the benefit of Hogan. He remained someone of significant interest, but they didn't hold him. I rationalized again. I had attorney/client confidences I felt obligated to keep.

I had a long discussion with Detective Monroe in the company of a detective from Chambers County, an FBI agent, and a woman from Customs and Immigration. I got the impression Monroe shared with the others that he thought I, or some client of mine, knew more about Shaw's business than I was sharing. I'd given them every scrap of information I could about Mina and Zoio Verenka and how they got to the States. After a torturous meeting, Monroe had the decency to get me alone. He implored me to share anything I had not yet shared. He told me that they were working on establishing a link between Shaw and those to whom he delivered girls but so far, had nothing.

I told him I had nothing that would help. I kept to myself the information about the man with a scar on his face. I hoped that bit of information, along with the other thing I had, might be the quickest way to find the girls. After all, I had one other thing the cops didn't have. I had the money.

Cathy Winwood and Bill Dodge met me at Petrol Station on a Thursday afternoon. I bought them both a Brash beer. We sat outside with nobody near enough to hear us talk.

I'd met with Cathy for lunch and told her about the twins being in the hands of the traffickers. I told her what I wanted to do and asked if she thought it was possible. She said she wasn't sure how to get it done and suggested we meet with Dodge that afternoon. She gave me a hug before she left.

Dodge, the mysterious, beer-loving Federal employee, was as cagey as before, but, as he sipped his beer, I watched his eyes. He listened closely to what I said. I just gave the facts. There were two specific girls in the hands of traffickers. I thought it likely the traffickers were eastern Europeans. I knew they did business in Houston, Dallas, Saint Louis, and Chicago. I didn't know about any other cities. The only description I had was of one man, in Dallas, with a scar circling from behind his left ear. And, in Dallas, they'd done their business in a warehouse painted in brown and green at least once.

"You don't have much, do you?" he said.

"No. I'm hoping somebody, somewhere has a connection that can get a message to somebody."

"And you want to do what?"

"I don't care about messing in their business. I want to do a deal for those two girls."

"You know, of course, you should come into my office. I'll invite the FBI, and you can go over your story in detail. I'm sure we can make it an active case of the task force."

"Thank you for the invitation, but no. If I have to, I'll run ads in the papers of all those cities offering a substantial reward for those girls, no questions asked. I'll see if that works."

"Not wise. You might get them killed. You might get yourself killed."

"Won't be the first risk I've taken in this adventure. If you give me your personal assurance that your task force has an eighty percent chance of getting them out safely before they are damaged beyond repair, we'll do it your official way."

He snorted and took a sip of beer.

He turned to Cathy and asked, "What are you going to do?"

"What I can. Talk to every lawyer I know who's represented anybody in the country charged with trafficking. Go visit anybody I can get to in prison for trafficking."

"Yeah," he said, "maybe the lawyers. You might want to hold off on visiting prisoners. I don't like many people. I like you. I don't want you killed" To me, he said, "Mr. Locke, I will make inquiries as I can in Dallas with your description. Maybe somebody has a confidential informant who can pass along your offer. Are you willing to financially reward an informant who does that successfully?"

"Yes."

"Go get a phone that cannot be traced to you and give Cathy the number."

I gave him copies of the before and after pictures of Mina. I told him their names and their hometown.

He left. Cathy gathered her things to leave. She said, "You know our chances are slim, right?"

"Yes. I'm open to suggestion."

"Can you put together the money it will take?"

"Yes."

"I'll get started tonight. I know a couple of defense lawyers in Dallas I can call. They will know others. We'll try, but most lawyers will not help. After all, they're lawyers. People they represent will be skittish. I'll do my best. So will

Bill. I know he doesn't say much, but he'll try hard. He had a situation once. He lost somebody who was trying to play by the rules. He'd like to see you succeed."

I BOUGHT A PREPAID CELL PHONE under a fake name and called Cathy to give her the number.

I was afraid what I was trying to do would take too long, and I agonized over what I should do instead. I noticed the *Soliez* disappeared from the database of working freighters. I created the wording for an advertisement to run offering a substantial reward for information leading to the girls, no questions asked. I called Cathy Winwood too many times. She never complained.

I'LL NEVER KNOW WHAT WORKED WHERE, but two weeks after our discussion at the Petrol my phone rang with an unknown number on the Caller ID. I answered.

The caller said, "Three hundred thousand dollars." And he hung up.

I called Cathy Winwood. She said, "Be careful. It could be somebody after the money. It happens. Meet them in public."

I had nothing to do but wait for another call.

The next afternoon my regular phone rang. Caller I.D. said "Moore, P.C." When I answered a most professional female voice said, "Mr. Locke, this is to confirm your appointment in the offices of Gilbert Moore at three-thirty in the afternoon tomorrow. Do you need directions?"

I did. I recognized the name but did not know where to find his office. I knew the call from Moore's offices had to be related to the call the day before. I had no appointment with one of the best criminal attorneys in the state of Texas.

Gilbert Moore's offices occupied one end of the twenty-sixth floor of a thirty-two story building in Dallas. I got there right on time. The door was heavy, solid wood. The waiting area was nicely appointed. The entire office exuded wealth, but unlike a lot of offices, I didn't feel like it was done to impress clients. Everything seemed to be more personal, reflecting the personal taste of a very successful Gilbert Moore, Attorney at Law.

Moore's was the only name on the door. He was a former prosecutor with a very successful criminal defense practice. He did not give interviews to the press, even during his most notorious trials. Unlike many well-known criminal attorneys, he did not seek the spotlight. What he did was win a lot of trials for which he was paid very substantial fees. He was a Texas legend.

I introduced myself to the very attractive receptionist, and she smiled as if I was the most important client the firm had ever had. She showed me and my briefcase into a conference room every bit as richly appointed as the waiting room. She offered coffee or soft drinks or bottled water. I declined and she left, quietly closing the door behind her.

In the conference room, there was an elegant clock on a side table with a second hand making precisely timed jumps from number to number. It took me a moment to realize that the clock made no noise whatsoever.

I sat quietly for twenty minutes, my hands folded on the table in front of me. There was nothing else to do. At least it was unlikely I would be murdered in the offices of Gilbert Moore.

Finally, the door opened and a sharply dressed young man entered. His dress shirt was crisp and white. It actually had pleats where it folded at his sides to tuck into his pants.

"Did you get some coffee?"

"No, I declined."

"I understand you practice in the Houston area. We're happy to extend the courtesy of our conference room to you."

I looked at him, trying to decode what he was saying. They'd called me.

He continued, with a tight professional smile, "Do you expect the others soon?"

Before I could even formulate an answer to that, he said, "Well, I'm sure they'll be here soon." And he left.

Then, I understood. All the office of Gilbert Moore was doing was providing me, a fellow attorney, with a meeting place. They had no idea what was going on or with whom I was meeting. If they were ever forced to talk about me being there, that was the story they would tell. Fine. I didn't care. Everybody creates the fictions necessary to sleep at night. All I wanted was to get what I'd come to get.

Fifteen minutes later the door opened and two men entered. One was short and dressed all in black and carried a leather briefcase. I thought the other must be the muscle. He was stout, dressed casually. Both must have been in their thirties. They had dark eyes and coal black hair cut short. Neither had a scar around an ear.

Surprising me, it was the stout man who spoke. "Do you have it?"

I hoisted my briefcase to the table, clicked it open and turned it to face them across the table. They did not blink at the stacks of cash there, three hundred thousand of Benjamin Shaw's dollars in tight little stacks. I'd banded it with new currency bands I bought at an office supply store. Just in case Shaw's bands could be recognized. They didn't need to know where I got the money.

The big man nodded to the smaller man and without a

word the man in black transferred the money from my briefcase to his.

The big man took the case and walked to the door. Turning, he said, "Wait here for an hour. My friend will keep you company for thirty minutes and then leave. You will wait for another thirty minutes and then go to the address he will give you. We do not expect to hear from you again."

He left. I thought it probable that I'd just been ripped off to the tune of three hundred thousand dollars. But it was my play and I would play it to its conclusion.

The man in black and I waited. Time turned on the clock without a word being spoken by either of us. It was the most excruciating silence I've ever endured. His eyes never left me. I just stared blankly at the wall wondering if the day was an expensive waste. Hopefully, we were just going through some security procedure, giving my silent companion's friend time to make sure the money was real and all there.

After thirty minutes my chaperon took a folded piece of paper from his shirt pocket, dropped it on the table and left, never having said a word. I never even saw him look at the clock.

The paper said: This building. Suite 1300.

I stood up and paced for another thirty minutes toying with the note, my pulse rising and my mind racing with thoughts of what I should have done.

As I left, the lovely receptionist smiled and said, "Have a nice day." I nodded.

I rode the elevator to the thirteenth floor. The entire floor was vacant and being redone. Sheetrock was stacked against the walls, wires dangled from the ceiling where acoustic tiles were in disarray. The door to suite 1300 was a plain, wood grained door and unlocked. I took a deep breath and opened the door.

Inside, there was nothing. The floor was concrete, the walls beige and scuffed. The light switch worked to flood the room with cold, fluorescent light. I walked over to the window and looked outside. The number of vehicles on the streets was growing. The rush hour approached. Perhaps they scheduled our appointment to take advantage of rush hour, to make it harder to follow them. They needn't have worried. I'd not told anyone I was meeting them. I was alone in an empty room with an empty briefcase. I was at a dead end and turned to leave.

A door at the end of the room opened and a head hesitantly appeared.

"Mr. Locke?" she said with surprise in that richly accented voice of hers. "You are here?"

My voice caught in my throat and I had trouble speaking at first. "I came to get you. Is your sister with you?"

The door opened wider. Mina pulled Zoio into the room and walked slowly toward me. They did look alike.

She walked right up to me, dropped her sister's hand, wrapped both arms around me, buried her face against my chest and started to cry.

"Come on," I said. "It's over. Let's get out of here."

I would never know who got word to whom. It didn't matter to me. I'd probably broken a couple of more laws by purchasing two human beings at the two for one price of three hundred thousand dollars.

I understood less than half of the excited conversation on the drive back to Houston.

CHAPTER TWENTY-THREE

IT WAS LATE SUMMER, almost fall. I'd canceled my plans to cruise to Key West at Christmas. It was a warm day. I stood at the controls topside, watching for water hazards and enjoying the visual distraction of Patricia, up front on the deck in a deliciously skimpy black bikini.

The Mississippi River stretched long, fore and aft. *The Lonely Star* fit in well with her fresh-water cousins. We'd left Surfside several weeks before and made our way down the Intracoastal to where the Mississippi empties into the Gulf at New Orleans. We'd spent a harrowing time dodging barges on the lower part of the river. We were two days past St. Louis. The river had slowed, controlled by dams and locks. On the upper part of the river, civilization is closer than it is on the lower reaches. We'd slowed down accordingly, enjoying fewer campsites on sandbars and more quaint inns and restaurants.

We had a deadline, but no time schedule. While we cruised, others were at work. Cathy Winwood continued to impress with her amazing resources. I'd learned from her that, in addition to the dark webs of evil encompassing the globe, there are other groups. There are groups of people who don't make speeches, who don't pontificate at the UN, people who don't waste a lot of time worrying about ineffective governments and laws when it comes to humanity and what's right. They get things done, often glossing over certain legalities. Cathy was plugged in and put some of those people to work.

Mina and Zoio were in Canada, living with a family Cathy described as a couple of ex-hippies. I'd been strongly opposed to letting them out of my sight, but the occasional snooping of various officials convinced me to follow Cathy's recommendation. While the girls lived temporarily in Canada, others created paper, official paper that documented their adoption by Patricia in Ukraine. At some point, the girls would stop being illegal residents in Canada and would become legal residents of the United States, residing with their adoptive mom.

After a long dinner during which I explained most everything to him, Uncle Harlan contributed a few resources of his own. The girls would arrive in America with a trust fund, maintained in a bank in another country. He and I were the local trustees. We'd taken to calling it the Zero Halliburton fund, naming it after its source.

Patricia and I had prepaid calling cards. They left fewer tracks than cell phones. We would stop from time to time and call a number we'd been given. A nice woman did something and connected us to either the girls or to Cathy. I knew that one of these days, Cathy would give us the word. It would be time. Patricia would catch the closest plane and fly to meet the girls. I would have to decide whether to turn around and take the boat back to Texas alone or fly back and pay somebody to deliver it to me.

Patricia and I didn't really talk about that time. We both knew we were enjoying an intense but brief time together. She had a new job that would start in the spring. She would be living and teaching in Illinois. I would be building barbecue pits in Texas. Our future beyond that was a mystery. Meanwhile, we enjoyed each other, the slow days on the greatest river, and the satisfaction of making one small difference that would have been important to Mary Elizabeth.

Down on the deck, Patricia rolled over and propped

her head up on her hand. She noticed me watching and smiled with self-aware pleasure.

She said, "It's getting breezy, isn't it?"

"The wind is freshening a bit."

"Do you think it will help keep the bugs away if we park this thing in some secluded spot tonight?"

"It could very well do that."

She stretched out on her back, popped a red jelly bean into her mouth and lifted her shades to look at me. "I want to spend the night on the boat. I want to sleep outside under the stars, but I don't want the bugs biting me in embarrassing places."

"If they try, I'll brush them off."

She smiled again, dropped the shades over her eyes, lifted her face toward the sun, and said, "I bet you will."

She has a wonderful laugh.

Bonus Material, A Preview

Continue reading to enjoy a sample from the second Samuel Locke novel, *The Blues and Ballet*.

CHAPTER ONE

I LISTENED TO THE BLUES and watched ballet the night they fed the dead guy to the alligators.

The Jackson Ballroom was in Houston's Fifth Ward on the banks of the Buffalo Bayou. The big windows to the left of the Ballroom's stage framed the skyline of the city. When I arrived that night, the internal glow of Houston's downtown towers had started to outshine the glow of the sun setting behind them. The windows were open to capture any breeze in the humid night, but the air in the room moved mostly because of ceiling fans. The musty scent of the Bayou complemented the century-old patina of the ballroom.

A hot Friday night in June was perfect for slowly sipping a whiskey while listening to the blues, but I was there to see a client. As I walked in, I caught the eye of the bartender, Jake, and pointed at the coffee pot. He nodded. A few minutes later he brought me a mug of strong coffee laced with chicory. I wrapped my hands around the mug and breathed deep. The dark and rich scent of the coffee gave me goosebumps of anticipation. I sat back to enjoy the music.

My client William "Thumper" Lee, an eighty-something-year-old African American, did not look my way. But I knew he'd seen me. Soon after I sat down, he traded his electric guitar for his battered acoustic six-string and started singing his composition "My Wife Called a Lawyer." I know the song. The lyrics include a line, *I called up my lawyer, he set a court date*. That night, Thumper sang, "I called up my lawyer, he showed up late."

Thumper finished the song and made his way to my

table. I said, "Cute, but I wasn't late."

He smiled as he sat down. "Hey, Samuel, the lawyer man. Good to see you. You drinking coffee? Here? At this time of night?"

"You said you had some legal stuff to talk about. I thought I'd stick to coffee."

"You're coming up to the river with me, right? Hope so. I need a ride home. You came ready to spend the night like I said, right?"

"Yep, I'm ready."

"Good. We'll talk about the legal stuff up there. Have a drink."

Thumper's invitation to spend a couple of nights at his place on the Trinity River intrigued me. When I measured clients by the size of collected legal fees, Thumper was by far my best client, but we rarely socialized outside various blues bars in and around Houston.

Although invited, he'd never been to my place on Galveston Island. I'd never even been invited to his place on the Trinity River. I looked forward to the visit. The summer had a melancholy slowness, and visiting his place would be a welcome diversion. Besides, I enjoyed doing legal work for him. His legal stuff was different from my other work. Some time ago I gave up trying to convince him to find a lawyer who knew recording and performance contracts when he told me, "You did me pretty good taking on the company. I reckon you got me enough money to die with. I'm happy. I don't much like lawyers, but you're better than most. It ain't about perfection, you yon zanmi, man. Yon zanmi."

I had to look up yon zanmi. It means "a friend" in Creole. I've since heard it in the lyrics of a Zydeco song. It pleased me that Thumper called me a friend.

That night at the Jackson Ballroom, I said, "Let me get

this straight. You had me come up here because you need a ride home? How'd you get here?"

"I had a ride. I need lawyer help. Right now, though, you're about to see something special. You just wait and see. It has to do with what I need you for."

He got up from the table and walked through the room, greeting a few people on his way to the door that led backstage. I admired the beer in frosty glasses sitting in front of the couple next to me. It was a hot night. I went to the bar and got one for me. After Jake handed me my beer, he came out from behind the bar with a push broom and started sweeping the dance floor in front of the stage.

The drummer, a white kid who looked about sixteen years old, started playing around on his drums, brushes shuffling on his snare with a rim-shot on the backbeat. The bass player, a skinny black guy known as Lefty Tom, got up from a table, picked up his upright bass, and started playing in time with the drummer, slowly walking the notes up and down. The percussive beat caused most everybody in the place to start keeping time with feet tapping on the floor or fingers on tabletops. Thumper returned to the stage, plugged in his electric guitar, and joined the percussive rhythms with chords, soft and slow and gentle.

Thumper said, "Now, you dancers out there, do me a favor. Sit this one out and just watch. You are about to see something special."

He kept playing the unformed song and looked with irritation toward the corner behind me. There, at three tables shoved together, eight people were having a good time enjoying their drinks but not paying attention to the music. They tried to talk over each other, and noise from their table got louder and louder.

"Hey," Thumper said. "Hey, y'all back there in the

corner. Listen up."

Several of us turned to look at them. One or two of their crowd poked the others and let them know they were being spoken to from the stage.

"Hey," Thumper repeated. "I know y'all are having a good time. That's a good thing. But do something for me. We're about to have something special up here. Something you ain't never seen here in the Hall. Keep it down, will you?"

The noise lessened. The crowd's attention returned to the front of the house. The song took shape. I listened to a lot of Thumper's music. I recognized the repeating chords of his song "She Walks On Water."

Jake turned off most of the lights, leaving on those over the racks of bottles behind the bar, several small spots shining up against the wall behind the band, and a couple of spots making the dance floor the center of attention. Thumper started to sing.

> She walks in the morning,
> But you can't see her cry ...

A ballerina appeared from the backroom to a collective murmur of surprise in the room. She glided to the front of the stage balanced on her toes in that magical, ballerina way. She wore a cornflower blue bandeau top and brief shorts. Shimmering drapes of pale rose-red and white floated and flowed around her. Her skin glistened under the spotlights like silk. She was gorgeous. Not a sound came from the audience. She mesmerized us with her dance.

> She walks in the morning,
> But you can't see her cry ...

Thumper and the band played a little softer than usual. Everybody in the place watched the dancer. Even Jake. Jake was usually in constant motion. If nothing else, he polished glasses or wiped down the bar top. For this performance, he leaned with both hands on the bar and did nothing but watch the dance.

She walks in the morning most every day,
She walks all alone and nobody sees her cry,
She walks in the summer, the winter too,
She walks all alone and nobody,
No, nobody,
Sees the tears in her eyes.

I recognized the dancer. I enjoyed ballet. My Uncle Harlan, a benefactor of almost all performing art associations in Houston, shared his tickets to the performances. Plus, I occasionally went out with Carol Smithers, a vice-president at Texas Commerce Bank. Carol danced ballet from the age of two until she was seventeen. On our first date to a ballet, Carol told me, "When I was a junior in high school, my boobs grew too big to dance ballet. I was the only girl at my high school crying because her boobs grew."

Harlan had a box where the performances were enjoyed from a distance. Carol's tickets were up close. With her, I couldn't see the entire stage at once and tended to focus on individual dancers. I heard more of the effort. I saw past the stage expressions and noticed the intense concentration on the faces of dancers. I saw the sweat. I appreciated the strain and focus. I noticed the dancers as individuals.

I recognized Angelique Cambray dancing to the blues of Thumper Lee that night. She was a soloist with the Houston Ballet.

Thumper's trio made the song a little longer than usual by sticking a harmonica solo by Thumper in the middle. The soulful wail of the harmonica perfectly accompanied Angelique's sensual movement. The music sped up during a guitar solo and Angelique's body carved fast, graceful curves in space. Suddenly, the song slowed with the final lyrics.

> *Take pity on the girl,*
> *I say,*
> *Take pity on the girl.*
> *She walked on the water in the morning,*
> *She walked on the water,*
> *And the river,*
> *The river washed her tears away.*

With the last two lines, Angelique sank to the floor, the multicolored drapes pooling around her. A tear coursed down her cheek. I'd seen ballet done to blues and jazz in the magnificence of Houston's Wortham Theater accompanied by the orchestra. But on that hot summer night, in a century-old blues hall on the banks of the bayou with music provided by Thumper's music, Angelique danced the most moving ballet I'd ever seen.

That was about the time they were cutting the dead guy into pieces for the alligators.

Angelique did a simple curtsy to enthusiastic applause and ran off into the back room. Thumper walked over to my table, wiping his face with a handkerchief.

"Thumper, that was one of the best things I've ever seen."

He smiled. "Yeah, she's something, isn't she? She's the reason you're here."

"Why? What's up?"

"I done told you, we'll talk about it later, up at the river. First, I want you to meet her."

He went backstage. Thumper takes his own time to do things. Curious about what kind of legal help Angelique Cambray needed, I knew I'd have to wait until Thumper decided to tell me. He's my richest client. I could be as patient as necessary.

I'd met Thumper Lee at the Ballroom a few years before. I'd seen one small ad in the Houston Press announcing a performance he would give on a Thursday night. I'd heard of him. He was a famous Texas blues musician. Up to the day I noticed that small ad, I thought he was dead. I'd seen a story or two that mentioned him being murdered in some mysterious way years before I was born. Out of curiosity, I went to the show expecting some kind of tribute performance, but it was the real deal. Before his last set, Thumper came out from backstage and talked to Jake who nodded in my direction. Thumper walked over to my table.

"Jake tells me you're a lawyer man."

"I am."

"Stick around after the show. I want to talk to you about something."

I stuck around. Thumper became my client, my first really good client since I'd left the law firm where I went to work right out of law school. Meeting him resulted in a lucrative relationship.

Like me, a record company thought he was dead. The company even won a Grammy Award for a collection of what they promoted as the lost recordings of Thumper Lee. Turned out they weren't lost to Thumper. The record company owed him money, not just for that record, but for years of recordings.

It was a lot of money. We stirred up some trouble, and the publicity made his recordings even more popular. I helped him get what they owed him plus some damages. My fee paid for my boat, *The Lonely Star*, with a lot left over. I easily put up with his idiosyncrasies.

Thumper and Angelique Cambray came out of the

backroom. She'd put on a pair of black parachute pants and a light blue jacket. He carried his two guitar cases. I stood when they reached my table.

Thumper introduced her, "Angelique, this is our lawyer, Samuel Locke. Sam, Angelique."

She extended a hand. A thin sheen of perspiration on her face reflected the lights in the room. Her eyes were large and dark and beautiful. She smiled, but there was something off about her demeanor. Her shoulders slumped a bit, and her smile seemed forced. She looked directly at me when introduced. After that, she looked around nervously, not looking at one thing with focus. Despite the heat of the night and the effort of her dance, she crossed her arms, hugging herself as if cold. I got the impression meeting me was a command performance, and she'd rather be somewhere else. Once, when I met her and spoke to her at a meet and greet hosted by the Houston Ballet, she'd been much more relaxed and animated.

"A pleasure to meet you," she said.

"Likewise. That was an incredible surprise. It was amazing."

Her restrained smile grew a millimeter, and she quit looking at Thumper to look directly at me. "Thank you."

"I've enjoyed your dancing before, but I've never seen anything like that."

She nodded and Thumper said, "She has to go, but I wanted you to meet her." Turning to her, he put an arm on her shoulder. They were the same height and eye to eye. "Are you going to be okay?"

"Yes."

"You go where you told me you were going, and you stay right there until we call you. Understand?"

"Yes. Straight there."

They hugged. She took a deep breath and looked like she was about to say something. She glanced at me and back at Thumper.

He said, "Go. It will be okay. Sam and I will get things fixed up. Don't you worry. Sam, I'll be right back. I'm going to walk her to her car."

Something needed fixing. I'd thought Thumper called me about something related to his music, another recording or concert contract. But the wordless communication between Angelique and Thumper suggested something more complex and emotional than a business deal, something darker. I'd worked on a lot of business deals with Thumper without him ever inviting me to his place for the weekend. That, plus the fact that Thumper knew and had a relationship of some kind with a soloist with the Houston Ballet, was unusual. I knew something interesting was happening.

He returned and said, "What did you think?"

"That was impressive. Beautiful."

"Yes. She is amazing." He looked at Jake behind the bar and raised a finger. Jake nodded and raised a bottle of Wild Turkey.

"How did you meet Angelique?" I asked. "How did this thing get started?"

"Now, there's a story. I need to fill you in about that."

Jake delivered him a shot of whiskey and he downed it. "Come on," he said. "I'm not going to do anything else here tonight. We'll talk on the way up to the river." He picked up his guitars and headed for the door.

Another group of musicians worked on stage, making tuning noises and doing sound checks. Thumper greeted a few people on the way out and signed two autographs.

He slid his two guitar cases into the back seat of my

Range Rover, opened one, and took out a letter-sized envelope. He got into the passenger seat.

"Where am I going?" I asked.

"Head up toward Liberty. My place is on the river north of there. Up pass Moss Hill."

I left the dirt parking lot of the Hall and drove through the Fifth Ward toward the highway.

"So," I said. "You know Angelique Cambray."

"Yeah, ain't she something?" He was quiet for a moment, looking out the window and nodding his head at thoughts he finally shared. "When I was ten years old, I used to sit outside the Ballroom listening to the music. At twelve I earned a quarter a night on weekends clearing tables and mopping up spilled beer and whiskey."

"Tell me more. How in the world do you know Angelique? What kind of legal work do you need?"

"I know her through family. You know, I used to walk along here to get home about this time of night. I'd walk into Houston, play on corners for tips, and walk home. It wasn't really dangerous when I started doing that, but it got that way. It got so dangerous I went to New Orleans to be safe." He laughed. "Can you imagine that? Moving to New Orleans to be safe."

"I know it was really bad down here."

"New Orleans had its problems, but at least its lawlessness had rules. For a while, there weren't no rules in the Nickle."

We left the Fifth Ward, nicknamed the Nickle, and got on the highway. Thumper seemed determined not to talk about whatever legal work needed doing. I didn't mind. Instead, he talked about growing up in the Nickle, about the musicians he'd enjoyed, and about playing in blues clubs in Europe in the forties and fifties.

At the time of our lawsuit against the record company, I learned he'd spent time in Europe, disappearing from the States for a long time. But I'd never heard him reminisce in such detail about his history. I did that night as we traveled the dark highway leaving Houston. I treasured the moment and wished I could tape the oral history he shared. He got quiet as we entered Interstate Ten.

We weren't on the interstate long before I exited to State Highway Ninety. We continued riding quietly without talking much until we crossed the San Jacinto River. Thumper finally decided to let me know a little more about what we were doing.

"You liked that dancing, huh?"

"Yes. It was a great idea to have a ballet done with your blues."

"That was actually Angelique's idea. She thinks we ought to take it downtown to the Wortham."

"Good idea."

"Yeah. It's time for Thumperly to get into ballet."

Thumperly Efforts L.L.C. is the name of the company we set up as Thumper's production company.

"I'll start studying up on what we need to do."

He nodded. He had a look on his face, and he was holding that envelope, tapping its edge against his knee. I knew him. Something was coming about whatever was in the envelope, something about the tension between him and Angelique. I had to wait him out. We had time. He'd said his place was north of Moss Hill. The small town of Moss Hill was at least an hour away. I passed a sign advertising a service station just ahead.

"I'm going to pull off for gas. Want some coffee?"

"Sure. Coffee would be good."

"Anything you want in it?"

"Nothing they'll put in it."

I filled up the Range Rover, took my travel mug from the console, and went inside. I filled my mug with the questionably named house blend and bought a large cup of the same for Thumper. I settled behind the wheel and handed Thumper his coffee. He opened his door and dumped out some of his coffee. Taking a flask out of his jacket he put a healthy dollop of whiskey in his cup. My truck smelled like hot coffee and whiskey.

"Want some?" He offered me the flask.

"Nope. I can just breathe it in. I hope I don't get stopped."

"Me, too."

Back on the highway, there were fewer and fewer lights. We drove into the darkness, the air conditioner holding off the humid heat of summer. After the lawsuit with his record company, *Texas Monthly Magazine* did an article profiling him. They called him a Texas legend. Thumper frustrated the writer who wanted to do a feature-length article about his history, his disappearance, and his re-emergence. Thumper would not cooperate with any discussion of his past. The deadline loomed, and the article ended up being a one-page profile accompanied by a really nice photograph. His record sales in Texas bumped up a bit after the article appeared.

It felt good driving in the dark of East Texas with a certified Texas legend. I felt lucky to have the moment. The scent of whiskey and coffee fit the moment perfectly.

"You know what," I said, "give me a little. Very little."

I held my cup out, and he topped off my coffee with a splash of Wild Turkey from his flask.

"Hey, what if I want to give Angelique some of Thumperly? I can do that, right?"

"Yes, you can do that. What exactly is it you want to do?"

"Take care of her."

Was he falling prey to some crazy attraction to her? Was she after his money? Things were starting to sound strange. Something was up.

Before I could formulate a way to probe his motives, he said, "I need you to represent her about something."

"What would that be?"

"Here, take this." He held the envelope my way.

"What's that?" I kept both hands on the steering wheel. I did not want to touch the envelope until I knew what was going on.

"It's a check for ten thousand dollars and a letter from her asking you to be her lawyer."

Ten thousand dollars. Uh oh.

"Thumper, I cannot agree to be her lawyer without knowing what's going on."

"That's what I'm going to do up at the river. Fill you in on what's going on. But we need that lawyer secret thing in place."

That lawyer secret thing. Uh oh.

"If I'm supposed to represent her, I have to talk to her. Not you."

"You will, but everything I do from now until the day I die will be to take care of her. In fact, I need you to change my will up so she gets everything."

Uh oh.

"We'll talk about it. Thumper, who is she to you? What's going on?"

"She is my granddaughter. Take the check. It's mine, not hers."

I took the check. Thumper was the grandfather of

Angelique Cambray. That surprised me as much as any one thing could. The weekend promised to be very interesting.

"We'll talk about it tomorrow," he said. "I'm tired. Wake me up when you get to Moss Hill." He leaned the seat back.

We drove silently into the dark.

By that time, they'd fed the dead guy to the alligators.